EMILY HILDA YOUNG

(1880–1949) was born in Northumberland, the daughter of a ship-broker. She was educated at Gateshead High School and Penrhos College, Colwyn Bay, Wales. In 1902, after her marriage to a solicitor, J. A. H. Daniell, she went to live in Bristol, which was to become the setting of most of her novels. Her first, *A Corn of Wheat*, was published in 1910, followed by *Yonder* (1912), and *Moor Fires* (1916).

During the First World War Emily Young worked in a munitions factory, and as a groom in a local stables. However, after her husband's death at Ypres in 1917 she left Bristol for London, going to live with a married man, Ralph Henderson, Head Master of Alleyn's school in Dulwich. She continued to write. *The Misses Mallett*, published originally as *The Bridge Dividing*, appeared in 1922, preceding her most successful novel, *William* (1925). Then came *The Vicar's Daughter* (1928), *Miss Mole* (1930) – winning the James Tait Black Memorial Prize, *Jenny Wren* (1932), *The Curate's Wife* (1934) and *Celia* (1937). She lived with the Hendersons in South London until Ralph Henderson's retirement at the time of the Second World War when he and E. H. Young went, alone, to live in Bradford-on-Avon, Wiltshire. Here Emily Young wrote two children's books, *Caravan Island* (1940) and *River Holiday* (1942), and one further novel, *Chatterton Square*, published in 1947, two years before her death from lung cancer at the age of sixty-nine.

Virago publishes *The Misses Mallett*, *Miss Mole*, *Jenny Wren*, *The Curate's Wife* and *Chatterton Square*.

VIRAGO
MODERN
CLASSIC

NUMBER
242

CHATTERTON SQUARE

BY

E. H. YOUNG

WITH A NEW AFTERWORD BY
BEL MOONEY

Published by VIRAGO PRESS Limited 1987
41 William IV Street, London WC2N 4DB

First published in Great Britain by Jonathan Cape 1947
Copyright E.H. Young 1947

Afterword Copyright © Bel Mooney 1987

British Cataloguing in Publication Data
Young, E.H.
    Chatterton Square. — (Virago modern
    classics)
    I. Title
    823′.912 [F]   PR6047.0465

    ISBN 0−86068−629−9

Printed in Finland by
Werner Söderström Oy, a member of Finnprint

CHAPTER I

CHATTERTON SQUARE belied its name. It was really an oblong and, at that, it was unfinished, for one of its longer sides was open to the road which, rising a little, led southwards to the Green, and northwards, dipping a little, to the short curving hill on to the Downs. What gardens the houses possessed were at the back; in compensation, the inhabitants of the Square were free to use a railed oval of grass fringed with evergreens. It made a pleasant patch of greenness but, as the gates were locked and the householders were apt to mislay the keys and the spiked railings were high enough to thwart stray urchins, there was seldom anyone inside the enclosure and there was very little traffic in the Square. It had seen better days. That was evident in the delicate tracery of the fanlights over the doors and the wrought iron balconies breaking the plain fronts here and there, but now most of the houses were in need of paint and, though there were no printed cards in the windows advertising lodgings to be let, the shabby young clerks who blossomed out into bright sports clothes at the week-ends and the old ladies with over-trimmed hats who took their slow daily walks were certainly not householders. Fashion and prosperity had deserted this corner of Upper Radstowe where all the houses had basement kitchens and anyone walking round the Square at cooking times would have seen these caverns lighted as though for some underground festivity.

It was the balconies, although his own house was not favoured with one, the fanlights, the atmosphere of an earlier and, as he thought, a more gracious day which, in spite of his wife's gentle objection to the basement, had induced Mr. Blackett to rent a house in the left hand corner of the Square. It was in good repair and had an added though, he had to admit, an incongruous attraction in an extra, flat-roofed room filling the space there had once been between his house and the one, at right angles to

9

it, on the long side of the Square. He needed that extra room for his books. He had been collecting them all his life and at last, on his promotion to be manager of the Radstowe branch of the business with which he had always been connected, he had found harbourage for them and solitude, when he needed it, for himself. This excrescence was ugly but its oddity was rather pleasing. It had the effect of being swung between the two houses for it was on a level with the pavement while they had their basements some feet below it and their first-floor rooms a few feet above it. Thus, to reach it from his dining-room or the passage, it was necessary to descend three shallow steps and he always enjoyed descending them for in this house of his choice there was that difference from other houses which matched the difference from other people he felt so strongly in himself. And he did not regret the absence of a balcony. The one decorating the Frasers' house next door, though he admired its beauty from a distance, was used too often and rather vulgarly, he thought, by Mrs. Fraser. It was just wide enough to accommodate a chair and long enough to accommodate several and there, on fine days, she would sit, reading or sewing, and no doubt missing none of the few happenings in the Square. He would not have cared to see any member of his family in so conspicuous a position and one so conducive to idling and gossip. His wife's drawing-room was at the back of the house with a little staircase leading into the garden, and she loved a garden. She was, or ought to be, as well content with her room as he was with his and she was the least curious of women. It would have given her no satisfaction to sit on a balcony and watch the comings and goings of the neighbours. She lived in a little world of her own with a home and a husband and three children to care for, and a peaceful, well-ordered world it was, good to come back to after a tiring day and these were troublous times. Mr. Blackett refused to liken his home to an oasis in a desert; that was too obvious a simile for his literary taste, but he gratefully took the refreshment he found there, only disturbed, half pleasurably, by the bigger Fraser encampment next door, with no apparent male chieftain at the head of it.

'I suppose,' he said to his wife, soon after their arrival in the Square, 'that Mrs. Fraser must be a widow.'

'I suppose so,' Mrs. Blackett replied.

'Ah, poor thing!' he said. He pitied widows but he distrusted them. They knew too much. As free as unmarried women, they were fully armed; this was an unfair advantage, and when it was combined with beauty, an air of well-being, a gaiety which, in a woman over forty had an unsuitable hint of mischief in it, he felt that in this easy conquest over, or incapacity for grief, all manhood was insulted, while all manhood, including his own, was probably viewed by that woman as a likely prey. But he knew how to protect himself. He had made that clear on her first friendly approaches and, though he hoped he was a humane man, he had a little spiteful pleasure in detecting her vulnerable spots. He doubted whether she was aware of them herself, but he saw them in her two tall sons. He was thankful his own three children were girls. If war came, and as he privately admitted in his more candid moments it threatened, distantly, it might involve them in suffering but it could hardly involve him in their loss. There, certainly, he had the advantage over Mrs. Fraser but it was not until he had been living in Upper Radstowe for a year that the conviction was forced upon him. At the time, he merely said, 'I don't think she is the kind of woman you would care for, Bertha.'

'No?' she said half questioningly. She was very rarely unwilling to accept his judgment and her beautifully chiselled lips, now as always, were set in the serene lines of her contentment, and then, unexpectedly, she asked, 'Why do you say that?'

Mr. Blackett smiled. He laid a hand on her shoulder. Its firm pressure emphasized what it was unnecessary to explain. She must trust his wider experience. She had had a sheltered girlhood in her father's vicarage; she had been sheltered as a wife and it would have been beneath his dignity and hers to have told her of the little attacks he had had to parry, easily enough, from women secretaries and clerks and typists. No doubt this sort of thing occurred in most offices where the sexes, unfortunately, mingled. Perhaps his share of it had been unusually large, but he could not change his appearance for the easing of these troubled young women: it was not his fault that he looked like an elegant poet with his pointed, little black beard, his slim figure in well-cut clothes and his hat just a fraction of an inch broader in the brim than the hats of other men. And he was neither the hearty business man who was jolly with the girls nor the suave man of affairs who treated them like machines. They knew he was different. He was a man in uncongenial surroundings who had made himself master of them and they found him interesting. Circumstances had forced him into trade and his humorous consolation for missing a literary career was his concern with the manufacture of paper for the making of books someone else would write.

'Conceited ass,' said Rosamund Fraser as, from her balcony, she watched him opening his front door.

'You say that,' Miss Spanner said, 'because he snubbed you.'

'No, he snubbed me because he's a conceited ass. I knew he would.'

'Then I wonder you gave him the chance.'

'Just to tease him,' Rosamund said lightly. 'He never knows whether I'm going to speak to him or not. He hopes I will and then hates me because I do and he thinks it's very common to call to him from the balcony.'

'Asking him for the news, too, when you'd just been listening to it on the wireless! You ought to be ashamed of yourself.'

'I am, a little. But I'm only forty-three, like you, Agnes. We're mere girls. We must have a little fun sometimes.'

'You're putting on weight though,' said Miss Spanner.

'Just the suitable amount for the mother of a family.'

'And I'm as slim as ever I was.'

'You're not slim, Agnes. You're skinny. Exactly the same back and front. If you hadn't a face I shouldn't know which was which. You've never eaten enough and of course you were half starved as a child.'

'Don't talk such rubbish,' said Miss Spanner. 'No child could have been better cared for.'

'I've had meals in your house, haven't I? Plenty of them, but never plenty at them. Why, I used to come home and raid the larder! But you're benefiting from all that parsimony now. You've got the money you might have eaten and worn and laughed with. They were a mean old pair, your parents, weren't they, now honestly, Agnes?'

Miss Spanner gave her slightly crooked nose a knock. 'It little becomes you to say so and I wonder at myself for bearing with you. My father gave Felix his articles, didn't he?'

'Yes. Conscience money,' Rosamund said.

'And what d'you mean by that?'

'Nothing criminal, but he took most of the firm's profits and my father did nearly all the work.'

'He was the junior partner.'

'While yours sat on chapel committees and hopped into a pulpit whenever he had the chance. Oh, I'm sure he got some business out of it. One eye was fixed on Heaven, booking seats for himself and your mother there, but the other was concentrated on Mammon. And how I wish I had his belief in the hereafter! It would do me good to imagine their dismay when they found the good seats had not been kept for them and to see their sweet smiles turning sour. And God was very good to you, Agnes, when he took them to his bosom within a few days of each other.'

'It was a great blow to me,' Miss Spanner said piously, but the slight cast in her right eye became accentuated into a squint, a sign with which Rosamund was well familiar. But for that squint, she and Agnes would never have become the friends they were. Even in the old-fashioned, odd-looking little girl, an only child born to her parents in their middle age, that squint commented on the sentiments she quoted from them, on the restrictions they set to her liberty, on her pretence of willing obedience to them. Agnes, in those days, Rosamund soon divined, was very far from being what she seemed. Sometimes she would give a sudden hoot of laughter, startling in its derision and painful in its young bitterness. Yet only in one matter, and then secretly, had she actually rebelled, for the old Spanners were people of character and together they were formidable. There was a steel-like quality under their smiling sweetness and though, in their own way, they adored and even cosseted her, they were determined to have the kind of daughter they wanted, one who would minister to them in their old age. She had arrived as an almost immodest inconvenience; she must survive as a comfort. They were too much for one lonely little girl to combat. She bore patiently with the pinafores she was made to wear; she went, without demur, to a little private school while Rosamund had a full and exciting life at a big one, but books she had to have and she soon exhausted the parental library. In this matter Rosamund and her father conspired with her and she spent many a happy hour in the very house where she was living now. She was asked there to tea, and her parents could hardly refuse an invitation from Mr. Spanner's useful partner, but she was left to herself with the books while Rosamund rushed round the roads on her bicycle or scamped her homework in another room.

'The direct intervention of Providence,' Rosamund said, 'like the walls of Jericho and that Red Sea business.'

'I'm very grateful,' said Miss Spanner, 'and I wish he'd be up to some of those useful tricks again, for more important matters than me, but he seems to have given up that sort of thing. Now a thoroughly catastrophic earthquake or a completely devastating plague on the continent would come in very handy.'

'Yes,' said Rosamund, 'and then we'd all settle down and trust the conjuror to do it again next time. What's the matter with us all, Agnes? And anyhow, what can you and I do about it? We can't do anything and so we don't even think about it, at least not much, not enough. I know what's happening, I know what may happen, but I'm fairly happy all the time and really I give more concentrated thought to planning my summer clothes and I suffer more acutely when they go wrong than I do when I face the future. But the future's so indefinite and I can do something about the clothes.'

'You've always thought too much about them.'

'And you've never thought enough. D'you know that the shoulder seams of that dress are halfway down your arms? You look frightful and you've had your hair in that teapot handle on the top of your head ever since you put it up.'

'What does it matter?' Miss Spanner asked. 'You can't make a silk purse out of a sow's ear.'

'A very nice pigskin one, though. And, after all, beauty's important. Let's have as much of it as we can get. And,' she added after a pause, 'if the worst does happen, Fergus will be in it again, by hook or crook.'

'And you'll make a hero of him,' Miss Spanner said with a snort.

'He'll make a hero of himself, as he did before,' Rosamund said. 'I won't have you being spiteful about Fergus.'

'I oughtn't to be,' Miss Spanner said. 'If he hadn't gone I'd still be alone in the dear old home. But after the war —'

'Don't be so definite,' Rosamund begged.

'After the war,' Miss Spanner persisted, 'and it really began when we let them march to the Rhine, there'll be a general reconciliation here and I shall be turned out. He's gone off before now, in a temper, and come back again.'

'He won't come back this time,' Rosamund said. 'I'd never have asked you to come and live with us if I hadn't been sure of that.'

'You can't be sure of anything with Fergus.'

'Of course you know him best,' Rosamund said with gentle sarcasm.

'And I was a fool,' Miss Spanner continued, 'to let myself be uprooted, but I've been a happy fool.'

'And you can go on being happy.'

'And a fool,' Miss Spanner said.

15

CHAPTER II

'BUT Mr. Lindsay,' said Miss Spanner, 'can't be in another war, can he? Not by any hook or crook. I'm glad of that. He can't hide his limp or his face wounds.'

'No,' Rosamund said, folding up her work. It was time to see about the family's supper and she went through the drawing-room and down the stairs — these were wide and shallow and the mahogany banister rail was smooth under her hand — and so through the hall and down the steep, dark staircase to the base-ment. Dark though it was, she did not need a light to guide her. She had been born in this house and lived in it with her father until the war ended. Felix and James and Chloe had been born here too but sometimes it seemed to her that she had never left it and had suddenly found herself supplied with a large family to share its occupation. Her children were the fourth generation to live in it, for the house had been her grandfather's, and she had a simple pride in her modest inheritance. She had been glad to come back to it when Mr. Spanner's offer to give Felix his articles and train him in his office — another pleasing piece of continuity — had coincided with Fergus's decision that he was tired of selling motor cars and the chance that the house was standing empty. All her roots were here, she thought, her feet prepared for the unevenness in the stone-flagged passage, and she had almost forgotten the dreadful bungalow with the corru-gated iron roof which had been her first home with Fergus. Like many another man returned from the first world war, he was bent on chicken farming. As he was equipped with nothing but enthusiasm it had not been a success, but they had had a lot of fun in that bleak field sprinkled with hen-coops and wire enclosures. They had always managed to have fun together, she thought, and checked a sigh to exclaim, 'Oh, Sandra!' for there was a light in the kitchen. 'What are you doing? This is my job, you know.'

'Enjoying myself. Making soup,' Sandra said, her head, like a tawny chrysanthemum, bent over a saucepan. All the Frasers were either red-haired like their father or dark like their mother and Sandra and Felix were the red ones. 'It's good for Chloe,' she said, stirring busily. 'Sometimes she's too tired to eat solid food straight away after the stuffy shop and the train. I wish she didn't have to work in Wellsborough.'

'You ought to be the mother of the family,' Rosamund said. 'But have you done your homework? Where's Paul?'

'He's got toothache.'

'Oh dear! Badly?'

'I don't know. You can never tell with boys, but I put some brandy on cotton wool and he's put it on the place.'

'He has no business to have toothache,' Rosamund said with annoyance. 'He went to the dentist in the holidays.'

'He eats too many sweets.'

'Such a horrid pain,' Rosamund murmured, leaning against the table.

'Would you have it for him if you could?' Sandra inquired. 'I wouldn't, not for Paul. It's funny, I would for any of the others but somehow, with Paul, I can't feel it matters very much.'

'I don't think it's at all funny. I think it's horrid.'

'I didn't mean funny like that. I meant queer.'

'Very queer,' Rosamund said. 'Don't you like him?' she asked in a troubled tone.

'Of course I do, only he doesn't seem quite human, not as human as a dog. More like a tadpole, something that's going to turn into something else.'

'Well, that's just what he is.'

'And I feel as if he hadn't any feelings.'

'You're quite wrong there. It's just that he can't sort them out. He's a nice, messy, ordinary schoolboy,' Rosamund said, her eyes following the geometrical pattern of the linoleum, black on a brown ground. 'What wonderful stuff this had been,' she said. 'I remember when it was put down.'

'Yes, darling, you've told us that several times already,' Sandra said.

17

Rosamund sat down rather heavily. 'Am I a bore?' she asked. Sandra's thin little face wrinkled with amusement. 'You're lovely,' she said. 'I'd like to kiss you, under your eyes.'

Rosamund held up her face obligingly. It was broad where Sandra wished to kiss it with a generous yet fine line to the chin and it would still be beautiful when she was an old woman. It depended on its structure, not its colour, though her big mouth was red enough without assistance and her eyes were more blue than grey.

'But don't drip soup on me,' she said. 'Put the spoon down first. And you didn't answer my question. You mustn't let me be boring. I think about the past so much because I was so happy. I suppose I was spoilt, but nothing nasty ever happened to me in this house. I can't remember being hurt or sad or lonely. Perhaps I was thick-skinned. Perhaps it made me a little careless about other people. I always expect them to get along as happily as I did.'

'So we do,' Sandra said stoutly.

Rosamund shook her head. 'It's a different world. There's too much in it, too much of everything, except time. And yet, for Agnes, there must have been far too much of that. More than forty years in that dreary house on the Green and chapel twice on Sundays as well as Sunday School! And blancmange and apricot jam for supper, the cheapest kind of apricot jam, every Sunday of her life! And the smug smiles of those godly old skinflints!'

'Is she happy now, d'you think?' Sandra asked anxiously.

'She says so.'

'I don't see how she can be really, she looks so funny and she has nobody of her own.'

'She has dozens of cousins and aunts and uncles and I just saved her in the nick of time, she was so used to doing what she was told, from going to live with the worst of them.'

'She must have changed a lot then,' Sandra said. 'She isn't a bit meek. I call her prim and rather disapproving, but somehow nice.'

Rosamund laughed and went to lay the supper table. This was in a pleasant room behind the kitchen and on a level with the garden and the use of it saved much carrying up and down the stairs. What should have been the dining-room was the bedroom of the elder boys and this was one of the arrangements which met with Miss Spanner's disapproval. She said it was like cheap sea-side lodgings to have people sleeping on the ground floor and she was ostentatious in shutting a door apt to be left open and reveal intimate garments hanging on chairs. What troubled her more, coming as she did from a house where affairs of the toilet were a secret and her father and she carefully avoided meeting each other unless fully dressed, was the Fraser habit of emerging from their bedrooms, scantily attired, and having animated conversations on the landing and Rosamund was as bad as any of them though, merely because it became her figure better, she did wear a flimsy dressing-gown. The family never seemed so talkative as when they ought to have been asleep and Miss Spanner wished to make a necessary excursion across the passage. It was a sign of the times, she thought, evidence of the slackness, the absence of standards, which had brought the country to its present pass, when nothing was really important or urgent and everything would turn out allright in the end. But much of what Sandra called her primness and disapproval was, in fact, the disguise for a sort of shy bewilderment. She was on unfamiliar ground. She had known these children from their babyhood. For years after Rosamund left Upper Radstowe, Miss Spanner had spent a fortnight's holiday with her until she found it easier to stay at home than to endure the veiled reproaches, the astonishment that she should care to leave her ageing parents, the reserve of their welcome when she returned and, when the Frasers came back to Upper Radstowe two years ago, Felix and James were young men and Chloe was a young woman. Chloe was like her mother, with the same modelling of the face and soft, dark hair, but her eyes were more grey than blue and she had not the gaiety and sparkle of Rosamund at that age. She seemed remote and a little mysterious to Miss Spanner and her air of withdrawal, not severe but elusive and no doubt alluring to the young men who pursued her; seemed to the older woman who only reached her outposts, a little affected, a trifle disdainful. It was different with the boys, for Miss Spanner was a woman, after all, and what she did not understand in them was their chief attraction. She felt a thrill of pleasure when they teased her with grave courtesy, a sensation she had felt for a short time, long ago, when the young man who taught the big boys at the Sunday School and wore collars much too large for his thin neck, had gone out of his way to walk home with her. He was very tall and she remembered how he had bent down to hear what she said as though this were precious to him, but she remembered it as seldom as possible. Her one little success had changed to a pitiable failure, for when he called at the house on some pretext or other, Mr. Spanner had made short work of him and he avoided her thereafter. Perhaps he had thought it would be a good thing to ally himself with Mr. Spanner who was somewhat higher in the social scale than most members of the congregation and known to be a man of means but he had made off at the first rebuff. Loving her for herself — and why should he? — an army of Spanners would not have quelled him. He had married soon afterwards and now he had a family of boys, all with dangerously thin necks, and they might have been even worse, Miss Spanner reflected, if she had been their mother. On the whole, things were just as well as they were; she could have contributed nothing in the way of physical beauty and as her admirer had, inevitably, become a deacon, she would have been tied to the chapel for life. Now she was as free as air, no one in the world could be freer and, as she took her place for supper, she marvelled at the ease with which Rosamund carried the responsibilities of her family. She sat at the head of the table and, in the last resort, she was authority; until that moment, she might have been another daughter of the house. She did not cast a quick maternal eye on her children, divining their moods and the degrees of their fatigue, watchful for signs of trouble. It was Sandra who did that. Paul had gone to bed with a swollen face and a sleeping pill and there was nothing more to

be done for him but, before she could eat with appetite, she had
to make sure all was well with the others, Felix in a good temper,
James no more silent than usual and Chloe no more tired, and
she had already been told that Miss Spanner, if not actually
happy, was less unhappy than she might have been and that
was comforting. Chloe said, 'Good soup,' and sent a nod of
thanks across the table and, thus encouraged, for there were
times when it was not safe to question Chloe, Sandra asked, 'Did
you sell anything nice to-day?'

'Not much.'

'Luxury trade,' said Miss Spanner significantly.

'People have to be clothed.'

'Not at your Miss Pringle's prices.'

'But it's important to be dressed properly.' Chloe refrained
from glancing at Miss Spanner. 'It ought to be considered as an
art.'

'But you don't design the dresses.'

'No, I show them off.'

'I call it a most undignified occupation,' Felix said, frowning
and pausing in the doorway with a pile of plates. It was the boys'
turn to clear away and fetch the dishes, the girls' turn to wash up.

'You wouldn't think so if you saw me doing it,' Chloe said,
'but there wasn't much of that to-day. Miss Pringle played
Patience behind the screen and I pretended to be busy in case
people looked through the window, and the Patience came out
three times and that put Miss Pringle in a very good temper and
she said perhaps she'd take me to Paris, flying, next time she goes.'

'Lovely!' Sandra said enthusiastically.

'She'd better go soon,' Miss Spanner said in hollow tones.

'Why?' Chloe asked. She looked round the table . Felix was
frowning, he was a ready frowner; James had lowered his eyelids.
'Oh, I see,' she said vaguely, 'but I don't believe it,' she added, at
the sight of Miss Spanner's tightened, down-turned lips. Miss
Spanner had an irritating air of knowing more than she cared to
say. She looked important as though she had special information
she must not divulge. It was quite enough to produce scepticism

or the pretence of it. That was the effect it had on Rosamund.

'Don't be gloomy, Agnes,' she said, and in that quiet room at the back of the house and the back of the Square, the little garden meeting the longer one of an invisible house, with birds singing in the bushes and a distant, homely sound of hammering from someone who was mending his fence, preserving his possessions, maintaining decency and order, the squabblings, the shoutings, the comings and goings and the threats in a land so very far away and no concern of theirs, seemed like an old story of another age and not quite real.

'Allright,' said Miss Spanner. 'By all means let's be merry ostriches while we can.'

CHAPTER III

BUT Felix had frowned and James had dropped his eyelids for their own reasons, not for the one Miss Spanner attributed to them. They had faced the probabilities of the future, they knew what part they would have to play in it and had no illusions about it. They were proud of what their father had done in the last war but they did not want to emulate him. They were a generation too late to see war as a gallant adventure, worth while for itself. They knew that, leaving out the chance of death or mutilation, the lives they had planned would be disrupted, perhaps ruined. Felix was soon to take his final examination in law, James was studying agriculture at the University; he had always wanted to be a farmer. Let those who would be less directly involved talk about it if they chose. These two, knowing without words that their views were identical, had hardly discussed it between themselves. In their close companionship confidences were quite unnecessary and they made no comment on Miss Spanner's little gibe as they left the house together.

Months ago, on her first arrival in Upper Radstowe, Flora

Blackett, across the road, had noticed the regularity with which these two young men strolled by and she was always at the window of her bedroom to see them go. That she might not miss them, she had given up having the coffee her mother made in her father's study after the evening meal, at one time a much valued privilege which her younger sisters did not yet enjoy.

'It keeps me awake,' she said.

'But we should like to have you with us,' said her father. He looked forward to this hour when, his day's work done and his spirits restored by a good meal, he could enjoy the company of his favourite daughter and they could talk together or he would talk to her of the things that interested him. He assumed that they also interested her and she had always been responsive, following his lead, ready to adopt his enthusiasms, and he could not offer her anything better than his books and his comments on them, yet, when she said, 'Just for a few minutes, then. I must work, you know,' his disappointment was cancelled by his approval. She was to go to the University in the autumn and had preparatory work to do. It was true that her father's window looked on to the Square but what would she have seen of the Frasers from that position? She would see nothing but their backs, while, from her own room, she could indulge in anticipation, in the hope that they, or at least one of them, would look up and see her and determine to see her again. She soon learnt that on one night they would appear at about eight o'clock, half an hour later on the next, and so, alternately throughout the week, except on Sundays. The late nights were those on which they washed the supper dishes and a peep into the basement kitchen would have revealed them with their coats off and their shirt-sleeves rolled up, busy at the sink, young gods turned scullions. She would have been horrified and then touched by their condescension, just as she was heartsick at their lack of curiosity, even when she flung the window open, and full of admiration for their masculine indifference.

This was her first experience of the kind. Without brothers, with parents who, for their different reasons, did not encourage

23

social exchanges, she had been almost as segregated as a nun and her feelings, abnormal only in their suddenness and consequent intensity, gave her a sense of guilt, secret and delightful. She began to find her father very dull and the animation he was accustomed to seeing and still saw in her face as she listened, now came of an almost spiteful amusement at his innocence. Did he really think she cared about his views of Pope as a poet, illustrated by extracts read in the special, sonorous voice he assumed for verse? She hardly heard what he said. She was sure her mother was not listening, either, and her father addressed what was practically an empty room. But he must not know it. She thanked him and slipped away as though reluctantly. She had work to do.

'This place suits Flora very well,' Mr. Blackett announced. 'I was told we should find the climate enervating, but I have never seen her look better.'

'She is growing quite attractive,' Mrs. Blackett said, looking down at the sewing with which her plump, pretty hands were busy.

'Attractive?' Mr. Blackett got up and looked into the Square and then Mrs. Blackett looked at him, silhouetted against the light. He did not like that word; he did not like its implications. He had an unacknowledged but profound distaste for any thought of Flora involved in courtship and marriage. There was a sort of indecency in it and, in connection with this repugnance, he had set himself against her first ambition to be a doctor. He would not hear of it. It was an unsuitable profession for a woman. She must take her degree and qualify as an almoner. So she would use all her best qualities and be a truly useful member of society. And now, when all arrangements had been made for her to go to Radstowe University, he began to wonder whether it was wise. It was that word which had upset him and the sight of two young men going past his window pointed his indecision. If they had been walking quickly, with purpose, as he always walked himself, he might not have noticed them. It was the leisurely swing of their movements, their loose tweed jackets, their bare heads, much, from a different angle, of what Flora saw in them, that made him turn to his wife, half angrily, as though she were responsible for their appearance but, before he could speak, she said quietly, looking down again, 'She is very much like you.'

This remark astonished him. It was of a personal kind so unusual from her that he did not know what to do with it. It made him momentarily uneasy; then he laughed and said, 'Well, Bertha, I think that is the first compliment you have paid me since you did me the honour of marrying me. Do you mean that Flora is like me in appearance.'

'Yes.'

'Thank you! And in character?'

Now she dropped her work and faced him fairly. She seldom did that. She was almost as shy as when he married her, still, it seemed to him, a little abashed by so much intimacy, and he found a recurring piquancy in a relationship for which he gave some credit to his own skill.

'In character?' he repeated hopefully.

'More than she realizes,' was Mrs. Blackett's odd reply.

He did not know what to do with that remark either and he did not speak of his doubts about the University. He shrank from giving them expression; indeed, he had to put them from his mind. His plans for Flora were not changed and what, he asked himself soon afterwards, would have been the sense in changing them? Here, almost on his doorstep were just such people as he wished her, the whole family, to avoid and Bertha had been to blame for breaking the crust of politeness which was more than enough to offer them.

He liked to take a walk on a Saturday afternoon with Flora for his companion, across the bridge, pausing there to look leftwards at the spreading city far below, the tangled waterways, the warehouses, the ships, the medley of houses and trees lifted to the heights of Upper Radstowe, and on the right where the gorge narrowed, to see the river sluggishly making for the Channel between banks of glistening mud on which was reflected, now and then, the white swoop of the gulls; or, at high tide, to hear the hooting of a siren and watch the ship coming slowly round

25

the bend. It was a scene of which he did not tire for it was never twice alike. The form, the opaqueness, the colour or absence of clouds had their way with it, darkening or lightening the trees on the farther cliff and the splashes of red and yellow rock on the nearer one. And his pleasure in all this was increased because he had won it for himself by his energy, by subjugating his inclinations to necessity where many another man would have found an easy excuse for failure. Then, stepping off the bridge, he found himself in another county where the air was changed, still soft but with a secret wildness in it even before he had left the houses and found himself in open country. Rosamund Fraser could have told him that he had farther to go to reach it than she had needed to travel in her young days. There were wire fences now, and warnings against trespassers, barring the fields where once she had walked freely. The wide, rough track edged with brambles and bracken from which she had seen the Channel and the pale hills of Wales had been smoothed into a road and there were houses instead of open country where she and her father had often eaten their picnic lunch on summer Sundays. But Mr. Blackett was very well pleased with what he found. This was better than a park in a London suburb and, humbly, he carried in his pocket three small volumes from which he might fill the gaps in his knowledge of birds and trees and flowers. Hitherto, his walks had been for exercise, for the sake of his slim figure; now he had the opportunity for new, delightful interests too and he was anxious for his children to get them earlier than had been possible for him. But on this particular Saturday, Flora flagged.

They cut their walk short and returned to find a shabby car outside their house and confusion within, Mrs. Blackett on the drawing-room sofa with a wrenched ankle – she had tripped on the iron staircase that led into the garden – attended by Mrs. Fraser and Miss Spanner, who had been fetched by Rhoda Blackett, – and a man at the sight of whom Mr. Blackett halted in his solicitous stride towards his wife.

'Did you notice that?' Miss Spanner said afterwards to Rosamund. 'There was something queer there.'

'There's something queer wherever you look,' Rosamund retorted. 'It must be that cast in your eye.'

There had certainly been no pleasure in Mr. Blackett's surprise. He did not like his wife's cousin, a man entirely dependent for attention on his limp and his showy facial wound. He must have been amazingly inconspicuous before he was thus labelled as a hero and the label was flagrant and most disfiguring. The wound had barely healed when, just out of hospital, he had appeared at the Vicarage the very day before Mr. Blackett's wedding. This, of course, was a great opportunity for display, but it was not fair to the bride who vexed Mr. Blackett for the first and, he hoped, the last time, by the tenderness and care she lavished on Piers Lindsay. He must have the most comfortable chair, he must go to bed early, a special place must be kept for him in church. If he had been the bridegroom she could hardly have been more affectionate, and Mr. Blackett did not properly recover from his annoyance until he and Bertha were in Florence whence Flora got her name and where she had been conceived. Mr. Blackett had seen Lindsay again at the funeral of Bertha's father. He had actually been in the Vicarage for a week, waiting with Bertha for his old uncle's death, but Mr. Blackett had not been aware of this. He had simply noted Lindsay's liking for appearing at ceremonies and since then he had never heard and rarely thought of him. And here he was — and Mr. Blackett could not imagine where he came from — with spectators again provided in the shape of Mrs. Fraser and Miss Spanner. These two had slipped away, however, before Mr. Blackett could put his surprise into words and his displeasure into his smile. It was difficult to distinguish Lindsay's own smile from a grimace of pain. The left side of his face was drawn up by a scar running to his temple, his right profile was normal with half a firm mouth and a straight nose, while, seen in full face, he looked like the true clown, with humour overcoming sadness. Thus he seemed to have three faces, to be disconcertingly three men who constantly changed places.

'It was fortunate for me but unlucky for Piers that he should arrive just now,' Mrs. Blackett said from the sofa.

27

'And Rhoda's fetching a doctor,' said Mary. She was twelve years old, the youngest of Mr. Blackett's daughters and, knowing he liked to think of her as his baby, she drew down her mouth piteously. 'Because perhaps Mother's leg's broken,' she said, ready to cry.

'Nonsense!' Lindsay said briskly, displaying, Mr. Blackett thought, an undue familiarity with his wife's ankle. 'Nothing broken, but a nasty wrench.'

'Are you in pain, Bertha?' Mr. Blackett remembered to ask. 'And what doctor?'

Mrs. Fraser, it appeared, had recommended her own and after he had been and gone and the family sat down to a belated tea, Piers Lindsay had still offered no explanation of his presence. He was remarkably sure of his welcome, Mr. Blackett thought, and not in the least embarrassed, rather pleased, by Mary's fascinated gaze and Rhoda's steady stare.

'I thought you were in the Midlands somewhere,' Mr. Blackett said at last, unable to control his curiosity any longer. 'Farming, isn't it?'

'Hardly that. One cow and a few pigs and fowls and fruit and vegetables.'

'Ah, a sort of hobby,' Mr. Blackett suggested.

'We manage to make both ends meet,' Lindsay said cheerfully.

'Then you have a partner?'

'No, there's just George and me. He's my servant and a very good cook and then there's odd help now and then—all we need.'

'And now you are having a holiday,' Mr. Blackett told him.

'No, I've just moved into Somerset, not far away, a few miles across the bridge. A nice cottage and good land. I'd have been here sooner but it took me some time to settle in.'

'Did it hurt?' Mary asked suddenly.

'What? Settling in?'

'I meant your face.'

'Oh, I've forgotten all about that long ago,' he said.

Mr. Blackett was doing finger exercises on the tablecloth. 'I think your cousin's cup is empty, Flora,' he said.

Rhoda opened her mouth to speak and shut it again. She had not seen this cousin of hers before but she had heard about him. She had heard too about the batman who had dragged Piers Lindsay into safety and been wounded himself in doing so. George must be that man, she thought, but something warned her not to ask. There would be other opportunities and her cousin departed with genial invitations to them all to visit him. He would come and fetch them in the car. He was hoping to get a regular house to house sale for his vegetables in Upper Radstowe and one day, when he finished early, he would take them to the cottage and they could try George's cakes.

'How perfectly awful!' Flora exclaimed when he had limped into the car, waved a hand and rattled off.

'What?' Rhoda asked.

'His face,' said Mary, 'but I like it.'

'No. Selling vegetables,' Flora said. 'It's not very pleasant for us, is it?'

'Pooh!' said Rhoda. 'Who cares?'

Mr. Blackett had gone into the drawing-room where his wife still lay on the sofa. 'I think I had better help you up to bed,' he said, 'now that our visitor has gone at last. He made himself very much at home. Were you aware of his having moved into Somerset?'

'Oh yes,' Mrs. Blackett said. 'Of course.'

'Of course? But you didn't tell me.'

'Didn't I?' She seemed to search her memory. 'How stupid of me.'

'It's not of the slightest importance,' Mr. Blackett said loftily and put out his arms to raise her.

'No, Herbert, I can manage very well myself with the help of a chair and I can get up the stairs by sitting on them,' she said and, in his irritation, it pleased him to see her, who usually moved with an old-fashioned swaying grace, compelled to so ungainly an ascent.

CHAPTER IV

NEARLY a year had passed since that unfortunate Saturday afternoon and Mr. Blackett had graver matters for worry than the friendly communications established with the Frasers and the proximity of his wife's cousin. And he had seen very little of him. Saturday afternoon, one of the likeliest times for selling vegetables, was not one of those Piers Lindsay chose for driving into Upper Radstowe, a fact which had not escaped Miss Spanner's notice. After living vicariously for so long in books she was finding a new pleasure in the study of the immediate human scene and supplying herself with her own fiction which might or might not be less strange than the truth. And she had not let slip the acquaintance she and Rosamund had made with him in Mrs. Blackett's garden when he had appeared just in time to help them to get her into the house and all formalities were dropped in the general amusement, shared by Mrs. Blackett, as they tried different methods of reaching the drawing-room sofa. Since then, when Miss Spanner saw him in the Square she always discovered that the household was in need of vegetables and he always insisted on carrying them down the area steps and into the kitchen where he was quite willing to linger and sometimes lingered so long before he went into the Blacketts' house that the construction of Miss Spanner's plot was endangered.

Of his comings and goings Mr. Blackett heard very little. Mary, who was garrulous, was the only member of his family who ever mentioned Lindsay. Flora's anxiety about the social aspect of a cousin who hawked greenstuff vanished when she found he was on friendly terms with the Frasers, the only people who mattered at the moment, and Rhoda followed her mother's silent lead. Then the winter had closed down and by the time Mr. Blackett reached home his curtains were drawn against his other annoyance. He did not see the young men from next door; he was spared the irritation of watching Mrs. Fraser pass his window as she went to the pillar box at the corner of the Square, always with that air of happiness to which he considered she had no right and moving with the ease of good health and the certainty of her pleasant appearance. In his opinion she wore her skirts too short and he particularly disliked the little ornaments in her ears, small turquoises or gold filigree in an intricate pattern. In the winter he rarely saw her. It was in the summer that the Frasers became evident, strolling about the Square, talking to their friends outside the house, behaving, in fact, as though the place were theirs, but the winter enabled Flora to see more of her neighbours than her father would have cared for. She could walk home from the University with James Fraser and loiter with him on the pavement in the sheltering darkness and when he chose to wheel his bicycle beside her instead of hastening home on it, she felt a happiness she had only dreamed of a few months ago. But she was careful with it and with him. She let him do all the talking, though sometimes they were both silent, and that was very romantic, as they turned from the busy streets, the omnibuses and the shops into the quiet roads of Upper Radstowe where in James's company, every sight and sound was dimmed or sharpened into beauty.

She had soon realized the strategic importance of her father's study window; it raked the front door and the top of the area steps as well, but not when the curtains were drawn and, as it was the orderly habit of the young Blacketts to leave and enter the house by the basement where they put on and off their outdoor shoes, it was easy for Flora to slip in and out, easier than to leave by the front door which she could not open again without the key she did not possess. Besides, her father might have heard her. Why he should object to the Frasers she did not know. He took every opportunity of uttering or looking slight, half humorous disparagement, as though they amused him while they were hardly worth his notice, and she rebelled against the absurdity of having to do by stealth what other people could do openly. Why should her home be treated like a castle and everybody else like besiegers who must be repulsed? Sometimes Flora felt very lonely. Her father had always been her friend but now all her young impulses stood between him and her and in her mother's unvarying kindness she felt a hint of effort, as though she had to remember to be loving. She was different with Rhoda, less careful in her gentleness. Rhoda was her mother's daughter as Flora was her father's and she was at a stage most unsympathetic to Flora. Moreover, she always showed a faint antagonism towards her father, staring at him with studious calculation while he talked, rousing all Flora's loyalty to him and putting another barrier between the sisters. There was no one she could talk to about her own concerns, no one she could laugh with and it was when these necessities were strongest on her and she was supposed to be working in her bedroom that she would run out and ring the Frasers' bell. And this, which was adventure to her, was the ordinary, natural thing to them and though she might find no one but Mrs. Fraser and Miss Spanner and Sandra and Paul at home, she would stay in the long, rather untidy living-room, for a little while, before she tiptoed back again, wondering, to her shame, whether the Frasers' house felt so free because there was no father in it. Yet her own was not an ogre. He expected people to be happy in his own way, not in theirs, that was all, and his way was certainly not across the road or walking home under the flowering trees, on pavements strewn with fallen petals. His way proved, at the moment, to be much farther afield.

'This is the year,' he said one evening, 'when I had planned to take you all abroad.'

'Me too?' Mary cried, jigging up and down.

'Yes, you too,' he said benignly. 'We haven't been abroad since we were in Florence, have we, Bertha? How would you like to go there again?'

'Oh,' Mrs. Blackett said, growing pink. 'Oh no!'

'No?' he said, smiling teasingly at her across the table. He liked to see that blush, evoked by memories to which she never referred but evidently did not want to have overlaid by new experiences. 'Well, perhaps not,' he agreed, looking for a shy glance he did not get. 'I had thought, too, of the Loire country. What about that, Flora?'

'Yes,' Flora said doubtfully.

'H'm, no enthusiasm anywhere, except from Mary,' Mr. Blackett said, looking from one face to the other. 'Then perhaps it's just as well that I can't plan anything definitely. I thought I was going to delight you all and specially you, Flora.'

'It would be lovely,' Flora said feebly, 'only — '

'Only what?'

She took a short breath, lifting her finely pencilled eyebrows, parting her lips, and for a moment, in the full realization of her prettiness increased by her embarrassment, he forgot that he was awaiting her answer. Hers was not the fashionable prettiness of that girl next door; it had a character of its own. She was different from other people, as he was himself, with her sleek, dark hair plaited round her neat head and her big greenish eyes, again like his own though his were smaller and, fortunately, he had not her feminine lashes. He saw, too, with less pleasure, what his wife had meant in calling her attractive and he said more sharply, 'Only what?'

'I know,' said Mary, nodding her head importantly. 'It's the war.'

'The war?' Mr. Blackett asked suavely. It might have been a new word to him and it was one he much disliked.

'Because there may be one,' Mary went on. 'She told me and what a shame it would be if James got his face spoilt like poor Cousin Piers, when he's so handsome.'

'I didn't say he was handsome,' Flora exclaimed, unwisely showing her anger.

'Well, anyhow, you said he had a lovely face.'

'They are both very nice-looking boys, I think,' Mrs. Blackett said smoothly.

'May I,' Mr. Blackett asked politely, 'be told about whom you are all talking and by his Christian name?'

'Mrs. Fraser's sons,' said Mrs. Blackett, and she earned Flora's gratitude and immediately changed the nature of their relationship by turning to her and saying, 'I don't know which

33

I think more charming. Sometimes one and sometimes the other.'

'Yes,' Flora said quickly.

'But James is the one she likes best,' Mary said.

'I know him best,' was Flora's ready answer and, under her mother's protection, she jerked her head back in a gesture of gay self-confidence.

'I haven't the pleasure of the young man's acquaintance,' Mr. Blackett said slowly, 'or of the other charming gentleman's but do assure either or both of them, those of you who are on such easy terms with them, that wounds are not altogether a disadvantage. For one thing, they carry a comfortable pension with them and a disfigured face has extra compensations. It gives distinction to what it may have lacked before and assures its owner of admiration, solicitous and probably unwarranted admiration.'

Without turning her head, Rhoda turned the eyes which had been watching her father towards her mother and intercepted the glance Mr. Blackett did not see and in the very short time it lasted, Rhoda saw in it a concentration of emotions which she could not analyse and which half frightened her. There was a cold anger in it, but she thought there was a kind of pleasure in it too.

'And as for war,' Mr. Blackett said, doing finger exercises on the table, 'this great country will not be led into that enormity through the foolish stubbornness of an unimportant small one. Don't let us have any talk of war.'

Yet he had meant to hint at it himself, under a less definite name, when he spoke of his uncertainty about holiday plans. Flora's lack of enthusiasm had quite another cause. How could she leave Upper Radstowe now? This very evening and for the first time, James had kissed her. They had taken an omnibus to the Downs and suddenly, breaking away from his own words, he had kissed her under the shelter of a hawthorn tree. Flora was no judge of kisses, but it seemed to her that he had set the seal of perfection on this one by making it short and hard and calmly continuing his conversation. Lingering over that kiss, repeating it, would have spoilt it, she thought, and she had the wit to accept it in his manner though she was drowsed with joy and the sweet smell of the blossom. They had parted as usual, by common, unspoken consent, before they reached the Square. James was as anxious to avoid Miss Spanner's eye as Flora to avoid her father's. And now she was threatened with being taken from him, hundreds of miles away for what would seem like hundreds of years, to places she had always longed to see but were less desirable to her to-day than the meanest corner of Upper Radstowe. Perhaps, though the chance was poor, her father, after this evening's reception of his proposal, would decide to go off by himself. Nothing would suit her better than that, after Mary's indiscretion. It had been foolish to talk to her of James. She had simply felt an imperative need to hear herself speaking of him to someone else and the only possible someone had been Mary. But her mother had helped her and Flora tried to thank her with her good-night kiss.

'Good night, my child,' said Mrs. Blackett, looking at her with the tiniest glint of amusement on her calm face, a new look for Flora that sent her happily to bed. Her mother, she decided, was not quite the person she had always imagined her to be.

The same thought kept Rhoda awake, not happily, a little bewildered. Of course it was right for her mother to be angry at that hint of her father's about Cousin Piers; he was always unkind about him, but there had been more in her mother's look than honest anger and what it was Rhoda did not understand. She knew she would meet obstacles on the broad road of life she saw stretching before her, dangers too, and she was not afraid of them, but she had not expected to come upon dark narrow passages, crossing each other, in which one could get lost, a kind of maze, and she wished it were the morning when things might be clear and simple again. As for the talk of war, she would ask Cousin Piers about that. He would tell her the truth; so would Miss Spanner. She had made friends with Miss Spanner and this might give her another chance to see that strange bedroom of hers, like a clean secondhand shop.

CHAPTER V

MRS. BLACKETT went to bed in expectation of having to hear a good deal about Flora and the young man across the road, but Mr. Blackett proved to be in a sentimental mood which she found much more disagreeable and, as she reflected later, when after his usual spell of lying on his back, his beard like the ace of spades against the sheet, he turned on to his side and the gentle whistling through his nose had ceased, he seldom attacked when he was alone with her. Most of his darts, and there were not many of them, were loosed in the presence of the family. Was that, she wondered, because he knew she would be loyal and refrain from a retort and he would have the final, unchallenged word? This evening, she had made her uncontrollable silent comment and she hoped Rhoda had not seen it. Flora certainly had not; her eyes had been elsewhere and Mrs. Blackett smiled towards the window through which she could see a light still burning in Mrs. Fraser's bedroom. How pleasant, she thought, gently moving nearer to her edge of the bed, to have a bedroom, even a bed, of one's own, to be able to toss and turn, to put on the light and read, to know there was a whole night in front of you in which to be alone. Trying to multiply three hundred and sixty-five by twenty and then doing some subtraction but not much, Mrs. Blackett calculated, with difficulty and probably with error, the number of nights she had spent in that bed with Mr. Blackett. There might be just as many more to come and she felt very envious of Mrs. Fraser in her solitude. But at this hour Rosamund was not often alone. It was the happiest time in Miss Spanner's day when the young Frasers were finally shut into their bedrooms and she could seek Rosamund in hers and she would emerge, though still cautiously, in her modest dressing-gown, her hair hanging in two lank plaits, and find her friend propped up in bed and waiting for her.

Nobody knew how much Miss Spanner, casting disapproving eyes on Rosamund's bare neck and arms, enjoyed the sight of her. Very early, she had discovered for herself the beauty there could be in words; it was Rosamund, in her teens, who first gave her consciousness of beauty through her eyes. This was when, walking slowly up the Avenue with her mother, she had descried Rosamund on her bicycle, free-wheeling down the hill, her hair a dark halo for her glowing face, her skirt above her knees, a hand waved gaily at her less fortunate friend who saw beauty and freedom and happiness expressed in that flying figure. And Agnes stood still to watch her while Mrs. Spanner, with a disparaging little cough, walked on, taking short, hard steps to emphasize her opinion of this exhibition. And afterwards, as though some film had been peeled off her eyes, Agnes saw beauty elsewhere, too, and there was much of it close at hand, but she still found the best of it in Rosamund for it was bound up with the deep, concealed affection she had felt for her since they first went out to tea at each other's houses, and if Mrs. Blackett had known these two were together now, she might have envied their companionship as much as Rosamund's solitude.

'What's the matter?' Miss Spanner asked, taking her usual seat.

'Nothing,' Rosamund said.

'All right. Don't tell me. I'm not curious.'

'No, not a bit,' Rosamund agreed effusively.

'I suppose it's about Chloe.'

'Chloe?' Rosamund said.

'She hasn't come home yet, has she?'

'Considering you sleep at the back of the house, you don't miss much of what goes on at the front or, in this case, what doesn't go on, do you?'

'I have very sharp ears,' Miss Spanner said complacently. 'Sharp eyes, too.'

'I know. You can see through a brick wall. You can see things that aren't there.'

'I wish I could see Chloe,' Miss Spanner said gloomily, folding her arms across her flat chest.

'About something special?'

'Now don't try to be clever,' said Miss Spanner. 'You know you're worrying about her too. It's very late.'

'I knew she was going to be late.'

'Oh,' Miss Spanner said. She tried another line of attack. 'She isn't looking very well.'

'Not enough fresh air,' Rosamund said.

'H'm,' said Miss Spanner. She would not readily believe an explanation as simple as that, and though this might be another of the brick walls, she would see through it in time.

Rosamund picked up her knitting. She knew Agnes had not nearly finished yet and she could go on with her work and her own thoughts while she waited for another suggestive remark.

'I don't think Mrs. Blackett's very happy,' Miss Spanner said at last.

'Very? I shouldn't think she's happy at all. How could she be?'

'There's no accounting for tastes,' Miss Spanner said. 'I mean not as happy as she was when she came here first.'

'I don't see any difference. She always looks to me like a photograph of my grandmother, complete with bustle. I can never quite believe that she isn't really wearing a bustle and a bonnet. That's the impression she gives, married, submissive and settled for life.'

'I should hope so,' Miss Spanner said severely.

'And she can't be any older than I am, she's probably younger. I'm beginning to think it's a mistake to marry as young as she and I did.'

'I told you so at the time.'

'Yes, for your own silly reasons, not for mine.'

'And what may yours be?'

'Well, here I am with a full-grown family and I'm really at exactly the right age for marrying for the first time. At least that's how I feel.'

Miss Spanner's right eye took a sudden dart towards her nose. 'And what are you going to do about it?'

'Go on darning socks, I suppose, and making puddings and trying to keep out of debt. I don't know what I should have

38

done if my nice father hadn't saved as he did for me and he would have saved much more if your nasty one hadn't saved so much himself. But I'm getting some of it back. You pay me far too much and we both know it, so I keep my head above water. And I believe Fergus has sent me another cheque. I've got a letter from him, under my pillow.'

'And you haven't read it?'

'Not yet. I found it here when I came to bed. Sandra must have seen it on the mat and brought it up. I expect she thought I'd hate the whole family to turn it over. And now, of course, she'll be lying awake and worrying about what's in it. I wish she wouldn't worry so much.'

'Then,' said Miss Spanner cunningly, 'why don't you read it and find out if there's something nice to tell her?'

'And if there isn't? It has the same French postmark. Strange to be getting letters from France again. I used to get so many. I hope he isn't going hungry.'

'Living on the fat of the land, I expect, and gambling too, I shouldn't wonder.'

'The only time he ever came near gambling,' Rosamund said indignantly, 'was when he gave most of his capital to those raw-boned sisters of his to start an hotel. Perhaps it's paying dividends at last, but I'm sure they'll keep them back if they think I'll get any of them. I wish you wouldn't talk as though he's a wastrel when really he's so decent.'

'H'm,' said Miss Spanner, a favourite sound with her. 'I don't call it decent to go off and leave his children to fend for themselves.'

'It was the best thing he ever did for them, poor lamb, except giving them some of his good looks. Peace, perfect peace! And as for fending for themselves, that's ridiculous. How much of it have they had to do? And, though you won't believe it, he had a sense of duty. You needn't snort. When he left one job it was only because he thought he'd make more money for us in another.'

'You told me yourself he was sick of trying to sell motor cars.

People don't leave their work because they're sick of it,' Miss Spanner said virtuously.

'The more fools they. Life isn't meant to be sick in. And he wanted to write.'

'It's a common complaint,' said Miss Spanner, 'but the rash doesn't always develop satisfactorily. And the complaint is often an excuse for staying in bed, speaking metaphorically, if you know what that means.'

'You're a spiteful old devil,' Rosamund said, 'and you might remember he has a head wound as well as a few others here and there. People's memories are very short. Don't we owe him something, you and I?' she asked with heat. 'My own memory was too short. I didn't make allowances enough.'

'In fact,' said Miss Spanner, 'he's a perfect character.'

And in that suggestion, Rosamund thought, lay the chief part of the trouble, perhaps the whole of it. He was not perfect, he knew he was not, but, through some mental or moral twist, he expected other people to find him so, in spite of his tempers which Rosamund herself took lightly for, between him and her, there was no real divergence. But he would not brook fault finding or criticism. That was why he did not put his own name to the stories he had begun to write with some success — he would acknowledge nothing but the best — and why he sneered at his own efforts, forestalling sneers from anybody else and not aiming too high lest he should have to confess to failure. But he could not use a pseudonym in the home: his faults and his tempers had to be his own; his children, as they grew older, were his critics. He had been charming with them when they were little and not jealous as she had feared he might be though she had given him little cause. It was when they began to develop their own personalities and wills that he grew irritable, when he saw them weighing him up and suspected that they found him wanting. Then he allowed arguments, often reasonable enough, to develop into quarrels, and Felix, too, had a temper which seemed to indicate that Fergus had not only his wound to blame, though Rosamund had laid stress on this, hoping, too optimistically, for tolerance from the young. And at last Rosamund who had been placatory, who was always convinced troubles would pass, intervened too late and much too emphatically, and watched his astonishment at this disloyalty turn to rage, not the hot anger that burnt itself out and soon turned, with her, to laughter, but a cold one she had not seen before; his love, and he had never ceased to love her, turning to what must be hatred. It frightened her but it did something else more lasting. It made him more formidable but, oddly, smaller than she had believed him and cast a little shadow of befoolment on the memory of the days when he really had seemed faultless, when, and for long afterwards, she had first seen him, marching round the Green with his men, arrogantly swinging his kilt and almost stopping dead when he saw her smiling from the pavement. She had always smiled at the soldiers when they passed; it was all she could do for them; but her smile faded at the sight of Fergus. It was like seeing Fate go by and the look he gave her assured her that this was how he saw her too.

'No, not perfect,' she said now, 'but he used to make me laugh. We did a lot of laughing, even when those awful chickens died. Nothing serious seemed to matter. It was good to be young.'

'Very Heaven,' said Miss Spanner.

'Yes,' Rosamund said, surprised. 'What made you say that?'

'Just a quotation. You wouldn't know it. Not,' she added grimly, 'my personal experience. Still,' she said, after a moment, 'what you lose on the swings you gain on the roundabouts. I've had my books and while you've concentrated on six people, six ordinary people,' she said, and paused for contradiction but Rosamund, as usual, disappointed her and nodded pleasantly, 'while you've only had them, I've made hundreds of friends, yes hundreds of them, good and bad and all interesting. They can't possibly die before I do. I'm sure of them for as long as I want them and when. There's somebody for every mood and though they don't go off in tempers,' she said, giving Rosamund one of her meaning looks, 'and leave you in the lurch, you can send them away when you've had enough of them, as you'd do with me now if you weren't afraid of hurting my feelings. You're waiting till I go to read that letter.'

'There's no hurry about it and as for not hurting your feelings — what a funny expression that is, by the way — I don't think I could hurt them if I tried, or you mine. Ours is the best relationship in the world. We haven't to be careful. We haven't to think before we speak.'

'You never did, did you?'

'I'm learning,' Rosamund said. 'You have to, with children and husbands.'

'I don't, not with mine,' Miss Spanner said triumphantly. 'No, I wouldn't change places with you, for all your happy youth. I've had an exciting life. Quite a lot of love affairs, too,' she said, squinting violently.

'And I've only had one. It seems rather a pity.'

'Now,' Miss Spanner said warningly, 'you leave well alone.'

'But I don't call it well. I'm used to being made a fuss of and I miss it. I'm like an actress without an audience. There's nobody to appreciate my technique.'

'I'm not so sure of that,' Miss Spanner muttered.

'Are you referring to my innocent little dallyings with Mr. Blackett? You know I wouldn't touch him with the tongs though, I admit, I should like to make him thoroughly miserable, not for ever, just for a little while.'

'But what about making Mrs. Blackett miserable.'

'I should think she'd be rather pleased, but I'm a civilized person, as much as any woman ever is, and I can control my primitive impulses.'

'Then mind you do,' said Miss Spanner.

'And you,' said Rosamund, 'had better stick to the fiction you get in your books. I don't think much of the home-made variety. If we knew the truth we should probably find that Mrs. Blackett adores her husband.'

Miss Spanner had cocked her ear towards the window.

'There's a car coming now,' she said. 'D'you hear it? That must be Chloe at last.'

'Come away from those curtains,' Rosamund said sharply. 'I won't have you peeping. Suppose the young man saw you? And go to bed.'

'Plenty of time,' said Miss Spanner as she heard the click of the brake, but almost at once the front door was opened and shut and Chloe's quick feet were on the stairs.

CHAPTER VI

SHE stood in her mother's doorway looking rueful but matter of fact. 'I'm sorry I'm so late,' she said. 'We had a puncture.'

'One does,' Rosamund said.

'Oh, this was a real accident. I mean he didn't stick a nail into the tyre or anything. He wouldn't think of that or, if he thought of it, he wouldn't do it.'

'Wouldn't he?' Rosamund said and she wondered at the young man as she looked at Chloe, sitting now on the end of the bed, her head rising flower-like from the big upturned collar of her coat.

'Much too conscientious,' Chloe said.

'That sounds rather nice.'

'Oh yes, plenty of niceness, nearly all niceness I should think. The kind of young man who has been a good son and so, I don't know why, will be a good husband. That's what your mother-in-law says when you get engaged to him and doesn't think you're half good enough. I don't suppose I am.'

'And are you engaged to him?'

'No, but he asked me to marry him while he was changing the wheel. With hands like that! Suppose I'd said yes? But then if I'd had to, if I'd wanted to, I shouldn't have cared if he'd been covered with grease, should I? How awkward things are! It would be so suitable. He's quite well off, by our standards; he

43

went into all that very thoroughly and I nearly laughed, and then, he'd be so safe. I'm always afraid of losing my head over some attractive cad. But that would be like marrying a policeman because you're afraid of burglars.'

'You might just as easily lose your head after you were married.'

'I might,' Chloe agreed, 'but I'd stick to my bargain. Anyhow, I don't really want to marry anyone for ages.'

'Then don't,' Rosamund said.

'But I want to have a lot of children.'

'Then do,' said Rosamund.

'But wouldn't it be rather awful never to have been terribly in love?'

'Yes, I think it would.'

'Well, he may get me in the end. He's very persistent.'

'Then he didn't take his dismissal meekly?'

'Of course not. Would you? If he'd done that,' Chloe said, 'I shouldn't even have bothered to tell you about him. Do you think Sandra's asleep?'

'No, I'm sure she wouldn't go to sleep till she knew you were safely back.'

'What a nuisance the child is! Now I shall feel I can't stay out as late as I want to.'

'But you mustn't stay out late.'

'I didn't think you minded.'

'I don't, on Saturdays, when you can stay in bed the next morning.'

'Is that all? I was afraid, for a minute, you were being a proper kind of mother.'

'I know I'm not a very good one,' Rosamund said.

'Don't be so silly! I didn't mean proper like that. I meant prim. You're just the kind I like. I shouldn't think Flora Blackett can talk to her mother as I do to you.'

'Perhaps she has no need to,' Rosamund said, and when she saw Chloe steadying her eyes a little too carefully, she laughed and said, 'All right. I'm like Agnes. I'm not curious.'

'Poor old Spanner! No, you're sweet,' Chloe said, and dropped a light kiss on her mother's hand.

'I've tried not to stick my claws into you,' Rosamund said, but when Chloe had gone she wished she had not seemed to be taking credit for what had come quite easily to her. She was not passionately maternal. Her children had followed each other quickly and without difficulty or pre-natal yearnings. They were the natural results of her marriage, not miracles, and she had been and remained too much occupied with Fergus to lavish over anxious care on them – it was years before she thought of buying a thermometer – and she was too young and ignorant and happy to watch for worrying psychological developments. It was much later that she realized the accidental wisdom of this detachment. The children did not depend on her unduly. Chloe had been confidential with her this evening because her emotions had not been roused – when that happened, for happiness or sorrow, she doubted whether she would hear anything about them. All the children were frank on the surface; they kept their deeper feelings, if they had any, to themselves and even Sandra's worries were indicated rather than expressed. And this, Rosamund thought, was as it should be. They were separate people, standing on their own feet, needing no parental props, and all their difficulties lay ahead when she would not be able to help them and, ultimately, every human being was alone. Yet, she wondered, were they all missing what she had withheld, first through light-heartedness and then by design? They had been brought up, too, as she had been herself, without any religion except what could be had at school. Had she wronged them there? She did not think so. If they felt the need of it, they could go and find it now, when nothing could be imposed on them by authority. Truthfulness and courtesy were what she had insisted on and these virtues included many others. Ought she to have marched them off to church on Sundays as Mr. Blackett marched his family? It might have been good discipline for the children but it would have been intolerably boring for herself and if they had asked her why she took them, she could not have given them a satisfactory answer. Whether she had been right or wrong, she could find little fault with the results. They were good children and they had, she decided, discipline enough in uncomplainingly doing without the indulgences most of their friends took as a matter of course.

'If there's a nice cheque inside this letter,' she thought, drawing it from beneath her pillow, 'I shan't spend a penny of it on necessities. I shall squander it all on the children. No, I shall give it to them to squander any way they like.'

Something of the same kind occurred to Miss Spanner when she returned to the bedroom Rhoda Blackett found so fascinating. It was a pleasant room with two low windows looking on to the garden. It would have graced fine old furniture or the productions of modern craftsmen in pale woods and Rosamund, enthusiastic about both schemes, was eager to help Miss Spanner with either. Nothing except her books, she said, ought to be brought from the dismal house on the Green. She must sell everything in it and shake the dust of it from her feet. But Miss Spanner, who had some sense of fitness, could not see herself moving elegantly amid eighteenth-century furniture and she said she was too dowdy to associate with the pale woods.

'Then why be dowdy?' Rosamund said.

'Too much bother to change,' said Miss Spanner, 'and not likely to be successful.'

Moreover, she prized much in her old home that Rosamund despised. There was the tiger-skin rug, for instance. Her great uncle had shot the tiger. It was something to have an uncle who had done that and when the boys asked her whether she was sure he had not bought the trophy in a London shop, she could show them a faded photograph of him seated on the tiger. Two smaller felines, more victims of his prowess, had always hung limply, as though disgraced, over the backs of armchairs in the drawing-room and Miss Spanner took all three skins to the Square. And she was thrifty. She was not going to sell good solid stuff for a mere song and she had only been restrained from laying down a good Turkey carpet, not long enough for the room and much too broad, by the certainty of providing a happy home for moths in the bulky fold which would be necessary. The tables, the top of the chest of drawers, the mantelshelf and the walls were all covered with ornaments and pictures she could not bear to part with and her only new possession was the electric reading lamp beside her bed. There had been no electric light in the house on the Green. The gas jet had hissed at some distance from her bed and, for reading there, she had been compelled to the use of candles and had always been in fear of gentle chiding if discovered. She had not yet lost her pride and pleasure in switching that light on and off and she was completely satisfied with her room.

'You'll have to dust it all yourself,' was Rosamund's comment as she eyed this collection with amusement and dismay.

Miss Spanner did more than that. She behaved, Rosamund complained, as though she were the paid help instead of the paying boarder. The only paid help was a lethargic charwoman who lived in one of the basements in the Square and, leaning on her broom, gave Miss Spanner all the news of the neighbours, thus enabling her to create exciting dramas round people of whom Rosamund had never heard. Sandra need have had no qualms about Miss Spanner's personal happiness. Nothing within this house was wanting to it and that conviction, coming over her as she turned on the light and saw it flooding her little Paradise, seemed to demand expression, not in words, for agreeable ones from her would have been out of character, but in some kind of unexpected treat for people who had made the place a home for her, accepting her as part of theirs. 'Why should they?' she asked, catching a glimpse of herself in the glass. She had been sure of Rosamund but what could she seem to the others except a rather peculiar and sour old maid? Yet Chloe, meeting her just now at her mother's door, had said 'Good night, Miss Spanner,' in a voice that was almost tender. 'Perhaps she's sorry for me,' Miss Spanner thought. 'And no wonder,' she added, getting another glimpse of the drab dressing-gown and the thin plaits. But Chloe was wrong, she decided,

47

sitting down and resting her head against the flattened head of one of her great uncle's cats. She had nothing to lose except her present happiness and already she had enjoyed it for a year and more. 'Manna from Heaven,' she said to herself. It was more than that for she had passed out of the desert too. She took her good fortune gratefully while it was vouchsafed, she would not grumble if it were withdrawn and that was possible, it was even likely. She could not share the complacency of her countrymen, their comfortable belief that those who yelled and threatened must be playing a big game of bluff, that foul ideas could not actually develop into fouler action. To respond with soft words and reasonable suggestions seemed to her like trying to divert a mad dog by whistling to him cheerfully but because men in high places did whistle optimistically, the rest of the country seemed to be content. Or was it merely that it was indifferent, morally and mentally weakened by the inertia that had fallen on it since the last war? And what could she do about it? she asked herself, feeling cold with anxiety and huddling closer into her chair. She was not suffering from physical fear though she had imagination enough to foresee that there might be bitter cause for it. Secretly and very deeply, she loved her country, its virtues and its faults. She was proud of it and, looking back, she saw its history studded with great names and great deeds and round these the force that created them, the character of its people. Had the strength gone from it, leaving only the tolerance and good humour which could be a weakness? The people were allowing themselves to be led by amiable old gentlemen who apparently thought their own pacific leanings were a safety in themselves. Meek sheep, that's what we are, Miss Spanner thought, trotting after the shepherd into wild country with nothing but his pleasant smiles for protection against wolves. It was not war Miss Spanner feared, except for these young ones whose hopes would be shattered, their bodies too, their children unborn and their work never accomplished. War was horrible, but there were worse things. Indeed, in conditions of her own choosing, Miss Spanner would not have shrunk from it. The age for

48

combatants, if she had the making of the conventions of war, would start at about forty-five and there would be no limit at the other end. All but the halt and the blind would be in it and she saw this army of her creation, with grey hairs and wrinkles under the helmets, floundering through the mud, swimming rivers, trying to run, gasping for breath, falling out exhausted or deciding it was time for a truce and a nice cup of tea. She felt quite equal to dealing with an enemy of her own age. She would last out better than most of them, she was very wiry, a bullet would go through her as though she were tissue paper and there was a strong strain of pugnacity in her character. 'I shouldn't be at all surprised if I got a commission, on the field,' she thought and, for a few minutes, she lost her consciousness of present time and place as she saw herself, cool and resourceful, the insignificant Miss Spanner a distinguished figure amid the rabble. Meanwhile, the young and the strong would be getting on with the real business of life and war would surely end for ever in tears and laughter. 'Once make it ridiculous and that would finish it,' she said. But there was no chance of that and there seemed to be nothing for her to do.

'Except to fill up that form,' she remembered, and as the church clock on the Green struck twelve and a siren hooted on the river, twelve solemn notes and one defiant one, she pledged herself to the service of her native city. 'But I shan't tell anyone,' she thought. 'They'd laugh. And perhaps I shan't be needed.'

Then she said her prayers, hoping that more than she dreamed of might be wrought by them.

CHAPTER VII

MR. BLACKETT, coming home rather earlier than usual one evening, found the vicar clipping the privet hedge in his front garden. This, near the church, faced the Green, so did Mr. Doubleday's study and he kept the hedge at a height that did not impede his view from the window and made it easy, when busy with his shears, to see the passers-by and have a chat with those he knew and smile at anyone, known or unknown, who gave him the opportunity. At the sight of Mr. Blackett, regular in his church attendance though, enviably, only once on Sunday, Mr. Doubleday laid his shears on the flat top of the hedge and Mr. Blackett, who despised the old gentleman's sermons and would have been surprised to learn that Mr. Doubleday thought nothing of them himself, was held to the ransom of a little talk by the vicar's beaming smile.

After glancing at a passing aeroplane, Mr. Doubleday straightened his face and referred to the European situation, a topic he seemed to think suitable to Mr. Blackett's air of gravity, and he relinquished the subject gladly when he received a somewhat curt reply. He had not really wanted to talk about it and he was much happier when Mr. Blackett spoke of the beauties of Upper Radstowe, then of the houses in the Square and so of some of the people in them. It was the first time in his life that Mr. Blackett had conversed, though he listened more than he spoke, across a garden hedge, but he was rewarded in thus breaking his code of manners and excused by the respectability of Mr. Doubleday's clerical hat and he walked home at much less than his usual sharp pace. It was only a short distance to the Square and he had a good deal to think about, with a good deal of pleasure, before he reached it. When he did reach it and, following the curve of the Oval, could see the Frasers' house and his own, he was startled to see too a muddled group of people clustered round a motor car and he hastened towards the scene of what he feared, for a short minute, must be an accident. Then the group resolved itself into Piers Lindsay with his car and trailer surrounded of course, Mr. Blackett had time to reflect, by a collection of women among whom, to his astonishment and what, on another day, would have been disgust, he saw his wife. Mrs. Fraser, taller by an inch or two, was there, and Miss Spanner, like a draped stick. This might have been a gathering in some mean street, where the front doors were all open, the women gossiping and chaffing the huckster while the children, all eyes and ears, joined in the fun, for Rhoda was watching Lindsay as he weighed something in the scales at the back of the trailer and Mary was sitting at the wheel of the car. It only needed a barrel organ, thought Mr. Blackett, and the little red-haired Fraser dancing to it, to complete the picture, but it was his own children, not the Fraser girls who were present.

'Get into the car and I'll take you for a drive,' Mary called to him, acting the baby for his benefit.

Smiling, he shook his head at her, removed his hat and acknowledged his neighbours gravely, but he looked longer at Mrs. Fraser than was necessary, longer, indeed, than was quite courteous, and then he turned to Lindsay.

'Trade seems to be good,' he said.

'Not at all bad,' he replied. 'Relatives and friends all rallying round. No, I'll carry this for you, Bertha,' he said, and she and Rhoda followed him down the area steps while Mr. Blackett let himself through the front door.

'Most unfortunate,' said Miss Spanner. 'One late and the other early.'

Mr. Blackett in his bedroom, changing his business suit for easier garments, took a discreet peep into the road. Miss Spanner, clasping a lettuce, was going towards the house; Lindsay and Mrs. Fraser were talking somewhat earnestly, it seemed to Mr. Blackett; then they appeared to settle something between them; Lindsay fastened up the end of the trailer, hustled Mary out of the driver's seat and took it himself, but instead of driving away he manoeuvred the car into position opposite the Fraser's door and then, with Mrs. Fraser, entered the house.

'Just so,' Mr. Blackett said to himself, 'just so,' jerkily tightening the knot of his necktie and, contrary to Rhoda's expectations, he was in a very good humour at the supper table. Meanwhile, the cousin's car stood outside the other door and it seemed to her very hard and all wrong that he should be there instead of here, though, she admitted, it would not have been very nice. What

51

she would have really liked would have been to cross the road herself and spend the evening with him and Miss Spanner. The other members of the family did not interest her. It was not comfortable to meet Sandra Fraser outside the school for, within it, she was a member of the sixth form, a prefect, a person of importance who had had occasion to reprove Rhoda who vaguely blundered through her work, broke rules through inattention and was only noticeable for her lapses. She envied Sandra for all the qualities she did not possess herself and thought it unfair that she should have Cousin Piers as well.

Mary, too, seemed to begrudge him to the Frasers. 'He's still there,' she said, turning in her chair. 'He must be staying to supper.'

'No doubt he sings for it,' Mr. Blackett said pleasantly.

'Sings for it?'

'Yes, in his own way,' Mr. Blackett said.

'But how?'

'Ah, I've never been privileged to hear him, but it's a sort of reversal, I imagine, of the sirens' song.'

'I don't know what that is,' Mary said.

'But without the wax,' Mr. Blackett continued with a smile.

'I don't understand,' Mary complained.

'Never mind. Just my nonsense.'

Here was an opportunity for instruction missed. Rhoda, looking at him with her considering stare, as she might have looked in a shop window and wondered whether she liked what was displayed there, noticed this omission and determined to trace the allusion which had some hidden place in her memory. Flora, who would have been sure to remember it, was fulfilling one of her increasing number of engagements.

Mr. Blackett himself was not satisfied with his analogy. He liked to be accurate and this one was confused, for the singer, in this case, was not the siren, who was assuredly making for the rocks and Mr. Blackett was not going to warn him of them:

'Nice people, I believe,' Mr. Doubleday had said of the Frasers.

52

'Mrs. Fraser's father was much respected in Upper Radstowe. Not a churchgoer,' he said and added quickly, 'unfortunately. And old Mr. Spanner,' here he looked grave without difficulty, 'was a nonconformist, but a very good firm of solicitors — Spanner and Brookes.'

Mr. Blackett had now learnt the connection between the two women next door, the one offending by her unattractiveness almost as much as Mrs. Fraser did by the consciousness of her ability to charm, one neglecting the obvious mission of a woman, the other making it a kind of sport, worth while for its own sake even if she brought nothing home. But he had discovered more than that. His instinctive distrust of her was justified.

'What, is her husband dead?' Mr. Doubleday had cried when Mr. Blackett sympathetically remarked on her widowhood and family cares. 'No, no, that can't be. I should have heard of it. One hears everything, you know. Can't avoid it,' he said, sighing and smiling together. 'Some little trouble, I believe. So my wife tells me. What a pity! What a pity! But it will blow over,' he promised, beaming again. 'These little matrimonial troubles often do, I find,' and he picked up his shears. Mrs. Doubleday's drawing-room faced the garden too and he had been idle long enough.

This was what had caused Mr. Blackett to walk home slowly and to be cheerful at supper, in spite of that scene in the street. He was a thoughtful man: he wrestled with problems over which Mr. Doubleday, for instance, found no difficulty, the existence of pain and evil, of God himself, and if he did not discuss these matters with his children, it was because he had no solutions to offer and he confined himself to subjects on which he could speak with personal certainty. But, curious as he was about many matters, there were regions of his own mind which he did not care to explore with thoroughness. He knew he might find things there which, as a conscientious person, he ought to remove, but their effects were pleasurable and he preferred to leave them undisturbed. He liked to believe that, in any case of an absent husband, the woman must be to blame. If he strayed, it was her fault for not being agreeable or clever enough to hold him; if she were guilty as, with Mrs. Fraser, seemed most likely, because this was how he wished to find her, then no excuse was possible, and he had the right to look at her a little longer, with a shade less respect than he would have wished anyone to look at Bertha. But — he watched her as she made the coffee, her pretty, plump hands moving slowly and deftly — Bertha, he was thankful to know, would never attract errant glances and she would, very properly, have resented them if she had recognized them. She was quite definitely his and everything she did and said acknowledged a settled contentment in her situation and the impossibility of imagining any other, and he felt a moment's irritation at her implied assumption that he was as well satisfied as she was. He was, of course, completely satisfied; no other kind of wife would have suited him; she was perfect, yet it would have enlivened existence to have her less sure of him while he remained sure of her, to see her taking a little trouble to keep a lover as well as a husband. But she had never played any feminine tricks, she was too profoundly innocent. And how silent she was, another valuable quality; yet, again, now that he was silent himself because he was afraid of saying what he would regret, he wished she would introduce some topic interesting in itself or capable of being made so. And he was sorely tempted to startle her out of her calm by Mr. Doubleday's shocking news, but then, in her gentle way, she would pass it on to Lindsay for his good and that was what Mr. Blackett did not desire. He did not tell himself why. Here was another of the regions he would not explore too far. He could not, however, resist the pleasure of hovering at the edge of both. They had been entirely separate, they were now intermingled, and they made a fascinatingly complicated country.

'He seems to make friends easily, your cousin,' he remarked. 'Gets bored with his own company, perhaps. One can understand that.'

'One of Mrs. Fraser's sons wants to be a farmer,' Mrs. Blackett said.

'Interesting,' Mr. Blackett said blandly, 'and I hope the young man will be successful, but I don't quite see the relevance.'

'Piers may be able to advise him.'

'Oh, I see. Yes.' Asking advice of a man was the surest way of flattering him. 'But the greengrocery trade is rather a far cry from farming, isn't it? And you know, Bertha, I'm not narrow-minded and I don't consider myself conventional, but is it really necessary to cluster round the vegetables as I found you all doing this afternoon? It was rather a vulgar spectacle and how the ghosts haunting this old square must have shuddered! Why not get your vegetables sent to you decently from a shop?'

'These are freshly gathered and I want to help him,' Mrs. Blackett said.

'He ought to have avoided giving you the opportunity.'

'Why?' Mrs. Blackett asked.

He lifted his shoulders. 'That's a question impossible to answer. It's a matter of feeling, it can't be put into words, and as for helping him, you know very well he has a pension and no responsibilities and the pension must be adequate or he would have found himself a real job long ago, or,' Mr. Blackett said slowly, 'have induced someone to give him one.'

'Why,' asked Mrs. Blackett as she collected the coffee cups, 'do you dislike him so much? But perhaps,' she added quietly, picking up the tray, 'that's another question it's impossible for you to answer.'

Mr. Blackett stared at the door she had shut behind her. It certainly was a question impossible for him to answer truthfully without acute discomfort and he blinked it away. What he did face was his surprise, his slight uneasiness, that it had come from Bertha. She had laid — was it accidentally? — some emphasis on the personal pronoun. 'Still waters run deep,' he found himself saying and then in annoyance, first for his own triteness and then for applying it to Bertha, he left his chair and went to the window.

The shabby car and trailer were still there and the car, he thought, looked like some patient old cab horse drowsing between the shafts, taking what rest he could get, and this was all part and parcel of Lindsay's make-up, the old car, the humble occupation pursued with such cheerful simplicity, the limp, the whimsically distorted face, and Mr. Blackett was obliged to acknowledge the artistic perfection of the performance. He turned away impatiently but he could not settle down to a book. He missed Flora. What with amenities connected with the University, and there seemed to be a lot of them, and the new friends she had made, there were a good many evenings when she was not at home. And Bertha had not returned with her sewing. It always soothed him to see her at it and he went to the drawing-room in search of her, but she was not in the pale, sparsely furnished room with everything in its place and nothing without a certain impersonal elegance. The room was not like her, he thought, pausing to look about him, and he had had no hand nor had he paid for anything in it. She had brought some things from her old home, the water-colours in their narrow gilt frames, the old-fashioned work table with its silk bag, a small walnut bureau and a few stiff chairs: the rest she had bought with her small legacy from her father. It was not like her, he thought again, wondering that he had not noticed this before. Bertha was essentially a wife and mother and it was strange that she had not impressed her characteristics on a room of her own choosing.

'Almost uninhabited,' he muttered and went to the door at the top of the steps down which she had been careless enough to fall last year.

She was in the garden with Rhoda and they were both working on the borders. It was so small a place that Mr. Blackett would not have bestowed more care on it than was necessary to keep it neat, but they were going to make it very gay. That was all very well, but had Rhoda done her homework? Something in the happy absorption of these two who had their backs towards him, stopped him from calling to her. Rhoda was a clumsy mover, thunderous on the stairs and apt to collide with the furniture, but he noticed that her hands were as deft as her mother's, and she touched the plants with surprising gentleness. Bertha, of course, had inherited her love of gardening from her father and she seemed to have passed it on to Rhoda and, as clearly as though they had told him, he knew their happiness in the work was doubled by doing it together. He felt lonely and isolated and unwontedly dissatisfied with himself as he stood at the top of the little staircase and he stepped back into the drawing-room before they could turn round and see him.

CHAPTER VIII

THE young man who wished to be a farmer was not present to hear any advice Piers Lindsay might have to give and there was not much of it.

'I'm buying some more land myself,' he said. 'There'll be a lot of food wanted if things go as I think they will. It won't be what you could call farming, though. Chiefly potatoes. Still, I shall need more help and if he's on the land already there's just the chance that he might not be taken off it.'

'What did Mr. Blackett do in the Great War?' was Rosamund's reply.

They were upstairs, in the drawing-room, and she had just lighted the fire, for it was hardly summer yet and the room felt chilly, and, tending it from her knees, she turned and looked at him as she asked this question. A stranger would not have known whether he was amused or grieved, but he was not a stranger now and she was learning to read expressions through the fixed, half-humorous mask.

'He was doing work of national importance,' Lindsay said gravely.

'Exactly! And that's my reply to your kind offer. I'm surprised you made it.'

'But I knew, pretty well, what you'd say,' he assured her.

She found this remark very warming and she was in need of

57

warmth; she was in need of recovering some sense of her own value, for it was a sound instinct that had bade her postpone the opening of Fergus's letter. He had made it clear that he did not intend to come back, that he did not wish to do so and was getting on very happily where he was. It was wonderful, he said — the whole letter was cheerfully friendly and this she found very daunting — it was wonderful how much more and how much better work could be done in sympathetic surroundings, and that remark, more than his suggestion that they should be legally parted as the present situation was senseless, had really hurt her because it touched her where she had a weakness. She had adopted his own light attitude towards his writing and he must have wanted encouragement, wanted to be taken seriously, to have a higher standard raised for him than he had dared to raise himself, and she had failed him while she thought all was well between them because they had never ceased to be lovers or to find pleasure in each other's company. That had been a great deal, it was more than most people had and it had seemed to satisfy him but, when she had seriously angered him — so she had worked things out in many wakeful hours — then he remembered faults in her she had never suspected and he had never mentioned. But, she excused herself, whatever they may have been there had not been much time, in her life with him, for more than she managed to do. It had been hard work with five children to rear and very little money to stretch for their needs. She had had a Victorian family in post-war circumstances; he ought to have thought of that and she suspected him of exaggerating her omissions in justification of himself. And, if that was necessary, there was no more to be said, though much to be thought of and she found she was able to think of his sympathetic surroundings with more fear for him than any other emotion; yet it was quite possible that his present surroundings were what he had always needed. She had loved him too simply, she supposed, taking everything for granted, never wondering whether he wanted anything he did not ask for. Why should she? She had not wanted more than he had given her. That was where she had been stupid and unimaginative, she decided, and it was humiliating, more humiliating than the loss of her physical hold on him, to look back and see him bearing patiently with her mental deficiencies. But, if that were true, she thought with amusement, it was the only provocation under which he had exercised that virtue. And he might find – here she was a little spiteful – that being loved simply was better than being loved with cunning. In the meantime – and she had always insisted with Agnes on his decency – he was worried about the money. He had not sent a cheque for fear it might prejudice her case but when he had heard from her lawyer – how absurdly distant that sounded – he would see what could be done. He seemed very sure of her acquiescence. She supposed she would have to oblige him and, truly, she did not want him back. She did not see how she or the children could readjust themselves to his presence. This break in the chain they had forged together could not be properly mended, not, at least, without clumsy signs of welding, yet it was sad that all the links should fall apart and what had been a solid entity should be disintegrated so easily. And, naturally, she suffered in her pride. That was why Piers Lindsay's words were grateful to her and she gave him a big, honest smile of pleasure, without self-consciousness, without realizing the charm of her attitude and her smile until she detected, for she was practised in such matters, his unmistakable appreciation.

This was warming, too, warming enough to make her turn to the fire again and say, 'And I suppose the war and all that is why Mr. Blackett dislikes you?'

'Does he?' Lindsay said mildly. 'I don't see why he should. It's all a very long time ago and he knew his own business best.'

'Yes, I know that's the correct thing for a man to say, a man who fought himself, but it's not what women think, not those of us who remember. And I remember. It's all discredited now and the people who avoided fighting are better off than those who didn't and the whole world flopped and everything seemed to have been wasted and you were all fools for your pains. That's what the younger generation believes, though I've tried to teach mine better, but when they look around them what else can you expect? It was a great time to have lived in, all the same, though not a very nice one for Mr. Blackett to remember,' she said, getting easily to her feet.

'You're hard on him, aren't you? He's not the only one.'

'He's the only one who lives next door to me and I don't like him. Do you? Oh, you needn't answer! And here's Chloe with the coffee.'

'But I ought to be going.'

'Just when I've lighted the fire?'

'I shall get into trouble with George, you know. He'll be very reproachful. A good supper spoilt.'

'Well, tell George – does he bully you? – not to cook it in future, on your Upper Radstowe days, until you get home. Then you can stay when you want to without upsetting him.'

'May I?'

'Of course, and next time you come I hope James will be here.'

James, at the moment was, unknowingly, giving Flora a hard lesson in love. Already, one of her disappointments had been his lack of money; not that she wanted him to spend it on her; in fact, she told herself romantically, she loved him all the more for having none, but it did hamper their movements. He could not often afford a meal outside his home, he told her frankly, or many visits to cinemas and theatres. Besides, here was the masculine touch, he did not like them. He liked being out of doors.

'Oh, so do I,' Flora said, quickly adapting herself. She would have been an ardent playgoer at a word from him, and he had found her wonderfully interested in what he could tell her about farming; indeed, but for her father, she would have switched over to that University course herself. Knowing this and thinking all the better of her, he had no scruples against giving her detailed reports of his lectures. A silent person at home, he did not spare this listener. Often she wished he would change the subject to herself and look at her sometimes, but it was she who looked at him, keeping an intelligent half ear open to the action of different chemicals on the soil, the other half hearing the quiet tones of his voice, her eyes studying each line of his face and noting each characteristic movement, and this was her reward for the little shifts and stratagems to which she was impelled. Her mother never asked any questions, but her father's interest in her doings was very inconvenient; he must always know what subject had been discussed at the debating society and what music she had heard at the music club and, as she foresaw that her answers would tax her ingenuity and might lead to her undoing, she had wisely told him there were no such meetings during the summer term, just informal ones among friends. And was not that true enough? Was not James her friend? She had to answer the second question with an affirmative too emphatic for her happiness. That first kiss under the hawthorn tree had been as sacred and significant to her as a betrothal but she had had to realize it was not that to James. She had had no experience, and she was slowly to discover that kissing was quite a commonplace amusement to many of her generation. Even more passionate encounters were treated lightly. Hitherto she had known very little about her contemporaries and while, inevitably, she was shocked, she was excited by this new world where people acknowledged and indulged emotions of which she thought she ought to be ashamed. She had to tell herself that James's love was of more valuable mintage than the current coin and his undemonstrativeness, the rareness of his kisses, were the highest compliment he could pay her. When he did kiss her it was with the same matter of fact suddenness he had shown under the hawthorn as though he might as well enjoy the clearness of her skin, the natural redness of her lips. It was a simple, unpremeditated act and she was attractive with her dark hair and red mouth and greenish eyes and lately she had cleverly counteracted the somewhat artistic arrangement of her hair by wearing clothes as fashionably severe as her dress allowance and her parents' prejudices would permit. Nevertheless, it was she who instigated most of their secret meetings; the secrecy was nearly all of her choosing; and on the evening when Piers Lindsay was supping comfortably in the Square, Flora had arranged to have a picnic meal in a nook overlooking the river.

'Won't it be too cold?' James had said with cruel honesty. Then, seeing her face fall, he had agreed, but it was far from warm there and it was not a good meal. She had had to buy what she could and the second course, jam tarts, had too much resemblance to the first one of meat pies.

'Now, if only we had something to drink,' James said, wounding her a little, 'I'd drink Miss Spanner's health.'

Backed by trees and bushes and then by the broad stretch of grass on one side of the Avenue, they sat near the edge of the cliff and looked down at the river, now a narrow channel between muddy banks, and across at the trees climbing the opposite slope. All shades of green were there, from palest to almost black, and here and there the trunk of a silver birch looked like the ghost of a tree among the living ones. On their left they could see the great pier supporting the farther end of the bridge, but a bastion of rock on their right screened off a more extended view of the river.

'It's nice here, isn't it?' Flora said hopefully.

'Yes, but we're sitting on the best side instead of looking at it.'

'Then why didn't you tell me?'

'It doesn't matter, does it?'

'No, not really,' Flora said with a touch of tenderness. 'Why do you want to drink Miss Spanner's health? Is it her birthday?'

'Not that I know of, but she's made it a kind of birthday for all of us. Given us some money for our holidays.'

'Oh,' Flora said, and added feebly, 'How kind!'

'I hadn't expected to have one, but now Felix and I can go off in September. Grand, isn't it?'

It was a moment or two before Flora could say, 'That's just when we may be going abroad.' Now all the trees seemed to have turned black, the sluggish strip of water and the grey banks were melancholy and the hoarse cries of the gulls as they searched for garbage had a cruel mocking note.

'Looking at churches and things?' James said with a grin.

'Not necessarily,' Flora replied. 'I expect it will be very gay. I expect we shall have quite a lot of fun,' but she saw herself under a glaring sun, trying to keep pace with her father, gazing at cathedrals and trailing on tired feet through picture galleries while Rhoda, looking glum, followed some way behind, Mary wanted to go somewhere else and her mother walked calmly, with her peculiar, somewhat swaying gait and pretended not to be hot and weary, a sight-seeing family with only one member of it enjoying himself. And sometimes, they would sit outside a café and have an ice for a treat. But what did it matter? Here was James, happy in his plans for going away and a little while ago she had felt sick at the threat of being parted from him.

'The Loire country, that's what we thought of,' she said. 'All those lovely castles and beautiful scenery.'

'And we're going to the mountains — at last,' James said.

'Switzerland?'

'No. Wales.'

'Oh,' said Flora in a slightly disparaging manner.

James did not notice it. 'I saw them once, from a long way off,' he said, wiping his fingers on the grass, then clasping his hands round his knees and staring in front of him. 'From our O.T.C. camp,' he said.

'My father thinks those O.T.C.s are very bad things,' Flora said. 'He says they make people war-minded.'

'Does he?' James drew his inward gaze from the invisible hills and looked at her. He was not exactly handsome, she thought. Perhaps Felix was really better looking, but then Felix had never taken more notice of her than the barest courtesy required, and she did not think a man ought to have red hair. James was dark, his features were good but roughly finished and their shape seemed to change with his moods. It was his height and his broad shoulders and the strong ease with which he carried himself that moved her. 'Oh, does he?' he repeated. 'Well, if messing about in the mud and sleeping in a leaky tent makes you war-minded, he's quite right. And seeing those hills,' he said, turning from her again, 'and not being able to get at them. But I always meant to. So did Felix. And then, when we had our birthday presents this morning —'

'When's your real birthday?' Flora asked.

'Never mind that, April, we both knew what we were going to do. And there'll be enough money for the boots as well.'

'Boots?'

'Yes, with proper climbing-nails in them. Very expensive. We don't know anything about it but we're going with a man who does, and living in a sort of hut where we do our own chores and cooking. Cheap. And September's often the best month in the whole year. A little bit frosty in the early morning sometimes and blazing hot in the middle of the day.'

He paused, relishing this prospect, until Flora asked him, 'How long will you be away?'

'Only a fortnight, I'm afraid, but we might stretch it to three weeks.'

In her disappointment and desolation, she was mercifully able to despise him a little. He did not look like a young god now, desirable and remote, nor like the tall young man who sometimes kissed her: sitting there, hugging his knees, he looked like a boy, the corners of his mouth compressed with pleasure.

'We're going to do some good long walks to get into training,' he said. 'Let's go up to the hill now, shall we? We can see Wales from there if it's clear enough. Not the real mountains. They're much farther north, but you get a sort of promise of them. And it's cold here. Rather damp, too,' he said, getting up and rubbing the seat of his trousers. 'Coming? It will warm us up.'

'No, I'm going home. But we must bury all this first,' she said, gathering up the paper bags and feeling she was burying something else as she pushed them into the hole he found for them and laid a stone on the top.

'Why, what's the matter?' he exclaimed, as they straightened themselves from their task. He held her firmly by both arms. 'I believe you're crying. Are you? What on earth for? What's the matter?'

'It's all been so horrid,' Flora said. Big tears rolled down her cheeks. 'And I meant it to be so nice.'

He let go her arms and put his own round her comfortingly. 'It's been a very nice picnic and we've had a good talk, haven't we?'

'Have we?' she said, jerked by a sob. She did not wipe away her tears. She expected him to do that in the obvious manner, but there, too, he failed her, though he took her hand kindly as they walked across the grass and let it linger in hers before they parted. But she knew his thoughts were on those hills and it had been a boring mistake to cry.

CHAPTER IX

AFTER seeing his wife and Rhoda in the garden, Mr. Blackett went back to his study. He was quite deserted. Mary had gone to bed, Flora was out, the only available companion was Connie in the kitchen, the patient car still stood outside and his unaccountable feeling of dissatisfaction with himself changed to one of irritation with his family, with Piers Lindsay and that woman next door. And what was Flora doing? Curious as he was about her mental development, he had never considered what effect these new friends of hers might have on it and on her character. In fact he was very little concerned with her character. He took for granted its being everything he desired and these friends of whom she spoke existed, for him, very vaguely. While he could keep them like that they were of no importance either to him or her. They were too shadowy to be asked into his house or to make any impact on his private world. But to-night, in his loneliness, he did wonder what charms they had to keep her from the pleasant intercourse there had been between him and her and he decided, not to go in search of her, any idea of that vain pursuit did not occur to him, but to take a walk, since no one wanted him at home, a long walk which would keep him out late and make Bertha a little anxious.

Thus it chanced that when he came to the bottom of Chatterton Road on his way to the Downs and there, where several roads met, looked this way and that before he braved the crossing, he saw his daughter on the wide path of the Avenue, her hand just dropping from that of a tall young man he recognized as a Fraser and while she stood and gazed after him as he went striding up the hill, Mr. Blackett, as quick as lightning, turned the corner on his right and he was round yet another corner before he paused. It was difficult to explain an instinctive flight from a situation he did not know how to deal with: he did not want to admit to a liking for knowledge which some other person did not wish him to have: he told himself, and it was true, that he needed time for thought, that here was something to be delicately handled and must not be attempted while he was in a state of anger and disappointment and disgust. Disgust was paramount, disgust at deceit and at the remembrance of those linked hands. If this was the public behaviour of his daughter and that young man who came from a home he thoroughly distrusted, what would they not do in secret? Terrible visions passed through Mr. Blackett's mind and at that moment, as he thought of her in any sort of physical contact with a member of his own sex, a thought he had hitherto avoided, he felt a violent distaste for his daughter; he did not want to see or touch or speak to her but she presented herself in his imagination and, for the first time, as another man might see her; he understood what his wife had meant when she said Flora was attractive. She had also said Flora was more like her father than she knew. He had accepted these words as compliments but had they implied more than they said, about Flora, about himself? That would not have been like Bertha and he was distracted from these conjectures when he realized that he was standing stock

66

still and must be an object of interest to anyone who passed, so he walked on, reaching the Downs a little farther eastwards than he had intended, mounting the rough ground there with the energy of his emotions, and finding no relief for them.

It was after nine o'clock, still light, but the slow approach of darkness could be felt and those who could not or would not wait for it, who sat or lay in the doubtful shelter of the hawthorn bushes, presented Mr. Blackett with hateful possible replicas of Flora and young Fraser. Though he kept his head high, his beard thrust forward, he could not keep his eyes completely shut and through their lowered lids he got glimpses of forms close pressed, dark arms clasping pale bodies and pale arms stretched across dark coats. And there were girls and men sometimes in pairs, sometimes in groups for greater ease and safety, not yet lost to everything except each other, and from these came voices and loud laughter, slaps responding to snatched kisses, make-believe skirmishes before surrender, and all this was abhorrent to Mr. Blackett, yet he did not make his way to one of the intersecting roads where he would not have been offended by these sights and sounds, nor did he connect them with the decent couples, followed by a tired child or two who ought long ago to have been in bed. A few years ago these men and women whom, if he had thought of them at all, he would have respected for their bonds of matrimony and the fruits of it, might have been rollicking or oblivious among the bushes, and while he realized that there were varieties of approach to the married state and to that family life of which he much approved, almost any approach seemed to him objectionable for his daughters and the thought of their marrying was only endurable if it could be achieved without preliminary dallyings and with mutual attraction of a purely intellectual kind. And already Flora had shown herself unlikely to oblige him in this way. She was not what he had thought her and the puzzle was whether he should find relief in speaking of his disgust or enjoy the subtler pleasure of pretending ignorance, but there was danger there and Mr. Blackett, beyond the hawthorn bushes now and on a bare stretch of grass, checked himself in his stride. The bare possibility of the impossible made him feel sick with fury and if he had not been spared the sight of Flora's tears he would have been certain that the horrible worst had happened. But he was able to calm himself: he was exaggerating matters. He knew most parents would accept such a situation lightly, but then he was not like other people. Hardly a day passed that did not bring this fact home to him. It was inconvenient, but he would not have had it otherwise and, in this happier state, he reached the edge of the cliff where it dropped away in two hundred feet of bare rock. Protected by railings, Mr. Blackett could look down without fear. Slowly the tide was coming in and the light from the lamps on each side of the river struck steadily across the mud and waveringly across the water and slowly the different greens on the opposite cliff were becoming one, gathering together for the night and leaving the silver birch trunks still more solitary and ghostly. It was very quiet down there. The lamps from a car on the road immediately below the cliff sometimes flung a big beam across the water and seemed to sweep away the lesser lights, but the car passed on and the lesser lights remained, waiting to guide the ships which would soon be coming up the river. And on the road behind Mr. Blackett a car sometimes went by, and that too passed, after holding him for a moment, as though he were a figure on a stage with a spotlight turned on him. That gone, only a pair of lovers sitting decently on a bench shared this high place with him and he was soothed by the beauty of the scene and cooled by a little breeze, coming just then when he needed it, and he took off his hat to let the wind blow through his hair. He was a little ashamed of his late excitement but Flora must be protected from undesirable young men — he hoped she need not be protected from herself — and, as he turned away, a very pleasing idea occurred to him and carried him briskly homewards.

Here he found a dark, quiet house. Far from being anxious about him, Bertha had gone to bed, and the streak of light under Flora's door vanished as he topped the stairs. There was no light under his own and he did not turn it on until he heard Bertha saying, 'I'm not asleep.'

'Aren't you feeling well, Bertha?' he inquired.

'Yes. Why shouldn't I?'

'I thought you couldn't be,' he said blandly. 'What time did Flora get back?'

'I'm not sure. I've been in the garden all the evening.'

'Ah, no wonder you are tired,' he said as Mrs. Blackett shut her eyes. 'But — are you laughing, Bertha?' he asked as, clad only in his shirt and socks, he approached the bed and saw the agitation of the bed clothes.

'Yes,' she said, her eyes still shut.

'I'm afraid I don't see the joke.'

'No,' she said. 'That's just it. You can't.'

'This is certainly fatigue,' he said, as the bed clothes continued to move. 'And I hope I have as much sense of humour as other people, and considerably more than you have yourself. What is the matter?' he asked testily. 'Has anything upset you?'

'No. I was only thinking of those old Snap cards we used to play with when we were children. But perhaps you didn't. Those funny ones. I can't remember many of them, but there was one that said "Who'd be a doctor?" in his nightshirt and I think that's the one you look like now.'

Looking still more like the rueful doctor, Mr. Blackett stared at her for a moment before he decided to say with marked lack of enthusiasm, 'I'm glad I amuse you.'

'Yes,' she agreed. 'It's better to laugh than to cry.'

Mr. Blackett, more like himself in the pyjamas he had hastily put on, lifted his eyebrows. This catchword came strangely from her and it was the kind of remark he particularly disliked. He considered it slightly vulgar and it ignored the possibility of the middle course, the one any civilized person would prefer. Bertha, whatever she might say, was quite evidently not herself. He could hardly believe she had really likened him to that ridiculous playing card. She had always treated him with a charming, old-fashioned courtesy, as he hoped he had treated her; it astonished and displeased him that she could see him in a comic aspect and it was impolite to tell him so. The Bertha he knew and trusted would have ignored the less dignified details of the bedchamber or accepted them as among her privileges. He defied any man to get undressed without being, at some moment, an object amusing to unfriendly or ribald eyes, eyes, for instance, which were not brown like Bertha's, but of a changing blue and all too ready to find humour in what they saw. The little lines at their corners, he decided, came of that readiness, and he glanced at Bertha whose eyes were now shut and saw that with her such lines were wanting. Hers was not a girlish face, that would have been unsuitable, yet there was hardly a mark on it which was not there when he first saw her, in her father's church, decorating it for the Easter festival. No more perfect setting could have been found for her, no better augury for the future. She had looked like a flower herself, he thought, as innocent and candid as the pheasant's eyes she was holding. The work was nearly done. Here and there a patch of sunlight settled on the dimness of the old church: very softly, someone was playing the organ, practising for to-morrow, and the sounds and the heady sweetness of the flowers and the sight of the girl who was not aware of the stranger who had strolled into the church, held the young Mr. Blackett in a charm which was not broken when she spoke. The whole thing would have been ruined by an ugly voice or accent, but everything was as it should be, even to the discovery that the vicar, appearing for an absent-minded inspection of the decorations, was her father and an easy person to approach. As an actor in this episode, Mr. Blackett missed its flavour of the novelette and had not detected it since. It was exactly what ought to have happened: his courtship had been carried on in the same atmosphere of calm and beauty: it had all been flawless except for the passing irritation of Lindsay's battered appearance at the wedding and there had been no disappointment in his marriage. Now, as these memories passed rapidly through his mind, he was more puzzled by his wife's laughter than vexed by his daughter's behaviour. Bertha laughed very seldom. Never before had he seen her unable to control her amusement and, on this unique occasion, it had been directed against himself. For an instant, though he was standing under a strong light, he seemed to be looking into darkness, into unpleasant places where he might lose his way. But he would have none of that. He refused to be tempted into uncomfortable situations and, in connection with Bertha, he would not admit the possibility of their existence. But, though her laughter had ceased and she lay still, her lips settled into their usual contented curves, he could not be sure that her present mood was one in which to talk seriously to her about Flora. She might find that a laughing matter, too. On the other hand, she might worry herself unduly and, on the whole, perhaps it was not necessary to say anything about it. He was quite capable of managing the affair alone. Then, with a feeling of satisfaction and anticipation, he drew up the blind. As usual, there was a faint glow from Mrs. Fraser's bedroom window. She kept late hours. This, too, gave him a feeling of satisfaction. It fitted in with everything else he had discovered about her character.

CHAPTER X

AND long after Mr. Blackett had ceased his gentle snoring and turned on to his side, Rosamund was still awake. Miss Spanner had had to make her nightly visit later than usual. First Chloe and then Felix had forestalled her.

'What lovely stuff money is,' Chloe said. 'And I didn't know Miss Spanner was an angel in disguise. Two nice, clean crackling five pound notes! They seem so much more real than a cheque. What made her do it, do you think?'

'She wanted to give you pleasure, I suppose.'

'While we can get it? Was that the idea? But Peter says — '

'Is that his name?'

'Yes, isn't it a mercy it isn't Pringle as well?'

'Why should it be?'

'Darling, didn't I tell you he's Miss Pringle's nephew and an accountant and does her books and that's how I got to know him? He's called Stephens. I'm surprised at your forgetting anything as important as that.'

'Oh, it's important, is it?'

'I'm not sure, but it ought to be, to you.'

'So it is and I hadn't really forgotten. Just for the moment. I've been rather muddle-headed lately.'

'Tired?' Chloe asked.

'Yes, a little, perhaps.'

'I don't know how you manage it all,' Chloe said. 'It rather puts me off having a big family and I want one. Seven people to feed and the house to look after and all the odds and ends to do and never in a hurry and never bad tempered.'

'Why should I be? And why shouldn't I have a full-time job? A man takes that as a matter of course.'

'Yes and when he comes home he has nothing more to do. He doesn't sit up in bed and do the mending. I think you ought to have a holiday. You must be sick of us all. Have it when I have mine and I'll stay at home and look after the family.'

'Where on earth should I go?' Rosamund said, but before Chloe could answer, she had pictured the sort of place she wanted, somewhere high above the sea where she could walk for miles on the cliff edge or lie for hours among the little flowers and herbs that look brighter and smell more pungent for their nearness to the sea, as though they stole some of its colour for themselves and mixed its saltness with their own scents. 'And who with?' she said and she knew the answer to that question too. The companion she would choose would be Piers Lindsay. It was rather absurd, but there was no doubt about it. Quite definitely, she did not want Fergus. He had wounded her, but that was not the reason. Even if he had not done that, if there had been no rupture in their union, she knew, to-night, she did not want him on those cliffs. But then, if there had been

72

no rupture, she might not have realized, as she did now, that she had, as it were, grown out of him, that he was the garment of her youth and, quite startled by this confession, she exclaimed aloud, 'I must be getting very old!'

Chloe laughed. 'What makes you say that?'

'I was imagining such a middle-aged sort of holiday.'

'And you'd like it?'

'Yes,' Rosamund said.

They would not talk very much, she decided. They would not need to be polite, giving way to each other's fancy for this or that. They would go their own ways when they liked but, she thought, what one chose would probably be what the other wanted. It would all be easy and natural and comfortable, as though they had always known each other and there was nothing to explain or discuss. But what a foolish dream! And how horrified the poor man would be to hear of it!

'Then do go,' Chloe begged. 'With Miss Spanner, perhaps.'

'No, nobody,' Rosamund said.

'But you'd be dull alone, wouldn't you?'

'I'm not going alone, either.'

'Is it the money?' Chloe asked. 'You can have mine, you know.'

'Yes, your nice, crackling five pound notes and all the fresh air you ought to have after living in that stuffy shop. What an idea! But thank you, Chloe, very much,' Rosamund said gently. 'And you were going to tell me what that Peter of yours thinks about things.'

'Oh, he's not mine yet. At least, I'm not his. He's so frightfully sane. It must be because he's always balancing accounts. I think it's very boring when people are so determined to see the other person's point of view that they positively have to squint.'

'And is he squinting?'

'Inclined to,' Chloe said.

'Like Agnes, but she sees straighter than most of us.'

'He says we've got out of so many difficulties, we may get out of this one.'

'He means we've wriggled out,' Rosamund said scornfully, 'and we may wriggle out again. Does he like that prospect?' she asked and Chloe heard an unaccustomed hardness in her mother's voice and saw the straight line of her lips as she roughly pushed away the needlework lying in front of her.

'I didn't know you cared like that,' Chloe said almost timidly.

'Of course I care! Of course I care! Though it's not the fashion. It's almost bad taste. Either nothing matters or there is nothing wrong. The result's the same. We ought to be on the top of the hill with our heads up and instead of that we're sliding down, quite pleased to accept a helpful shove from anyone who chooses to give it. Anyone! And such anyones! My God, how are the mighty fallen!' She sank back against her pillows. 'What an outburst!' she said.

'But you sound,' said Chloe, 'as though you want a war.'

'How could I? I know too much about it, but it's not as bad as believing that any concessions, however cowardly, must be better.'

She had, in this connection, a great longing for Fergus. His language would have done her good, but there was now no possibility of that pleasure. He had, she supposed, deserted her, but not for very long and she did not know whether it was long enough or what other grounds for divorce were necessary and whether he had given her any, in the matter of those sympathetic surroundings, for instance. It was just like him to be vague; it would be just like him to change his mind and it would serve him right if he changed it too late. The impulse of her pride and her affection was to gratify him speedily, yet the past asserted its claims, not to keep him for herself but to watch over his future and to go slowly lest he should act too hastily. And she had no idea what view the children would take of such legal proceedings or what they thought of the present situation. They had made no comment when she told them he had gone. For themselves, even for Sandra who looked wan and anxious, the relief was evident. Perhaps they assumed that it was a relief for her too as, in a complicated way, it was. They had taken care not to embarrass her with questions and now, just as she was wishing there were some wise person to whom she could talk freely, but not Agnes, who had always been prejudiced against Fergus and perhaps jealous of him, Felix knocked at her door and came in. Here was someone wise, at least, in the law and, but for an air of responsibility he sometimes wore nowadays as the male head of the family, he might have been Fergus himself and it was half pleasure and half pain to look at him. And it was as the male head of the family that he had come.

'Who's this latest swain of Chloe's?' he asked.

'I don't know much about him. I imagine he's quite respectable. But sit down, Felix. Don't stand over me so threateningly.'

'Well,' he sat down, 'I think you ought to head him off.'

'That's so likely, isn't it? When have I tried to head off your young women or James's?'

'That's altogether different and as far as James is concerned, it will be Father Blackett who'll do the heading off if necessary.'

'Father Blackett?'

'Didn't you know?'

'I always try not to know, on principle. But, dear me, how extraordinary!'

'Why? She's rather an attractive wench. Not my type, though. She's too much like an enamel – green eyes and black hair and red lips and sort of burnished.'

'So she is. And you like something more elusive, I imagine. Well, I hope it isn't serious. I shouldn't like any Blackett blood in the family.'

'Of course it isn't serious. They've come across each other at the University and I should think she's rather a limpet.'

'She's just like her father to look at. Take away Mr. Blackett's beard and you'd see Flora. And he's feminine, too. That's what's the matter with him, perhaps. Not effeminate. Feminine. Very bad in a man, I think.'

'Not so bad as the masculine in a woman.'

'Yes, yours must be the elusive type,' Rosamund said. 'This isn't curiosity. It's deduction. And I expect you'll end by marrying a big-footed, flat-chested, tweed and felt, loud voiced, thoroughly good sort.'

'It would be the end of me all right,' he said. 'And perhaps you'd better not let James know I told you.'

'Of course I won't. And I shan't tell Chloe you are taking an elder-brotherly interest in her affairs.'

'You mean I'm butting in where I'm not wanted.'

'She might think so, but I don't. I'm glad you came. I'm always at home to visitors at this time of night, you know, but Agnes is my only regular caller. And about this Pringle. That's not really his name. I generally call him the conscientious accountant.'

'Accountant? I thought he was some kind of farmer.'

'You're not,' Rosamund asked slowly, 'talking about Mr. Lindsay, are you?'

'Of course. Who else?'

'But — ' Rosamund began. 'Well, really, this is a very surprising evening. And I don't think, though he has been in and out of the house often enough, he has ever seen much of Chloe.'

'He was making the most of his first chance, then.'

'Was he? I didn't notice it particularly, but I can well believe it. She's very nice to look at.'

In the mirror opposite to her bed, she could see herself, a Chloe grown middle-aged. Naturally, he would look at the younger edition, but this one, she thought impersonally, was worth some consideration too.

'I don't suppose she found it easy to look at him, poor chap, and then, he's old enough to be her father. That's why I said you ought to head him off.'

'And it seems to me,' Rosamund said, suddenly angry, 'that you're being perfectly idiotic. Can't I ask a friend to the house for fear he should fall in love with Chloe. He wouldn't be so stupid. You're very grandmotherly, Felix, to-night. What's the matter with you?'

Under this attack he looked more than ever like Fergus.

There was trouble in store for some woman in the future, Rosamund thought, but she would have a great deal of happiness, too, as she had had herself.

'I think,' he said, nervously determined to speak his mind, 'it would be better not to have friends like that in the house. Better for you, I mean.'

'Better for me?'

'Yes. Well — I hate saying it — but you're in rather a peculiar position, aren't you?'

She did not answer immediately. She was astonished, amused, hurt and angry all together, but she could not help being pleased when he added awkwardly, 'And still so young-looking and pretty.'

'I thought it was Chloe you were anxious about.'

'Chloe? No, she's in no danger, but he might be and people might think you were.'

She tried not to laugh. 'So you're guarding my reputation.'

'Yes,' he said stubbornly.

'With dear old Agnes for a chaperon and two grown-up sons? Felix,' she was gentle with him, 'surely this caution is unnecessary. I think my reputation, if I have one, will stand more than an occasional visit from Mr. Lindsay, when he brings the vegetables. And if it doesn't, well, it can go hang. No!' she cried, sitting up with a jerk, 'I'm not going to be locked up like a nun, no, not even if people talk — and why should they? It's too silly and if they do and you are embarrassed by it, you'll just have to bear it. I never heard such nonsense. Does James feel like this? Does Chloe? I don't believe it. You must have inherited some puritanical taint from those awful aunts you've never seen. They'd convict me of sin if they saw me smiling at the butcher. And I do smile at him and he gives me the best cuts of meat. One must use what weapons one has. And I believe the policeman on point duty by the church would hold up a royal procession for me.'

'That's just it,' Felix said. 'You're so — so gay.'

'The word they use for ladies who are no better than they

77

should be, poor things. I always think it's so ironic. And I'm in danger of being mistaken for one of those? You think I ought to look humble and depressed? Well, I'm neither. And I like Mr. Lindsay. He's a friend and I'm going to keep him if I can. And with a daughter like Chloe in the house what busybody's going to suspect an old woman like me? You said, yourself, he was looking at her all the time.'

'Yes, but you were looking at him.',

'So that's it, is it? Why didn't you say so at once.'

'It wasn't easy.'

'I should think not. And you're wrong. I know perfectly well how I look sometimes, but I don't do it with Mr. Lindsay. I don't want to.'

Felix shuffled his feet before he got on to them. 'I didn't mean that,' he said. 'I meant you suddenly looked so happy. And it made me angry, but not with you. Oh,' he said, when he saw that while she was laughing there were tears in her eyes, 'I suppose I'm being a fool, but there's no one else to look after you, is there?'

She shook her head. 'Nobody,' she said.

'And you're not cross with me?'

'No, no. I think you're sweet. Kiss me good night.'

How young he was and how clumsy, she thought as she watched him go, how much more conventional and perspicacious than she had imagined and, she admitted it, how right!

'Oh, come in Agnes,' she said as Miss Spanner poked an aggrieved face round the door. 'I'm sorry you've been kept waiting but I've had rather a busy evening.'

CHAPTER XI

SHE had a queer feeling the next morning when she rose as usual, at six o'clock. There was a hush on the Square and in the house at this hour and to-day it seemed to be a little stealthy,

78

telling her to move quietly and, still more urgently, to keep her mind closed against the quick perceptions of these strangers with whom she lived. Never, in all her life, had she been self-conscious, except, by choice, with Fergus, when she evoked response from all his senses as a kind of exercise in her power to charm him. Otherwise, she went her careless, natural way, growing a little more cautious when she had to act the buffer between him and the children, but not suspecting their possible interest in her own character and reactions. Until lately she had not been interested in them herself. Now she feared she must be alarmingly transparent if Felix thought it necessary to warn her against herself, and it occurred to her suddenly that, since he had reached an age when he could fit effect to cause, he had never before last night seen her so radiantly at ease. She must have shown more signs of strain with Fergus in the house than she had known and it was natural for the boy to see danger in her new aspect. Nevertheless, she ought, she supposed, to have been annoyed at his presumption, but it seemed to her rather pathetic and it must have needed courage. What chiefly concerned her as she stepped on to the balcony and looked into the quiet square where all the windows were like the eyes of sleepers, then went downstairs to do some tidying and dusting before she woke the household by turning on her bath water, was the light Felix had thrown on his own character, the comparative darkness in which the characters of all her other children remained, the likelihood that in their different ways and for different reasons they made their silent criticisms. Even Paul, who blundered in and out of the house, whose real life was in his school, to whom the family was of not much more importance, at present, than the furniture, must see her from his own peculiar angle and she did not know what it was. She did not know how any of them saw her and she had no doubt she saw them all askew. She had always been vaguely conscious of this and she had nothing to complain of, for one of the few definite rules she had made for herself, and easily kept, was to avoid soul searchings with her children. She had sense enough to know that she was more likely to crystallize than to dissolve a trouble by first discovering and then discussing it. Moreover, their troubles were their own possessions; she could only share them when they were offered and she had not expected to find in any of her children the discernment Felix had shown. She wondered whether he had heard any disparaging remarks, any suggestion that her conduct had driven Fergus away and, knowing her native city, she could well imagine how certain of his elders, and she could name them, had put him to occasional and what they thought skilful questioning. Yes, she thought, and she damned their prurient curiosity, something more than Piers Lindsay's visits and her own pleasure had inspired Felix's warning but, as she had told him, she would not be influenced by provincial gossip, even for the greater comfort of her children. They were all involved in what he called a peculiar situation and they would all be impoverished by a cowardly discretion.

She carried her cup into the garden-room and stood by the open door. It was a grey morning, but the birds were pleased with it. They had their troubles too, she supposed, and very anxious times bringing up their young but, after a little while, their responsibilities were over. The early days of her own young had been her most light-hearted and her responsibility for them would never end. It would grow heavier as their lives became more complicated, when, for instance, as was more than likely, they married the wrong people. She had not married the wrong man. It would be mean and disloyal and untrue to pretend now that he had not been everything she wanted and, without children, their undeniable claims and what, to him, was the burden of them and the pressure of their personalities, she and Fergus would have been together still and in all probability nothing would have happened to reveal the faults of either to the other. But they were not together and it seemed to her that there was a monstrous moral tyranny in social and religious conditions which could penalize two mature people who chose to part. And the funny part of it was that the one person to

80

whom she could adequately express her feelings on this matter and be sure of sympathy, was Fergus himself, and she sighed as she turned reluctantly from the open doorway. The porridge had to be made, the table to be laid for breakfast, Paul to be dragged out of bed, reminded to clean his teeth and got off to school in time, innumerable little tasks had to be done, though marriages went awry and the whole of Europe threatened to go up in flames. It sometimes seemed that Providence had arranged things very inconveniently, but actually the tiresome and perpetual business of keeping people fed and clothed and clean was a merciful dispensation and life, she thought, as she began to hear human signs of it in distant rumblings and the nearer clatter of the milkman's cans, had an extraordinary charm, as though, in the gloomiest moments, the sufferer was upheld by something less definite but more certain than knowledge, a willingness, even in rebellion, to accept unhappiness in the unconscious realization that it would drop into its place with all other experiences and enlighten or leaven them.

'But I am not unhappy,' she said to herself as she went about her business yet, during that day, she thought very often of her father, wishing she could have his counsel, or rather, for he had always hesitated to give it, she wished she could know he was aware of her now and wanting the best for her. She was thinking of him when she went on to the hill at about six o'clock that evening. There was hardly a place within eyeshot or for miles beyond where at some time or other she had not been with him, but how careful he had been not to impose himself on her, to retire as she made friends of her own age and, while he made no claims or forced on her any offerings of love or service, she had always been conscious of him as a pervading wise beneficence. She had tried to be as little intrusive with her own children, but she had not his selflessness and she doubted whether she were capable of so much love and, while she looked on the scene they had so often enjoyed together, she thought of Piers Lindsay, in whom she fancied she had found something of that beneficence and selflessness, and she thought of him with a warmth she did not try to deaden, until the crunching of footsteps distracted her and she saw, approaching her, Mr. Blackett, of all people the most inappropriate to her mood.

For himself, Mr. Blackett did not believe in luck. He saw it squandered on other people; his own good fortune could always be attributed to some creditable quality or effort; to foresight and making the best of his opportunities and, as he walked home that evening, he saw Mrs. Fraser, making her way across the Green, as an opportunity and he did not let it slip. How to find her alone had been a puzzle and he solved the puzzle as he followed her slowly, pausing to look upwards at the grey clouds, to admire the copper beech, now at its most beautiful, presenting himself to anyone interested as a man refreshing himself with natural beauty after the confinement of his office.

It was not exactly refreshment he experienced when, after losing her round a bend in the little hill, he came within close sight of her. Her hands, one of them holding her gloves, rested lightly on the railing and there was something in her stillness which prevented him from accusing her of a studied pose and might have persuaded him to turn back and leave her to her contemplation, if the sound of his footsteps had not already disturbed her. And when she saw him he did not get the smile he had expected. Her lips parted, but no greeting came from them and, after a little nod of recognition, she looked again at the woods across the water. This he found more irritating than the smile would have been. He could account for the smile in his own way and at once: what was practically a dismissal demanded a little thought before he could transmute it into something he liked better. Until then, he was angry enough to persist in his purpose and he halted beside her.

'A delightful view,' he said.

The grey morning, heralded so gaily by the birds, had developed into a characteristic Upper Radstowe day. Until an hour or two ago there had been a very fine, steady drizzle and wisps of mist were hanging about the trees, like giant thistledown caught in the branches. The water and the banks of mud and the low, motionless clouds all had their varied density of greyness which seemed to muffle the sounds of traffic in the roads and the slow progress of cars and carts across the bridge. And to-morrow, if the sun shone and the wind blew, this sombre scene would be changed to one of colour and movement and the day after that it would be different again. But she would not discuss the view with Mr. Blackett; it vexed her that he should be privileged to see it. However, she smiled when she thought of Felix. Surely being alone on the hill with Mr. Blackett, for there was no one else about, was much worse than entertaining Mr. Lindsay in a house full of people, and Mr. Blackett, looking at her profile, saw half that smile and thought it was very sly. At the same time, studying her in a rough tweed coat and skirt of indefinite blues, he wondered why Bertha's clothes never had this suitably casual air. Bertha, he had lately discovered, always gave the impression that she was going to a tea party which had taken place a good many years ago, but she did habitually wear a hat and he was glad to be able to find fault with Mrs. Fraser's bare, delightful head, and he wanted to find much graver fault than that, to disturb her easy, assured poise, without driving her away.

'I am very glad of this opportunity to speak to you,' he said.

'But,' she said, turning to look at him, 'we are always within easy reach of each other.'

'Alone,' he said solemnly.

'Really? Well, here I am.'

'About your son,' Mr. Blackett said, and she remembered what Felix had told her and then made her forget.

'Oh,' she said regretfully, 'has Paul been on your flat roof again? He can drop on to it, you know, from the bathroom window, and I'm afraid he drops other things sometimes and then has to go and fetch them. I do hope he hasn't disturbed you.'

'Not in that way,' said Mr. Blackett. 'Indeed, I do not think that is the young man's name and that is not the way in which he has chosen to amuse himself. I find, to my great disgust, that

83

one of your elder sons is having clandestine meetings with my daughter.'

'Is he? How old fashioned that sounds! And how very foolish.'

'Foolish!' Mr. Blackett exclaimed. 'Is that all you have to say about it?'

'Yes, it's so unnecessary.'

'Your son evidently thinks not.'

'My son? Why not your daughter? That's possible, you know.'

'My daughter has been very carefully brought up,' Mr. Blackett said coldly. 'Anything so contrary to my wishes and our general standards as secrecy of this vulgar sort would be quite incompatible with everything I know of her.'

'Yes, I can believe that,' Rosamund said.

'Therefore,' he went on, 'you must realize that it is your son who is to blame.'

'But I don't. Incompatible with all you know of her, yes, but then, how much do you know?'

'How much do I know of her? What unpleasant suggestion,' he demanded, 'are you trying to make?'

A bright pink spot appeared on each of Mr. Blackett's cheeks and with these dabs of angry colour above the silky blackness of his beard and a glimpse of very red lips he, too, Rosamund thought, looked like an enamel and she made a guess that what he did not know of his daughter was what he would not acknowledge in himself, that what was healthy and natural in Flora was manifested here in the perverse pleasure of trying to irritate where he would have liked to charm. One way and another, she had given a good deal of thought to Mr. Blackett because she knew he had given much to her and her baser nature would thoroughly have enjoyed provoking this man to indiscretions for which he would later loathe himself, a salutary experience for him, but her baser nature was well under control and she determined not to encourage his by allowing him to quarrel with her.

'Unpleasant?' she said. 'No sort of unpleasantness occurred to me. I hope it didn't to you. I meant, well, what you must have discovered for yourself, that all of us know only a very small part of the people we know best.'

'In my case, that is not true,' Mr. Blackett said firmly, and he thought of Bertha. Her pure mind was fully open to him he was sure. It was true that she had puzzled him last night with her laughter, but she had explained that, at once, at his request, childishly and not pleasingly, but with the simple frankness he expected of her. 'It is not true,' he repeated.

'Isn't it? How nice. Then why worry about this little affair? I don't suppose,' she said, looking across the river, 'it's of any more importance or much more clandestine, as you call it, than our meeting here to-night. You could so easily have found me in my house.'

She looked at him and saw his lips open and shut and his colour heighten before he said, with a hint of confusion, 'What certainty of privacy could I have there?'

'And that,' Rosamund said slowly, 'may be the very question Flora asked herself.'

'I do not believe it. She must have been instigated to such deception. I saw them myself, last night, evidently emerging from the trees beyond the Avenue.'

'Perhaps they had been admiring the view,' Rosamund said softly.

'And,' Mr. Blackett went on, 'they were walking hand in hand, like — like — well, it seemed to me very vulgar. And, this is what troubled me, there they parted and went home by different routes.'

'I can think of a dozen good reasons for that,' Rosamund said. 'I don't think you understand the younger generation and, dear me, if everybody took these little affairs as seriously as you do I should have half the fathers in Upper Radstowe on my door-step.'

'And I don't suppose,' said Mr. Blackett with an unpleasant smile and she thought his lips grew redder still, as though he were about to eat a dainty he had long desired, 'I don't suppose you would have any objection to that.'

Long ago, she had dropped her hands from the railing and now she lifted the one that held her gloves, wondering whether she should flick them across his face. It would have given her great satisfaction for a moment but she knew she would regret it. Laughter was the best rebuff, so she laughed, saying, 'I should be delighted. Most of them are old friends and I went to school with their sisters and their wives. And now I must hurry home. Shall we go together?' she asked gravely, 'or,' she quoted him, 'shall we go back by different routes?'

Mr. Blackett blinked. 'I shall stay here for a little while,' he said, 'but Mrs. Fraser,' he knew she had had the best of it and his pride, or his discretion, forced him to an appearance of generosity, 'please tell your son that when he wants to see my daughter my house is open to him.'

'I will, certainly,' she said pleasantly. 'I think that's wise and kind, too. We can't tell how much longer these poor young things may have for pleasure.'

Mr. Blackett's face closed up like a trap. 'No, not much longer,' he said angrily, 'if many people encourage that point of view.'

CHAPTER XII

She thought of Fergus with another sudden gust of longing as she ran down the hill. She knew how willing he would be to smash the blandness out of Mr. Blackett's face. The physical difference between the two men was that between a tomcat and a tiger and she would have been glad to show Mr. Blackett what kind of man she had married, a brave man with all his wounds in front, incapable of a sneering insult and if she had seen him coming towards her at that moment, lean and lithe, as he had been when she first saw him in this very place, she would have flung herself against him and burst into tears. And soon afterwards, he would have become an intolerable nuisance and she would have wanted to be rid of him. The power responsible for the world to whom she had been grateful, early that morning, for the necessary tasks imposed on men and women, had evidently determined that nothing should be perfect. Even a fine summer evening must be ruined by midges, in the desire, perhaps, to create a divine discontent and the hope of a midgeless life hereafter. But, in spite of every kind of pest, Rosamund again asserted her hearty liking for the world she lived in. She was enraged with Mr. Blackett almost to crying point, she felt herself slightly besmirched by that smile of his, yet how interesting the episode had been and how well she had managed it! But Felix must be right. She did do something not quite suitable in a deserted matron; she liked using her power over men and she certainly had deliberately teased Mr. Blackett when she had the chance, so no doubt it served her right that, too respectable for any other sort of impropriety, he had found his pleasure in the indication that he could have it otherwise if he chose, but as it was just possible that James might be really fond of that girl, there was an added cause for satisfaction at having kept her temper.

She was glad to be in her own home again and she stood for a moment, enjoying the familiar atmosphere and the sense of her own and her people's past. It did not go very far back, but far enough to give her a feeling of security and pride, to restore what Mr. Blackett had tried to take from her.

'Oh,' said Sandra, appearing from the kitchen stairs. 'I was wondering where you were.'

'And you were expecting a policeman, I suppose, to tell you I'd been taken to hospital.'

'Yes, something of that sort,' Sandra admitted, 'but all the same, I've put on the potatoes.'

'Good girl. I think I'll have a bath.'

'You haven't caught a chill, have you?'

'No I have not,' her mother said emphatically. 'I feel rather messy, that's all.'

'But you look rather pleased.'

'I'm thinking what a nice staircase this is and how we've done nearly all the polishing of the rail ourselves. People's hands! Your great-grandfather's and your grandfather's and your mother's.

'And we've worn the carpet out too. People's feet!' Sandra said, lightly mocking her mother.

'Ah well, that's been in several houses. The staircase has never been anywhere else, but I can't expect you to feel as I do about that.'

'And the carpet,' Sandra went on, 'will be worse than ever if Felix and James walk on it in the new boots they're getting. They say they've got nails in them like claws. I rather wish Miss Spanner hadn't given them that money and I think she wishes so too. They've been showing her pictures of the sort of places they're going to and they look very dangerous.'

'I like people to do dangerous things,' Rosamund said.

'Yes, it's nice that they want to, but I wish they wouldn't. Miss Spanner says it's tempting Providence.'

'She must have a very poor idea of it or him, whichever it is. I don't believe he or it is as weak-minded as all that, or as mean. Does she think it's tempting Providence to cross the street? That's just as dangerous. Where are they all? In the drawing-room? Then I'll go and encourage the boys just to spite her.'

'After she's been so kind?' Sandra said reproachfully.

'She'd be miserable if no one disagreed with her,' Rosamund said, and she went quickly up the shallow stairs, pausing once to look down at Sandra and make a little face at her and then Sandra had to smile.

There were times when she felt years older than her mother who seemed to this grave and anxious young person a little irresponsible though, in the service of her family, there was very little she forgot or left undone. It was her gaiety, only just under the surface at her most serious moments, her readiness to go up-stairs now and tease Miss Spanner, which seemed to Sandra a little inappropriate in a mother. But she was lovely, Sandra thought, going back to the potatoes, a person to be proud of, especially at school functions where she could be compared with other mothers who were also, but much more definitely, old girls. She had felt the same kind of pride in her father. He might be tiresome at home but, outside it, she had never had to wish he would be different or to fear he would embarrass her. She had not known the acute suffering of seeing her parents with other people's disapproving or scornful eyes. That would be much worse than having a father whose disappearance was a little difficult to explain, a little difficult but not impossible like bad manners or illiteracy which some people had to bear. Moreover, Sandra believed he would come back some day, miraculously changed, like people in tracts, and everything would be perfect, no, not quite perfect, for his return would involve the departure of Miss Spanner who would not want to go and Sandra, while she watched the potatoes, had to set to work for the solving of this problem.

Miss Spanner had retreated to her bedroom before Rosamund reached the drawing-room and she found the boys, each in a big armchair, absorbed in books and maps connected with their holiday. They did not look up when she came in; she doubted whether they knew she was there and, marvelling at masculine powers of concentration, she went away without interrupting them. More and more, as the days passed, she was jealous for all the happiness they could get and she was touched by their past concealment of desires they knew she could not gratify without a strain on her resources they would not ask her to make. She fancied Mr. Blackett's good tidings for James would fall rather flat, but she had to pass them on.

'I want to see you to-night,' she said to him after supper. 'Pop in before Agnes has a chance.'

'Anything serious?' he asked.

'You will be able to tell me that,' she said, and at once, when he appeared, she told him she had a message from Mr. Blackett.

'Blackett? Oh, next door.'

'He says if you want to see his daughter — it's Flora, isn't it? — you can go to his house to do so.'

'What for? I see her nearly every day already.'

'He says he finds you are meeting her clandestinely, that's his own word.'

'Good Lord! Why should I?' He was thoughtful for a moment. 'I've been for walks with her,' he said. 'She's interested in farming.'

'I see,' Rosamund said, and she looked down to hide how much she saw. He was pathetically simple. He did not know the first rules of the game but she would not cast doubts on an enthusiasm which, she thought, looking at him again, she could well understand.

'And last night,' said James, 'we had a sort of picnic.'

'Just you two?'

'Yes.'

'Chilly, wasn't it?'

'Yes, I'm afraid it was, rather,' James said with a grin. 'You see — well, never mind. The man's mad. I was afraid you were going to tell me we couldn't go to Wales for some reason or other. We've decided to go by night. That'll give us two extra days. And then there's ten miles to walk unless we can get a lift. But it won't be a bad thing to walk. We'll get into training and break in our boots. You'd hardly think there was anywhere nowadays, would you, ten miles from a station? And not a shop for another four. So we'll send most of our stuff by post.'

'For the postman to carry?'

'That's all right. There's a mail van.'

'Then you won't be entirely cut off. You'll be able to get your love letters. And how I envy you!'

'What, the love letters?'

'No, I don't think they'd be up to the standard I'm used to. And James, I'm sorry to persist but I think I'd better know. When you go for walks I'm told you don't come back together.'

'We often come home together but we always part short of the Square. I don't really care except that I'd rather the Spanner didn't see us, though really she deserves a bit of fun, doesn't she? But look here, I can't go and call like a suitor, can I? It's too silly. And why the blazes did he want to bother you about it?'

To that question Rosamund made no reply. 'And you don't feel like a suitor?' she said.

'Good Lord, no! What d'you think?'

'Not that, certainly. But I wonder whether he's told Flora he has given me this message. I think you'll have to go. It would be cruel to make her look foolish and I should hate Mr. Blackett to think you're afraid of him. Can't you make some sort of excuse? Take her a book or something?'

'And how often,' James asked gloomily, 'shall I have to do that?'

'Oh, once or twice, perhaps, and then you'll have your holiday.'

'And after that,' James said, 'I may be otherwise engaged. I only hope it won't be before.'

'Mr. Lindsay says you can go and work on his land at once if you like.'

'And of course you accepted the offer.'

'Oh, of course!' Rosamund said.

'That's all right then.' He kissed her good night. 'Did old Blackett make himself disagreeable?'

'I don't allow people to be disagreeable unless I choose,' she said.

'Anyhow, he must be a rum bird.'

'Very. I don't know where he perched himself last night but he told me he saw you in the Avenue, hand in hand.'

'Did he? Bad luck.'

'And I must say it sounded rather affectionate.'

'Well, what can one do — sometimes? Mind, she's a nice girl. It's all my fault, what fault there is.'

'And not much of that?'

'No, of course not,' James said impatiently. 'And what sort of book shall I pretend I want to lend her? He's sure to have a look at it, nosey old fool.'

'Obviously one about farming,' she said.

He glanced at her, faintly suspicious, but she was quite grave. 'The whole thing's too obvious and what rot it all is! Why can't we go in and out of each other's houses naturally, if we want to, without all this fuss?'

'Ask Mr. Blackett.'

'He must have a bee in his bonnet.'

'Several, I should think. And Rhoda Blackett often does come here, to see Miss Spanner, though he doesn't know it. They've taken a great liking to each other.'

'And I've taken a great liking to Miss Spanner. We've ordered the boots — did I tell you? But we shan't need a rope. Smithers will have that.'

'I hope Smithers knows what he's doing.'

'Oh yes, he's had a lot of experience.'

'Then I wish he'd take Mr. Blackett into some really nasty place and scare the life out of him.'

'Vindictive old woman!'

'Good for his soul,' Rosamund said. 'I don't suppose he's ever been physically frightened in his life. He seems to have avoided the perfect opportunity. Yes, it would do him a lot of good.'

'Funny ideas you get,' James said, going to the door.

'But it's a good one, this. It's just occurred to me, the value of being stripped bare by panic and seeing how puny you are without your clothes and how unimportant.'

'Well cheer up,' James said. 'It looks as though there'll be a general improvement in the human race before long.'

'In what's left of it,' she agreed.

'A sort of answer to prayer from your point of view,' he said dryly.

'Well that's one way of looking at it. No, I should call it penance for the penitent, but how many of us are that?'

CHAPTER XIII

'Why are you looking so pleased with yourself?' Miss Spanner asked.

For the second night running she had had to wait, with her door ajar, until Rosamund's children left the coast clear for her own visit. Last night, first Chloe and then Felix had delayed her and to-night it was James. This was unusual. 'Something in the wind,' she thought, giving her nose a knock.

'Because I'm feeling pleased,' Rosamund said. 'I was thinking what nice children I have.'

'H'm,' said Miss Spanner, 'it's early yet to be sure of that.'

'It's not early to say they're nice now, at this minute, you old curmudgeon. And little as you may think of them, you've been very good to them.'

'Pooh!' said Miss Spanner. 'There's nothing easier than giving away money when you have more than you need yourself.'

'Queer, then, that so few people do it.'

'And as a matter of fact I've been regretting it. Those boys are determined to break their necks.'

'Well, they're their own necks and they'll break them in a happy moment.'

'That's a silly way to talk.'

'Yes it is, rather.'

'Affected.'

'Just a bit,' Rosamund admitted amiably.

'You're unusually agreeable to-night. What's the matter with you?' Miss Spanner asked sharply.

'Nothing.'

'Nothing from a woman,' Miss Spanner said sagely, 'always means something. It's a way of saying I'll tell you if you go on asking questions.'

'You'll ask them all right without any encouragement, Agnes dear. What do you want to know?'

'All this coming and going. A long talk with Chloe and another with Felix and now James to-night, and I hope none of them's coming back again.'

'If you'd get a decent dressing-gown and do something to your hair you wouldn't mind if they did.'

'On the contrary, if I adopted your standards of what you call decency, I should mind much more.'

'I'm only wearing a sort of modest evening dress,' Rosamund said, glancing at herself in the mirror.

'And I've never had an evening dress in my life. Since I put up my hair and long before that no one except my mother —'

'Your dear mother, Agnes. That's the proper way to speak of the departed.'

'Yes, my dear mother,' Miss Spanner said, squinting a little, 'no one else has seen me not fully clothed.'

'You mean covered.'

'Yes, covered. Now, don't tell me they haven't missed anything. I know that well enough.'

Frowning, Rosamund tightened her lips. 'I wish you wouldn't, you really oughtn't to say things like that at this time of night. I shall never get to sleep for anger. Nothing, not even Mr. Blackett —'

'What's the matter with him?'

'He exists, doesn't he? Nothing makes me so furious as thinking of your youth. And I can't do anything about it. That's what's so infuriating. I'd like to do terrible things to your father and mother. I'd like to push them into a bed of nettles. Oh, but that's not nearly bad enough. I'd like, yes, I'd like to shut them up in a room with rats. That's the nastiest thing I can think of.'

'You're very childish and you're wasting your energy,' Miss Spanner said calmly. 'It's all over.'

'That's just it.'

'And I rather like thinking about it. It amuses me. Anyhow, I learnt to be self-sufficient and to love books. This generation seems to care very little about them, but I'm bringing up that little Rhoda Blackett in the way she should go.'

Rhoda Blackett, essentially honest, had been a little disingenuous with Miss Spanner. Not naturally an ardent reader and with a father who had quite a little library at her disposal, she was borrowing books from Miss Spanner because so she gained an entrance into the bedroom like a secondhand shop, and she was reading them because that was the way to secure Miss Spanner's friendship and, whatever her appetite might have been for literature, she would always have felt that what her father offered her was slightly tainted: the same book from Miss

Spanner must have a different and more wholesome flavour. And she had permission to walk when she chose into the Frasers' house, and upstairs to Miss Spanner's room and when there was no answer to her knock she went inside, by permission again, and took a book from the shelves. This she laid open on her knee in case Miss Spanner arrived, but her attention was for the knick-knacks, the photographs of bearded men in frock coats and ladies wearing jet ornaments, the old-fashioned watch, its key attached to a gold chain, on a watch-stand beside Miss Spanner's bed, the nightdress case embroidered in a design of bright pink roses. All this pleased Rhoda unaccountably but very much. She seemed to be living, when she sat there, in another time, not a distant but a very different one from her own and it was the nearness with the strangeness of it that gave it charm. She might so easily have had a mother who wore jet ornaments and her father actually had a beard, though not of the shape favoured by Miss Spanner's relatives, and Rhoda was not sure whether she had fortunately escaped or unhappily missed a period in which people looked like this, solid and sure of themselves and their opinions and their place in the world. Even in the photographs, it was possible to see how firmly their feet were set on the ground. She felt at ease in this pictured company, more at ease though less exhilarated than she was with Miss Spanner. These people on the walls who stared at her glassily or kindly could not find her wanting and decide they had had enough of her and make it plain she need not come again and, because this would be a disaster, she who at sixteen, young in some ways for her age, went blundering, half asleep, through her work at school, was determined to keep her mind alert and found it less difficult when she was with Miss Spanner. And this was a different alertness from the one she practised on her own family. There she was quick to understand or, at least, to puzzle over what was going on in the mind of her father and mother and Flora but she was quite indifferent as to what he and Flora might think of herself. She knew her mother would think nothing that was not kind and wise. She and her mother were

95

sure of each other and verbal communication was almost unnecessary; with Miss Spanner, Rhoda had to be on her mettle, while her instinctive good sense warned her not to affect more intelligence than she really had. And she was a good, because she was a fascinated, listener. Part of Miss Spanner seemed to begin with the people in the photographs, another to linger in her own youth and the rest to have reached beyond the youth of the people in the house. Her clothes would not have come very much amiss in the earliest period, the modesty of her habits belonged to the middle one, but her mind had ranged a good deal farther than she chose to let the young Frasers know and farther than Rhoda could go with her. The Frasers, as Miss Spanner was aware, liked her very well, accepted her as she appeared to be and laughed at her oddities while they respected her character, and she was fond of them, but they had a lightness of touch, an apparent frivolity of outlook which made them, with their beauty, a little unreal to her. This clumsy girl, endangering the precious ornaments when she came into the room, gave Miss Spanner a self-confidence she secretly lacked. Rhoda's eyes were not much concerned with outward appearances; it was the inside of Miss Spanner she wanted to see and Miss Spanner produced the best of it. It was not learning, for she had none; it was not wisdom or wit, though these were not altogether lacking; it was the desire for affection and the power to give it and an unspoken sympathy which, with an effort, was also scrupulous, for if Rhoda had been a little disingenuous with Miss Spanner, so had been Miss Spanner's first approaches to Rhoda, but the questions she had meant to ask were never uttered, the probing she had meant to do remained undone. The child liked her, she knew that, and it was not with the tolerant, amused liking of the Frasers, but with some surprising pleasure in her company, and, in payment, curiosity must remain unsatisfied. This was the more easily done because Miss Spanner found herself the object of interest to someone else and she told the truth when she said she could now enjoy looking back on her youth. It provided her with entertainment for Rhoda who seemed to think it neither sad nor funny. Staring at Miss Spanner, she listened greedily to anything she was told and Miss Spanner would hardly have been human if she had not exaggerated a little. Where she showed restraint was in limiting the quantity she offered at a time and she would often catch herself up in a reminiscence and change the subject, thus whetting an appetite which was persistent but not exacting. Rhoda accepted these breaks in Miss Spanner's narratives but, sooner or later, brought her back to the story.

'As you can imagine,' Miss Spanner said one day, 'we were a great family for wearing mourning. If we lost a third cousin, my father's hat band had to be changed. My mother nearly always wore black anyhow. The difficulty was to rig me out, without expense, but they always managed it.'

'How?' Rhoda asked.

'Oh, I'll tell you about that another day. You'd better go home now, hadn't you?'

Rhoda was not hurt by such abrupt dismissals. This was the sort of treatment she liked, but her actual arrivals and departures always made her a little nervous. What she feared most was encountering the young men of the house. She was aware of Flora's interest in them and she herself was in an intermediate state which despised such interest but made her self-conscious when she met them, distrusting her own clumsiness, sure she would collide with something or drop the book she carried and look foolish, knowing she could not possibly produce the suitable light word in passing. She was old enough to know she was too young and too unattractive to get more than common courtesy from them; that was more than she wanted, and she was, therefore, surprised and momentarily embarrassed when one evening, a few days after Mr. Blackett had made his concession, James waylaid her in the hall and said, 'I'll come over with you if I may. I've got a book here for Flora.'

'I'll take it for you,' she said sensibly.

He hesitated as they stood together on the doorstep. Mr. Blackett had been more successful than he had expected or perhaps intended. What with this parental fuss and the exciting prospects of his holiday and Flora's silly, somewhat claimant tears, James regretted his slight indiscretions and felt the beginnings of distaste for a girl who seemed to take them seriously. It was just possible, he found himself capable of this thought, that she had carried her distress to her parents, but it would be unchivalrous, though he did not use the word, to break with her abruptly and he must show old Blackett he was not afraid of him and so, in spite of the temptation of Rhoda's offer, he refused it.

'No, I'd like to come,' he said.

'What is it?' she asked, peering for the title, and when she saw it she uttered a dubious 'Oh!'

'You'd think it very dull, I suppose,' he said.

'No, I like that kind of thing.'

'So you are interested in farming too.'

'Too?' she said. 'Like you, you mean?'

'Yes — and Flora.'

Rhoda, staring in her steady way at James and finding it surprisingly easy to do so, did not say anything. It would have been natural to her to give a blunt denial to this ridiculous assertion but, though she did not really like Flora and had always thought she was a fraud, acting the part which, at the moment, served her best and this particular part seemed more flagrant than usual because it was appropriating something of Rhoda's own, she had never been a tell-tale and if she looked sceptical it was not on purpose. She would not even tell him that her own interests were out of doors and she meant to be a gardener, but she would have liked him to know. He had a nice face, he was not at all the grand kind of young man she had imagined and suddenly she wanted him to see her as more than an insignificant neighbour and Flora's sister. But she could not bring herself to do anything towards that end.

'Well, come on,' was all she said.

CHAPTER XIV

'WHEN I was courting you, Bertha,' said Mr. Blackett, 'what would you have thought if I had offered you a technical book on paper making?'

They had finished their coffee. Flora had drunk hers hastily and disappeared. James's visit had been short. He had left the house just as Mr. Blackett reached it and Flora, having awkwardly made them known to each other, had been living since then in apprehension of her father's adverse comments. She had seen him pick up the book she had not had time to hide and drop it with a light, disdainful movement. If he could have flicked away so heavy an object, he would have flicked it, but he had said nothing then or at the supper table.

'What would you have thought?' he repeated.

'I expect I should have felt rather flattered,' Mrs. Blackett said.

'Oh.' It seemed, for a moment, that he had left something undone, but he quickly saw a way out of this difficulty. 'I hope,' he said, 'I should never have done anything so egotistical. I think what I generally brought you, Bertha, was flowers.'

'Yes,' she agreed. 'But that nice boy from next door isn't courting Flora, as you call it.'

'Then what is he doing? And I'm sorry you don't like that expression. I think it is a charming one.'

'Just being friendly, I think,' and Mr. Blackett made a sceptical noise. He knew more than she did. 'And even if they do have a little flirtation, it won't do Flora any harm!'

'Flirtation!' Mr. Blackett exclaimed with disgust.

'Yes,' Mrs. Blackett said calmly. 'Until lately, she has had a very dull life for a girl.'

'You have never surprised me more,' he said, pursing his lips and, in his irritation, he rose from his comfortable chair, straightened a picture with nervous fingers and sat down again.

'Have I ever surprised you at all?' she asked.

'No.' He remembered that playing-card. 'Well, very rarely. And why should you? And this surprise is very great. A dull life! Do you realize what you said? She has had everything I could give her — everything!'

'Too much, perhaps.'

'Too much!' He heard himself like an echo, but what else could he say?

'Not enough variety,' said Mrs. Blackett, 'and very little fun.'

He just managed to stop himself from repeating her last word. 'I set my face from the first,' he said slowly, 'against this modern mania for amusement.'

'I meant at home, among ourselves,' Mrs. Blackett said. 'We can't help it, I suppose. We haven't got a proper sense of it, you and I.'

'I deny that,' Mr. Blackett said. 'I'm as ready for a joke as anybody.'

'And we can't do anything about it,' Mrs. Blackett went on as though she had not heard his last remark, 'so I want Flora and the others to find it where they can.'

'And you suggest flirtation! A strange suggestion, Bertha, and a strange word, from you!'

'Yes, it was the wrong word to use and the wrong thing to suggest. Flirting is out of fashion nowadays. Young people are too frank and girls have too much liberty and too much sense to want that kind of excitement; but then, Flora hasn't had much liberty and I don't think she has much sense.'

Astonishment at this calm and unexpected remark kept Mr. Blackett silent for a moment before he said, 'I don't understand you. I don't understand you at all,' and then, remembering what Mrs. Fraser had said to him on the hill and refusing to acknowledge that she might be right, he modified his statement by saying, 'I don't understand you to-night. What will you say next? Flora is unusually intelligent. She always has been. I wish I could say as much for Rhoda. And of course I want them to have pleasure, but I shall be very much disappointed, I shall be displeased, if you encourage her to neglect her work for it. And how much gaiety did you have in your own youth?'

'Not nearly enough,' Mrs. Blackett said with unusual emphasis.

'I don't agree,' he said. 'How can I when I see what you are now? And, after all, Bertha, what is life for?'

Mrs. Blackett raised her head and looked round the room as though, vaguely, she searched for something and with a slow shake of her head she said, 'I don't know.'

'And yet,' he said, looking at her very kindly because, suddenly, she seemed a little pitiful and he had never seen her look like that before, 'in everything you are and do, that knowledge is implicit.'

'Oh, don't say that!' she exclaimed quickly. 'Don't talk like that!' and, if she had looked at him then, she would have seen his tender smile changed to a complacent, teasing one. But she did not look at him. She was hurriedly gathering the coffee cups together with a little less than her usual neatness.

'No Bertha, don't go,' he said, and still with that smile and lolling back in his chair, he stretched out a hand towards her. This was a happy moment for him. It was her humility he found so touching and his power to confuse her with a word of praise was much more gratifying than it had been before he married her. It assured him he had not lost his art: moreover, the reward was more immediate.

'Bertha, come here,' he said. But with a little hunched up movement of her shoulders, as though she held herself close instead of letting him hold her, she picked up the tray and went away without a look or word.

Even Mr. Blackett could not attribute this disappearance to the modesty he so much appreciated. His next resource was to fear or rather, more comfortably, to hope she was not feeling well, but again he remembered Mrs. Fraser's words and he remembered her too, with some of the feeling he had wanted to bestow on Bertha. Mrs. Fraser, he was quite sure, would have welcomed it. And Bertha's behaviour not only forced him to the thought of the other woman; it justified him in lingering over the remembrance of her as she stood on the hill, before she saw him, her hands on the railings, her body leaning back a little from them, motionless, yet with an effect of eagerness. That was how he always saw her, eager, with the pulse of spring in her, yet with a ripeness suitable to her age, like fruit at its perfection, still on the tree but very willing to be picked and, suddenly, he wondered whether she had been waiting there by appointment or in hope. That, of course, would account for the coldness of her manner towards him and why else should a woman with a family to look after and the hour for the evening meal approaching, be standing there, bare-headed, on a damp evening? She had been hurrying, too, when he first caught sight of her and it gratified him to think that the expected person had failed to appear, which must have been humiliating, or had been driven off by his own presence. Thus, inadvertently in this case though not as a rare occurrence, he had been on the side of the angels and he felt a glow of pleasure which sent him cheerfully, forgetting Bertha's offence, in search of company, to the drawing-room which was empty, like the garden, and then to the dining-room where he found Rhoda standing at the window, a scattering of school books on the table behind her.

She turned, smiling, as he entered and he saw her face fall.

'Oh, I thought it was Mother,' she said, and feeling hurt, he checked the inquiry he would have made about her homework, the half-playful reproach for idling and, worse still, for looking out of the window. Though she always puzzled and irritated him, he would have been glad, at this moment, if the smile had been for him and he felt a desire to show her he deserved it.

'Anything interesting in the Square?' he asked genially.

'Nothing particular,' she said, moving away, but when he took her place – though, discreetly, he kept further back – he said bitingly, 'I entirely agree with you,' for he saw Piers Lindsay at some distance from Mrs. Fraser's door and felt sure he had not limped so badly before he turned the corner.

'Quite the pedlar to-day,' he said, 'and that, Rhoda, is a word one might think was connected with the foot, but really, I believe derives from one meaning a basket. He has no basket, not even the modern equivalent for one in the shape of his ramshackle car. Why is that, I wonder? But,' he went on, 'he is not altogether without his stock in trade. Well, let us welcome him. Go and open the door to him. You will save Connie a journey. But no,' he said sharply, 'I see that will not be necessary. New friends for old! I don't like that, Rhoda, do you?' he asked, smiling at her with his teeth set. 'I'm afraid your mother will be hurt.'

'Why?' Rhoda asked, though she felt a bitter disappointment herself.

Mr. Blackett parted his teeth to make a little exclamation of vexation. Communication with Rhoda was impossible. She was extraordinarily stupid and he wondered how he could have fathered such a child and what suitable work in life he could find for her. He turned to look at the books on the table and shook his head at her sprawling handwriting.

'I don't know what we are to do with you,' he sighed.

'But I know what I'm going to do with myself,' she said.

'Really? This is interesting and as you may need my help perhaps you'll tell me what your plans are.'

'I'm going to be a gardener.'

'A gardener?' he said.

'Yes. There are places where you can be trained but,' Rhoda said eagerly, 'if you can't afford to send me there, I don't mind just doing jobbing work, by the day, you know. I could easily do that already.'

'Well Rhoda,' he said slowly, 'I think this is quite a good idea.'

'Do you?' Her surprise and gratitude ought to have touched him. 'I'm sure I'd get a lot of work. Heaps of people would be glad of me. And then,' she went on, for he was listening with interest, he was looking at her gravely, almost respectfully, 'if only I could get a lot of houses together, a whole row of little ones, I could sort of make them agree with each other. Of course I wouldn't have them all the same, but I could make them look more like one big garden instead of ugly little separate patches. The people in those little houses always have their flowers too bright. They ought to have more nice soft greens and greys against their staring bricks, and blues, not reds and yellows. It would really be better to do that than to be a gardener in a grand place where everything is lovely already. Don't you think so?'

Mr. Blackett did not reply at once. He seemed to be looking at someone he saw for the first time. The girl looked quite pretty, he thought. Her eyes were bright and the aggressiveness of her short nose had become alertness.

'Of course you must be properly trained, but I shall have to talk to your mother about this,' he said, and Rhoda had the good sense to refrain from telling him that she and her mother had talked about it many times. 'And you must work harder at school,' he added.

'I'll try,' she said. He had been nice to her, nicer than he had ever been before and she must be nice to him and she was generously ready to believe that all their little differences had been her fault.

'We seem,' Mr. Blackett continued, 'to be turning into quite an agricultural little community, what with a daughter who wants to be a gardener, a cousin,' and now there came a familiar twist into his voice, 'who hawks vegetables and another daughter who seems to take an interest in farming.'

And again Rhoda was loyal to Flora yet, in spite of that warning in her father's voice, she was trustful enough to say, 'I'd like to be a farmer myself, but that would be more difficult. I don't suppose you'd like that. Still,' she said, 'perhaps I'll have to be.'

'Have to be?'

'Yes, if there's a war we'll all have to do something and I'll work on the land. Perhaps I could help Cousin Piers.'

'You certainly won't help your Cousin Piers. I doubt if he would let you. I think he would consider,' Mr. Blackett half glanced over his shoulder, 'that other people had prior claims. And there will not be a war.' The little pink spots appeared on his cheeks. 'You may be sure of that. Fortunately, we have wise men at the head of affairs and they will save us from that wicked folly. And who has been putting that idea into your head?'

Miss Spanner's entertainment of Rhoda had not always been of a reminiscent kind and as her political opinions were exactly opposite to Mr. Blackett's, Rhoda had readily adopted them, but her friendship with Miss Spanner must be concealed from her father — even in her trustful mood she knew this — and she said now, defensively, 'Well, I read the newspapers.'

'When? I've never seen you doing that. I've often wished you would.' After a glance at *The Times* while he breakfasted, he carried it to his office and though he brought it back each evening and at one time Flora had obediently read the articles he recommended, no one else had ever asked for it and Mrs. Blackett seemed quite content with hearing what he chose to tell her.

'I'm afraid,' Mr. Blackett said, 'the extent of your reading is the sensational stuff you see on the placards. You ought not to call that reading the newspapers.'

'I don't. I always look at Mother's paper before I go back to school in the afternoon,' Rhoda said indignantly, but she saw at once, from the expression on her father's face that, somehow, she had made a mistake, and again she had a fleeting conviction that life was an intricacy of dark and narrow passages in which she could never be sure of the right way.

CHAPTER XV

'AND so,' Rosamund said to Felix when Sandra came running down the stairs to say that Mr. Lindsay had arrived, 'I suppose I must try to look glum,' and after practising in the little mirror on the wall she turned to him and said, 'How will this do?' But already the lips she had tried to turn down had sprung up again. The structure of her face resisted any effect of gloom and she won a reluctant smile from Felix.

'Don't be absurd,' he said.

'And anyhow,' she took off her apron, 'Agnes will do all the glumming that's necessary.'

She was, in fact, a little afraid of what Agnes might do. Impelled by a sense of duty, she was quite capable of making unmistakable references to Fergus for, with her faith in Rosamund's powers of attraction, she considered that Mr. Lindsay was being welcomed under false pretences. But this view of the matter, on Rosamund's part, would have implied a quite unwarranted belief that she was the magnet drawing him. And yet that was what she wished to be, with the natural desire of a woman deprived of her rightful opportunities to exercise her gifts. Fergus's unfailing appreciation of them had done much, too much, she thought now, to compensate for his faults and if he had been less satisfactory as a lover she might have taken earlier steps to improve him as a father. She had been selfish, she was selfish still, she decided unrepentantly. She knew it was just possible that she was misleading Piers Lindsay, but he was old enough to take care of himself and she had too much personal dignity, too much respect for him and she was too much of an artist in her own line, to be anything but simple and frank in her manner towards him. Moreover, he evoked such behaviour and in the long room where the whole family was gathered, everybody was at ease except Miss Spanner who had isolated herself as far as she could and wore the disagreeable expression of a consciously poor relation upheld by a sense of her moral value. This expression was unintentional but she was isolated by much more than a few feet of carpet. She had seen Rosamund's happy youth and contrasted it with her own; now she saw the youth of Rosamund's children, less happy because their world was more confused; the old certainties had become doubts and this alone put their lives immeasurably distant from the one spent in the dark house on the Green where only her innate independence and covert rebellion had prevented Miss Spanner from thinking, as she had to live, according to inviolable rule. And that life had stiffened not her mind but her manner. She had had no practice in gracious social dealings. No one had invaded Mrs. Spanner's drawing-room except an occasional deacon, on chapel business with Mr. Spanner to whom she was chillingly polite, or, very rarely, the minister himself who expected and received a proper meed of laughter for his little jokes and rather pitied her for having a daughter who, though devoted, seemed somewhat stupid and lacked the soft ways he looked for in young women.

To-night Agnes was stiffer than usual in disapproval of Mr. Lindsay's visit, but she was a woman and not an old one and, half ashamed to confess it, she wished she could make some contribution of beauty to the scene as these others did, beauty of feature or voice or pose or that transfiguring anxiety for other people's happiness which made Sandra's sharp little face as vivid as her hair, and as she cut away the cobbles Rosamund had made in the boys' socks and filled the gaps with the fine darning she had learnt under her mother's sharp eye, she was deeply resentful of her physical imperfections and, in rebellion against them, she lost consciousness of her surroundings in what was almost a determination to send her clothes to a rummage sale, put her head into the hands of a good hairdresser and the rest of her body into those of Chloe and Miss Pringle. The processes would be humiliating and uncomfortable and in the end she would not be beautiful but perhaps it was her duty to try and she might, at least, be elegant and distinguished looking and these words had no sooner passed through her mind than she came to herself and let out a short bark of laughter, and at that the conversation, which had been a shelter for her thoughts, immediately ceased and seven pairs of eyes looked at her with astonishment.

She patted her throat. 'Just a sudden choke,' she said and several pairs of eyes looked at her with sceptical amusement.

'Shall I get you some water?' Sandra asked with tender malice.

'For a moment,' Felix remarked gravely, 'I was afraid you were laughing at the masculine futility of our conversation.'

'Not at all,' said Miss Spanner. 'Most interesting.' She patted her throat again and nodded reassuringly and Paul, between a squeak and a grunt, picked up the talk where it had been dropped.

They were talking, she discovered, about cricket. Cricket! she thought, and to her, who had been brought up in a world where games were considered a waste of time, this seemed a strange subject to be discussing now, but while terms and names were bandied to and fro, much less familiar to her than those of

European statesmen and trouble-makers, she took heart at the remembrance that Drake played bowls and in the belief that the young men of to-day, in spite of disillusionment and apparent indifference to matters more serious in her view than cricket, would still be true to their breed. It was the old ones she distrusted. And what a lot there was to say about a game and how meekly the women kept silence under a topic they seemed to consider sacred, as in truth to some extent they did, and how impatient and scornful the men would be, Miss Spanner thought, if she and Rosamund and Chloe started a discussion about cooking, a skilful occupation of much more real concern to men than cricket was to women. 'But they always get the best of it,' she grumbled to herself and at once she added 'And they deserve it,' for it was not she who had one leg a little shorter than the other and her face was not disfigured though that, in her case, would not have made much difference, indeed, it might have been an advantage. She would have had three faces and people would have found in her the fascination she found in Mr. Lindsay as the faces came and went, the normal profile giving way to a comic ruefulness and then to a strained and almost tragic aspect.

It was the normal profile she saw as he rose and said he must go and see his cousins before he fetched his car. George was usually able to deal with its vagaries but this time he had failed and it had been necessary to take it to an expert. So that, Miss Spanner thought with satisfaction and Rosamund with none, accounted for this visit, but Miss Spanner's satisfaction was tempered with disappointment. After all, he had not come on foot to spare Mrs. Blackett's feelings and Miss Spanner, anxious for propriety in the household with which she was connected, could not willingly relinquish her determination that there should be a three-cornered drama across the road, complicated by an abortive one here. It had to be abortive here, for personal contact with such an affair would be inconvenient and somewhat sordid but, at a little distance, like some thrilling story of crime, it would be transmuted into romance by the skill of the artist who, in this case, was Miss Spanner herself.

'But if you go now,' Sandra said, 'you won't hear the news.'

'George will be listening. He'll tell me all about it,' he said, and Rosamund felt an unreasoning enmity for George. He seemed to be a universal provider.

'And do you know anything about knots?' James asked.

'Knots?'

'Yes, for ropes. Climbing ropes,' he added.

It was rather pathetic, Rosamund thought, that eagerness of a reserved person to speak about his holiday now that he was assured of it. Like a child, he had been impelled to make an opportunity for introducing the subject and it was something of a reproach to her who ought, she supposed, to have divined a longing he had chivalrously concealed.

'I did do a little climbing, once,' Lindsay said. He seemed to be amused by the recollection and then, as he turned his head, to be distressed by it.

'Didn't you care about it?'

'Yes, very much but I'd only just begun. I was having my first climbing holiday when the war started. I only had three days of it and after that I'd have been rather a nuisance on a rope so I didn't try again. But I can't imagine anything better,' he said, remembering the dusty smell of heather on an August morning, the gritty warmth of the rocks, the blue arch of the sky and the sheep calling, the perfect peace but for that sound and the rasp of nails on the rock and an occasional word from the man in front of him. But that peace had suddenly become ironical when, at the top of the little mountain, the climb over, some inferior being who had walked up and was scattering orange peel, gave them the news and, chiefly because of the orange peel, they had made no comment beyond a grunt. What unfriendly snobs they had been! They had coiled up the rope and hurried down by the quickest way to the little farmhouse lying now with an air of unreality in its security at the foot of the mountain. They had gone down through thick heather, still saying nothing, but when they reached the stream threading the valley they had stopped with one accord and stripped and bathed in water like iced silk. Though none of them would have acknowledged the feeling, it was as though, now that they were more accessible, they could afford themselves a little leisure before they packed their sacks and tramped to the nearest station. The smells and sights and sounds of that day were pungent and clear to him now. There could never have been a bluer sky or a brighter green than that of the moss bordering the stream: it was a cushion of softness too, and the sounds of the water, trickling here and gushing there, making a lovely, callous song, and still doing it no doubt, was the best music he had ever heard, though his real youth ended by its banks.

All this passed through his mind in the few seconds before he spoke again. 'But that was a very long time ago,' he said, and had a momentary impression of constraint in the room.

It was Paul who explained it. 'And it'll be funny if the same thing happens when Felix and James go climbing in September.'

'Oh Paul!' Rosamund said softly, in protest against this embarrassment of a visitor.

It was never safe, Lindsay thought, to mention that old war. You met the smile of incredulity or impatience, you seemed to boast — and perhaps that reference to his injuries had seemed like boasting — and when the whole thing was not discredited you touched somebody on a tender spot. And now there was this new danger of uttering omens.

'But it might easily happen,' Paul persisted, not without hope.

'Yes, we know,' his mother said.

'And if we only get three days, like you,' James said, 'it will be something.'

'It will be a great deal,' Lindsay said.

'And Drake played bowls,' said Miss Spanner. She was glad she had remembered that. 'And I wish you'd play them too, instead of these monkey tricks you're after. What was good enough for him ought to be good enough for you.'

'But he got his adventures in other ways,' Felix said.

'And you'll get plenty when you're a pilot,' Paul assured him.

'Oh, shut up!' Felix said, looking like his father.

But Paul was accidentally wiser than the others. Nobody was afraid of the subject, but everyone thought someone else might be and Rosamund decided it was time to put an end to all this delicacy.

'I wish you could have your holiday now, at once,' she said. 'I do so want you to have it.'

'Smithers can't go any sooner.'

'Bother Smithers! Well, perhaps it will be all right,' she said, and, while a derisive sound came from Miss Spanner, she looked at Lindsay, hoping for a comforting word. She would not have believed it but she would have liked to hear it and she liked him all the better for not saying it.

'Nice man,' said Felix, coming back from seeing him off.

'But dull,' Chloe said.

'And very lonely, I should think,' Sandra said.

'Now don't be sorry for him.' Rosamund spoke a little sharply. 'It's a kind of self-indulgence and I'm sure there's not the slightest need for it. That George of his seems to be a complete family as well as a cook and a handyman and if necessary, no doubt, a nurse too.'

'But he isn't a real family,' Sandra said, 'and that's what everybody ought to have.'

CHAPTER XVI

MRS. BLACKETT had done her best to brighten Connie's cavernous kitchen. With walls painted yellow and curtains and table cover to match there was an effect of sunshine under the electric light and blessed, as it was, with the added comfort of a cushioned expanding chair, Mr. Blackett could not understand why Connie was not content to stay there until a reasonable hour in the evening instead of going to bed as soon as her work was done and leaving some member of the family to answer the front door bell. It was very seldom rung at such a time and Mr. Blackett, unwilling to admit her right to go to bed when she chose and never sure whether she had gone or not, had failed to appoint a definite substitute for this task. The result, this evening, with Piers Lindsay on the doorstep, as he could see from his window, was a pause for the sound of Connie mounting the basement stairs and then a rush from various parts of the house and what Mr. Blackett considered a most unnecessary gathering in the hall to greet the visitor and one likely to give him quite a wrong impression. Mrs. Blackett was there smiling serenely; Flora, hoping for the arrival of a different visitor, and Rhoda with her faith in Cousin Piers restored. After all, he had not come on foot in a sort of secrecy as Miss Spanner, too, had suspected and, although it was a pity he had wasted any time on the Frasers, she did not grudge him to Miss Spanner and he had not, as her father suggested, altogether exchanged old friends for new.

'And Mary, I suppose, is in bed,' Mr. Blackett said from the background, using the most urbane notes of his voice in comment on this gathering and Flora, in disappointment, gave him a sympathetic smile with a little lift of her shoulders. She felt just as he did about this enthusiasm and almost recovered the credit she had lost with her father. She had been smirched in his eyes by her physical contact with that young man: it was impossible for his imagination to halt at a handclasp and he had avoided looking at a daughter who had provoked him to such unpleasant thoughts, yet there could not be anything seriously wrong with a girl who took his meaning so swiftly and shared his feelings and he smiled back, acknowledging her as his own again.

This little episode was not noticed by the others. 'I saw you,' Rhoda said, 'but I was afraid you wouldn't be coming.'

'Of course I was coming,' he answered, wondering why she should care, seeing a faint likeness in her pleasure to Bertha's in the old days when they met after a parting, a little startled by this evidence that, stumbling through life and going rather blindly, it was possible to pick up treasure as well as miss it and he was warmed by the discovery that, as was fitting, Bertha's child had a liking for him and he thought the lack of reason for it was its chief charm. But there was a formality in Mrs. Blackett's pale drawing-room in strong contrast to the friendly ease in the Frasers' house. Rhoda's now sullen face made him doubt whether, a few minutes ago, he had read it truly, while Mr. Blackett, wearing a politely receptive expression, seemed to await some explanation of this visit. Flora, following his lead, looked faintly amused and Mrs. Blackett never had much to say, but she did her best with the weather and inquiries after his crops and he responded with inquiries about her garden and went to the door to look down on it from the top of the little staircase.

'Let's go down and see it properly,' Rhoda said.

'No, no, it's beginning to get dark,' her father objected.

'That's when a garden looks nicest.'

'And those steps are dangerous, as we know to our cost. To my very considerable cost,' he added. 'Now, be careful, Bertha,' he said as she followed the other two and he watched her to the bottom. 'Your cousin,' he said, turning back to Flora, 'is agile enough when he chooses. There are occasions when he forgets to limp. Well, I think we've done our duty by him and he, no doubt, thinks he is doing his duty by us. A sense of duty can be very misleading, Flora. Modesty ought to accompany it and I can honestly say that I do not value myself enough to believe I should be doing my duty in paying a call on a single soul I know, and especially not at this time of night.'

'But he's a cousin,' Flora said, 'and Mother's very fond of him.'

Mr. Blackett laughed a little. 'Fond?' he said. 'Your mother is very loyal and very courteous, two great qualities,' he said, and he went back to the door to take a look at her.

They were all at the farther end of the garden; he could hear the murmuring of their voices and as the three figures moved through the dusk in their absurdly concentrated scrutiny of the flower beds, he saw his wife slip a hand under Lindsay's arm and check their pacing to look up at him and laugh, clearly and happily. He stepped back at once in instinctive horror of eavesdropping, but why, he asked himself the next minute, should it seem like eavesdropping to hear his wife's laughter? He did not answer the question. He blinked away the memory of the confidence with which she had put her hand under Lindsay's arm and his resentment turned more safely to Rhoda's remark about her mother's newspaper. He would have to look into that matter for it seemed to be vaguely connected with everything else that puzzled him. And he remembered again how she had laughed at him last night, not clearly and not happily. Moreover, she had repulsed him to-night and for a second or two he felt as Rhoda had felt a short time ago. He saw life as a more complicated journey than he had believed, much more complicated than any journey he undertook ought to be, and when, with difficulty, he turned from this unpleasing prospect it was to find Flora looking at him with curiosity.

'Don't you feel well?' she asked.

'I always feel well,' he replied, taking all the credit for his excellent health.

'Because you looked rather funny,' Flora said.

Mr. Blackett gave his quiet little frown. 'I'm glad I amuse you,' he said, and though she hastened to tell him that her remark was not intended in that sense, he found some relief to his irritation by asking her smilingly how she was getting on with her agricultural studies.

Adroitly, she answered him with a little grimace. He liked that: it was reassuring, yet he hardly knew how to reconcile it with that scene in the Avenue, in fact, he thought, shutting himself up in his study, nothing was quite what it seemed or what it ought to be. He did not share Rhoda's relief at the candour of Lindsay's behaviour. It did not fit the situation as he wanted it and he was enraged at the man's freedom to be frank, to come and go as he chose and, worst of all, Bertha was not herself and what with her newspaper and her laughter and her cousin, the annoyance of having to allow the son of that woman next door into his house and the thought of that woman, coolly in command of herself and of him as they stood on the hill, there was turmoil in his mind though, just for a moment, he admitted the pettiness of his affairs, the little he had to complain of and his own insignificance in comparison with more horrible tumults and unhappiness much greater than he was likely to know.

'And all unnecessary,' he thought, not referring to his own troubles but to those made by other people far away and threatening to affect the order of his life and he turned to his bookshelves to find escape in noble poetry and to believe that, because he appreciated fine sentiments, they were those by which his life was governed.

And in the garden where the pale flowers shone out proudly among the darker ones whose colours were being stolen by the night, though their sweetness came, now and then, in little gusts of scent, Mrs. Blackett and Piers Lindsay and Rhoda still lingered, chatting casually about this and that, the elders remembering little happenings of their youth, egged on by Rhoda who was a charmed but, finally, not altogether a contented audience. Her mother, she found, must have laughed much more then than she did now, talked more too and been, it was evident, much happier and this was another little shock to Rhoda. In spite of that strange, puzzling look she had once seen her mother give her father, she had always assumed that her parents and most other adults must be happy. They could do anything they liked and what more could anybody ask? But Rhoda, though slowly, was growing up. She remembered that look and compared it with what she could see now of her mother's face; she compared past moments of tension which she had mistaken for calm with what she could feel of relaxation in the atmosphere here, and there had been that other queer look, this time of her father's, yet she had never heard a harsh word from one to the other. And perhaps people who were married did not exchange little comfortable nothings as her mother and her cousin were doing now; perhaps, with children, life became too serious; perhaps it was all her father's fault. His presence curbed her own spontaneity — there had been a rare exception that evening before he spoilt it — and it might curb her mother's. He seemed to put a cork into people's mouths and only some special eagerness could eject it and suddenly, as though the cork had been applied, there was silence in the garden until Mrs. Blackett said, on a downward breath, 'It's time we went in.'

'Why?' Lindsay asked. 'And what's time, after all? It's our servant, not our master?'

'Is it?' Mrs. Blackett said, a little sadly.

'Ought to be, anyhow. And it's nice out here. I like to be in a quiet place and hear noises in the distance. It makes the quietness quieter.'

There were rattlings and rumblings in roads far beyond the Square and then a steamer on the river hooted its call of melancholy triumph.

'It's high tide,' Mrs. Blackett said. Men were going out to sea or coming home from it, and nearer, startlingly near, there was another and an alien sound, melancholy too, but angry, the roaring of a lion in the Zoo.

'Hope and despair,' Mrs. Blackett said, and there was silence again until, as she started reluctantly for the house, Lindsay said, 'You're lucky in your neighbours, Bertha.'

'Am I? Oh yes,' she agreed hastily, 'they are charming people but I'm afraid I don't make friends very easily. I'm not like you, Piers,' she said with peculiar gentleness.

'No, just like yourself,' he said. 'But I wasn't thinking of the Frasers —'

'And Miss Spanner's far the nicest anyway,' Rhoda said.

'You think so?' he said, giving this opinion due consideration. 'What I meant was that you were lucky in not having gramophones and loud speakers on each side of you to spoil a night like this.'

'Yes, a lovely night,' Mrs. Blackett said, looking up to see an impatient star or two and taking in her cousin's face in passing. 'And isn't it a wonderful thing?' she said and stopped.

'What?' Rhoda asked.

'A lovely night,' her mother replied but, before she remembered Rhoda's presence, she had meant to record the blessedness of being able to keep certain hours and incidents inviolate, to enclose them in a frame of memory and put glass over them, safe from the contamination of less happy times. 'And I've never asked you to have anything to eat or drink,' she said, at the foot of the stairs. 'Shall we go into the kitchen now and make some coffee?'

'That would be fun,' Rhoda said.

'No, no, George will make some for me if I want it.'

'And I'm so glad you have George to look after you,' Mrs. Blackett told him.

She and Rhoda watched him out of sight and Mr. Blackett, hearing their farewells, listened for that halting footstep to stop at the Frasers' door, but with mingled pleasure and annoyance he heard it going on until it became a faint tapping and then nothing.

'You,' said Rhoda to her mother, 'and Miss Spanner and Cousin Piers are the nicest people I know. I wish they'd get married to each other and then, when I saw one of them I'd see them both.'

'Oh Rhoda,' Mrs. Blackett protested, 'that wouldn't do at all!'

'Well, why not? I know she isn't very pretty, but I don't think he'd mind about that.'

'Don't you?' Mrs. Blackett said slowly and with interest.

'No, he has too much sense. And I expect that's why he goes there such a lot.'

'But he doesn't go so very often, does he?'

'Oftener than he comes here,' Rhoda said. 'And who wouldn't?' she added with youthful bitterness, a remark to which Mrs. Blackett made no reply.

CHAPTER XVII

THAT night, when Miss Spanner had gone to bed, Rosamund wrote a long letter to Fergus. She wrote it very quickly, not once hesitating for a word, then read it, laughed, with tears in her eyes, and tore it up. She had never intended to send it. She had written it for her own relief and the clearing of her mind, but she knew such an out-pouring would have made him laugh too and without tears, for their love, ardent as it had always been, had always had, she saw now, an astonishingly light quality. They had taken it naturally, as children take sunshine and rain, asking no questions, and he would have received sceptically and, she hoped, angrily, the news that she had more to give another man than she had given him. She had not been asked for it and never would be. It was buried treasure, but it was not altogether wasted. She set a slightly higher value on herself for being able to love without hope of reward and without melancholy, acknowledging Piers Lindsay as the man who, she had slowly come to believe, would have satisfied her completely in her maturity. And yet, in a way, she loved Fergus still. She could not imagine his physical presence without a little stirring of her senses, though her mind rejected him. He was her youth, her happiness, her laughter, and it would have been false and graceless to repudiate the past because, now, she could give a different allegiance to a man who, all that evening, had hardly spared her a glance, who, she thought, with amused annoyance, had everything he wanted in that George of his and would be very foolish, even if he were tempted, to exchange his easy freedom for the complicated situation in which love for her would involve him and she tried to think she cared for him enough — his quietness, his underlying, rarely expressed humour, the feeling of safety he gave her — to be glad nothing should disturb him. She did not succeed in doing that, but the letter she had written and destroyed was a farewell to the youth which was still so strong in her and would seem ridiculous to anybody else. And meanwhile, Fergus was setting out on a new adventure. It would be selfish not to help him on his way, undignified to betray the pique she could not deny, and she wrote another letter, telling him she would do as he wished when he gave her the necessary information, and finding some comfort in the knowledge that in serving him in what was likely to be a doubtful enterprise, she was not furthering any ends of her own.

'And after all,' she told herself, 'I have had much more

already than most people ever get,' and leaving her bed, she put on her dressing-gown and went on to the balcony.

It was a warm night and very still. Nothing moved in the Square. The evergreens in the Oval, testy things, always ready, given a chance, to scratch their neighbours and express their irritation with dry rustlings, did not stir. The lamps burned steadily and in all the houses the lights were out except in the one behind her. It was like looking at a darkened stage before the actors had appeared and the only sounds were those heard earlier from the Blacketts' garden, the noise of traffic, more intermittent at this hour, but astonishingly clear. The lorries and the steamers might have been in the road just beyond the Square and it would hardly have surprised her to see a lion slinking from the bushes. That possibility had often occurred to her in her childhood, but it was the snakes she had really feared, often picturing one of them as it sneaked out of the Zoo and came, in terrible strong loops, up Chatterton Road, into the Square and up the balcony and fancying she would wake to see its flat head near her pillow in this room she was occupying now. But her father had had a strong wire door made to fit the French window and let the air in while it kept the snakes out and here it was still — she put out a hand to touch it — flat against the wall, broken here and there and rusty, but she would not have it taken away.

'You are very sentimental,' Chloe had told her.

'Perhaps,' she replied, 'but if there's any such kind thing I've done for you that you can remember when I'm dead, and I'm afraid there isn't, I shan't have lived in vain.'

'But you've been wonderful in never doing too much,' Chloe said.

'There are such a lot of you.' Thus Rosamund tried to reject this unexpected and welcome praise.

'And quite right too,' Chloe said. 'I'm going to have a lot of children myself, even if we're poor like us. I've no patience with these ones and twos and a car. I think it's one's duty to have more than that.'

'Duty?' The word came strangely from Chloe.

'Yes. And look at us. We scrape along very happily, don't we?'

'Yes, we scrape along,' Rosamund said.

People, especially her own children, were very surprising. Chloe took all the gaiety she could get; the rest of her spare time was spent in fashioning pretty clothes with the skill and success of the single-minded and she might very well have looked on marriage as an opportunity for more gaiety, much more leisure and clothes she did not make herself, but she was prepared to sacrifice the figure on which she set such store, do without the luxuries towards which she was inclined and face a life of hard work and even hardship from a sense of duty. And she was one of a generation in disrepute as pleasure-seeking, lax in certain matters, according to old standards, indifferent to everything outside its own affairs and living carelessly in a world adrift on a strong sea, but then, Rosamund thought, though the older generation might have sterner rules of behaviour, they were adrift too and were either unaware of their danger or, conscious of their ineptitude, pretended all was well with the ship. And as she stood on that balcony where once she had had to peer through the railings instead of looking over them, whence she had watched Fergus come and go and come back again to stand under her window on such a night as this and assure her that he, like the snakes, could easily reach her, she remembered that his generation, too, had been viewed with dismay by its elders and confounded them by its gallantry and endurance. It was the same old story. The difference lay in the probability that, nowadays, Fergus would not remain on the pavement. Almost as a matter of course he would be with her and she was rather glad Chloe slept on a higher story, though she doubted whether the conscientious accountant would try to storm a fortress. Neither, she thought, would Mr. Lindsay, even with his physical powers unimpaired — he had too much fundamental decency — and Mr. Blackett, though he might toy with the idea, would not have enough skill or courage or impetuosity — but Fergus would. He had worked out the route long ago, by way of the area railings and a water pipe, and remembering him with painful vividness and thinking she could hear his light, strong footstep, she shut her eyes and told herself she would keep them shut until he was beside her and they were sure of each other again for a deceptive hour or two. She gave him time but he did not come. Those imagined footsteps stopped short of the house though she had half lifted her arms in welcome, and she could have cried out in her disappointment and desolation. Then, impatient with her own foolishness and her disloyalty to another love, she turned indoors and picked up the letter she had addressed and stamped. It was impossible to recover the past but for Fergus this letter was the future, and she must let him have it though she saw an arid one for herself, and putting on a coat, she went downstairs and let herself out of the front door.

She lingered beside the pillar box when she had dropped her letter within. It was a sturdy and respectable little structure to be near in the solitude of the night, and the night was too good to leave for the confinement of the house. The sky was thick with stars. She could not really believe they were great impersonal suns at an immeasurable distance from the earth, these little golden points. She still thought of them as she had done in childhood, as lamps put out in the daytime and lighted again at night, an expression of God's desire to please and comfort human beings by filling every possible space with beauty. And to her they were not impersonal. There seemed to be a mind in each one of them, maliciously amused at times but always essentially friendly. God, she thought, must have used a sort of pepper pot for placing these things he had created so lavishly, some of them closely clustered, others scattered as though in a last fling of the pot, and in comparison with the immensity in which they were poised she knew she was smaller than a speck of dust, she was invisible and yet that acceptance of her own unimportance did not make life less interesting or, at times, less painful, and knowing she would not be invisible to the person, most likely a policeman, who was approaching with a dull official

121

tread, she slowly went back to the house and the church clock struck twelve as she reached the door.

She had left it open; she now found it shut. She must have forgotten to put up the latch and the door had swung to, as its habit was. She could not tackle the climb to the balcony, she would have to wake the boys, but first she tried the area door, hoping someone had forgotten to bolt it as, many a time, she had discovered when she came downstairs in the morning. To-night, of course, it had been remembered, the kitchen window was locked, too, and then, as she stood down there, she heard the rapid footsteps she had been listening for a little while ago and as her heart leapt in her breast and she shrank further into the darkness, she hoped that this, too, was an illusion. The mood in which she could have abandoned herself to him had passed. Now she would not know what to do with him. He did not belong to her any more and she would be bitterly angry if he climbed up to her window. But he was not going to do that. She heard the jingling of coins and keys and calling breathlessly, 'Don't shut me out!' she emerged on to the pavement.

The figure, the bare head, the pose were those of Fergus, but it was Felix's voice she heard.

'What on earth are you doing there?' he asked.

She took a step towards him and, laughing a little over the violent beating of her heart, she was glad to lean against him and to feel his arm go round her.

'And in your nightgown!' he exclaimed between anxiety and reproach.

'Yes, shocking, isn't it?'

'But what's the matter? What were you doing? I can feel your heart pumping. Have you been frightened?'

'No. Yes. Just a little. How absurd this is! But rather nice. Did you ever see so many stars? I thought you were in bed hours ago.'

'I thought you were.'

'So I was and then I had a little walk. Well, why not? And

when I came back the door had shut itself and the area door is bolted. And then I heard you coming but I didn't know it was you so I stayed down there until I heard your key. That was discreet, wasn't it?'

'It all sounds very stupid to me,' Felix said, gently propelling her towards the door, 'and you ought to know my step by this time.'

'Yes, but I don't often hear it quite so early in the morning,' Rosamund said smoothly and, fumbling for the light, she switched it on and looked at him under raised eyebrows, the only form of question she would put.

He did not answer it but, with unconscious effrontery, he put another. 'What were you really doing?' he asked.

'Just saying good-bye to my young man,' she said.

Looking displeased, he shrugged that nonsense away. 'I hope no one saw you,' he said and went into his bedroom without wishing her good night.

She sat down on the bottom stair. She did not know whether to be amused or angry. Again he had that mixed effect on her, the primitive part of her pleased by this masculine arrogance, the other annoyed by his presumption. It would never have occurred to Chloe to express disapproval. She would simply have laughed indulgently and hoped she had not taken cold and tucked her up in bed, but Felix, as a man, thought he had the right to criticize and punish her with stern looks, and the angry part of her nearly took control, urging her to follow him and show him what she could do herself in the way of scolding, but she did not obey this impulse. She went back to her bedroom, wishing this odd son of hers, who gave no account of his own night wanderings, had been able to laugh with her and kiss her and so, though unknowingly, to comfort her.

CHAPTER XVIII

IT was still something of an adventure for Miss Spanner to have a meal in a restaurant. Nothing would have induced her to go alone into a place where there were men as waiters; she knew what they would think of her and how they would treat her and she had not the special kind of courage which could combat them, but in a teashop, where there were home-made cakes and young ladies in cretonne overalls, she was comparatively at ease when she had defied and conquered a slight feeling of guilt. Very rarely, while her parents lived, had she partaken of as much as a bun and a glass of milk outside her home and a sense of undue extravagance, almost of frivolity, had accompanied these little excursions. The old Spanners had been eloquent on the sanctity and sufficiency of the home. There was no need to eat outside it, a modern tendency they deplored, and no good reason for leaving it and it was on her return from one of those holidays she had at last relinquished that Miss Spanner had found, hanging near her bed and framed, the assurance that home-keeping hearts were happiest. The embroidering, in red and blue cross-stitch, of this remark had occupied Mrs. Spanner during her daughter's absence and had probably made it well worth-while. Neither of them ever mentioned it but every night, when she went to bed, Agnes had turned its face to the wall. She had the same pleasure in doing that as her mother had had in working it and her chief annoyance in giving up her annual holiday was Mrs. Spanner's belief that the text had done its gentle work. It was the first thing she put on the bonfire she made in the little garden at the back of the house when the receipts and correspondence of two lifetimes had to be destroyed. The cheap white frame crackled venomously and took some of the secret venom from her heart, the canvas lasted a little longer and there was a sort of sadness in watching the disappearance of this evidence of something which had been perfect in its way. Her mother's self-satisfied, unconscious selfishness had been without a flaw and Miss Spanner could not rid herself so easily of its effects;

a tiny, gnawing worry spoilt any little pleasure she gave herself, but she fought it bravely and gradually became a little bolder.

Once a month she set off for a bookshop kept by an attractive young man in a street leading off the Slope. He made her very welcome and she generally stayed there for an hour or two before she departed with her chosen book. She would have been daunted by his charming ways and suspected him of laughing at her if she had not known she was on her own ground there, was better read than he was and had a sounder judgment and she did her best to improve his which had a leaning towards anything unpleasant or obscure, when he was not busy and they could talk. On the arrival of another customer, she settled herself in a comfortable chair, for his shop was almost a parlour, read one of the books she did not intend to buy, and then, having decided on her purchase, she walked richly home.

On this particular afternoon, two days after Rosamund had posted her letter, rain started heavily just as she was making ready to go and she hesitated at the door.

'But you mustn't go out in this!' the young man exclaimed with solicitude.

'No,' Miss Spanner agreed, for she was flimsily clad, but at that moment, the door was opened and there bounced into the shop, shaking her wet curls, a laughing girl.

'Not to buy one of your old books, darling,' she explained. 'Just to shelter.'

'Whatever it is,' the young man said in a voice quite embarrassing in its tenderness and, as he patted the girl's damp shoulders with a gay silk handkerchief, he offered Miss Spanner the loan of his umbrella.

An hour or so later, when she returned to the Square, the rain was still falling in a steady slant and in spite of the umbrella, which had chiefly protected the new book, the lower part of her body was very wet when she went down the area steps into the kitchen.

'You look as though you're wearing trousers,' Rosamund said, as she saw the thin frock clinging to Miss Spanner's legs. 'Get them off quickly and I'll make some tea for you.'

'I've had tea,' Miss Spanner said portentously, 'and this is the bookseller's umbrella. He practically bribed me with it to get me out of the shop. A girl, of course.'

'Pretty?'

'A healthy lump. She looked as if she'd never read a book in her life,' Miss Spanner said scornfully. 'Well, he's not the only one to neglect his business — or his work —' she added with emphasis, 'for the sake of a pretty face.'

'I hope not,' Rosamund said.

'Do you?' Miss Spanner asked. 'Yes, at a distance, I daresay, but not when it comes nearer home. Very much nearer,' she said with a violent squint.

'If you don't go and change,' Rosamund said, 'I shall have to nurse you through pneumonia and I should hate it.'

'And such a wisp of a thing, too,' Miss Spanner said, going towards the door. 'More like thistledown than anything I've ever seen before. That's the attraction, I suppose, but I wouldn't mind betting she's really as hard as flint.'

'I thought you said she was a healthy lump.'

'I'm not talking about her. I'm talking about the one I saw in the teashop. I had to pop in to get out of the rain and there they were, in a corner, Felix and this flippertygibbet, with no eyes for anyone else.'

'There was probably no one else so good to look at.'

'But they were so serious! That's what I didn't like. I thought that was a bad sign and I'd better warn you. I slipped out before they would have to pass me, but I needn't have worried. I expect they're there still, and the worst of it is I was so startled that I let some of the butter from my crumpet drip on to my new book.'

'Then, if that's the worst of it, there's no need to worry.'

'You never had any real respect for literature,' Miss Spanner said, and left Rosamund to pass in mental review all her children's friends known to her and to find no one who could be likened to thistledown or suspected of being as hard as flint. Well, she had always made up her mind not to interfere or show curiosity in such affairs, but she would have been happier if she had not discovered the puritanical strain in Felix's character. There was danger there and Agnes was probably right in distrusting the seriousness of the pair. And what sort of girl could this be, she wondered, of whom he had never spoken, and how endlessly tiresome children were. When they were babies she had looked forward to the time when they would not need constant care and now she found that keeping them out of the fire, from falling downstairs and eating unsuitable substances was nothing to the inaction she had imposed on herself, the advice she must not offer, the knowledge that they would never consider themselves in need of it. Life, it seemed, had been planned to make the experience of one generation useless to the next and for all her pretence of casualness she saw her responsibilities lasting as long as she did and she was troubled by the thought of that piece of thistledown. Thistledown floats elusively but when it finds a resting place to its fancy it can show a surprising tenacity and, as she looked at her son that night, she decided that no one could be blamed for adherence to him. She thought he had grown graver lately — there was cause enough for that without personal complications — and she admired him for not flicking an eyelid when Miss Spanner, squinting at him, spoke of the excellent tea she had had that afternoon and recommended the shop.

'I know it,' he said. 'Were you there too? I didn't see you.'

'And I'm not surprised at that,' Miss Spanner said grimly.

'And didn't you see me?' he went on, and Rosamund silently commended this attack.

'I'd just bought a new book,' Miss Spanner replied.

'Well, of course I couldn't compete with that,' he said. 'But what a pity! We could have had a nice little party.'

'He got the better of you there, Agnes,' Rosamund said that night. 'And serve you right.'

'It's just as well he should know I know and would be sure to tell you,' Miss Spanner said airily.

'It's not just as well he should think you an interfering old cat. I don't want the boys to get those horrid ideas about women.'

'He'll get horrider ones, sooner or later, from that girl of his, you mark my words.'

'You'd say that about any girl he took out to tea,' Rosamund said, hoping she would be given some of the information for which she would not ask.

'And it would be true of most of them. You can't even tell nowadays whether a girl's what we used to call respectable or not. They daub themselves up until they all look alike.'

'They don't feel properly dressed without all that stuff on their faces.'

'Then Felix's young woman must like going about naked. She looked unnaturally natural.'

'Oh, I do hope she isn't dowdy,' Rosamund said earnestly.

'There you are! That's always the way with you. Clothes first and character afterwards. Now, if I had a son — '

'Yes, I wonder what he would have been like?' Rosamund said thoughtfully, and Miss Spanner, remembering the tentative suitor her father had driven away, replied with resignation, 'He would have been very odd. Not handsome. A long thin neck and a big head, outwardly timid but inwardly very arrogant and not at all nice to me.'

'But Agnes, what an extraordinary person to invent!'

'I know, but I can't help it. He always turns out like that. I've tried other kinds but they're never right. What else could you expect? And it's one of the consolations of my life that I see him like that and haven't really got him. I'm much better off as I am and I'm coming to the conclusion that the happiest people are the ones who have missed everything they thought they wanted. Look at me,' said Miss Spanner, gathering her dressing-gown more closely round her, 'I'm as bare as a monument and as invulnerable. And I don't envy you in the least. I used to, when I was young, but not now. All my unnecessary lumber, and I never had much, just drops off as I get older and you'll carry yours with you to your grave.'

'Exactly what I've been thinking, too,' Rosamund said. 'However, well, I may as well tell you now as later, I shall soon have a little less of it. But lumber! What a word to use in connection with Fergus, or with any of them, for that matter.'

'Fergus?' Miss Spanner said sharply. 'But you're rid of him already.'

'Not in the eyes of the law. Now, you're not going to pretend to be shocked, are you? When the holy bonds have worn as thin as ours have it's much better to break the last threads, isn't it? Agnes, don't look like that!'

'You don't mean you're going to divorce him?' Miss Spanner said with horror.

'That's what he wants me to do.'

'Don't do it,' Miss Spanner begged earnestly. 'Don't do it.'

'But what difference will it make? What difference, Agnes?'

'All the difference in the world,' she replied in a hollow tone, and pursing her lips and huddling against the back of her chair, she shut her eyes and did not see the dismay on Rosamund's face, the lips which so seldom drooped, parted woefully. And for a few seconds, Rosamund, too, shut her eyes, squeezing back the tears that suddenly pricked them. She had never believed that Agnes would fail her in the mind or in the flesh or that the prejudices of her upbringing lay so near the surface, but nothing, it seemed, was permanent or secure, not even this queer, life-long friendship, and pain and astonishment kept her silent.

'I knew, all the time, I ought to have stored my furniture instead of selling it!' Miss Spanner exclaimed at length.

'There's quite enough in your bedroom to furnish a whole house,' Rosamund said.

'And you said I was here for life!'

'And aren't you?' Rosamund asked sadly.

'Well, is it likely?' Miss Spanner asked in the loud voice of her distress and went away without another word, but outside her own bedroom door she paused, remembering the unhappiness on Rosamund's face. She could not bear that, she must go back, she thought but, as she turned, she heard a sound on the upper staircase and saw a pale figure running down and looking, Miss Spanner thought afterwards, like a winged victory with her arms outspread in the wide sleeves of her wrapper, and a moment later she found those arms enclosing and firmly holding her in a warm, sweet-smelling darkness.

'Oh, Miss Spanner, I'm so sorry,' Chloe said, loosening but not relinquishing her hold. 'I was coming down, so fast that if I hadn't caught you I should have knocked you down. Are you all right? Did I hurt you?'

'No, no, just a moment's shock,' said Miss Spanner, and Chloe's arms tightened gently.

'I'm so sorry,' she said again as Miss Spanner seemed to welcome her support. 'Shall I see you into bed?'

'Oh no!' Miss Spanner exclaimed. Under the electric light, she doubted whether Chloe would be so tender with her.

'Mayn't I? And you're sure I haven't given you a black eye or broken your nose or anything? Then good night, Miss Spanner. I was just going to see Mother for a minute.'

'Be kind to her,' Miss Spanner said.

'Why yes. But is anything the matter? Does she need kindness, specially?'

'We all do,' Miss Spanner said severely as she went into her room.

She did not turn on the light. She wanted to keep, for as long as possible, the dark sweetness and warmth in which Chloe had enfolded her. This was the nearest thing to an embrace she had ever experienced. Rosamund's hugs were lovingly matter-of-fact and, though Chloe did not love her at all, she had given the impression that she was holding something precious and Miss Spanner let out a quivering sigh for everything she pretended she was glad to have missed. And Chloe's softness and gentle strength, her laughing yet solicitous voice, the faint smell of flowers that came from her, made Miss Spanner bitterly envious for a moment, before she groped her way to her bedside lamp and settled down to her new book, to a pleasure that lasted far beyond youth and beauty and the desire to love and to be loved.

CHAPTER XIX

YESTERDAY'S rain had given the world a thorough cleaning. There was a polish on the evergreens in the Oval and every tree Rosamund could see in her little garden and beyond it had lost its air of beginning to be bored with its own abundance. In middle-age, a little spurt of new interest in life seemed to have been given to them, a state strongly contrasting with her own as she prepared breakfast for her large household and saw years ahead of her through which she continued to supply four meals a day, a task requiring mountains of plates and dishes and a huge armoury of knives and forks. But perhaps it would not be like that, she thought, pausing in her work to look into a different future and the time might soon come when she would wish she had so many large appetites to satisfy. In the meantime, she could not forestall that longing, that nostalgia for the past. She was concerned with the present which did not please her. She and Fergus between them had made a mess of their marriage, she had to publish the fact and she foresaw that Agnes would have to carry her sacred virginity elsewhere. Fergus's desertion had not hurt her so much. She was able to take part of the blame for that and so justify the love she had given him and keep the memory of it sweet, but Agnes's attitude was unbelievably petty in the desire to protect a reputation no one would trouble to assail. Rosamund had expected indignation against Fergus, a show of being shocked and an assurance of sturdy faithfulness and there was a nightmarish quality in last night's disappointment. And she would be lonely without Agnes. She would miss, too, her generous contribution towards the household expenses but that was quite definitely a smaller matter. She could get another lodger if she must; she would never get another friend. And the sense of failure with Fergus and with Agnes, her fond belief in her power to hold them without any care or conscious effort, her assumption that because there was love there was safety, when she should have recognized it for the frail thing it was, hung round her like a cloud and she could not disperse it when she heard Sandra on the basement stairs.

'It's chiefly bad temper,' Rosamund said, in answer to the anxious widening of Sandra's eyes. 'I'm sure I shall burn the bacon.'

'Then I'd better do it. But you're never bad-tempered.'

'Tired, perhaps.'

'Yes, perhaps,' Sandra said in a politely sceptical tone. 'Has the postman been yet?'

'No. So you see I haven't had any bad news. That's a possibility eliminated, isn't it? Now you'll have to think of another. Can't you let me be a little cross sometimes without jumping to worrying conclusions?'

'I'll try,' Sandra said, 'but Chloe stayed with you for a long time last night and I thought there might be something the matter.'

'You would, but there isn't, and in case you think I've been run over or murdered or that I've decided I've had enough of you all – '

'And I expect you have, really,' Sandra said.

'Don't be surprised if I'm not here when you come back from school. I'll leave everything ready for you. I'm going to have a picnic all by myself. I've just thought of it. Now that's the truth and nothing but the truth. Do you believe me?'

'Of course,' Sandra said. 'But the ground will be very wet after all that rain. You'd better take a mackintosh to sit on.'

'I'd rather not sit,' Rosamund replied.

She found it a little difficult to behave normally with Agnes who had suddenly become half a stranger and was pathetically propitiatory that morning. She was eager to help; she would look after the family; she would do the shopping.

'You'd better go house-hunting,' was Rosamund's ungracious reply, regretted as soon as it was uttered and cancelled, she hoped, with a hasty kiss.

Then she set off across the bridge. To take any other direction did not occur to her. This was the inevitable way and though, on the other side of the water, there were more houses than there used to be, more fences and locked gates and warnings to trespassers, the soft, wild flavour in the wind was the same. She was in another county, another world, the one in which her kind, grave father became gaily inconsequent long before they stopped at the inn for lunch, with cider for him, fizzy lemonade for her and bread and cheese for both. But soon she left the houses behind and, prevented by the new wire fences from taking the old short cut across the fields, she walked on the horse track beside the road until she came to higher ground, within sight of the inn and everything else as it had always been. The lane she followed towards the Monks' Pool was a lane still, with grassy hedge-topped banks. On one side was a field of dull gold whence the hay had been gathered; on the other, grey-green oats rustled and whispered like an expectant crowd and, under a sudden gust of wind, they all swayed in the same direction and whispered with more vehemence, as though what they had been waiting for had arrived at last. But for that whispering and the short notes of birds and the occasional rumble of traffic in the road she had left, the world was very quiet and she went down the sunny lane until, when she looked back, the hedges seemed to meet and shut her in and to shut out everything that troubled her. And she was alone. With surprise she realized the delight of solitude, the relaxation of every nerve in this freedom from the impact of any other mind or the proximity of any other body. Perched on a gate and eating her sandwiches, this pleasure seemed to flow over her to the rhythm of the light breeze, the fluffy, leisurely clouds, the sibilant movement of the oats behind her. On this first day of July the air was spring-like and the resilience of her own nature met and mingled with it. She felt young and carefree, glad simply to exist in the sunshine as it drew earthy smells from the damp banks and sure that life, which had always been good to her, would continue this excellent habit. The sound of a car coming up the lane was an annoying intrusion. A car had no right in her lane but, when she recognized it, drawing its trailer, it was forgiven and its driver, when he recognized her, drew up and alighted.

'I was hoping to see you soon,' he said, 'but not here, and this is better.'

'This is very good,' she agreed. She slipped from the gate and turned to rest her arms on the top rail as he did. 'Why, of course, this is one of your Upper Radstowe days. I'd forgotten that,' she said, and she was pleased with herself for having forgotten, she felt charmingly innocent as she had felt long ago when she looked frankly into the face of a passing policeman, assuring him that she, at least, had done no harm. She wondered if Lindsay were pleased too. He was looking at the oats, no doubt reckoning what sort of crop they would make.

'There are more beautiful places than this, all round about,' she said, 'but it's one of my favourites. I haven't been here for a long time though, and never alone before. There was always someone with me when I was young, my father or a friend or — or someone and to-day I was having a happy time, discovering how nice it was to be all by myself.'

'And then I came and spoilt it.'

'It doesn't seem to have made much difference,' she said contentedly.

'No, I suppose it wouldn't,' he replied, humbly taking her in the wrong sense. The uninjured profile was next to her and when she looked at it she saw a twitch of amusement at the corner of his mouth. 'So I can't hope you were on your way to see me.'

'No, I wasn't,' and again she felt clean and innocent. 'I just came here from a sort of homing instinct, I think.'

'Well,' he said, 'my cottage isn't far from here. Past the Monks' Pool, the first turning on the left.'

'I knew it was somewhere near the Monks' Pool, but there's no turning there.'

'There wasn't until I made one.'

'I suppose you had to do it,' she said after a pause. 'It's foolish to resent changes, and quite useless. Look at that!' she said as an aeroplane roared overhead. 'There were no such things when we were young. We did still have the sky to ourselves. It looks lovely in the sunshine, but why do all the new things have to make a noise?'

'I think they might seem more sinister if they were silent and at this moment,' he said gravely, 'I wish there were enough of them to blot out the whole sky. But nobody seems to be in a hurry about it.'

'And they ought to be?'

'I haven't much faith in inactive good intentions and their power to influence a people gone mad. I don't know whether kind words have ever been really effective with a maniac and I'd rather put him in a strait jacket. An unpleasant thing to have to do, but I wouldn't take the risk of simply hoping his better nature will prevail.'

The aeroplane had gone with a last twinkle as the sun caught it and except for the low flight of birds which seemed almost earthbound in comparison, the sky was empty again.

'But let us be happy to-day,' Rosamund said in a low voice.

'That's all too easy,' he said.

'Yes and it's the way I've always lived, thinking it's not worthwhile to make a fuss to-day because everything may be all right to-morrow, but it isn't. And it won't be, will it?'

'Not possibly.'

'How comforting you are!' she said.

'But what else can I say?'

'Nothing. That's why you're comforting. I'm frightened by all these people who have bandaged their eyes and pretend they're having a nice game of Blindman's Buff. And I've no one to talk to about it. No man. Only Agnes. The boys are so discreet and considerate, I might be half-witted or an invalid who mustn't be worried. As though I don't know far more about it than they do! They were born in one war and it looks,' she said, beating the bar of the gate with both hands, 'it looks as though they'll have to die in the next. All right, I won't,' she said as he made a little gesture of pity and appeal, 'but wouldn't it be wonderful — and what a hackneyed remark — to wake up and find it isn't true?'

'Yes, but not just yet. I don't want to find I'm not here after all.'

'Neither do I,' she said, and the frank smile she gave him changed to an uncertain one, retreating before the eagerness she could discern, as she had learnt to discern most of his expressions, through the fixed, comic mournfulness of his face. Moreover, his injury had not touched his eyes and with astonishment she recognized in them the look she had told herself she would never see. The retreat had been an instinctively conscientious withdrawal, and then, in a spasm of rebellion against caution and fairness and common sense, she let him take his chance while she took her happiness. She dropped the defences she might have raised against the sweetness of the unexpected moment, the tenderness she felt for him and her trust in him. Yet, with her hands in his, she was critical and watchful. Behind her was the experience of a love-making in which neither she nor Fergus had seemèd, to each other, to make a false movement or utter a jarring word. They had been inspired in their first raptures to an artistic perfection which was considered, if that were possible, while it was spontaneous, dèliberate even in ecstasy. Nothing like that could ever come again and she wondered if Piers, too, had a past which could not be recovered and feared, as she did, an awkward ardour and self-consciousness. These thoughts came too quickly to be framed in words and went as fast. She, at least, had nothing to fear. Whether through practice or instinct, she did not care which, his technique was good, too good to be accepted under false pretences, and she said reluctantly, 'But then, you see, there's Fergus,' and mercifully he did not drop, he tightened his hold of her hands. She nodded in confirmation of her words. 'I ought to have told you before, but that would have been conceited.'

'Conceited?'

'As if it would matter to you one way or the other. But it was partly because I thought you might be too discreet to come and see me if you knew. And I wanted you to come.'

'Are you telling me,' he did drop her hands now, 'you are still married?'

'Yes. I'd better tell you everything and try to be fair to him,' and they turned again to lean against the gate and the oats seemed to listen greedily and nudge each other as they heard the story.

'And now,' she said, when she had finished, 'I don't think I shall like this place any more.'

'I won't have you saying that. I'd like to put a fence round it and keep everyone else out,' and she thought that was a strange thing for him to say for she remembered with a pang how Fergus, in one of his mad moods, had chalked a circle round the place on the pavement where she had been standing when he first saw her and said it was sacred ground.

She glanced over her shoulder at the little car. 'I don't know why it always looks like an old cab horse but it does,' she said. 'I feel rather like one myself. And your customers will be wondering where you are.'

'They can go on wondering.'

'Yes,' she said. 'We can give each other a few more minutes.'

'Years, surely. Thirty or forty of them, perhaps.'

She shook her head. 'No, no. This is all my fault. I drifted with Fergus and I've drifted with you. I ought to have limited our acquaintance to cabbages. But how did I know what would happen? And yet,' she cried with anger, 'why should I deny myself something good?'

'And why should I have to do without it?'

'Because it's entangled with so many other people.'

'We can straighten the tangle.'

'Perhaps. Perhaps it will be straightened for us. Last night Agnes told me she thought the happy people were those who had missed what they thought they wanted. It would be better to miss this than to spoil it.'

'Much, but it won't be spoilt.' He started the engine. 'Go and ask George to give you some tea,' he said, and drove off in an abrupt departure. But it was the right one for the moment and she told herself again with a curious detachment that his technique was certainly good.

CHAPTER XX

MISS SPANNER had not forgotten that this was one of Lindsay's Upper Radstowe days. She was surprised and pleased that Rosamund should have chosen it for her solitary expedition and she was able to tell herself that a person in doubt about a line of conduct could rely on Providence either to reserve judgment, in which case the doubt must remain unresolved, or to point the way and the way had been clearly pointed. Her own mind was in a careful state of confusion. She had collected enough conscientious motives to smother the one which was insistent and irresistible, the one which induced her to go shopping in a recklessly placatory spirit and return with a large piece of salmon, several pounds of raspberries and a jar of cream.

'Good Lord!' said James. 'Will the housekeeping money stretch to it?' He was at home, for the University term was over.

'It won't have to stretch,' said Miss Spanner. 'It's my own little treat for to-night. Your mother will be tired and hungry.'

'I'm glad I haven't missed it.'

'Why should you?'

'Because I'm going away, farming, to earn an honest penny till it's time for the other little treat you've given us. Plenty to do on a farm at this time of year and I can't stay here doing nothing for months, can I?'

'How do I know what you can or can't do?' Miss Spanner said, finding, as usual, a difficulty in expressing approval. 'But I hope there'll be a good harvest. We'll need it. And you'd better get into training. If I were you I'd go for a nice long walk this afternoon.'

'No you wouldn't, Miss Spanner. If you were me you'd go to the pictures. Let's go together and my treat this time.'

Miss Spanner gave her nose a knock to hide her pleasure. 'Anything good on?'

'I don't know, but you can always shut your eyes when there's anything unsuitable.'

'Then I might as well go prepared for a long nap,' she said. 'It would be a good deal cheaper and much more comfortable to have it here. Besides, I'm in charge of the house. No, you go and tell me about it afterwards. Or take someone else,' she suggested brightly. 'One of the Blackett girls.'

'Which?' James inquired, eyeing her cautiously.

'Rhoda,' Miss Spanner said promptly.

'The one who stares?'

'Does she? Well, she's the best of them. I don't care for that Flora. Self-conscious and conceited, like her father. But Rhoda's different. She's getting the right ideas about things too. From me,' she added. 'But no, you can't take her. She'll be at school. Take the other one. I don't suppose she knows what to do with herself any more than you do. I see her sitting at her window for hours on end.'

'You don't miss much, do you?' James said with a grin.

'No, I'm a great student of human nature,' she said with modest pride.

'And what this house chiefly needs,' he went on with apparent irrelevance, 'is a way into it and out of it at the back, through the garden.'

'Yes, I daresay that would suit you very well,' said Miss Spanner acidly, 'and I'm glad your mother's spared that anxiety.'

'But you'd hear us, wouldn't you, from your bedroom? You'd be able to let us in and help us upstairs when we came reeling home.'

'I don't like that kind of talk,' said Miss Spanner. 'I don't think it's at all funny.'

'But you started it, by implication. I'm sure I can't be fit to take any girl to the pictures and I'm not going myself. After all I think I'll go for your nice long walk.'

'Much better,' said Miss Spanner.

'And see if I can find Lindsay's place.'

'Yes, that's a very good idea,' she said with enthusiasm. 'And, oh dear, I forgot to bring a cucumber! If you've really nothing to do at the moment, would you mind running out and getting one?'

'I'll go with pleasure but I won't run.'

'Well, well, it's only a way of speaking.'

'I know. It makes the request sound less exacting, doesn't it? A smooth or a knobbly one?'

'Knobbly, if possible.'

He hesitated in the hall. He was acutely conscious of Flora at her window and it was infuriating that he could not leave or enter the house without the likelihood of being watched. But she was somewhat on his mind. Should he look up, as though hopefully, and wave, or turn his back on her as quickly as possible? He felt he owed her a little attention, but that sort of debt had the peculiarity of increasing with every payment. He had been a fool to kiss her. It had been as natural and unimportant as biting an apple, but he had not wanted the whole of the apple and her father's formal permission to visit her had spoilt his taste for any of it. Perhaps that was what the old stickler wanted. Well, there were only a few more days before he would be on the farm and then there would be the mountains and then, who knew what? With chivalry towards her and comfort for himself he tried not to remember that she had cried and stubbornly he did not look up either going or returning.

It was while he was out that Miss Spanner's jaw gave a sudden drop. She wondered whether she had been a little hasty in believing Providence was guiding her. James was almost certain to meet that unmistakable little car and he would return with Mr. Lindsay. It would not surprise her if Rosamund returned with him too. That would account for this lonely picnic of hers. She might have known there was something behind this desire for solitude and it looked as though her plan, which now seemed more than ever urgent, was to be frustrated. But she refused to believe it must be a bad one just because it might meet with difficulties. Indeed, difficulty was inherent in any good cause, it was its guarantee of value; history showed that clearly. 'And anyhow, I don't care,' she said to herself. Nevertheless, this excellent argument did not prevent her from rejoicing when things were made easy for her: Piers Lindsay arrived unaccompanied and she was alone in the house. Sandra and Paul had gone back to school, Felix to his office, and James had started in search of the man who was busily uncovering his trailer and setting up his scales and, as she watched him, Miss Spanner was swept by an extraordinary confusion of feeling. She felt both hard and pitiful: for the first time in her life she had a sense of sin and welcomed this new experience while it daunted her. She was in a web of her own making and completely isolated in it. She knew that by her own act she must remain mentally isolated from the one person she wished to be near, yet the force of her night's thinking and her morning's scheming drove her on.

'Four pounds of peas,' she said. 'No, I'd better have six. By the time I've shelled them there won't be too many for such a family. Five of them, not counting Rosamund and me. Far too many in my opinion, and not one of them independent yet. A heavy burden.'

'Mrs. Fraser seems to carry it lightly.'

'Ah well, she's used to it, you see. That makes all the difference. And a lot of potatoes.'

He carried the potatoes into the kitchen and she shut the door.

'Rosamund's out,' she said, 'and I'm glad. I wanted to ask

you what you think of things. I don't like the news this morning.'

'No. They're another step farther on. They're consolidating.'

'While we're asleep.'

'No, not asleep. Drunk with optimism and noble aspirations.'

'Yes. You see,' she said hurriedly, 'I don't like to talk about it much to Rosamund. It's not a nice prospect for her, with those boys. And there's Fergus too.' She caught her breath and waited in vain for a question. 'Her husband, you know,' she said. 'He's in France at present. I expect she's told you and he'll be back soon if I know him. And, oh dear, I never saw two people more in love. And then there's Paul. Four years last time — how long this? I can't help wishing it would start soon and finish before he's old enough to fight and then she'd have one of them left. Still, I haven't a doubt Fergus will come through as he did before. He's that kind of man. Reckless, but lucky. She's very proud of him.' Miss Spanner sighed heavily. She was doing her best but she did not seem to be getting any response. From Lindsay not so much as a sympathetic murmur had reached her. It was dark in the kitchen, too dark to see him properly and when she turned on the light she did not catch the quickly controlled stricken expression she had expected. That might be because his expression was odd already, but there was a thoughtful kindness in his eyes. He seemed to be thinking more of her than of Rosamund and himself.

'She is fortunate in having such a loyal friend in you,' he said, and he looked at her with that thoughtful air for another second or two before he said briskly, 'Well, that's the potatoes and the peas. Anything else?'

'Nothing else,' Miss Spanner said. She felt strangely empty and exhausted and when she remembered that she had not paid him, she followed him with an effort, to get a friendly smile from Mrs. Blackett, now on the pavement, and a cheerful word from Mr. Lindsay as he accepted the money and fished the change from a pocket of his baggy trousers. This cheerfulness made a mockery of her little scheme. He had not needed the warning she had given him; she was perfectly safe from him and she had better, much better for her own comfort, have been silent. And after all, if it was not Mr. Lindsay it would be someone else, her security had gone and she had smirched herself for nothing, and she went back to the kitchen and turned off the light and sat on a hard chair in the dark. She was very unhappy and she was bound to be unhappy for the rest of her days. Sooner or latter she would be turned out and she had done what Rosamund would call a dirty trick. If that trick had been necessary it would not have troubled her much except for the fear, and this was great, of having it found out, but it had not been necessary and she was pretty sure that Mr. Lindsay had suspected some personal motive in her confidences. To her own ears, they had sounded rather forced, as though rehearsed, and he had put a peculiar emphasis on his remark about her loyalty, or had her own conscience stressed it? And though he seemed too innocent and simple-minded a man for so much subtlety and too decent to tell tales, she decided that it was never wise to reckon on the inferior intelligence of other people. No, it was she who had been stupid and Rosamund, if she knew, would tell her she had been wrong as usual. And what was the use of struggling? She could not fight a whole battalion of suitors and that there would be a throng of them when Rosamund was free, she could not doubt. There was nothing abnormal or even jealous in her love for Rosamund. It was her own late won happiness she was protecting, the companionship, the talks at bedtime, her growing affection for these young people of whom she pretended to disapprove, their charming, half-teasing ways with her. All that, since last night, had become precarious. Her own simplicity lay in the belief that every free and reasonable man would want to secure Rosamund for himself. Since that day when she came bicycling down the Avenue, she had meant warmth and beauty and gaiety to Miss Spanner and even the inconvenience of five children, so carefully indicated to Piers Lindsay, would not be a powerful deterrent for anyone who saw her with Miss Spanner's eyes. Rosamund with a husband, however loosely attached, meant security for her friend; Rosamund without a husband set Miss Spanner's world rocking. And like Rosamund herself a few hours ago, but silently, she cried out in rebellion against forgoing what she wanted.

'But perhaps it won't happen,' she thought, as millions of people were thinking about a greater matter.

CHAPTER XXI

WHEN the rattle of the car and its trailer had passed beyond earshot, Rosamund opened the gate and went into the field. There was a little border of bare earth between the oats and the hedge and she followed it, looking for a place where she could lie down and go to sleep. She had no thought of what had happened in the last hour or of what the future held for her; she merely felt exhausted. Sleep, at that moment, was the only thing she needed and when, in a corner of the field, she found the ground lifted into a bank, scooped out and pebbled like a tiny quarry, she accepted it without hesitation. This bed proved to be less hard and drier than she had expected and she had hardly put her handkerchief under her cheek and told herself she should have taken Sandra's advice and brought a mackintosh, before she was asleep but still half conscious that the sun was warm on her. She waked when a shadow seemed to come between it and her.

'Well, I'm blessed!' said the voice of James.

She sat up. 'What time is it!' She looked at her watch. 'Why, it's after four. I thought it was going to rain and it's only you. I must have been asleep for hours and I'm frightfully hungry.'

'Well, there's going to be a very good supper. Salmon. The dear old Spanner has let herself go.'

'H'm. Has she? I'm not surprised,' Rosamund said dryly, 'but it's a long time till then.'

'But what,' James persisted, 'are you doing here?'

'I went to sleep.'

'I know that. But what a place to choose!'

'The best I could find. I was nearly asleep on my feet, a queer feeling, I've never had it before, but I had just enough sense not to lie on the grass.'

'Did you have a bad night?'

'Yes, rather. What are you doing here yourself?'

He told her. 'But Lindsay isn't there.'

'No, it's one of his Upper Radstowe days.'

'I'd have thought Miss Spanner would have remembered. Still, I've had a look round, his man's there, and then as I came along the lane I saw a blue something and I thought I'd better investigate.' He sat down beside her. 'You do do funny things, you know. Suppose somebody else had found you.'

'It wouldn't have been nearly so nice. James, do you think we could go and ask that George to give us some tea?'

'No, hardly, could we? But there's the pub on the main road. Let's go there.'

'All right, we'll go there.'

'Wait till I dust you down. You're a bit earthy. And if you're crippled with rheumatism it will be your own fault.'

'Wouldn't that be horrid? I couldn't like myself any more. I never feel really kind about people who don't move well. It's a shockingly savage instinct.'

'What about Lindsay's limp?'

'Oh, that's quite different. That's something to be proud of.'

'Like our parent's bad temper,' James said. 'Same cause but more inconvenient.'

'Oh James,' she breathed. It was almost the first time any of the children had spoken of their father since he went away and she did not know whether the words were merely a comment on the irony of things or whether they held a reproach for her; it was as a reproach she heard them. She felt cold and miserable and mentally confused and as James saw the colour go from her cheeks and even her eyes seem paler, he put his arm through hers.

'Never mind, old dear,' he said. 'Come on. It's not your fault.'

'But I'm not so sure,' she told him and, finding it hard work not to weep, she laughed instead when he stopped and kissed her gently and quickly on each eye.

'To bring the colour back,' he said.

It was a pretty, surprising thing for him to do and while, in the softening pleasure of it, she was tempted to confide in him, it was perhaps the fear of more emotion which led him, still with his arm in hers, to talk uninterrruptedly until they reached the inn. The young did not want to know the troubles of their elders, to be bored with what could not be so very important. They could not believe that older people knew anything like their own intensity of feeling. And, actually, after the little shock James had given her, Rosamund, for the time, was incapable of more emotion. Whether it was that sharp reminder of Fergus, though she seldom needed one, or the sleep separating the present from the immediate past, something had left her high and dry on the prosaic shore of common sense. It was the natural reaction of a woman of her age and in this reaction she was bound to see something rather absurd and quite impracticable in the future Lindsay planned. A love affair between two middle-aged people was one thing and could be beautiful and satisfying: marriage between them when one of them had a large family and neither of them had much money, was quite another thing, unfair to the children and a muddle that might even become squalid. What, she asked herself, as she and James walked silently down the long road from the inn, did she and Piers imagine they were going to do? Did he intend to leave his holding and settle down to doing nothing in the Square, or was the family to be scattered? It was true that it was bound to scatter itself before long. Chloe seemed likely to marry the conscientious accountant and Felix and James would have to go to war or wherever their work might take them, but still there were Paul and Sandra. Were they to be sent to boarding-school while she went to live with Piers and George? Paul would like that, but she could not afford boarding-schools and she would be very dull among the cabbages and potatoes. At this moment she could not recover the happy excitement of knowing she was loved again, of living vividly under appreciative eyes and of being able to love, not with all the ecstasy of youth but with confidence and content. All that had fallen away. It seemed unreal, as though it were only part of her dreams when she was sleeping in the field and now the sun began to dip and the clouds it had kept at bay began to harry it, covering and uncovering it and chasing it again, as her own happiness was darkened and pursued by doubts.

'It's cold, isn't it?' she said.

"I expect you've caught cold,' James said severely.

He walked on the horse t rack; she kept to the road. Its hard surface and the sound of her feet on it suited her mood and neither of them spoke again until he exclaimed, 'Oh, here he's coming now.'

His masculine eye had recognized, far off, the bonnet of Lindsay's car and she thought, 'That settles it. I didn't hope I might see him when I started this morning and I never thought I might meet him now. I'm not having the right sensations. I want him to love me, of course, but it's too much bother ; it's all too complicated; I must be too old to love him as I should.' Yet when he stopped the car and she saw his odd face again and heard his voice and knew he would always act exactly as she would wish, giving her now no special look of understanding, but frankly glad to see them both and anxious to drive them home again, her doubts vanished and she remembered how Sandra, who was so often right, had said he was a man who ought to have a family of his own. He would have to be content with hers and she believed he would be. Somehow, all the difficulties would be solved, not by her but by his sensible, quiet selflessness.

'Mother's cold. We'd better walk,' James said.

'No, I'm quite warm again,' she said, and she heard the warmth in her own voice, 'but I'd rather walk. I want to be tired and hungry for my supper. James says it's going to be a good one.'

'I know you're going to have a lot of my green peas.'

'So you saw Agnes?'

'Oh yes, I saw her,' he said, and he gave the involuntary little blink of one eye which she had learnt to know as a sign that something puzzled, amused or troubled him.

'That's cheered you up,' James remarked blandly as they walked on again.

'Yes,' she admitted. They knew more about her than she had thought, these boys of hers; more than she knew of them, but James seemed to be amused where Felix was anxious. 'And why shouldn't it cheer me?' she asked.

'I'd be surprised if it didn't. He's a nice person and it's nice to see you enjoying yourself. On the whole, you have a pretty dull time of it.'

'Dull! I call that an insult. I shan't be dull until I'm dead and I even have hopes that I shall enjoy things then. Nobody is dull who hasn't a dull mind. I don't mean that I'm clever.'

'I think you are, rather.'

'Do you? How?' Rosamund asked with animation.

'Not intellectual —'

'No.'

'But, well, on the spot.'

'And yet, d'you know, I can never remember how much milk is a pint and sugar a pound.'

'That doesn't matter. We've got to have the stuff anyhow. But you understand people.'

'Oh no, James, I don't. I should have to be God to do that,' she said, and she thought of Agnes, so broad-minded about what she read, incapable of being shocked by the written word if it reached her standard of literary merit, turning tail at the prospect of continuing to live with what was called the innocent party to a divorce and thinking she could make up for this desertion with salmon and green peas. And why had Piers blinked at the mention of her?

'No, I don't understand people,' she said.

'What I mean is that you don't fuss.'

'Too lazy.'

'You work like a nigger.'

'Lots of dust in the corners, but who cares?'

148

'Not me,' said James.

They had come to the end of the long road and crossed another to take the curving way above the woods. The leaves were too thick now to allow more than an occasional glimpse of the cliffs across the river; the river itself was hidden, but it was good to know it was there, that not far away it reached the Channel and the Channel merged into the sea.

'In every other place I've lived in,' Rosamund said, 'I've felt a little trapped. Yes, even in that great bare field where we tried to have the chicken farm.' She laughed. She always laughed when she thought of the farm, the bungalow with its corrugated roof, the wind that had a chill in it on the hottest day, the wire enclosures for the hen runs and the determined mortality of the hens.

'Here,' she said as they reached the bridge, 'I feel I can get out. And so I don't want to.'

'How many did you start with?' James asked.

'Start with?'

'For the chicken farm.'

'Oh, I forget. I know how many we ended with.'

'Mad idea,' James said. 'I don't think that will happen again, whatever else does. People won't squander their gratuity money on jobs they don't understand.'

'No,' she agreed and, seeing him vexed with himself for having introduced this subject, she went on with it. 'But Felix will have a profession to come back to and you'll know a good deal about yours. I wish I could buy you a really nice farm.'

'Of course you can't. I'll have to start with a little place like Lindsay's. P'raps he'll sell me his.'

'Why should he?' She was a little suspicious of James's acuteness.

'He'll be wanting to retire soon, I should think. It's hard work for a man of his age.'

'But he's quite young!' Rosamund exclaimed. 'He can't be much older than I am. Yes, that amuses you, doesn't it? And when I was your age I thought everybody over thirty was practically dead. But we don't feel like that. We find ourselves just as interesting as we ever did and what happens to us seems just as important. But it isn't really. We've opened our oysters and eaten most of them, too. It's the ones you are going to open that matter now.'

James gave a satiric grunt, thus expressing his view of what his particular oyster was likely to be.

CHAPTER XXII

FROM her bedroom window and well aware that Flora — supposed to be deep in study, was looking out of hers — Mrs. Blackett saw Mrs. Fraser and James at the far end of the Square. They were walking slowly but not with the slowness of fatigue. There was an easy swing about their movements which gave her the impression that they were in no hurry to get home and that their unstrained companionship was pleasant to them both. It must be very nice, she thought with moderation, to have a tall son like that and nice for him to have a mother who could fit her pace and probably her mind to his. And then an ironical little smile disturbed the placid curve of Mrs. Blackett's lips. Piers had stayed with her longer than usual this afternoon and she realized that this attention must have been due to the absence of Mrs. Fraser who was now entering her house, while her son stood aside but, Mrs. Blackett noted, did not linger to give an upward glance at Flora's window and with a little pity for her daughter, because she was young, there was mixed a little cruel satisfaction because the pity was for that particular daughter. Trying to do the right thing by her and to think the right thoughts, she could not accompany these efforts with properly sympathetic feelings. By the time Rhoda and Mary were born she was comparatively inured to the process of their begetting; she could forget it in the happiness they gave her, but Flora was stamped with the surprise and disgust and despair she had known as she trailed through the picture galleries of Florence on her honeymoon and did not know how to face the future. Flora was stamped too with much of her father's character and appearance and for Mrs. Blackett she was rather like a child who had been taken into the family because there was nowhere else for her to go. That did not lessen, it increased her mother's sense of duty towards her. With Rhoda there was no such sense because there was love and understanding to transcend it.

Mrs. Blackett smoothed the hair which was never untidy and changed her morning frock for another, a flowered silk instead of a flowered cotton, and realized, as usual, that whatever she wore was always, though she did not know why, a little wrong, and as she moved quietly about her room the thought of Flora, on the other side of the wall fancying herself in love with a boy who was certainly not in love with her, led her to the consideration of the other threads linking her family to the one across the road. There was Rhoda's odd affection for Miss Spanner, there was Piers who, naturally enough, preferred that house to this one and there was her husband's secret interest in everything that happened there and she smiled again as she thought how astonished and humiliated he would be if he knew that she was not only aware of it but amused and sustained and pleased by it. And she understood it too. Mrs. Fraser had beauty, but for Mrs. Blackett, and probably for others, that was not the chief part of her charm; it was the sense of undiminished life in her. She must, Mrs. Blackett reckoned, be somewhere about her own age but she had not settled down into being the mother of a family with no more adventures ahead of her; she never would. She was ready for the next good thing that came her way and though it was a readiness that could easily be misunderstood, that possibility would not trouble or control her. For — and this was why Mrs. Blackett envied her — she seemed to have the right kind of freedom, one involving no defiance or any need to assert itself, a heritage taken for granted like the right to her share of the sunshine. But then, Mrs. Blackett thought, she had no husband, and she went down to the drawing-room where Mr. Blackett always expected to find her on his return.

151

He informed his family as it gathered round the supper table that he had expected the day's news. The annexation earlier in the year of a country speaking the same language and with many of the same ideals and traditions, was a natural development. The two nations were not foreign to each other, they were relatives: both would benefit through setting up house together, and that process had now been properly completed.

'Moreover,' he went on, 'good temper could not be expected of a hungry nation, or of a hungry man,' he added, smilingly offering himself as the exception to the rule. 'You will see,' he continued perseveringly, for the only response to this little sally was Rhoda's contemplative stare, 'how much pleasanter I am when I have finished this excellent meal. It will be the same in Europe or I am much mistaken. I hope you agree with me, Bertha.'

'You have not told us what you are talking about,' she said.

'But you know, don't you?'

'Yes, I know,' she said.

'And yet I carried off the paper before you had a chance to look at it,' he said, and Rhoda, knowing what he would be at, turned, not too quickly, to look at her mother. 'Or do you housewives discuss international affairs when you meet in the shops?'

Mrs. Blackett replied indirectly and with her usual calm, 'Piers was here this afternoon.'

'Oh, he was, was he? Well, no doubt he gave you the facts correctly, but I hope you were suspicious of his comments.'

'He did not make any,' she said quietly.

'In a hurry, perhaps.'

'No, he was here for tea.'

'And adapted his conversation to his estimate of feminine intelligence, was that it? You are not used to that, Flora. I'm surprised you put up with that.'

Like someone pulling in a kite, Flora dragged her thoughts back to earth. 'What?' she said vaguely.

The little pink spots appeared on her father's cheeks. 'When people are gathered together for a meal,' he said, 'it is common courtesy to pay attention to what is said and done there. Even if you are bored by it. Even if you think it beneath your notice. And here is something of real interest and importance.'

'Cousin Piers?' she said.

'Cousin Piers? Of course not!'

'But you were talking about him, and so — ' Flora saved herself by leaving her sentence eloquently unfinished and giving him a smiling glance. 'And I know about the news from Mother's paper.'

'I see,' said Mr. Blackett. 'And Rhoda too?'

'Yes,' Rhoda said.

'And what do you think about it?'

'I don't know enough to have an opinion.' She was relying on Miss Spanner to give her one when next she had a chance to go across the road.

'And as you think things are settling down so comfortably,' Mrs. Blackett said, 'what about our holiday on the Continent?'

'Oh, yes, yes!' Mary cried.

'It mightn't be safe,' Flora murmured anxiously.

'Perfectly safe,' Mr. Blackett said. 'I am sure the hungry man is now quite satisfied, but we can discuss the holiday later.'

It was very unlike Bertha to make a definite proposal, especially in the presence of the children, but then, it had been unlike her to laugh at him; it was unlike her to have a separate newspaper. How long had this been going on, he wondered, and there crept over him the horrible suspicion that they were all, yes, even Flora, humouring while they listened to him. And he had been doing his best, single-handed, to prepare the girls for intelligent citizenship. Bertha, with all her excellences, had never helped him there. She might, and this was an even worse suspicion, be actually undermining his influence with whatever inferior paper she allowed the children to read. But he rejected this idea at once. He was sure she was loyal, she trusted his judgment, it was very seldom she questioned his decisions and a little later, as he watched her pouring out his coffee, he knew that he depended on her loyalty and faith in him just as she depended on his acumen and knowledge. These, nicely mingled, were the foundations on which they had built their home. Perhaps she had her little moments of irritation with him, as he had his of disappointment with her, but that was to be expected in the happiest marriages and, in this conciliatory mood, he reproached her playfully for concealing her extravagance in taking a second paper. It was the best thing he could do about it.

'As though I should have objected!' he exclaimed.

'No, I don't suppose you would have objected,' she said.

'So I don't quite understand.'

'No,' Mrs. Blackett said, and, realizing that here he had come against a blank wall, he wisely turned away from it.

'And then,' he said, 'wasn't it a pity to raise the children's hopes about a holiday?'

'It is you who need one. I don't think you are very well.'

It is always difficult to choose between presenting oneself as a person nobly struggling against ill health or as one of magnificent physique; each aspect evokes admiration and, on the whole, Mr. Blackett preferred the more masculine one, but the little laugh he gave could refer, as she chose, to either.

'Restless,' Mrs. Blackett went on calmly. 'You don't settle down to your reading as you did before we came here, and you don't sleep so well. Perhaps the climate doesn't suit you. I wonder if you ought to see a doctor. But what you really ought to do is to go away, by yourself or with Flora.'

'I shouldn't think of indulging myself like that and leaving you at home.'

'Oh, we should be very happy, Rhoda and Mary and I. It would be quite a holiday for us too.'

'You are not very complimentary,' he said.

'And Connie could have hers at the same time. That would suit me very well. I think you might feel quite different when you came back. Your mind would be refreshed. You would have other things to think about.'

'But I don't want to feel different!' Mr. Blackett exclaimed irritably. 'And as for my mind, I wasn't aware that it showed signs of flagging.'

'Oh no,' Mrs. Blackett said pleasantly, 'it's too active,' and she gave him one of her rare, full looks. 'Like a squirrel in a cage,' she added and carried away the tray before he could reply.

He would not have known what to say if she had stayed, he did not know what to think. She had made an insulting simile and told him his mental state was hopeless and futile, referring, of course, to the worry of the times which no reasonable man could forget though he made light of them, but her words were apt in a different sense from that, a sense of which she knew nothing, though it was her fault that he knew so much. He left his chair and paced up and down the room. Her very virtues were her failings and now he freely admitted that the stress he had laid on her delightful modesty and the pleasant excitement he derived from it, was his noble effort to be mentally faithful to her. That sort of modesty in a woman of her age was simply ridiculous. It was not modesty; it was coldness. What wonder then that he should be obsessed by the thought of that woman next door, ripe and ardent and inviting, almost within his reach and only out of it because his conscience denied what his flesh affirmed, and there passed through his mind again all the little pictures of her he had collected. He saw her smiling teasingly at him from the balcony, standing on the hill, a different and almost a formidable person then, and, in bewildering contradiction, outside her own door at midnight with a man's arms round her. Mr. Blackett saw this picture less clearly than the others. He blurred it purposely. He did not want to find a simple explanation of this extraordinary behaviour. He wanted all the evidence he could get to confirm his conception of the woman's character. All this was his pastime and his torment and the prospect of leaving it for a holiday by himself was very bleak, with Flora it was even bleaker, but he could imagine one of a different kind, with another companion and in another country where it would be possible to forget the Square and Upper Radstowe and his office and his wife and children, where no one would look suspiciously askance and, under a warmer sun, he would shed layer after layer of the propriety and discretion imposed on him by his circumstances and his respectable upbringing, he would be the self no one had ever seen, rejuvenated and satisfied in every sense. And he saw himself in corduroy trousers and a coloured shirt, letting the latent Bohemian in him have proper play. Somewhere in France, he thought, though the words were not altogether agreeable; he had heard them too often in another connection. It was a country which, unlike many of his generation, he did not know. He was careful not to publish the fact. His only foreign excursion had been to Italy with Bertha and this had been a resource — there had been fighting in Italy — when people spoke of that now almost forgotten war. For a time it had been a tender and exquisite memory and so it would have remained if the bud he had taken there had ever opened into a flower. It had never opened; it never would; it had tightened like a rosebud caught by frost. But where had the frost come from? Not from him. It was in the very nature of Bertha herself and he had been wronged, he had been cheated, he was justified in anything he chose to do. Yet, he thought, as his sense of injury died down a little, this imperfection had one merit: no one could look at her and doubt her virtue and he was sure of her. In a touchingly abiding way, she loved him. Women did, he thought, straightening his tie in front of a glazed representation of Salisbury Cathedral which gave back his image, and behind his face with its little pointed beard, behind the spire of the cathedral he saw other scenes.

'But I wonder if I should really enjoy it?' he thought, with dismay for his limitations and pride in his high moral sense.

CHAPTER XXIII

It was a pleasant room, the one opening on to the garden, and Miss Spanner had taken pains with the supper table, setting on it a bunch of pink roses and their leaves to match the salmon and raspberries, the peas and cucumber, and she had polished the worn old silver.

'Is it a special occasion?' Sandra asked. 'We haven't forgotten your birthday, have we, and left you to do all this for yourself?'

'I don't consider my birthday worth celebrating, by me or anyone else,' Miss Spanner replied gloomily. 'And I was born in November, one of the nastiest months in the year.' She gave the salmon a prod with a fork. 'I hope it's done properly.'

'Yes, it comes away from the bone beautifully,' Sandra said. 'It's exactly right.' She looked anxiously at Miss Spanner. She was not sure whether she was really unhappy or merely embarrassed by her own generosity. She had been very sharp-tongued after she had given Chloe and the boys the money for their holidays. 'But,' she said, after a moment's thought, 'it would have been horrid for us if you hadn't been born at all,' and Miss Spanner's nose had to sustain another knock.

'It wouldn't have made the slightest difference to any of you.'

'What about Mother?'

Miss Spanner flushed under the eyes in an unbecoming way she had. 'Now, don't argue with me,' she said, 'but go and bang the gong.'

Sandra obeyed slowly. Miss Spanner was behaving as though she knew she had not long to live and must do all she could for other people before she went. Death was dreadful, Sandra thought. One forgot about it and then suddenly realized that it came, in time, to everybody, even to the young, even to the people one loved best, and she touched the gong very softly, as though a loud noise might precipitate disaster.

'That's no good,' Felix said as he and James came out of their bedroom. 'Let me do it,' and he took the stick from her and beat so loud a summons that Rosamund, at the head of the stairs, put her hands to her ears and Sandra, seeing her mother there, rejected her thoughts of death. This was life now coming down the stairs and the noise Felix was making changed from one of doom to one of triumph. He stopped with a final bang and gave Paul a light rap with the stick as he came, protesting, from the sitting-room.

'Go and wash your hands,' Felix said.

Mind your own business,' said Paul, preparing to dodge another blow, but Felix took the remark calmly. He was in a good temper, Sandra observed. That was a comfort. Sometimes he was rather glum or irritable and he was the kind of person whose moods affected his company.

'Let me see your hands, Paul,' Rosamund said. She had bathed and changed and smelt faintly of dusting powder.

'You'd think he might be responsible for them himself, at his age,' Felix said.

'You never were. You were the worst of the lot. Yes, they'll do. Now, come along. Let's make a party of it.'

'But where's Chloe?' Sandra said.

'We can't wait for her and when we've finished,' Felix said, 'let's drink Miss Spanner's health.'

'What in?' asked James.

'She wouldn't like it in anything but water.'

'No, don't,' Sandra begged. 'I think it might make her feel uncomfortable.'

'Of course it will,' Felix said cheerfully. 'That's part of the fun and she'll enjoy remembering it afterwards. In planning pleasure for yourself or other people, that's the important thing. Less pleasure at the moment but more next morning.'

Sandra looked at her mother for support but she did not get it. Rosamund was not feeling very tender towards Agnes. Besides, Felix was right. She would squint atrociously, but she would be pleased afterwards and now, at the sight of her anxious face, Rosamund forgot to be annoyed with her.

'Oh Agnes, how pretty it all looks!' she exclaimed. 'And what a meal! It's too good for anything but complete concentration. We won't talk, we'll just eat.'

'And when I want to do that,' Paul said, 'I'm told it's bad manners.'

'So it is. Let's all be bad mannered.'

'And without any restraining thoughts of fish cakes to-morrow,' James suggested.

'But leave some for Chloe,' Sandra said.

'And Agnes must sit at the head of the table,' said Rosamund. 'It's her party.'

'Oh dear, what a fuss about nothing,' Miss Spanner grumbled, but how happy she would be, she thought, if she had planned this little feast for yesterday. Then it would have been an honest gift; it was meanly and uselessly propitiatory to-day, and though Rosamund did not know everything – she did not know the worst – she knew enough to see this gift for what it was and in her gaiety, her sweetness towards herself, Miss Spanner fancied there was a spice of mischief. And yet it might be pure happiness that made her eyes so bright and, if so, where had she found it? James came rather near to answering this question.

'I had a nice walk, Miss Spanner,' he said, 'and I'm very grateful to you for making me go.'

'I didn't make you go anywhere,' she said with unnecessary heat, 'except to fetch the cucumber.'

'You influenced me though and, quite by chance, I found my mother in compromising circumstances.'

'No, not compromising, James. Unusual, perhaps.'

'All right, unusual, and I believe she would have been there still if I hadn't brought her home.'

'Yes.' It amused her to see Felix pricking up his ears and Agnes setting her wits to work. She wondered doubtingly whether James could possibly be producing these effects on purpose and she laughed at him across the table as though she shared the little conspiracy. 'Yes. I was very comfortable. A nice place and a nice day,' she said and steadied herself for what he might say next, but at that moment Chloe slipped into the room and into her chair with a murmured apology.

'Was your train late?' Felix asked.

'What? No, I don't think so.'

'But you are, very.'

'Yes, I walked home.' She did not notice or she ignored a tone she would normally have resented.

'All the way from the station? Couldn't you get into a bus?' asked Sandra, ready to be sympathetic.

'I didn't want to.' She looked like someone who had come out of very strong sunshine and was still dazed by it or, contrariwise, had been in a dark place and could not yet adapt herself to the light.

'I don't believe you know what you're eating,' said Paul with disgust.

'Oh, salmon. Yes, how nice,' she said.

'It's Agnes's party,' her mother said.

'How kind,' said Chloe, discovering Miss Spanner at the head of the table, and Rosamund, watching her, saw that she was beginning to come back from wherever she had been and pictured her walking rather blindly through the crowded streets, up the steep Slope and so to these quiet roads where, when the lamps were lit, the shadows of the overhanging trees made dark pools on the pavement through which one could walk dryshod. But this was a summer evening, the lamps were not lighted yet and Rosamund was sorry Chloe had not walked to-night, as she had so often done herself, through those pools of shadow, sometimes quite still and sometimes seeming to be ruffled by a little wind. For the continuance of a dream or the easing of trouble she had always found them good, she did not know why, unless it was because she got from them something of what Agnes got from poetry, something transcending self, in these reflections of what she called reality. But, whether Chloe was in need of solace or guarding her happiness in a mist of her own making, it was impossible to tell until she came into her mother's room that night and, because she came, Rosamund knew she was not bringing trouble. She would have battled with that alone.

'I've fallen in love,' she announced, 'and at first sight.'

'Oh Chloe, are you sure?' It was what she had done herself.

'Quite sure. Weren't you?'

'Absolutely certain.'

'Well then —' Chloe said with a little gesture of finality and, the next moment, Rosamund realized that she must be looking much as her own father had looked in similar circumstances, grave and anxious, for Chloe leaned forward to take her hands and cry, 'Don't worry. It's all right. It's the conscientious accountant! Funny, isn't it?'

Rosamund let out a sigh of relief. She liked the conscientious accountant and if anyone was ever safe, Chloe would be safe with him. 'But,' she said, 'at first sight?'

'Yes. Don't you think you see a person for the first time when, for the first time, he doesn't know you're looking at him, when he doesn't know you're within miles of him? I saw him, by chance, like that to-day, separate from me, probably not thinking of me, self-sufficient and dignified, though he has always been dignified, at his worst, so to speak. I couldn't stand anything else. And so nice. And good,' Chloe said, frowning in apology for this remark. 'And I fell in love properly, then and there, and I was terrified he might have fallen out of it.'

'And had he?'

'No. Wasn't it lucky? He's coming to see you to-morrow about getting married very soon. I didn't want him to come in to-night.'

'May I tell Agnes?'

'The whole world,' Chloe said gaily, and at the door she paused to add, 'I'm so thankful you're not the kind of mother one has to dodge for fear of being clasped to her bosom.'

'And wept over,' Rosamund said. 'But what a good day I'm having. James too expressed some approval of me this afternoon. Chloe, do you mind telling me what time of day it was when you made this pleasant discovery?'

'In the lunch hour. Why?'

'I was just wondering what I was doing then.'

'Did you have a telepathic communication?'

'No, but I was feeling happy.'

'Then it must have been some sort of communication,' Chloe said, and Rosamund let it go at that, thinking it was strange, and would seem ludicrous to Chloe, that they should have been having something of the same experience at somewhere about the same hour. There was no one to whom she could speak of her own, no one to whom she wished to speak of it, but if James had been the lawyer instead of Felix, she might have told him about Fergus and asked how best she could carry out his wishes. James would be tolerant towards his father; Felix had too many of his qualities mixed with a startling sense of propriety, in regard to his parents if not to himself, and she was determined not to have Fergus abused or misunderstood. She must find a lawyer who was a stranger to him and to her and as Fergus seemed to be in no hurry and had not answered her last letter, the affair might be delayed at least until Chloe was married and preparations for the wedding need not be contemporaneous with those for the final separation of her parents. It was entirely reasonable for people to part when living together meant unhappiness for both or either, but it was an unsavoury business, not necessarily for those concerned, who alone could judge it, but tainted for them by association and by the demands made by the law.

She sighed, wondering whether Piers too was propped up in bed and thinking of her or asleep already and whether he lay on his right side or his left, with his ordinary profile uppermost or the other. And Agnes was a long time coming. Little had been seen of her since her health had been drunk and she had retired in protesting confusion. No doubt Sandra was right, as usual, and Agnes had seen more mockery than kindness in the tribute, so, thinking there could hardly be a more solitary person in the world, Rosamund slipped out of bed and went bare-footed to Miss Spanner's door. There was a light under it and she knocked and went in.

Wearing the drab dressing-gown on which her lank plaits made two dark streaks, Miss Spanner was sitting in the midst of her possessions, like an unhappy child who had been sent for punishment to the lumber room and so forlorn that, for the first time, Rosamund thought of the future as it might affect her. She had been persuaded out of the gloomy house on the Green, she had been promised a home and had found one and now, though she might overcome the scruples of her ingrained respectability, what was to happen to her later? And it seemed to Rosamund quite impossible to desert her, to be warmed by happiness when she had stripped this poorly clad creature nearly naked. Life was very complicated. The simplest action seemed to develop a resentful personality to pay you back for having created it but, at the moment, there was nothing to be done about it except to be kind to Agnes.

'What are you doing?' she asked gently.

'Sitting,' said Miss Spanner.

'So I see. And I've been waiting for you.'

'Why?' Miss Spanner asked mournfully.

'Because I love you, my dear old idiot, and as you didn't come to me I've come to you. What's the matter? Felix didn't upset you, did he? He really meant it all, you know.'

'H'm,' said Miss Spanner sceptically. 'And if he did, he's wrong.'

'Well, get into bed and don't think any more about it.'

'I haven't wasted a moment over it. Is it likely?'

'Goodness knows,' Rosamund said. 'We're all unaccountable to each other. I should never have dreamt you'd react as you did last night.'

'Of course you wouldn't,' Miss Spanner said bitterly. What did Rosamund know about loneliness, its blessed cessation and the threat of its return?

'But why spoil everything now?' Rosamund said. 'Let's go on as though I hadn't told you. And I'm still quite respectable. I'm not divorced yet,' she said, and at that Miss Spanner very forcibly uttered the only expletive of her life.

'I don't care a damn about divorce,' she said.

'Oh Agnes!' Rosamund dropped to her knees and put her arms round Miss Spanner's narrow waist and her face against the dressing-gown. 'I'm hugging you for the language as well as for the sentiment,' she said. 'How I wish your dear parents could have heard them both! Let's hope they're listening. I shan't be-grudge them Heaven if they're allowed to do a little eavesdrop-ping.' Then, jerked by convulsive movements in Miss Spanner's chest which might have been caused by laughter, she sat back on her heels to enjoy this wholesome manifestation.

But Miss Spanner was not laughing, With tiny, very rapid agitations she shook her head. 'You don't know everything,' she hiccuped.

'And I don't want to. If there's anything I hate it's the way women think they can't be friends without pouring out the inmost secrets of their hearts. Keep your secrets to yourself, Agnes, and your sins, and I'll keep mine and for Heaven's sake get into bed.'

CHAPTER XXIV

'I SUPPOSE I must go and say good-bye to my young lady,' James said to his mother in the morning. 'It will be a long parting. I shan't come back, you know, before the holidays. I'm going to meet Felix and Smithers somewhere on the way. So I'm taking my boots.' He was greasing them as he sat outside the garden room and she was touched by the contented lines of his mouth and his earnestness as he rubbed.

'They'll be useful on the farm, I expect,' she said.

He looked at her with pity. 'And blunt these lovely nails?' he said. 'I thought better of you.'

'Yes, that was stupid,' she agreed. 'And by the way, did Chloe tell you she's engaged?'

'No. Is she? To Stephens? Good. You'll be getting us all off your hands soon. You'll be quite rich! I shouldn't be surprised if they take Felix into partnership before long.'

'You're optimistic. Suppose he hasn't passed his final?'

'Of course he has.'

'And perhaps he'll want to start somewhere else.'

'Not yet,' said James, wiping his hands on the grass.

That was a remark that might mean a good deal or nothing at all. She ignored it, but she wished James were not going away. They had always been on easy though not confidential terms and quite suddenly these seemed to have developed into a closer relationship. The schoolboy who had looked to her, as Paul did, for the material things of life, was left far behind: the youth not sure of himself and jealous of his freedom was gaining confidence; and happiness, the simple happiness of being able to look forward to the holiday he had always wanted, had loosened his tongue and enlarged his sympathies. Sorrow was supposed to strengthen human nature; she was sure happiness enriched it and, though she had a dozen household tasks to do, she lingered in the garden, pulling up a weed here and there while James finished his pipe, his arms round his knees, his eyes sometimes on the deep blue of the sky, sometimes on her, but oftenest on the boots, like shining black armoured barges, side by side on the grass. It would be something to remember, she thought, this little pause under the sunshine, this feeling of content and companionship.

'I must remember to get some dubbin,' he said at last, telling her where his thoughts had been.

'And I must do some shopping. I don't know what on earth to give Chloe's young man for supper.'

'Is he coming? Pity the salmon wasn't postponed.'

'No, that would have looked too much like an effort. He'll have to get used to the shepherd's pie and suet pudding standard.'

'Good enough for anybody,' James said.

After tea he went across the road to say good-bye to Flora. He thought this was a good time to choose. Mr. Blackett would not be there and with a guest in prospect and his packing to do, he would have to hurry back again. He found, however, to his half-annoyed relief, that there would be no difficulty in escaping. They were all in the garden, just finishing their tea there and when he had helped to carry the remains into the kitchen and done his share in a not very animated conversation, Flora looked at her watch and said she must get back to work.

'Good Lord! I haven't done a stroke since term ended,' James said.

'Perhaps you don't need to,' she said dryly, 'but I have regular hours and I stick to them.'

'And you are starting the practical side of your work to-morrow,' Mrs. Blackett said kindly. 'That will be hard work, too.'

'Yes, but easy, if you know what I mean. Just doing what I'm told.'

'Well good-bye,' Flora said. 'I hope you'll enjoy it.'

'I'm sure I shall. But you ought to have a holiday, you know,' he said, escorting her to the kitchen door, and Rhoda muttered through her down-turned lips, 'She'll start having one to-morrow.'

Mrs. Blackett caught the words and repressed a smile. It was just what she had been thinking. Neither she nor Rhoda was deceived by the long hours Flora spent in her bedroom. The little variations in her hair-dressing and the alterations to her clothes were proof of other occupations than her studies, and the poor girl, dealing coldly with this young man, out of pride or in the hope of making him want what he could not get, had given him a fine exhibition of priggishness.

When he came back to the group on the little lawn he seemed more at ease and he did not hurry away. Very few people are anxious to break off a conversation about their own concerns and though Mrs. Blackett fetched her hoe and busied herself at the flower beds, Rhoda had endless questions to ask and only the imminence of Mr. Blackett's return got James out of his deck-chair. And she asked the questions because she wanted to know the answers. Miss Spanner was quite right; she was the best of the lot, much the best, he decided, when she ran after him into the road with the book he had lent to Flora.

'She forgot to give you this and you may want it. I've read it,' she said, and with loyal untruthfulness she added, 'too.'

'Have you?'

'Yes. I like that kind of thing. I suppose you couldn't lend me another, could you?'

'Yes, rather. Come across now and I'll find something.'

'Shall I?'

'Yes. Come on.'

'In here,' he said, opening his bedroom door. 'It's in rather a mess because I'm packing. How about this one? It's a bit stodgy, though.'

'Nothing's stodgy when you like it,' Rhoda said.

'No, it isn't, is it?'

'But I read rather slowly.'

'That doesn't matter. You can keep it till I come back.'

'Oh thank you,' Rhoda said. 'I'll take great care of it.'

She was gone before he had time to take her to the door and, when he followed, it was only to see her popping down the area steps like a rabbit into its hole. Funny little thing but sensible, he thought, both in her tastes and the quickness of her disappearance and it was to his credit that he did not think of looking towards Flora's window to see whether she had witnessed this little episode. But she had seen it and, unable to control her angry pain, she went at once in search of Rhoda.

'Why did you run after Mr. Fraser?' she demanded.

'Is that what you call him?'

'Yes, to you.'

'How silly! He's only a boy.'

The whole of Flora's inside seemed to tremble with humiliation and anger. James was still very nearly the young god he had been when she first saw him, he was faithless but hardly less desirable, and to hear him described disparagingly by this clumsy schoolgirl was almost more than she could bear, but she had to bear it or betray what Rhoda's sharp eyes had seen long ago.

'He may not be much more than a boy,' she said, 'but I'm quite sure he thinks of you as quite a little girl. That's why he was so kind.'

'Was he kind?' Rhoda asked.

'How do I know?' Flora said impatiently.

'You don't. He was just ordinary,' Rhoda said, insulting the god again but stilling some of Flora's inward trembling. 'And I returned the book he lent you.'

'But I haven't finished it.'

'Or begun it,' said Rhoda, and Flora, obliged to drop her dignity, asked anxiously, 'Did you tell him that?'

'He didn't ask.'

'That's no answer.'

'Yes it is — from me,' Rhoda said. 'You might know I wouldn't bother to tell him, or be so mean.'

'Oh, I shouldn't have minded, but he's so enthusiastic he thinks everybody else must be, too. He does seem rather boyish in that way,' she conceded. Rhoda's words were having an effect. If he seemed like a boy to her, how much more boyish he should seem to her elder. Moreover, in self-defence she had to change the god who neglected her into the boy she could neglect, but she had not quite succeeded in doing this when she saw a thick book lying on Rhoda's bed. She picked it up. 'And I see he's lent you another,' she said with amusement.

And now Rhoda had to protect James. 'Because I asked him for it.'

'You asked for it?'

'Yes, I want to read it.'

Flora laughed again, turning the pages. 'It's all about fertilizers and chemicals,' she said. 'You won't understand a word of it. He must know very well why you borrowed it.'

'Of course he does.'

'And he won't think any the more of you. It's really very silly, at your age, to be running after him like that.'

'Oh, he's quite used to it from this family,' Rhoda said, and at that the book left Flora's hands to strike Rhoda on the shoulder and land with a heavy thud on the floor.

Rhoda's first care was for the book. It was a heavy one and might have suffered but it was not hurt and in the meantime Flora had gone. It was Rhoda who was hurt, not on the shoulder but in her mind. She had been a little shy and self-conscious with James at first because she thought he would despise her for her youth and lack of prettiness but, in their common interest, she had forgotten that. She hoped he liked her as she hoped Miss Spanner did, but she made little efforts to please Miss Spanner she would not have troubled to make with James, not knowing this omission was an unconscious resistance to nature's claims.

Consciously, she agreed with Flora. It was silly, she thought, it was rather common, for schoolgirls to be preoccupied with boys. It was bad enough at Flora's age; it was infuriating to be accused of it at hers. She was glad he was going away. She would be able to visit Miss Spanner without sneers and horrid hints from Flora. James was a nice person, she was sure of that, and the chief part of his niceness lay in the fact that he wanted to be a farmer. James studying medicine or anything else would have had quite a different aspect for her, as remote as the other Frasers, as most of the people she knew and among whom she pushed her way as she might have passed through a flock of sheep, though she would probably have found the sheep more interesting. But, hating this spiteful quarrel with her sister, she did cast a thought at the sisters across the road and wonder if they were friends. Then she became happily absorbed in the fertilizers, reading very slowly and neglecting her homework for them.

And Flora, on the other side of the landing, had a good cry. With it she washed away all thoughts of James except resentful ones. He cared nothing for her and she would not care for him. She had been very silly and simple, she admitted that. She ought not to have let him kiss her; she had not realized how unimportant an action it was to him. That was the fault of her sheltered upbringing; she would be wiser another time and she had always really thought Felix was more attractive. Then she bathed her eyes and did her hair again and peered into her looking-glass. There was no sign of her tears except for a greater gloss on her eyelashes and, pleased with her reflection, she was able to pity James for his stupidity.

CHAPTER XXV

'THIS is no time for getting married,' was Miss Spanner's comment, when Rosamund told her of Chloe's engagement and, almost in the same breath, she said, 'Did you see Mr. Lindsay yesterday?'

A little startled by the proximity of these remarks, Rosamund at once said, 'Yes.'

'I can't think how,' said Miss Spanner. She had recovered her spirits but she was still a little uneasy. She could not forget that calculating look in Mr. Lindsay's eyes. 'I've been trying to work it out.'

'You would,' Rosamund said.

'He was here all the afternoon so perhaps you saw him in the morning,' Miss Spanner suggested. 'Or when you were coming home. But then you were with James, weren't you?'

'Yes, we came back together. I wish he hadn't gone away.'

'Better if it had been Felix who had gone,' said Miss Spanner, compressing her lips.

'Don't you like him as much?'

'I wasn't thinking of my own preferences. I wish he was having his holiday now instead of later.'

'So do I.'

'But not for your reasons.'

'No?' Rosamund said with light indifference.

'And,' said Miss Spanner, annoyed by this airy manner, 'I wonder I don't hate the sight of you.'

'Perhaps you will some day.'

'Why?' said Miss Spanner sharply.

'Just satiety,' Rosamund said in the same light tone.

'Oh.' Miss Spanner was disappointed and returned to the attack. 'What I find so trying is that you never converse.'

'I hope not. It sounds awful.'

'I can't keep you to the same subject for two minutes. You won't even answer a simple question if you can help it.'

'Agnes, your questions are never simple but then, neither am I. And d'you know what I think you ought to do? Take a course of severe reading — philosophy or something — or learn a language. That would keep your mind occupied.'

'It's very well occupied, thank you.'

'It's occupied but not very well.'

170

'That isn't my fault,' said Miss Spanner primly. 'But I wish I'd learnt languages long ago.'

'You can get a nice little set of books that teach you in about three months.'

'Too late,' said Miss Spanner. 'I'd like to know what they're really saying over there when they sound like the Zoo let loose.'

'Oh, we know near enough. But it's a very large Zoo, and unfortunately there are no bars in it, or round it. I don't like animals to be kept in cages, but I'd fasten all those up without the slightest qualm and keep them fastened up, too. We've been pretending, all this time, that there are only a few dangerous ones among them; the others are quite harmless; nice, gentle creatures, almost pets. That's the part they played after the war and here they are again, following the bigger beasts and yelping enthusiastically when they roar, but they'll be quite ready to behave nicely again if necessary.'

'But will it be necessary?' asked Miss Spanner. 'That's the point.'

'Just misled, poor dears,' Rosamund murmured, then turning on Miss Spanner, she cried, 'Of course it will be necessary! I'd rather be dead than part of that menagerie.'

'Pray don't be obvious,' Miss Spanner begged.

'No, I needn't talk like that to you. But I'm sick of holding my tongue. We're all afraid of saying what we think about the things that really matter in case some other fool may call us obvious or sentimental or immoderate, or accuse us of bad taste. We're far too moderate and far too tolerant, so steeped in moderation,' she said, speaking very fast, 'that we refuse to believe other people are not, in spite of all the evidence. We mustn't think they're worse in any way than we are. That would be self-righteous. Judge not that ye be not judged. I think that was rather an unfortunate remark. Of course no one has any evil intentions. They are sheep in wolf's clothing, just dressed up for fun, that's all!'

'Go on,' said Miss Spanner as Rosamund paused for breath. 'I like to see you in a temper.'

'Do you call this a temper? I feel like screaming the place down! But we don't do that. We shrug our shoulders and hope for the best and believe in it too! But what's the good of talking, after all? I'm going to see the bank manager. I must have some money for Chloe's clothes.'

'Don't get too many,' Miss Spanner advised significantly.

'Don't croak,' said Rosamund.

'Well, I like that!' said Miss Spanner indignantly.

'But start writing a novel.'

'Me?' said Miss Spanner. 'As though I'd dare. I've much too high a standard.'

'Oh, you needn't try to get it published,' Rosamund said easily. 'I just thought it might get some of your funny ideas out of your system. If you wrote down all the mysteries you make out of nothing, you'd see how silly they are.'

'That would only be through lack of skill,' said Miss Spanner. 'They're not so silly as you think. For instance, there'll be trouble across the road, sooner or later.'

'Bound to be.'

'Why?' asked Miss Spanner, with jealousy for her own perspicacity.

'You know best, Agnes. You always do.'

'There you are again! I can never get a straight answer out of you,' Miss Spanner complained.

'I don't want to spoil your fun,' Rosamund said.

She went out into the Square and stood still for a minute, listening to the familiar sounds, the usual sounds of the traffic she could not see, an errand-boy whistling, footsteps, the church clock striking the half hour. Nothing came from the river, it must be low tide, and the beasts in the Zoo, here, were silent. Like the other beasts, in another country, it was at night they roared, but not with frenzy, not gathering for the hunt; theirs was the awful indignation of the wrongfully imprisoned who have no redress. And Mrs. Blackett, watching from behind the dining-room curtains and ready to follow Mrs. Fraser, as she often did, and meet her on their shopping excursions, saw her lift her hands a little way and drop them and imagined that the movement synchronized with a breath drawn and let out. And she was right for, whatever might be wrong with this country of hers, there was still freedom in it and Rosamund expressed her thankfulness with that sigh and made a token gesture of love with the raising of her arms. She had never set foot outside her native land, but that did not affect her certainty that there was none to equal it, either for the quality of its people or its beauty; the toleration she had abused matched by the landscape which, at its most spectacular, had a comparative restraint, and she did not believe there were any meadows like English ones, any villages as snug or old houses more gracious. It was possible that there were no worse slums and she knew that under those pale hills at which she looked so often from her own little hill above the river, there was a ghastly mess of deserted works, miles and miles of them, the iron of them ironically red with rust while the faces of the men who had worked there once and of the boys who had looked there for a living and been denied it were pale with the lack of iron in their blood. And they were patient, with bitterness but without violence, and these were some of the men who might be called on to fight. They would do it and, still without more violence than was inherent in the dreadful job, with too little anger against their enemies and too much belief that they were of the same stuff as themselves, unwilling and decent victims of necessity.

The gentle sound made by Mrs. Blackett as she shut the front door behind her broke into Rosamund's meditations and she looked round.

'How nice!' she said.

'Yes,' said Mrs. Blackett.

Her dress was not draped over a bustle and she was not wearing a bonnet but, as usual, she gave that impression and, as usual, Rosamund felt, though she did not believe, that this woman of another generation, like her own mother in an early photograph, should be deferred to a little and spared close contact with the thoughts and habits of a less sheltered age. She found it difficult not to take Mrs. Blackett's arm at the crossing near the church and pilot her safely to the other side, but the policeman on duty, saluting Rosamund, saw them over safely.

'I always feel very grand when he does that,' Rosamund said.

'But you must be used to that kind of thing,' said Mrs. Blackett simply.

'I've lived here for so long,' Rosamund said, 'and yet,' she reminded herself, 'as much out of it as in it. It's only, I suppose, because the important things have happened to me here. There was the war and Felix and James and Chloe were born here. I was living with my father in the house we have now.'

'May I ask you, please forgive me if I shouldn't,' Mrs. Blackett said gently, 'but I've often wondered whether he was killed, your husband.'

'Wounded three times,' Rosamund said, 'but he wasn't killed.' She laughed. 'If he had been how could I account for Sandra and Paul?'

'I hadn't thought of that. How stupid of me.'

'Or perhaps how nice,' Rosamund said, and their eyes met in a shared amusement. The bustle and the bonnet, Rosamund decided, were only a disguise. They had no correspondence with Mrs. Blackett's mind and she, sustaining her air of amusement, announced that wherever they came from, Mrs. Fraser had charming children.

'They seem so alive and so — so free,' she said, 'and yet they are never aggressive.'

'Not even Paul?' Rosamund said. 'I'm afraid he's rather given to jumping on to Mr. Blackett's flat roof. It's a great temptation.'

'I can understand that,' Mrs. Blackett said, with, Rosamund fancied, just a suspicion of dryness. And it suddenly occurred to her that she and Mrs. Blackett were missing a good deal through not seeing more of each other.

'Have you much shopping to do?' she said. 'I must go to the bank, but afterwards shall we meet and have coffee somewhere?'

'I'd rather meet you on the hill,' Mrs. Blackett said.

Would you? Much nicer. Then we'll wait for each other there.

It was Mrs. Blackett who waited and Rosamund, who had resented Mr. Blackett's presence on her hill, was glad to see his wife there, sitting very straight on a seat that faced the hidden Channel. She enjoyed the company of men; their presence enlivened her and whether she had detained the bank manager or he had detained her, she was not sure; but like many other women, she found her own sex more interesting. Their minds, being less direct, were more amusing to follow and the mind of a woman who had married Mr. Blackett, remained married to him and still seemed content, must either be nearly empty or else full of surprises.

Mrs. Blackett turned as she heard quick footsteps and, looking at Mrs. Fraser with her own share of curiosity, she noted again, with envy, the air of youth and enjoyment she wore about her, naturally, without the effort which might have made her foolish.

'I've brought some chocolates,' she said. 'Soft ones so that our cheeks won't bulge and we can get rid of them quickly if we see anyone we know. It's most undignified to be discovered eating.'

Mrs. Blackett dipped into the bag. 'I know very few people here,' she said, and she might have added 'or anywhere'. She might have told Mrs. Fraser that since the fleeting friendships of her schooldays she had never before spent a few idle moments like this with a woman to whom it would be easy to talk freely, not thinking carefully before she spoke or regretting her words afterwards, but the habit of reserve was very strong in her; she could not take proper advantage of this opportunity.

'Don't let's be polite with the chocolates,' Rosamund said. 'Let's eat as many as we want. Bad for the figure but good for the rest of one, not to be everlastingly holding back.'

'And yet,' said Mrs. Blackett, speaking in a low, toneless voice, as though to herself, 'there can be a very great pleasure in doing that.'

'A form of self-indulgence?'

'It can be that,' Mrs. Blackett said.

Rosamund took another chocolate. 'I approve of self-indulgence so long as it hurts no one else. It's a very harmless kind that doesn't.'

'There's one's own character to consider,' Mrs. Blackett said, still seeming to commune with herself, 'but that's one's own affair, or,' she turned to Rosamund, 'is that impossible?'

'Quite,' was the cheerful answer. 'We're all tied up together. The best things we do often have terrible results, so what's to be done about it? Be good and risk the consequences, or just do as we like and risk them again? Meaning to do right is one thing but sometimes it's quite another to recognize it. Perhaps we'll be judged by our intentions, though it's still rather hard on the people who suffer from them. What a speech! That's the second I've made to-day. Agnes had the benefit of the other,' and as Mrs. Blackett, remaining silent, seemed to put a closure on this discussion, Rosamund said, 'My Chloe is going to be married.'

Inevitably, Mrs. Blackett was drawn from her own meditations by this interesting information. 'She's very young, isn't she?'

'No younger than I was.'

'I suppose not. No younger than I was, either. I expect,' she said, and Rosamund thought Mrs. Blackett's brown eyes were pathetic but half hopeful above the serenity of her mouth. 'I expect you will find it difficult to believe that I was only forty on my last birthday,' and without stopping to think or to fear that Mrs. Blackett might be hurt, Rosamund said quickly, 'It's your clothes,' and then waited a little anxiously for a reply.

It came meekly. 'I know.'

'Was that rude?' Rosamund asked. 'You needn't answer. It was, but I couldn't help it. Chloe and I — she's in a dress shop, you know — always want to meddle with other people's clothes. My own are nothing; I can't afford good ones. I run these cotton things up myself and you'd be shocked if you saw them inside out, still, one gets an effect, and it angers me when superior people say such things arc not important. It's important to make everything as beautiful as we can.'

'I quite agree,' Mrs. Blackett said, 'if I put myself into your hands I'm sure you would do a great deal to improve me and I should like that, but,' she said, looking, Rosamund thought, rather odd, 'on the whole I think I get rather more fun out of looking as I do.'

CHAPTER XXVI

AFTERWARDS, Rosamund wondered whether Mrs. Blackett, half opening that door to intimacy, had been disappointed when her timid or tacit invitation had not been accepted; at the moment, it had been difficult to know how to respond and Rosamund had hoped her smile was adequate, suggesting interest without curiosity, but there had been more than tact in her restraint. It seemed unfair to encourage confidences when she meant to make none herself. There was even the possibility that Mrs. Blackett was more eager to receive than to give and offered something in the nature of a bait but, in spite of the natural frankness of her nature, Rosamund did not bite and Mrs. Blackett neither tempted nor appealed – whichever it might be – again. The smile could not have been adequate. Mrs. Blackett had very gently shut the door and Rosamund, with a little heartache, decided that she ought to have risked giving it a push. It was better to be snubbed, she thought, than to be unkind, though perhaps Mrs. Blackett considered she had said enough for the instruction of an intelligent person and Rosamund had a malicious pleasure that evening when she saw Mr. Blackett approaching the house in which his wife amused herself with a perpetual masquerade. 'Poor fool!' she thought, smiling down at him from the balcony. It was strange to think that in a short time she might be connected with him by marriage. It was something of a deterrent too and, stepping back into the empty drawing-room, she wished she could find Piers sitting there.

When she was with him she had no doubts. In his absence the situation seemed unreal, rather absurd, inconvenient and, for one of her upbringing, faintly improper. And she did not like secrets; she hated the necessity for discretion; nevertheless, she knew that when she saw him again she would think it a very good secret, well worth a temporary discomfort. But he was not here now, she had not heard again from Fergus and the whole thing seemed fantastic and something of a bother. What on earth was she going to do with Agnes and the children and particularly with Agnes? Even the younger children would soon be setting out on their own voyages, while Agnes thought she had reached a permanent harbour. She had been persuaded into it and she liked it and there would be a peculiar cruelty in turning her out of it. It would be easier, Rosamund thought, to deny herself and Piers the happiness they looked for. 'If she won't come where I go, I shall have to stay here with her,' she thought as she went to the top of the house to say good night to Paul and Sandra. With Paul this was a mere matter of putting her head round the door and telling him to hurry; to-night, with Chloe away, staying with her future mother-in-law, Sandra would expect a lengthy visit.

'Sit there,' she said, leaning from her pillows to pat the end of the bed. 'I do hope she isn't feeling unhappy.'

'Who is it this time?'

'Chloe of course. In a strange place, you know, and I expect her mother-in-law is awfully — awfully upholstered. Inside and out. And wears very strong, very long stays.'

'Yes,' Rosamund agreed, 'and she'll be horrid to Chloe. I expect she'll cry herself to sleep to-night and to-morrow she'll be like a young lady in an old-fashioned novel and say she can't marry Peter because his mother disapproves of her. And then she'll fall into a decline and die.'

'Don't make fun of me,' Sandra said.

'I certainly shall. What else can I do with you?'

'I'm not really pessimistic, only anxious about people I'm fond of. I like to be prepared for the worst and when it doesn't happen, it's such a lovely relief. And when the nice things I plan don't happen either, I'm not much disappointed.'

'This is the first I've heard of your nice plans. They might happen oftener if you told me about them.'

'Oh, it's not that I'm doing without things you might manage to give me, not that kind of thing at all.'

'They all lived happily ever after, is that it?'

'Yes,' Sandra said unwillingly. 'Is it stupid?'

'No, I don't think fairy tales are stupid.'

'Well, really,' Sandra admitted, 'I'm afraid it's more like tracts. Everybody good and happy all of a sudden, you know. And why aren't they always, anyway? That's what puzzles me. I mean why wasn't it arranged like that?'

'I'm glad it wasn't,' Rosamund said briskly. 'I think that would have been very dull. Most of the fun of life,' and she thought of Mrs. Blackett, 'comes from the impact of one person on another. Most of the sorrow, too. People may be charming separately but devils when they are together. That's interesting, risky too, and perhaps interesting just because it's risky.'

'Oh,' Sandra said. 'Yes, I see. So perhaps a plan I've made, in case of need, wouldn't do after all.'

'In case of need?'

'Well, you never know, do you?'

'No.' Rosamund laughed. 'That's another good thing. What's this plan of yours?'

It was, though Sandra did not know it, the plan Rhoda, for a different reason, had made already.

'I thought it might be very convenient, some day, and very nice too, if Miss Spanner married Mr. Lindsay. I don't suppose, at his age, he'd mind about her rather funny looks.'

'Don't you?' Rosamund said, thinking this child was much younger in some ways for her years than most of her contemporaries.

'Well, would he?' Sandra inquired. 'And though I like his face, he isn't handsome himself, is he? And then, Miss Spanner would take care of him. He ought to have someone to do that.'

There's that George of his,' Rosamund said.

'A woman would be better. They think of things.'

'And yet I hadn't thought of that,' Rosamund said, as though to herself.

'You have such a lot to think of,' Sandra said excusingly, but her mother had no sense of guilt. She was delighted to realize that her feelings for Piers were free of any maternal tinge. She was seeking her own happiness, she hoped he was seeking his, as young lovers did, as all lovers should, without any thought of giving care and kindness, though perhaps with some hope of receiving both, and Sandra, seeing the brightness of her eyes when she looked up and the serious yet soft lines of her mouth, characteristically attributed this air of tender pleasure to her mother's hope of good fortune for her friend.

'So you think it's a good idea,' Sandra said.

'I don't think Agnes would.'

'Oh well, it was just in case.'

'In case of what?' Rosamund asked quickly, but Sandra did not answer.

'It's funny,' she said, 'that what's good for some people has to be bad for others. A good thing oughtn't to be able to hurt anybody. When you get a prize, for instance, it means that some-one else doesn't. Or two people in love with the same person. One of them gets hurt. It seems as if there isn't enough niceness to go round.'

'Not all at the same time anyhow. I suppose the important thing is not what we get but what we do with it, or how we do without it.'

'Yes.' For herself, Sandra found no difficulty there. It was all the other people for whom she was concerned and, knowing this, Rosamund said, 'You can't bear everybody's burdens.'

'But we're told to.'

'Yes, if we can. I think that's the point. There are a great many that simply won't be shifted from one back to another and then it's no good worrying. Waste of energy. That's one of the few things I've learnt so far, though it was never one of my temptations to bother much. And another thing I've learnt is that you have to learn everything for yourself. Advice from one's elders is quite useless, so I won't give you any.'

'You've been giving it all the time,' Sandra said with pleasing pertness, and Rosamund went away, thinking it odd that she and Fergus, each with a strong sense of self, had produced this little creature who seemed to have none.

'If James and Sandra could be mixed,' she said to Miss Spanner, 'the result would be a person like my father.'

'But you can't mix them, so you'll have to put up with them as they are.'

'Willingly and gratefully,' Rosamund said.

'H'm,' said Miss Spanner. 'And you would have thought —'

'That's most unlikely. Keep to the first person, Agnes.'

'Very well. Then I'd have thought Felix would have stayed at home to-night.'

'Why should he?'

'To keep us company, of course; the place feels empty, and we'd be better company than what he's keeping, I'll be bound. What do you imagine he's doing?'

'I don't imagine anything, on principle.'

'Your principles seem to me to be a complete lack of them.'

'But you have plenty. There's no sense in two people doing the same job.'

She sat down, studying the familiar figure of her friend, rearranging her hair, stripping her of the dark blue dress patterned in large white zigzags, its open neck modestly veiled with muslin, putting her feet into shoes which had not belonged to the late Mrs. Spanner and coming, as usual, to the conclusion that it would be a form of sacrilege to tamper with anything unique.

'And you darn so much better than I do,' she added, watching Miss Spanner's needle going in and out. 'And pay me handsomely for letting you do it. It's not fair but it suits me very well. Still, when Chloe goes and Felix gets a salary I could easily manage with less.'

'Don't be too sure,' said Miss Spanner. 'I went to see about a wireless set this afternoon.'

'I don't see the connection.'

'Not yet,' said Miss Spanner darkly. 'I thought I'd get one of my own. There'll be a lot to listen to soon if I'm not much mistaken.'

'You are often very much mistaken, but I'm afraid you're right about that.'

'And I hadn't the faintest idea — how could I have? — so you can't say I was poking my nose where it wasn't wanted. It must have been the hand of Providence that led me there. You see, it wasn't the shop I'd meant to go to but, I don't know how, I found myself inside.'

'Was it very difficult?'

'What?'

'Getting in. You sounded rather tottery or as though there were obstructions.'

'Don't try to be funny,' said Miss Spanner. 'As I've said before, it's a queer thing that you and I can never have a straight-forward conversation and if you don't want to hear any more I won't bore you with it,' but before Rosamund could reply and thwart her, she said quickly, 'It's in that shop the will-o'-the-wisp gets her living. At least,' she added, 'one hopes so.'

'Will-o'-the-wisp?' Rosamund's questioning tone was genuine. Then she remembered. 'The girl who was having tea with Felix?'

'Yes. It must have been her early closing day.'

'And she works in a shop. Like Chloe. That's all right. I hope you bought something. I expect she gets a commission.'

'I said I'd go again to-morrow.'

'For another look?'

'To give you a chance, too,' and as this remark provoked no immediate reply, Miss Spanner looked up a little timidly, but only one eye was fixed on Rosamund; the other was intently examining her own nose.

'Yes, you may well squint,' Rosamund said at last. 'I hate to insult you, but that pretty idea is worthy of your mother. I'm sure she used to spy through the keyhole when she suspected the servant of having a young man in the kitchen. I daresay she spied through your bedroom keyhole too.'

'She couldn't. I took care of that,' said Miss Spanner, and Rosamund's scorn was changed to laughter.

'Well,' she said, 'I suppose I do lots of things you'd think much worse than that.'

'What?' Miss Spanner asked eagerly but again getting no reply, she said, 'And anyhow, it's all Paul's fault. That boy's nothing but a nuisance. He never leaves the wireless alone. I'm not going to have him touching mine. It was when yours had to be repaired that Felix must have met that girl. I'm pretty sure that's the shop he went to. I'll ask him, shall I? I'll ask him the best place for buying one and you'll see that won't be the place he recommends.'

'I'd much rather you didn't.'

'Very well,' said Miss Spanner, compressing her lips. 'Have it your own way. And if you like, as you're so scrupulous, I'll go to another shop myself.'

'No, don't do that. She may be hungry. Perhaps that's why Felix took her out to tea. Does she look hungry?'

'She looks like thistledown. Elusive. I told you that before. But she's a good saleswoman and that bears out another thing I told you. She's as hard as nails. But she'll get a surprise, won't she, when I tell her where to send the set? She may even get a bit of a fright.'

'How?' Rosamund asked.

'I don't look very prosperous, do I? That will be a disappointment.'

'You look shabby enough to be suspected of great wealth. But Agnes,' Rosamund said reluctantly, 'just tell me one thing. Has she a nice voice?'

'Voice all right,' said Miss Spanner. 'Vowels very refined

CHAPTER XXVII

MR. BLACKETT, when he entered his house that evening, took a look at himself in the hall mirror before he removed his hat and, trying to look without prejudice, he saw what would have arrested his own respectful attention. Observing this person with the neat beard, the black hat set at a very slightly rakish angle, the well-cut jacket, the bow tie, his carefully groomed appearance in interesting contrast with his other-worldly air, he would have been curious, recognizing this stranger as some-one very different from the ordinary Radstowe man of business. He would not have been amused, yet Mrs. Fraser's smile, when she looked at him from her balcony, had promised to develop into laughter. There were all kinds of laughter. There was the one of pure joy, though he had never heard it, and there was the painful laughter, almost like sobbing, he had heard once from Bertha, but he did not think Mrs. Fraser was threatened with that kind of hysterical outburst; had he not presented himself to her in his shirt and socks, reminding her — and he frowned angrily and hung up his hat — of some ridiculous playing-card? She had seemed to have some satisfactory little joke of her own about him, but he flattered himself that he was not the kind of man about whom little jokes could be made. No, Mrs. Fraser's attitude towards him could be otherwise explained. Like all inferior people, she had to mock at what intellectually and in every other way was beyond her reach and this thought took him brightly into his wife's drawing-room.

'And what have you been doing with yourself on this fine day?' he inquired.

She looked up from her sewing without troubling to smile. The natural set of her lips was already amiable enough. 'I did some shopping and then Mrs. Fraser and I sat on the hill and ate chocolates.'

'My dear Bertha! Couldn't you find some better use for your leisure?'

'How?' Mrs. Blackett asked so unexpectedly that Mr. Blackett was momentarily at a loss.

'Anyhow!' he exclaimed.

'Such a beautiful view,' she said.

'I grant you the view,' Mr. Blackett said generously.

'And a charming acquaintance.'

'Oh, acquaintance! I was afraid you were going to say friend.

'No,' she said gravely, 'I wouldn't take that liberty.'

Turning from her, he swung on his heels and felt strangely baffled. Usually, in his study, in the dining-room, that movement brought him opposite a window; here his outlook was blocked by the pale inner wall of the drawing-room. Two pale water-colours hung on it, one on each side of an elegant little settee on which no one ever sat and, facing that demure pallor, he seemed, for a moment, to be hopelessly imprisoned. But he managed to break out.

'And eating chocolates out of doors!' he said. 'Like school-girls!'

'Yes, it was absurd. I felt quite young,' she said, and Mr. Blackett heard another kind of laughter, a clear, unemotional sound evoked by the memory of a pleasant, unemotional moment.

'A decent courtesy towards a neighbour is one thing,' said Mr. Blackett, addressing the pale wall and looking, though he did not know it, like a child made to face it for a punishment.

'But going for a walk and having a talk with her is quite another,' said Mrs. Blackett to save him the trouble. 'But it's the other thing that is so attractive and sometimes,' she added on a higher but not a louder note, 'sometimes it's the other person,' and as though Mr. Blackett knew that the time for his release had not yet come and, docile, would not move until the word was given, he remained just as he was, standing quite still, but he gave a little laugh and said, 'I've never really looked at these pictures before. Where did they come from?'

'From home.'

'Home?' Mr. Blackett said in pained reproof.

'My old home.'

'Yes, of course.' His tone was a humorous comment on the

185

contents of that home. 'Well, one rather wonders whether the artist meant them to be looked at. I hardly think he can have expected it,' and turning at last, he saw to his surprise, an increased look of contentment on his wife's face. He had meant to hit her back for the little blow he thought she had directed against him, but perhaps it had been unintentional, while his own, carefully aimed, seemed to be accepted with enjoyment, and he realized his foolish readiness to mistake simplicity for subtlety. A little guiltily conscious as he was of his preoccupation – half pleasure and half vexation – with his neighbour, he was apt to find a meaning in Bertha's words which was not there, but how could she, in her innocence, suspect him of this teasing self-indulgence or understand it? She would be shocked and completely puzzled by it, as though she were reading intellectually erotic poetry and, with this comparison, Mr. Blackett found a happy, though vague explanation of his state. It satisfied him however; it excused what his respectability condemned. He had been thwarted in his ambitions and out of duty and necessity he had repressed them, but he was an artist by temperament, susceptible to every form of beauty. He had missed physical ecstasy too and it was mere chance that a certain woman's beauty, it might just as well have been another's, had stirred him into restlessness of mind and body, his mind wasting itself in speculations about a creature who, without intellect of her own, could have been a spur to his through the satisfaction of his senses. Denying himself what she seemed to offer, he found relief in the desire to humiliate and hurt her. No, it would be quite impossible, even if it would be wise, to try to tell Bertha that.

'So you agree with me about the pictures,' he said.

'They are not very good pictures,' said Mrs. Blackett, 'but one doesn't always like things because they are good. Or people,' she added.

'But one should,' he protested. 'That is why I like you,' he added with tender playfulness for, whatever temporary discontents she roused in him, he came back to the permanent security she promised and her accidental shrewdness always amused when it did not faintly startle him.

'And your companion of this morning,' he said, 'is like the paintings. Recognized as not very good, but agreeable to you in some way. But be careful, Bertha. You must trust me to know more of the world than you do and I don't care to think of you sitting up there on the hill with her in any kind of intimacy.'

'I can well understand that,' Mrs. Blackett said with warm sympathy, and Mr. Blackett did not quite know what to do with this remark. Its sincerity had a flavour of defiance, but there was none in her expression. She had laid down her work and this time she really smiled at him, pleased, apparently, to meet him on common ground.

'Then why — ?' he said.

'Why not?' she replied. 'I spend a great deal of time with my bad pictures. Why shouldn't I spend a little with Mrs. Fraser, even if she isn't very good? I like my pictures and I like her. And why don't you think she's good?'

'I know enough to persuade me of that,' he said, 'and I would rather you were not seen with her in Upper Radstowe. She is very well known here.'

'Of course. She spent her childhood in that house. So did her father.'

'Yes, that's the pity of it. I think it my duty,' he said regretfully, 'to tell you that Mrs. Fraser is not a widow.'

'Isn't she?' Mrs. Blackett cried. 'Oh, poor thing!' she mourned, in the most animated exclamation he had ever heard from her, but, a little fuddled with the pleasure of making this revelation, he heard nothing peculiar in her words or her look of grief. 'And she seems so happy!' Mrs. Blackett said.

'Yes, that's what one finds so distressing. Rather blatant.'

'Or brave,' Mrs. Blackett said. 'Is her husband in prison or something?'

Mr. Blackett laughed. 'I believe he is a perfectly respectable person. I imagine he has been obliged to leave her.'

'And what obliged him? His business?'

'His self-respect,' Mr. Blackett said.

Mrs. Blackett was silent for a moment. 'What a lot of it he must have,' she said.

'And what do you mean by that, exactly?' he asked, coming to himself.

'It must have been difficult to leave her,' she answered slowly. 'She's pretty, but it's much more than that. What is it?' she asked in innocent inquiry. 'I think it must be because she's so full of life, but not fussily, not noisily. She seems to have some secret way of enjoying every minute. She doesn't say anything particularly interesting, but she makes you feel that everything is. She's welcoming, she's warm,' Mrs. Blackett said, lingering on the words and, as he heard his own thoughts falling relentlessly from his wife's lips, it was all Mr. Blackett could do not to lift his hands to his ears and cry imploringly, 'Don't!'

'Like a ripe plum on a wall,' she added. It was what he had thought himself.

'Waiting to be picked,' he said harshly.

'Yes. We had them in the Vicarage garden,' Mrs. Blackett went on quietly. 'They seemed to fit and fill one's hand.'

'Or someone else's,' he said between his teeth, but he gathered himself together, 'So now, Bertha,' he said suavely, 'you will understand why I may have seemed prejudiced against Mrs. Fraser.'

'Yes, I understand that, too,' she said, 'and yet you haven't told me anything about her.'

He hesitated. From anyone else he would have thought that remark a little cryptic, but it was Bertha who had made it, who was giving him her candid gaze, and he said, 'There is no need to go into details. You must trust me. And you will remember?'

'Oh yes,' she answered solemnly, but when he had shut the door behind him she laughed silently. Then she stood up and taking, with both hands, first one and then the other water-colour by its gilt frame, she held it firmly and possessively. No, they were not good pictures, but their value was increased by his scorn of them and they were dear to her through association, through her sympathy for their pretty, gracious failure, her conviction that behind the trees that would be uprooted by a light wind, the haystack that was no credit to the farmer, the shaky legs of the cart horses and the bonelessness of the recumbent cows, there was much more than the painter had been able to express and she imagined that, as these pictures appeared to other eyes than her own, so she herself appeared to most of those who knew her, a little dim, harmless, not unpleasing, and deliberately she had informed Mrs. Fraser that though her execution might be feeble, it did not represent the impulses behind it.

She dropped her hands, thinking now of that woman who, less enviable than she had been, had become more interesting. She was not impressed by Mr. Blackett's hints; she knew their origin, but, if what he had tried to indicate were true, she did not care. There was more than one kind of virtue and Mrs. Fraser had the kind she liked.

At that moment, Mr. Blackett reappeared. 'Not a word of all that to your cousin,' he warned her. He smiled. 'The age of chivalry is not quite dead,' he said and, without waiting for a word of compliance, he went away.

When they met, a little later, at the supper table, he was surprised, a little vexed, to see her serenity unruffled. Was she, as he sometimes fancied, a little stupid? Had he not been explicit enough? It was true that he had made no definite accusation. Whatever he might choose to think or to suggest, he did not care to make, in speech, assertions he could not prove. He had respect for the spoken truth and he had been tender towards her innocence, but he would have been gratified by a few shy questions, a shrinking from the neighbourhood of impropriety: he would have borne patiently with the reminder that it was not she who had chosen to live in the Square, and he would have reassured and comforted her, adopting the air of a man of the world who had often encountered doubtful situations. But she did not gratify him, even when, sitting over their coffee, they saw Flora quickly pass the study window and Mr. Blackett jumped up to see and to report angrily that she was on the Frasers' doorstep.

'Is she?' Mrs. Blackett said calmly.

'And you don't mind?'

'Not at all. Why should I?' she asked, and he told himself that her simplicity did sometimes verge on stupidity. His delicacy had been wasted on her and then, as he told himself he was not altogether sorry, his certainty was pricked by a sharp little doubt as he heard her saying gently, 'But I am sure you would like to go and rescue her.'

CHAPTER XXVIII

FLORA would have been quite pleased to be rescued. She found her visit very dull with Mrs. Fraser and Miss Spanner sewing at one end of the long room and Paul and Sandra doing their homework at the other, and though Sandra left hers and joined the little group, she did not improve matters for Flora who was not interested in Rhoda's contemporary. She had not expected much amusement. She had seen Felix leave the house and, though she hoped for his return, she had called to prove to herself, but chiefly to show everybody else, that James had not been the only attraction there, that the family in general was what she liked. And James, in retrospect, had really been rather wearisome with his endless talk about farming, endured for the sake of the rare moments when he became conscious of her as something more than an attentive ear. She was worth more homage than that and already the little episode was like something that had happened long ago when she was young and ignorant. She had profited by it but she would forget it and though it was not very exciting to talk to two middle-aged women and a schoolgirl, she went away well pleased with herself, for Mrs. Fraser had been very nice and she was halfway across the road before Miss Spanner let out a long, low grunt which would have been a groan if there had not been a certain amount of pleasure in it.

'That means Miss Spanner doesn't like her,' said Paul.

'And perhaps,' said Miss Spanner, 'it expresses my regret that you and all the rest of you are not as charming.'

'But it doesn't. I know all your noises by this time. That means you think she's a fool and so do I.'

'Keep your opinions to yourself,' Miss Spanner said.

'Why should I?'

'Because at your age you haven't any worth hearing.'

'But what,' he asked, 'about the mouths of babes and sucklings?'

'I'm surprised you've ever heard of them. You haven't been brought up to read your Bible as I was.'

'And whose fault's that?'

'Ah,' said Miss Spanner, 'that's not for me to say, but times have changed. The very day I was born my father bought one for me.'

'You must have been pleased,' said Paul, but Miss Spanner was not to be ruffled. She seemed in particularly good spirits, Rosamund thought suspiciously, though she always enjoyed her arguments with Paul. 'And it's upstairs now with my name inside, in his beautiful handwriting, and the date.'

'That's no proof he bought it the day you were born,' Rosamund said.

'No, but when I was old enough, I was told about it.'

'No doubt. So were a lot of other people, I'm sure. And how lucky the shops were still open. I can't think why he didn't buy the Bible beforehand, but then, what a waste it would have been if anything had gone wrong! And it wouldn't have made such a good little story. I like this one, Agnes. It's one of your best.'

'D'you mean she's making it all up?' Paul asked. 'I can't see anything funny in it.'

'It's not meant to be funny. Just interesting. But you didn't know Agnes's parents as I did. I never tire of hearing about them and now that they are dead I get a lot of pleasure from remembering them.'

'So do I,' said Miss Spanner with a squint.

But Paul was not interested in the old Spanners. He went to bed and when Rosamund returned from saying good night to him and Sandra she heard about the wireless set and understood Agnes's good humour. She was never happier than when she thought she had made a discovery of a distressing nature and, particularly, when she hoped it would distress her friend, and Rosamund, lying in bed, listening for Felix's step, remembering how, not so long ago, she had persuaded herself it was Fergus's she would hear, wondering how she would feel now if it were his indeed, pondered on this peculiarity in Agnes, existing as it did with love and loyalty. No doubt a psychologist could find an explanation of it; she could invent quite a good one herself; but as there was no evident reason, she supposed there must be a subtle one, why they should be friends at all. That was the best, the safety, of it. They had nothing in common except a part of their past; their tastes were different, though their opinions often coincided; they seldom, as Agnes pretended to complain, had a straightforward conversation; they were perpetually sparring and never bore each other any malice and nothing either of them could say or do really affected their detached yet close relationship. Marriage ought to be like that, Rosamund thought, but it never could be. The bond was too obvious, the demands were inevitable, and the bond sometimes chafed and the demands were not satisfied. On the other hand, she thought with amusement, Agnes could not give her a moment's contentment of flesh and spirit. That, though it might dwindle to a memory, remained a bond. She would never be quite free of Fergus, never lose some sense of responsibility for him, she thought, as she heard footsteps approaching and, temporarily faithless to the lover across the river, waited for a quick, light step on the stairs or the fulfilment of that old threat to climb on to her balcony. But no one entered by the French window, the feet on the stairs were cautiously slow, and Fergus had never looked as grave as did this young man who had so great a physical likeness to him. They seemed to have named Felix wrongly, she thought, as she looked at him. They had labelled him with their own happiness, regardless of what the future might have in store for him, and he looked now as though it had nothing he did not dislike.

'What's the matter?' she asked a little sharply, for suddenly she felt irritated by his serious air, suggesting that he had some fault to find but meant to be kind and tolerant, and at once, with a quick frown, he became still more like Fergus, ready to take offence, more like himself when his father was at home and he was in constant expectation of a snub or a gibe.

'I saw your light,' he said, 'and I wanted to talk to you but of course any other time will do.'

'No time like the present,' Rosamund said flippantly. 'One of those silly sayings. It's often better to sleep on it.'

'As you will,' he said wearily, and she recognized the air she had resented as one of difficult self-control. His hard stare was not directed against her; it came of his determination to keep up the eyelids that would have drooped.

'What is it?' she asked gently, putting out a hand he did not take.

'The future,' he said.

'Oh, the future!'

'Yes, I know.' He sat down in the chair near her bed. 'But I suppose we must behave as though there is one.'

In the long mirror opposite her bed she could see herself and, level with her shoulder, she had a glimpse of Felix's red head, and she told herself this was another thing she must remember, like those happy moments in the sunny garden when James had greased his climbing boots. With him there had been an easy sense of companionship; here there was one of strain, but at least Felix had brought it to her. She would remember that and she hoped she would be able to remember that she had done all she could for him.

'Yes, let's behave like that,' she agreed.

'It's the financial situation,' he said.

'Is it difficult?' she asked, trying to speak lightly, thinking it would be just the queer way of things if this serious young man had plunged himself into debt.

'That's what I want to know,' he said.

'Oh, it's just as usual. I pay my way. Agnes is a great help, of course. I shall have to raise some money to equip Chloe decently and I've always reckoned on letting you and James have a little capital when you need it. But it will be very little, just about as much as I shall spend on her. There are still Sandra and Paul to think of. But I don't owe anyone a penny. I often wonder what my father denied himself for my sake and I have less scruple in being overpaid by Agnes when I think of the profits her stingy old father pocketed. Pious old brute! Your grandfather ought to have insisted on having more but he wasn't that kind of man. Instead, he stinted himself for me.'

'He must have been very far seeing,' Felix said acidly.

Rosamund shut her eyes. The justice of this remark did not make it more palatable and she felt a hot little worm of anger wriggling, like a live thing, in her breast. She had to control it and she did not open her eyes, and they seemed to be shut for a long time before the wriggling ceased.

'It's only fair to tell you,' she said quickly, 'that your father does send me money when he can.'

'Thoughtful!' Felix said, and the worm became very active again.

'Listen, Felix,' she said after another struggle. 'Don't judge him. You don't know enough.'

'I know he made Hell here.'

'Oh,' she said, 'if that's all Hell is, no one need fear it very much. And he isn't here now. I know,' she conceded, 'what's the good of pretending? — that he was often terribly tiresome!'

In derision of this understatement, Felix gave a hard laugh. 'And we mustn't forget his wounds,' he sneered.

This time, anger did take charge of her. 'Indeed you mustn't!' she cried, lifting herself straighter against her pillows. 'How dare you talk like that? You don't know what he did for you, for all of us, but you ought to know!' And again she shut her eyes, this time squeezing them tight, not trying to shut out those years of mud and slaughter when, horrible as they were, this present cynicism had not fallen like a blight on the world which tried to discredit even man's unbelievable courage and endurance, but concentrating on them in tribute, taking again what share she could of foul discomfort and fear and agony.

'I've never actually seen a really nasty sight in my life,' she said slowly, 'legs blown off and faces pulped and bits of a friend scraped together in a shovel. And neither have you. Who are you to judge?'

'Well, perhaps my time's coming,' Felix said sullenly, and at once she softened towards him, for indeed his time might be coming and she turned to look at him, to get his face off by heart before it vanished for ever or was spoilt.

'And anyhow,' Felix went on, 'he isn't the only one. Look at Lindsay. He's sane enough, with a face wound like that, too.'

'Yes, but then,' she said, looking at him slyly, 'Mr. Lindsay hasn't got red hair.'

'What on earth has that to do with it?'

She laughed. 'Danger signal. Didn't you know? Nearly always. Sandra seems to be an exception but you are true to type. Irritable — how would you contend with five children? — Impulsive — yes, though you may not think so. Sometimes,' she said this at a venture, taking a risk that seemed to be justified by the desperately tired look that had settled on his face again, 'sometimes acting too quickly and being too proud to retreat or, perhaps, too conscientious. And conscience can be the devil, quoting Scripture for his purpose. One has to keep a careful watch on conscience,' she ended lightly.

She had given him his chance to tell her what troubled him, but he would not take it, and she was shrivelled by the coldly amused look he gave her though she knew it was given in self-defence.

'All that's very interesting,' he said, 'but we've wandered rather far from the financial situation.'

'So we have. There's nothing more to tell you but I can let you have some money now if you want it.'

'Of course I don't want it,' he said angrily. 'Do you think I've come begging?'

'Oh, don't talk like that,' she said. 'How could you?'

'Yes,' he said with difficulty. 'I'm sorry.'

'I mean how could you beg from me? There's no thine and mine between us.'

But these words did not seem to comfort him. 'Soon,' he said slowly, 'I shall be getting a salary.' And then, with a rush, he said, 'What I really wanted to know was whether you were reckoning on it.'

'No, I wasn't counting on it. I should expect you to contribute something, though, if you lived here still.'

'But not unless.'

'Certainly not. Why should I? I've always realized that you might want to go away and then you'd have all you could do to keep yourself at first.'

'Well, that's all,' he said. He went to the door. 'I just wanted to know,' he muttered, as though to himself.

She called him back as he turned the handle.

'Oh yes, good night,' he said.

'No.' That was not what she wanted. 'Come here and take this little pill,' she said. 'It will make you sleep.'

'A drug,' he said with disapproval.

'It's quite harmless. I often have one.'

'Do you?' he said, and his face softened for the first time, for here, he seemed to realize, was another troubled human being who sometimes lay awake.

'Yes, I'll take it,' he said as he bent down to kiss her.

'And soon you'll be having your holiday,' she said.

'Perhaps,' he said, lifting his eyebrows and giving her a rather wavering smile. He kissed her again. 'Thank you very much,' he said, and she knew he thanked her for the help he would not take.

CHAPTER XXIX

THE harmless little pills were all too harmless for Rosamund that night and she wondered that she had ever lain awake before. Fergus's desertion, the sense of her own failure, the constant though not acute worry about him and what silly, impetuous things he might be doing, a certain amount of jealousy for the conditions he found so congenial to his work, the complicated happiness of loving again and being loved, all these which had often kept her wakeful seemed now quite soporific compared with this helpless anxiety for Felix. While things went well with the children she had been able to preserve her attitude of non-interference in deed and, to a great extent, in thought. It was, as Agnes had once told her, a sort of affectation. Nevertheless, she believed it was a good one. But how absurdly she had prided herself on what had been so easy, natural to her in the first place and favoured by circumstances in the second. They had always been extraordinarily nice children but no amount of niceness could guarantee a parent against trouble when a child came to man's estate and to that Felix had undoubtedly come with a strength against which a refined vowel had no power. He was not in debt, she could take his word for that, not, at least, of a monetary kind, but he might feel he was in debt of another; or, too well disciplined to have involved himself like that, he might feel impelled to a life-long commitment, knowing it was a mad one, for the satisfaction of a moment, exquisite but as frail as the thistledown to which Agnes had compared that girl. And that it was that girl or someone like her, someone whom he was ashamed to bring home or who refused to be brought, Rosamund became convinced and whether from duty after desire fulfilled or unfilled desire urging him pitilessly, he must mean to marry her. That, of course, was why he had wanted information about the financial situation, that was why his face was white and drawn. She knew the signs when she saw them. She knew that if her fleshly envelope had enwrapped a woman alien, even antagonistic, to Fergus in thought and upbringing and speech, he would still, defying his folly, have married her unless she had been one of those who could be bought. And then, surprisingly, for inevitably she had pictured the girl as a minx and was unfairly willing to believe in the hard as nails theory, it occurred to her that the girl too might be engaged in the same sort of conflict between sense and passion. She might be a very nice girl, in spite of the vowels, and Felix was an easy person to love, a little forbidding at times, an attraction in itself, and as charming as his father when he chose. But it might not be that girl at all. Why should it not be someone in her own semi-detached condition? And she felt a great distaste for that condition, a longing for everything to be clear and simple — an exorbitant demand to make of life — and at the same time she knew that Piers was the one person who could comfort her because there was no one else to whom she could take a trouble she could not name. All she knew for certain was that Felix was unhappy and though this was a common enough experience for youth, she deeply resented it for her son.

She did sleep at last but not before Mr. Blackett, waking in the early hours of the morning and raising himself on his elbow into the position he had found necessary, was able to see a familiar glimmer in the darkness and give rein to those fancies which he knew were extravagant and absurd but in which he found a strange pleasure and release.

He would have been very happy if he had known that the woman who was not a widow went in search of Piers Lindsay that afternoon. It was one of Upper Radstowe's characteristic days, with a warm drizzle and little gusts of wind that, vexed with this half-hearted rain, drove it impatiently for a few minutes and then gave it up in despair. It might go on for hours or it might tire of itself soon, but Rosamund and Miss Spanner both put on their mackintoshes. Miss Spanner also donned a mackintosh hood.

'I'm going to buy that wireless set,' she said.

'Oh yes,' Rosamund said indifferently, and then with the irritation Miss Spanner's appearance often roused in her, she asked, 'Need you really get yourself up like a cross between a middle-aged pixie and a dustman?'

'To be suitably dressed is to be well dressed,' Miss Spanner replied complacently. 'You're wearing very thick shoes,' she added suspiciously.

'Well, you see,' Rosamund glanced at Miss Spanner's feet, 'I don't possess a pair of my late mother's buttoned boots. Still, I don't mind walking with you as far as the bus.'

'I'd rather like a walk into the country myself,' Miss Spanner said.

'Not with me, Agnes. If it's exercise you want you can get it on the pavements,' Rosamund said, thinking there was no other person in the world to whom she could talk like that, knowing that though Miss Spanner put on an offended air as a matter of course, there was no grievance in her heart. 'You're an angel,' she said impetuously.

'Yes, I know,' Miss Spanner replied gently.

That sent Rosamund chuckling across the bridge, the soft rain in her face, the familiar scene subdued under the grey sky, the water leaden, but the gulls startlingly white against the mud where, crying harshly, they scolded and searched for food. She walked quickly resenting as usual the fences barring her from the short cut to the Monks' Pool, thinking how, in each period of her life, in childhood and youth and now in middle age, she had been happy as she passed this way or had found happiness at the end of it; with her father, with Fergus and with Piers and, under the influence of her memories, some of her anxiety fell from her as she walked on the horse track beside the high stone wall, but when she found herself at the turning into the lane where she and Piers had leaned over the gate, she did not pause reminiscently beside it. She had not come to see a lover, only to find a friend. Yet, when she walked down the lane and passed the Monks' Pool and discovered the carefully concealed turning to Lindsay's plain brick cottage and saw him kicking off his gum boots in the doorway, it was a lover who looked at her and the good resolutions with which she had set out became a

199

little shaky. Like Fergus, but differently, Piers did the right thing. A friend would have smiled and called out a welcome, an inept lover might have shown his joyful agitation with a fatuous grin; this man whose expression she could read through the pathetically comic distortion of his face, looked at her with the graveness of deep and unexpected satisfaction and gravely she looked at him. He, she knew, was not thinking of himself at all, except to be conscious of content, while she was trying to get behind his eyes and see herself as he saw her, in an old mackintosh and muddy shoes, an ordinary enough woman transformed by some peculiarity of vision into an extraordinary and the only one, and as he led her into a big room with a fire, on this damp day, burning at the farther end, she thought it was stupid to make Cupid blind. He was all eyes, but they were seriously astigmatic.

'I must shout for George and tell him to make us a good tea,' Piers said.

There was a low fender stool round the hearth and on this she sat, her back to the fire, her face to the room. She liked the room. There was a sort of order in what might have been a muddle — pipes and books, letters and catalogues and packets of seed on one table, a neat row of boots under another near the door, comfortable armchairs without extra cushions, a low wooden stool on which she had no doubt the tea-tray would be set, shelves with not many but very well worn books and, with its flaps down, a gate-legged table, a half-made knitted garment lying on it. Here was a lost opportunity for Agnes! She would have interpreted the disappearance of Piers as an errand of warning to someone who must not be seen, she would have watched him on his return, expecting to see him carelessly throw a newspaper over this incriminating evidence, but Rosamund asked at once, 'Who knits?'

'George,' Lindsay said. 'He isn't much of a reader. He likes a sensational newspaper and when he's finished with that he's had enough literature for the day. And then he knits.'

'In here?'

'Yes, we both sit here.'

'Do you talk?'

'He tells me the bits of news he's afraid I've missed. Crimes, mostly, and we discuss the whys and wherefores. He's quite a student of that kind of human nature.'

'He'd get on very well with Agnes,' Rosamund said.

Sandra's plan for Agnes only needed the small alteration of substituting George for Piers. That would be an altogether happy solution, for what else could be done with these permanent attachments who, wrenched from their places, would suffer cruelly? It was a thousand pities Agnes was not a faithful servant or George somewhat higher in the social scale. And yet, did it matter? In spite of being with Piers, the sense of unreality returned to her. She felt this was just an interlude or one of those confused dreams in which the worry of possessions lost and trains missed mingles with a wonderful happiness and the knowledge that it cannot last.

'I think you have all you want already,' she said, when George had brought in the tea. He, too, had a slight limp, but his waxed moustache gave him a martial air. 'I can't make scones like these. Piers, shall we pretend we never leaned over that gate?'

'Yes, if you like,' he said cheerfully. and added, 'If you can.'

'That's just it. I can't.'

'Why should you?'

'Because it makes me feel a little messy.'

'No it doesn't, but you know that's what other people would call it. If there's any mess, it isn't of your making.'

'No. I should have been faithful to Fergus as long as he was faithful to me.'

'But he hasn't been. That's my good luck.'

'Though of course,' she went on, 'I should still have wanted you to like me rather more than you should.'

'Nothing could have prevented that.'

'How nice you are,' she said. He had not touched her and there was a delicate delight in his restraint and her own.

'From that first day in Bertha's garden when she hurt her foot,' he said.

'Was it? And Agnes was convinced you were gazing with all that anxiety at your lost love.'

'So I was. But she was lost a very long time ago. When I came back from the war and found she was on the point of marrying Blackett. But I soon recovered.'

'Oh, what a pity! For her, I mean. Lovely for me, though.'

'And for me.'

'But oh dear, it's just as Sandra said. No one gets anything without robbing someone else. And I think Mrs. Blackett's miserable. I'm sure she hates him. I think she'd like to kill him, slowly. She'll never get rid of him in any other way. He won't give her a chance, he's too respectable, though he'd like to.'

'But she has the children.'

Rosamund laughed. This seemed to her a thoroughly masculine remark. But she had not come to talk about Mrs. Blackett; she had come to talk about Felix.

'What can I do?' she asked when she had done. 'Just trust in God? But then, you see, I have a superstitious feeling that He's more likely to help me if I behave myself — yes, I knew you'd laugh — if I do without — ' she made a little gesture, 'this sort of thing.'

'Funny idea of God!'

'And then, I shouldn't like the children to know about it. Not yet. And perhaps Felix is doing just what I'm doing myself.'

'Then he's being very good.'

'But I'm not in a strong position, am I?'

Thinking that her position, weak or strong, could make little practical difference, but realizing that there were other powers, he looked at her very tenderly. 'Well, let's pretend,' he said, 'if that's any comfort to you. I'm just the greengrocer again and I'll try to be obliging and polite, but I'll never say an unnecessary word, I'll never look at you.'

'Oh, I don't see why you shouldn't look, just now and then, just to tell me that you like me still.'

'No, not a look,' he said, speaking with cheerful stubbornness to a corner of the room.

'I shan't be able to bear it.'

'It's your own choice,' he said in the same tone.

'I'm disappointed,' Rosamund murmured, like an aggrieved child. 'I thought at least you'd protest.'

'Protest!' He jumped up and stood over her. 'Protest!' he repeated. 'I simply daren't begin. Do you realize how long, at the quickest, we've got to wait? And here are you and here am I — What does that man think he's playing at? Haven't you heard from him?'

'Not yet, but I expect there's some good reason.'

'Good enough for him, no doubt, but not for me. It's effrontery, to make a request like that and then ignore you.'

'Not effrontery. He's just erratic.'

'You're strangely tolerant about him.'

'And you ought to be grateful to him.'

'And so I am,' he said, but he did not let her go until she had promised to write again to Fergus that night. She would rather have let things slide and had as little as possible to do with the shaping of them. She had faith in her unassisted good fortune.

CHAPTER XXX

THIS easy-going optimism was a national as well as a personal attribute but, while she had it for her own comparatively small affairs, as though they were too unimportant to be dealt with seriously, she differed from the mass of her countrymen who seemed to see in the very greatness of the threat overhanging the world its impossibility of fulfilment, to find comfort, too, in the belief that a bully was necessarily a coward and a large volume of sound indicated very little action. They were admirable in their general decency and moderation, these people going about their business under a clear sky: they would have been more admirable if, as they were to do later, they had adopted that calm cheerfulness, the natural behaviour of people living in a reasonable world, as a symbol of determination and endurance, and it astonished Rosamund that anyone who had lived through the last war should be able to forget treachery, should refuse to believe that those capable of it and incapable of remorse, dead to the very idea of that emotion, amazed at having it expected of them, had obligingly changed their character; should refuse to believe, too, that beastliness within its own borders would not spread beyond them.

'It's that Black Forest,' Miss Spanner said.

'How?' Rosamund asked. 'Oh I see what you mean. Everybody so friendly and kind and such lovely scenery. And they enjoy such simple, innocent pleasures.'

On this subject, at least, there was no wilful misunderstanding between these two. Miss Spanner's wireless set had arrived and she spent much of her time in sitting with her ear close to it, for she kept the sound very low out of consideration for the people in the house and because she had the feeling that thus she was the recipient of special information.

'And did the young lady blench when you gave her the address?' Rosamund asked.

'Not she! Not a quiver!'

'Of course not. I don't suppose she knows it.'

'Cunning of him,' said Miss Spanner. 'But she knows it right enough and that thistledown effect is about as trustworthy as the amiability of the Black Forest.'

'I hope so, for her sake,' Rosamund said. 'It's a rude world.'

Yet for her it was being kind. She felt clean and innocent now when the greengrocer arrived in the Square. She let Miss Spanner do the buying of the vegetables and listened with amusement to her comments on Lindsay's longer visits to the Blackett household.

'There'll be trouble there,' Miss Spanner prophesied again with relish.

'I shouldn't be surprised,' Rosamund said, with an indifference very reassuring to her friend. There was still that vague horde of suitors threatening the future but the immediate danger had passed.

And one of Sandra's fears had been dissolved. Chloe's mother-in-law, as Sandra saw for herself when Mrs. Stephens paid an enthusiastic call on Rosamund, was not at all upholstered. Her floating garments seemed to adhere by magic to her small body and apparently she wore no corset of any kind. Chloe would be safe with her except, possibly, from too much love. James wrote cheerfully from the farm; Felix looked less strained and was oftener at home and Rosamund liked to think, though sceptically, that what Lindsay called her foolishness had had a hidden wisdom and influence in it, that Felix, too, was pretending to be a greengrocer for somebody but, with the puzzled hope that there was some sense in suffering, she would have been less sceptical if she had suffered more. She did not suffer at all. This watching for Piers and exchanging a few casual words with him, this doubting, at times, whether a man who loved her as she should be loved could be so persistently successful in avoiding her, her own refusal to trick him into breaking the word she had persuaded him to give her, all this she made into a sort of game, very amusing to herself, though apt to become monotonous, and quite unsuitable as the pastime of a woman preparing for her daughter's marriage. And, secretly, she was glad she could avoid telling him that there had been no answer from Fergus except a telegram saying impudently, 'No hurry.' This message had enraged her with its assumption that the choice was his alone but, she had to admit, it came as a relief; she need not take any action. She could go on drifting, trusting in her luck and putting no spokes into the wheel of destiny. Nevertheless, anger was her first emotion when she opened the telegram and then she laughed and Miss Spanner, who had a genuis for appearing at what, for her, was the right moment, asked sharply, 'What's the joke?'

'Something you wouldn't understand, Agnes dear.' She sighed. 'I don't really understand it myself.'

'But I suppose you can tell me who it's from.'

'No.' Rosamund smiled sweetly in a puzzled way. 'There's no name on it. Funny, isn't it?'

'Bah!' said Miss Spanner, marching to the window and then rapping on it loudly.

'What are you doing?' Rosamund asked. 'If you're cross, hit something more solid than my window.'

'I want to speak to someone with a little sense,' Miss Spanner said. 'That's Rhoda Blackett out there and I haven't seen her for some time,' and she went to the door to meet her. 'You've been neglecting me,' she said when they were in her room.

'It's examinations,' Rhoda said. 'Oh, that's new, isn't it?' she asked, looking at the handsome piece of furniture which was Miss Spanner's wireless set.

'Yes, and it's a very good one. Walnut, you see, and nicely polished. The top makes a useful table, too. I really needed another,' Miss Spanner said, as she cautiously squeezed her way to a chair. 'And I shall be able to spread out my ornaments a little. I think the ruby glass looks very well on it, · don't you?'

'Yes,' Rhoda said, thinking it was lucky Miss Spanner was so thin for, while there was more space for the ornaments there was decidedly less for her. 'We haven't got one,' she said, 'or a telephone either.'

'Your father doesn't like these modern inventions, is that it?'

'I suppose so.'

'H'm. I wonder you don't go to bed by candle-light. Not that I care about all of them myself. Now electricity,' she glanced at the lamp by her bed, 'I do appreciate, though I wouldn't have a telephone as a gift. But at a time like this I like to get all the news I can.'

'What sort of time do you think it is?' Rhoda asked.

'Serious,' said Miss Spanner.

'Tell me why,' Rhoda said, and Miss Spanner told her. 'But I expect you have heard all that before, from your father, perhaps,' and as Rhoda made no reply, she added, 'or from Mr. Lindsay. You see a lot of him, don't you?'

'He nearly always comes when I'm at school,' Rhoda complained.

'Oh, that's unfortunate,' said Miss Spanner, delighted with this piece of information but a little ashamed of having procured it.

'Yes,' said Rhoda, 'and I don't know why nice people are always so hard to get at.'

'Because other people think they are nice too,' Miss Spanner said with a startling squint. Then the wandering eye accompanied the other to look at Rhoda. 'And as I'm easy to get at I'm afraid I can't be nice,' she said.

'Oh, you are!' Rhoda exclaimed, 'but not very easy. I mean,' she said and then she stopped. She had to be loyal even where she disliked. She could not speak of the watchful curiosity and disparaging tricks of her father, but she felt the need, once expressed by James, of doors which did not open on to the Square. 'Besides,' she said, 'I've been working harder lately.'

'Quite right. Good girl,' said Miss Spanner.

'I always seemed to be sort of asleep at school,' Rhoda said. 'Or like not quite knowing where I was going in a fog. Breaking rules without meaning to, you know. And then I began to wake up. I suppose I was rather young for my age,' she said thoughtfully.

'Storing up energy, that's what you've been doing,' said Miss Spanner.

'Do you think that was it? I was afraid I must be extra stupid.'

'Certainly not!' said Miss Spanner. There was no stupidity in a girl who sought her company and while Rhoda still employed the steady stare so irritating to her father, there was a new alertness in her appearance.

'And,' she said, getting up to go and considering what route she could take with least danger to Miss Spanner's ornaments, 'James says —'

'James?' said Miss Spanner.

'Yes, your James. The one who lives here. I've had a letter and he says I can have a red book about farming on the bottom shelf

207

of his bookcase beside the door. Do you think you could get it for me, now I'm here?'

'Yes,' said Miss Spanner, 'I'll get it now.'

'It's the only red one,' Rhoda said, following her down the stairs, and waiting outside the bedroom door.

'Well, there you are. This must be the one,' said Miss Spanner, and patting her shoulder, she saw her out.

Though she was surprised, she had not asked a single question; she did not ask one of herself as she went upstairs. Rhoda's simplicity must not be sullied even in Miss Spanner's mind. Around that girl in the shop, round anyone already a little world-worn, she felt herself free to weave her unlikely plots, but not round Rhoda, Miss Spanner swore to herself as, sentimentally, she compared the girl to a daisy still hardly higher than its leaves, sturdy, round eyed and candid. She was sure that what she described as nonsense had never entered the child's head and she was determined to keep it out of her own, but Flora had already done what Miss Spanner would not do. Rhoda had tried to cast out the idea; she did not want it. It was Flora's invention and she could keep it. Flora was like that, Rhoda thought with scorn and she was glad she had found James's letter before anyone else could see it. Now she was careful to enter the house by the area door and conceal the book until she could safely carry it upstairs; the letter was already hidden there. It was a great possession. Very few letters arrived at the Blacketts' house. On birthdays and at Christmas there were messages from relatives, but this was the first really unnecessary one Rhoda had ever had. She rather wondered why James had written it. Probably James would have wondered too if he had thought about it at all. It was natural to write from a farm to a girl who was interested in farming, to tell her, with male egoism, what he was doing, to find a sympathetic outlet for his enthusiasm and while Rhoda accepted it in that way, it gave her a warm, happy feeling, a livelier continuation of the one she had when he lent her the first book and Flora had tried to spoil that simple kindness. He was another of the few nice people she knew, he was her friend.

Before she began to know him she had avoided him self-consciously, thinking he would despise her for her clumsy, unattractive youth, but now she did not give a thought to the effect her appearance might have on him because it did not occur to her that it would affect him at all. They liked the same things and through them they liked each other and the details he gave about the farm were almost as valuable as the writing of them. She did not look, and she would have looked in vain, for any sign of interest in herself and she was well satisfied with the assurance that he was hers sincerely, James Fraser.

She scrawled a reply without premeditation, under the cover of one of her exercise books. 'Dear James,' she wrote, 'thank you for your letter and for saying I could have that book. It looks easier than the one about fertilizers. I didn't understand all that. I do wish I was on a farm too, but Miss Spanner says she thinks there'll be a war and then I might be able to. She gave it to me this afternoon. Yours sincerely, Rhoda Blackett.'

Her marks for English composition had always been very low.

CHAPTER XXXI

FLORA was bored. Term was over and the acquaintances she had made at the University, pleasant enough when they met there, showed no anxiety to seek her now. Some of them had gone away on holiday; others, who lived elsewhere, had returned there, and what entertainment could she offer any of those who remained if she asked them to her home? Her father had three manners for young visitors — the playful, the instructive and the disapproving; her mother was sweet but dull; the presence of Rhoda and Mary would persuade the guests they had been asked to a children's party and anyhow there was nothing to do. Other people could have lawn-tennis parties, they had brothers who brought young men to the house and, only yesterday, she had seen a little group of students of her own year, men and girls she knew, pedalling across the Green on some sort of excursion. They had looked very gay, all bare-headed, some of them bare-kneed, the wind filling their shirts and blouses, turning them into sails and, as the small procession passed her and stopped pedalling to freewheel down the road sloping to the bridge, the humdrum bicycles had the effect of tiny ships setting off for an adventure, and she went sadly home-wards, taking with her the memory of lightly ruffled hair, red, smiling lips and laughter, the quick turn of a girl's head as she spoke to the youth beside her, the way he lifted his hands and dropped them again on to the handle-bars to emphasize what he said, the whole a picture of happiness and easy comradeship. And she had not been asked to join them. Perhaps, she hoped, that was only because they knew she had no bicycle. And why had she no bicycle? Why had she nothing she wanted, no fun, no friends, no chance of any amusement or excitement during the dreary months ahead of her? The Square was a desert. Old ladies toddled round it with dogs on leads, harassed-looking women, carrying baskets, emerged from basements to fetch food for their lodgers, the lodgers popped in and out, and the Oval was always empty. Its railings needed paint, the evergreens themselves lacked polish and except for that one corner where the Frasers' house met the Blacketts', the whole place was shabby and neglected, a fit refuge for impoverished old ladies and for the young men who, wearing stiff collars and dark suits, and always with cigarettes hanging from their lips, left early and returned late, to blaze out in their bright sports clothes at the week-end. Even Flora could not interest herself in them. She was disgusted at having to share the Square with people of that kind and her Cousin Piers did nothing to improve matters with his trailer full of vegetables and some of those landladies for customers. Yet, though James had gone and Felix went in and out with the speed of the lodgers and a preoccupied air, there were certain hours when Flora still liked to be at her window and one of these was when Chloe Fraser came home, sometimes alone, sometimes with the man she was to marry. When she returned alone a car was almost sure to follow a little later and stand outside the house until the drawing-room lights went out and then Flora, picturing those two as they went down the stairs and said their farewells in the hall, was filled with vivid envy. But she was never as lucky as her father had been when he saw Chloe's mother embraced on the pavement. She might catch a glimpse of Chloe's pale frock but that was all and, having learnt very little from James and his casual kisses, she had to get her information on such matters from the pictures she saw at the cinema where she sometimes went, unknown to her father. The more immediate knowledge she was always hoping for would have to be unknown to him too. She was like him; she had his impulses and through them she divined, though she did not understand, the horror he felt for love-making and marriage in connection with his children. She guessed, correctly, that when she was approaching middle age he would not altogether set his face against a decorous union; it seemed strange that he should have married anyone himself and she surprised her mother by asking her what he was like as a young man.

Mrs. Blackett did not answer for a moment. Then, 'Just like he is now,' she said.

'Not young at all, then.'

'I shouldn't say that. He is still very young in some ways.'

'What ways?'

'I don't think I can quite explain,' she said gently. She could not tell his daughter that he still saw things first and always as they affected himself, that like most young people he found himself the most interesting person in the world and that, in middle age, he was aggrieved when others did not share this view and estimated his fellows largely by their estimate of him and the coincidence of their opinions with his own. She could not judge him in his business but it seemed to her that, in his home, everything said and done bounced against him as a pleasant little tap or an offensive blow, but she could not tell Flora that.

'You see,' she said, 'you are growing younger and so, to you, he seems older than he did. You used to be a very grave young person. You did not criticize him then.'

'I'm grave still,' Flora said angrily. 'I have to be. I don't get a chance to be anything else. And I don't care what you say, he can't ever have been young properly, having fun and doing jolly things and going to parties and, oh, all the nice silly things like that. And I wish I wasn't growing younger. What's the good? I was much happier when I thought I ought to be serious all the time. And now it's just dull and horrid.'

'Yes,' Mrs. Blackett said, and this unexpected answer caused Flora to ask with interest, 'Are you dull too?'

'No, I'm not dull. I have my own ways of amusing myself.'

'Just looking after the house and sitting here and sewing?'

'We all have to find our own way,' Mrs. Blackett said.

'But that's so lonely!' Flora exclaimed, and again Mrs. Blackett said, 'Yes.'

'And not even a summer holiday,' Flora went on. 'Father said he might take us abroad but of course nothing's happened.'

'I thought you were not very anxious to go.'

'Well, I am, now,' Flora said, flushing a little. 'There's nothing to do here. I don't suppose it would be much fun, but it would be different.'

'Ask him to take you.'

'Just him and me!' Flora cried. 'Oh no! You won't suggest that, will you?'

'I did,' Mrs. Blackett confessed, 'some time ago, but I won't do it again,' she promised with a friendly smile.

Flora muttered an awkward 'Thank you,' because she did not know how to be gracious and natural with a mother from whom she had expected mild reproaches for speaking disrespectfully of her father, a little good advice and some perfectly useless suggestions, like polishing the furniture or learning to cook. She had become, for Flora, a much more important person than she had been, quite different from the one who took their temperatures when they were ill, saw that they were well fed and made sure the household wheels ran smoothly, but still only different in relation to Flora herself. She was her father's daughter and her interest stopped there, but this talk had made her a little happier, a little less discontented, when she went into the dining-room and asked Rhoda and Mary to clear away their books. She wanted to lay the supper table. It was Connie's evening out; it was also the evening when Rhoda wrote her letter and she was prepared to be amiable too, especially as Flora was not wearing her important elder sister's air. In an obliging hurry she gathered her things together and after removing one of the exercise books and putting it under her arm, she flung the rest on to a side table and went away. There was time to do a little gardening before supper.

Flora, who was neat, stacked up the books and with faint amusement for Rhoda's lack of scholarship, ruffled the pages of an exercise book and idly glanced at the notes in them, written in Rhoda's legible but ungainly hand. A loose sheet slipped out and as she put it back she read it, by accident at first and then deliberately, with so much blood in her head that her feet seemed to rest on nothing. It was a harmless, childish little letter but that there should be one at all, that she should be thanking James for one, was an insult to herself who had once loved him, who had once thought he loved her. Anybody would do for him, that was evident, and she had been one of the anybodys. Her anger was too great for rough handling of the letter. She put it back very gently, hating to touch it. Then she ran upstairs to Rhoda's bedroom and looked out of the window. Rhoda was in the garden, safely occupied. But where was James's letter? Lacking a lock to a drawer, where would she herself have put it? She found it at once under the lining paper and read it without a scruple, but when she had finished this dull report on crops and cows, she found herself weeping bitterly. She did not know why; she told herself she had nothing to cry for; she would have hated to get such a letter; there had been no need to hide it, but the very simplicity of both letters touched her to a new kind of angry envy, and because this one had been hidden she knew it must be precious to Rhoda, who was thus richer than she was herself,

Rhoda, who had nothing to offer anyone in the way of beauty or intelligence or charm!

Dabbing her eyes, Flora looked down again at this unattractive sister and felt still angrier because the discovery of the letters could not be used against her. It would have been pleasant to take them to her father, but while he would have been satisfyingly vexed with Rhoda, she would have humiliated and betrayed herself. She had to find what comfort she could in hoping that Rhoda, too, would have a bitter lesson to learn though, Flora looked at herself in the glass, with less excuse.

Facing her sister at the supper table, however, seeing her face more animated than usual and wondering whether James had had the bad taste to kiss it, she found it impossible to restrain herself. She had to do something to discomfort Rhoda and leaning forward, she asked, 'Why does Miss Spanner say there's going to be a war?' And she could see Rhoda puzzled by this question and suspicious of it, but the attack was intended to be an oblique one and, before Rhoda could answer, Mr. Blackett spoke.

'And who may this mistaken Miss Spanner be?' he asked, blandly ignorant of such a person's existence.

'The funny old thing who lives with the Frasers of course,' Flora said, and Rhoda retorted hotly, unwisely, as she knew, but with her loyalty stronger than her caution, 'She isn't very old and she isn't a bit funny, except on purpose.'

'And how,' asked Mr. Blackett, still ominously bland, 'are you able to give us this interesting information, Rhoda?'

'Oh, she's Rhoda's friend. You often go over to see her, don't you, Rhoda?'

'Yes,' Rhoda said stoutly. 'She's my friend. She's very nice and she knows a lot and she tells the truth.'

Mr. Blackett raised his eyebrows until they were almost out of sight. These were his own qualities and he spoke with the coldness of his indignation. 'I should hardly have thought you needed to cross the road for those benefits,' he said. 'Indeed, it seems to me a most unlikely place in which to find them.' Then, flooded by his consciousness of the endless irritation, in one way or the other, these people caused him, from Mrs. Fraser who had over-much femininity to the plain spinster who offended him by her complete lack of it, the dam of his self-control was broken and his words poured out against Rhoda who could not be content at home and must seek the company of people he distrusted; against those who spoke of war and thus helped to create it; against the ignorance of women in general and of Miss Spanner in particular. He spoke of his faith in the leaders of the country and the good qualities of the people who were being maligned. He knew there were some sections of the community who wickedly wanted war for their own profit, but what an obscure creature like this Miss Spanner hoped to get out of it he could not imagine. It was pure mischief making, the frivolous occupation of an empty mind.

This was a long speech and only Rhoda continued to eat her supper. The others had lost their appetitites or thought it rude to display any in the circumstances, but the ordeal was nearly over.

'And to prove I believe what I say,' said Mr. Blackett, inspired by his own eloquence to get the better of his discretion, 'I intend to go abroad next month and to take Flora with me.'

Flora, hoist with her own petard, carefully cast a piteous look at her mother and Mrs. Blackett, knowing that while she might serve herself she would not be serving her daughter by opposing this scheme, but must make some show of helping her, said quietly, 'Hadn't you better wait, Herbert, and take us all next year?'

'So you are one of the faithless ones, too, are you, Bertha? I'm surprised — and disappointed. No,' he said, as Flora began to move the neglected plates, 'as far as I am concerned don't trouble about another course. I am far too much upset.'

'Oh, that's fortunate,' said Mrs. Blackett.

'Fortunate!' he exclaimed.

'I mean,' she said with smiling meekness, 'because I know the pudding must be burnt.'

CHAPTER XXXII

WHILE her father talked, Rhoda had plenty of time to trace the origin of Flora's question and she was shrewd enough to know why it had been asked. With inherent distrust of her sister, she had meant to carry away the notebook in which her letter was concealed and in her haste she had taken the wrong one. Flora had read it and she was angry. That she might have sought for and found James's letter was a villainy of which Rhoda did not suspect her. She was willing to believe that her offence had been at least partly accidental and though she had been very mean in using it, she was going to be well punished. Rhoda could not imagine a much worse prospect than a holiday with her father for sole companion and, shrewd here too, she guessed that her father's decision was one of an irritable moment and his pride would compel him to abide by it. That was punishment enough and Rhoda decided to say nothing and this was not altogether out of generosity. She knew the kind of remarks Flora would make and, determined not to be troubled by them, she was pleasant and friendly while they washed the supper dishes together.

'Nice for us,' she said, 'but awful for you. You'll be staring at churches all the time.'

'Not awful at all,' Flora said. 'It's just what I should choose. I should hate to go trailing about with the whole family, everybody wanting to do different things.'

'And nobody,' said Rhoda, 'doing what they like. The best thing is not to go at all.'

'I don't agree with you,' Flora said. She could not allow Rhoda to pity her and, after all, it would be something to talk about next term, she would not have to admit to doing nothing and going nowhere when other people talked about their holidays and there was always the chance of the sort of adventure she wanted, but she realized that those chances would be lost without the exercise of tact, now and later, and Mrs. Blackett was surprised when, all smiles and eagerness, she brought the coffee into the study. This bright manner might be deplored as deceit or applauded as stoicism or unselfishness and it seemed to Mrs. Blackett that the virtues and vices had an extraordinary way of overlapping each other. It could hardly be called deceit in Flora to disguise her feelings for her father's sake, yet Mrs. Blackett would have bèen better pleased by a less sudden enthusiasm. She never felt sure of Flora's motives. But, from her own point of view, this enthusiasm was just what she wanted. It was infecting Mr. Blackett, loosening his pursed lips and adding a real desire to a petty impulse and, as she lifted her coffee cup she noticed that her hand was not quite steady. There had not been many occasions for excitement in her life, but this was one of them and she found herself saying childishly, 'Oh God, don't let anything stop them and, if there has to be a war, don't let it be just yet.' She was not praying that humanity might be spared untold suffering and grief; she was begging for a little time for herself. There was so much of it. It went on and on, developing, too, a deplorable elasticity within itself, stretching until it seemed it would have to snap, but it never did and, surely, it was not much to ask for a little of it for her own. In nearly twenty years of marriage there had hardly been twenty nights passed by Mr. Blackett outside his home and now, with any good fortune, there might be at least twenty evenings when he did not turn his key in the front-door lock, twenty nights when she would not hear him coming upstairs to bed and as many mornings when she need not suffer the absurd indignity of clambering over his recumbent figure because he insisted on having the bed pushed against the wall and on occupying the outside place. She would send Connie for her holiday, the house would belong to her and Rhoda, with Mary as an almost negligible addition, and already there seemed to be more light and air in it, as though the door had been opened into a bigger, freer world.

'But this is all very well,' she heard her husband saying, 'all very well for you and me, Flora, but a little cruel to be making plans which don't include your mother. And so, perhaps,' he said, for these plans were very different from the one in which

217

he had seen himself wearing corduroy trousers and coloured shirts and with another companion, 'perhaps we had better give them up.'

Mrs. Blackett prayed again, this time for guidance. 'Not on my account,' she said. 'It gives me a great deal of pleasure to listen to them. I'm very glad that you should go but, if you have come to the conclusion —'

He interrupted her. 'I came to a conclusion a long time ago, Bertha, and I see no reason for changing it.'

As far as he was concerned, she knew the affair was settled. More than a holiday and an educational experience for Flora, this was to be a declaration of faith and only some event beyond his control would turn him from his purpose. And as July slipped into August, a month when all the trees seem to be heavy with suspense, when one period is nearly ended and another must begin, there was a like feeling of suspense over the whole world, so heavy and yet so frail that Mrs. Blackett went her way very softly, lest a hasty movement or a loud noise should set up vibrations which would precipitate disaster and, try as she would to concentrate on great issues, it was her own little disaster she most dreaded, her own happy release towards which she looked with hope. But at last the day came when the suitcases were in the hall and the cab was at the door and Flora, for the benefit of anyone who might be watching, tried to look as though she were quite used to foreign travel, calmly entered the cab and was followed by her father who was quite sure he was being watched.

Mrs. Blackett with Mary, excitedly, and Rhoda, dutifully, beside her, waited while the cab turned out of the Square into the road and disappeared. They had gone, and she followed them in imagination to the station, to London where they were to spend the night and across the Channel, and even though bad news might send them back, and there seemed no immediate likelihood of that, she reckoned that she had the rest of this day and all to-morrow and perhaps the whole of the day after for herself. That would be a pittance compared with what she had been promised, but it would be well worth having. She counted the hours, determined not to lose a moment of enjoyment, to make each one last as long as possible, but she knew that time would be less elastic now; it would refuse to stretch.

She did not go in at once and Mary, seeing her standing still with her hands clasped, her face upturned and her eyes shut, thought she must be praying or, perhaps, trying not to cry.

'But you're not crying, are you?' she asked.

'I could, easily,' said her mother, smiling with her eyes still shut.

'Why? Are you anxious about them? Are you afraid the sea will be rough and they'll be sick?'

'I don't care if they are,' Rhoda said.

'Neither do I,' said Mrs. Blackett, opening her eyes. 'Not a bit.'

'Oh Mother!' Mary said reproachfully.

'It wouldn't last long and they'd soon get over it,' Mrs. Blackett said cheerfully.

'Then,' said Mary, referring to her mother's readiness to weep, 'it must be because Father's gone away.'

'Yes, that's it, exactly,' said Mrs. Blackett, and without looking at Rhoda, she went into the house.

Mr. Blackett was right. His departure had been watched, but not by Rosamund. At the sound of the cab, Miss Spanner had stepped to the drawing-room window. Then, with some pale silk over her arm and a few pins between her lips, she went downstairs to report.

'They've gone,' she said, first removing the pins and sticking them into her white overall. 'Grey flannel suit and grey felt hat. New.'

'I was hoping he'd get himself up in knickerbockers and strong boots.'

'Very sensible, too,' said Miss Spanner.

'Though, as a matter of fact,' Rosamund said, 'the conceited ass dresses very well. But I should have liked him to look ridiculous.'

'He'll look ridiculous enough if he can't get back. He'll look very funny in a concentration camp.'

219

'He'll get back all right.'

'H'm, I wonder,' said Miss Spanner. 'And I wonder if Chloe is ever going to wear this,' and she shook out the garment she was making.

With strongly expressed disapproval of the flimsy materials Chloe had chosen, she was putting exquisite work into the fashioning of them though she disapproved even more strongly of the patterns she had to follow and, arrayed in a specially purchased overall, she spent hours stitching in the seclusion of the drawing-room which happened, fortunately, to be handy for anything occurring in the Square.

'Yes,' said Rosamund, 'you and I do a lot of wondering but, for goodness sake, don't wonder aloud when Chloe's about.'

'I'm not an idiot,' said Miss Spanner, 'and, if it comes to that, neither is she,' and Rosamund remembered how Chloe, breaking into her own gaiety as she made plans for her wedding had said, 'This is rather funny. It's like planning a picnic for a day when you're practically certain there'll be a terrific thunderstorm.'

It seemed worse than that to Rosamund. It was like living in the neighbourhood of an armed madman mistaken by the police, and nearly everybody else, for a well-meaning citizen, a little noisy and harsh in his own house, but doing nothing to cause real anxiety or to warrant more interference than common-sense persuasion.

'It's abominable that she should have things spoilt like this!' she cried.

'Well, well, well,' said Miss Spanner, 'they are not quite spoilt yet and if they have to be, it's a small matter, after all.'

'I know that, but life, for most of us, is made up of small matters, and if they were not important to us we'd be half dead and the big things wouldn't affect us either, and what do we really know about measurements and comparative values? But I know I'd like to wring the dirty necks of those devils if I could do it without touching them.'

'And I'd help you,' Miss Spanner said. 'Now, how d'you think it would be to put some embroidery at the top of this? I thought,' she said somewhat shamefacedly and giving her nose a knock, I might do some true lover's knots, in blue, you know. She's going to wear this set on her wedding day and there must be a bit of blue somewhere about.'

'You're an angel,' Rosamund said. 'I've told you that before. You couldn't take more trouble if you were doing it for yourself.'

'I'd have taken much less,' Miss Spanner said. 'There's not much inspiration to be got from calico and that's what my underclothes would have been made of, nightgowns up to the throat and down to the wrists. And quite right, too,' she added, and returned to the drawing-room with her light burden.

Chloe was to be married at the end of September when the boys had had their holiday, but about that Felix had said nothing.

'I suppose you're going?' Rosamund asked him.

He had passed his examination successfully and that look of strain which at times she had tried to attribute to a natural anxiety, had changed to a rather grim one. 'Of course. Why not?' he said.

'Oh, I don't know. You never talk about it.'

'I don't talk much about my own affairs,' he answered with an irritatingly superior manner.

'No, I've noticed that,' she said dryly, and then, quickly, knowing this was not the way to deal with him, she said in what she hoped was the right tone, 'I often wish you would.'

But he changed the subject. 'I hope,' he said, 'you're not going to make a great fuss over Chloe's wedding.'

'Do you? Why?'

'I think it would be most unsuitable.'

'Fortunately so does she.'

'That's all right then.'

'So long as you are pleased —' she said, dryly again. Really, she thought angrily, he treated her as though she had deeply offended him and he could not forgive her. She wanted to shake him. But how childish he was under the severity that made him seem a prig. For some reason, he was offended with himself and,

like a small boy, he wreaked his anger on his mother. Nevertheless, she saw this treatment as part of her general failure. She
could not gain the confidence of her son, Fergus had left her and
Piers was altogether too true to his word, too cheerful under the
determination to keep it. She would have despised him for a
love-lorn look yet she felt it was her due and asked herself why,
since he was getting on so well without her, though she began to
be increasingly less happy without him, they should trouble to
think about the future. This was her mood of the moment.
Even Mr. Blackett's departure was a grievance: she was robbed
of one of her amusements.

'But the air does feel a little purer,' she thought when she
stepped into the Square.

CHAPTER XXXIII

'What a difference it makes when there are no men about the
place,' Rosamund said on the first of September. Felix had gone
off with the experienced Smithers, to meet James on the way;
Paul was camping with some friends and a young schoolmaster.
'Not nearly so much cooking to do, a reasonably tidy house and
the certainty that there won't be any trouble. Just you and me
and Sandra and Chloe. Very nice. Peace, perfect peace.'

'Not,' said Miss Spanner, looking up from her newspaper,
'what I should call a timely remark. But you're quite right.
There'd always be peace without them. You can't imagine
getting a gang of women together who'd carry on like this
pretty lot.'

'And yet,' said Rosamund, 'though men do the worst things
they do most of the best things too. There's no getting away
from that.'

'You wait till women have had a proper chance.'

'They'll never, in general, have the kind of chance you mean,
and quite right too, as you would, say. They've got something

else to do. If you'd been a boy, Agnes, — Oh well, I suppose you'd only have turned into a deacon and you're much better as you are.'

'Cumbering the earth,' Miss Spanner said with melancholy, and paused to consider the fruitlessness of her life before she said, 'And this best of yours doesn't do as much good as the worst does harm. How d'you account for that?'

'I never try to account for anything,' Rosamund said, 'not even my petty cash.'

She could account without trouble, however, for certain signs across the road, the front door, hitherto rigorously shut, often left open; a light burning late in Flora's bedroom, though Flora had gone away, and no light from the big bedroom on the other side of the door; an indefinable change in Mrs. Blackett's appearance, as though she had decided to discard her bustle and moved more freely without it; a definite change in a new morning frock with a shorter and less ample skirt. The masquerade, thought Rosamund, was in abeyance. Mrs. Blackett moved more freely but not more quickly. There was about her an air of leisure, of having all time at her disposal, but she could have told the acute observer who was her neighbour that this was something in the nature of sympathetic magic. By thus assuming that there was no hurry she might persuade time to linger. It seemed to her like an eager horse with a hard mouth and, pull as she might on the reins, she could not control it. Already it had galloped into September and, though she went to bed late and rose early, the days were still too short and they were in danger of being spoilt by the thought of the endless future. This was foolish wastefulness and she tried to be more thrifty; it would have been much easier if the future had not threatened her nearly every day with a letter from her husband who, considerately ignoring her assurance that she would be quite satisfied with a postcard now and then, gave her detailed accounts of all he and Flora did and descriptions of what they saw. These were garnished with historical and literary allusions and marked as passages to be read to the children. Thus warned, she had only to skim the rest of the letters, to note changes of address and learn that he thought of her constantly. She did not believe that. The only person of whom he thought constantly was himself and, after years of intensive study, she knew just how he was thinking of that person now and how he pictured himself as other people saw him, as a distinguished-looking man, probably a painter or a writer, probably, too, a widower, devoting himself to a pretty daughter whose delight in his company equalled his for hers. Her preoccupation for so many years could not be suddenly forgotten altogether; she could not cherish her happiness without dwelling on its cause and in the careful changing of her routine there was a sense of triumph not unflavoured with spite; the very neglect of the letters which lay where they had been dropped, until one of the children picked them up, was an acknowledgment of an effort to forget.

But all this was the undertow to the calmness of those days in the Square. She and Rhoda busied themselves or idled in the garden and Mary had the run of the kitchen and, showing a surprising efficiency as a cook, prepared the meals they ate there or out of doors and served them at any uncertain hour she chose.

'I wish we could go on like this for ever,' Rhoda said. 'I can't see why people aren't allowed to live just with the ones they like.'

'But you see,' Mrs. Blackett said, 'the people you don't want to be with may want to be with you.'

'But they don't,' said Rhoda, bluntly changing from the general to the particular. 'Flora doesn't and Father doesn't and I don't like them. Not a bit. I like you and Miss Spanner and Cousin Piers.' She hesitated for a second. 'And I like James Fraser,' she decided to say.

'So do I,' said Mrs. Blackett, 'and you're seeing a lot of us now, or most of us, aren't you?'

'Yes,' Rhoda agreed. There was no curious eye at the study window to be avoided and Cousin Piers came oftener and stayed much longer. He settled down. Sometimes he stayed to supper and Miss Spanner, resigning the drawing-room and balcony to the lovers, sat near the front window of the long living-room with one eye on his car and the other on the clock. But, to her regret, Rhoda was always there to see him off.

'Very discreet,' she said, 'but it doesn't deceive me.'

'And no doubt that's what they are trying to do,' Rosamund said. 'You're a coarse-minded old thing, aren't you? All this mock modesty about natural things — I don't suppose anyone's ever seen you in your bath — '

'I should hope not!' Miss Spanner exclaimed. 'It's all I can do to bear seeing myself!'

'I didn't suggest that anyone wanted to see you there,' Rosamund said gently, 'but, I repeat, you have a coarse mind.'

'I haven't. It's filled with beautiful things you've never heard of.'

'Not quite full though. You've left room in it for your horrid little intrigues.'

'You know they amuse you.'

'Sometimes,' Rosamund agreed.

'And you must admit it's a bit odd, a bit significant, one car outside our door and we know why, and another outside theirs, and we can make a good guess.'

'Perhaps he's lonely,' Rosamund said, 'and has nowhere else to go. Perhaps he's tired of studying criminology with George and looking at that awful waxed moustache. It bristles quite alarmingly. I found myself dodging instinctively when he approached.'

'What's that?' Miss Spanner said sharply but quietly. 'I didn't know you'd ever seen him.'

'No, you don't know everything,' Rosamund said, moving to the other end of the room and followed by a cry she could not hear without pity.

'I don't know anything!' Miss Spanner keened. 'Nothing at all,' she said, bringing down her voice to a lower, mournful note and looking about her vaguely as though the fears she had conquered were surrounding her again. And she remembered, she had never been able to forget, because she had not understood, that look Lindsay had given her. He must have seen through her bright confidences and he had looked at her with pity because she had made them, because they had never been necessary or because already they were useless. But she pulled herself together. She was taking fright at the mere mention of a waxed moustache. Meanwhile, Mr. Lindsay was spending a long evening with the Blacketts and all the facts of the past weeks corresponded with her fancies better than with her fears, all the facts except those walks of Rosamund's into the country.

'I suppose,' she said, 'you've been to Mr. Lindsay's house.'

'Clever Agnes! Guessed it in one!'

'But he doesn't come to yours any more. Funny, that. I should call that a bit of a snub. And going next door instead! That's a slap in the face.'

'Yes, most humiliating,' Rosamund said.

She found it very tantalizing to picture him there, puffing at his pipe and fitting into his surroundings as he always seemed able to do because he completely lacked self-consciousness, and it was all very well to say the house was better without its masculine element. She missed the boys' voices and their comings and goings; she even missed the nuisance Paul so often made of himself, but what she wanted most was not their noisy youth or Lindsay's assurance that she was still beloved. She wanted the contact of a mature male mind. He could tell her no more about events abroad than she and Agnes already knew and his view of them was much the same, but discussing them with the wisest possible woman would have been less satisfactory to her than talking with a reasonably intelligent man. There was the slightly different angle from which he saw things, the elimination of the violent personal hatred she felt for those people who were cruel and rapacious and treacherous and showed these vices in their faces, and there was her own femininity which believed his must be a more balanced judgment. And Mrs. Blackett, if she wanted it, was getting the benefit of all this. Rosamund was restless and uneasy. She remembered that

Piers had once been in love with Mrs. Blackett and she was jealous, though not afraid, of his memory of those days, of the early memories the two must share and speak of, in the twilight of the garden, with the tenderness of people who are beginning to grow old. She had no past to share with him, perhaps no future; all her young memories belonged to someone else and he had carried some of them away with him.

'We might pay him out,' said Miss Spanner after a long pause, 'by refusing to buy his vegetables.'

'Ingenious,' said Rosamund, referring to the remark, not to the idea. 'Go on making a few more suggestions. They are more successful than direct questions, more like goads, and even I have to react to them at last.'

'Well,' said Miss Spanner, thus encouraged, 'I suppose it was easier to tell him in his house than here.'

'Much. You weren't there, for one thing.'

'And you were quite right to tell him.'

'I thought so.'

'Did he know anything about it already?'

'Not a word,' Rosamund said.

'Oh,' said Miss Spanner thoughtfully.

'You seem surprised.'

'Not at all,' Miss Spanner said hastily. 'In fact, I'm not quite sure what we're talking about. And as you won't confide in me, I won't confide in you.'

'Why should you?' Rosamund said with sympathy.

'Because, though I don't want to worry you, I think you ought to know.'

Rosamund said nothing. She only had to wait until Agnes could contain her news no longer and almost at once she said, 'That girl's gone away too. She wasn't in the shop when I went there this afternoon.'

'What did you go for?'

'To make some inquiries about my wireless set, of course,' Miss Spanner said self-righteously.

'I don't believe that,' Rosamund said angrily.

'Well,' Miss Spanner confessed, 'I did think it would be interesting to know. Having her holiday, they told me, and though I said she looked as though a little sea air would do her good, I didn't get any more out of them. All tarred with the same brush, I daresay.'

She looked round at the sound of the door being sharply shut and found herself in an empty room.

Rosamund walked out of the house and paused for a moment on the pavement. Darkness had not fallen yet but it was coming and in the general greyness of the Square, pierced here and there by a lighted window, the evergreens in the Oval made a strong black curve, the two cars, black too, looked like large animals abandoned by their owners but faithfully and patiently expectant of them. She felt rather like that herself and spared them a glance of sympathy before she walked out of the Square and up the road. She stopped at the top of it before she crossed on to the Green. She had seen it under almost every possible condition, through all the seasons, at all hours and in all weathers, but it looked strange to her to-night. It was the Green she knew arranged as the setting for a stage scene or as she might have seen it in a dream, put down in another place where absurd, irrelevant things might happen for which she would know, even in her sleep, she had no responsibility and they could have no issue. And as she looked at the dark grass and the tall trees, their lower branches gilded where the lamplight touched them, the branches immobile and the lights steady, with a glimpse beyond of the row of houses once graced by the presence of the Spanners, the quietness of the place within a circle of moving cars, their strong lights making the Green more remote and more inviolate, she lost some of her angry impatience with Agnes and her discoveries and, though some of the anxiety they roused remained with her, she accepted it and in doing that lost still more of it. She accepted her own state of uncertainty and restlessness, longing and reluctance, in the momentary vague conviction that she, like everybody else, was a sort of vessel into which experience and emotion was poured according to its capacity and its readiness to receive and that by receiving in this fashion, and letting the contents of the jar mingle and ferment or undergo any other change inherent in the mixture, the spirit was fed as truly as the body with material food. And this, she knew, was a different kind of passiveness from the one which resented definite action; it was not the usual resource of her natural indolence; it was the stuff out of which the right action could emerge if it were left alone with patience. It was her old faith that things would turn out as she wished changed into the belief that, though they might not turn out well for her, for Felix, for Piers, for all the people with whom her life was bound, they would not necessarily be bad as tiny contributions to the common stock.

She lost her uncertain grasp of this idea in the practical problem of getting across the road, but her mood had altered. Gone was the impulse to run away, to be rid of her responsibilities if only for an hour, her half-formed plan to waylay Lindsay at the bridge, to get into his car and later, far out in the quiet country, into his arms. The desires remained, but one runaway in a family was more than enough and though physically she was still ardently alive and the art of attraction she loved to exercise was impatient of continued restraint, she knew her regrets would last longer than her pleasure, she remembered that Sandra would be distressed at finding her nowhere in the house, so she simply crossed the Green and skirted it on her homeward way and waved, as he passed, to a Piers who did not see her.

CHAPTER XXXIV

MRS. BLACKETT now had the benefit of her husband's newspaper as well as of her own. She had also the comments, denied to Rosamund, of a man whose judgment she trusted. As she read, the personal effect of events was still for her shamefully paramount and, as she listened and rejoiced in his company, she wondered he could spare so much of it when Mrs. Fraser was just across the road. Had he, like Herbert, discovered she was not free for him? Recognizing her own temporary gain, she regretted the loss for him, if such it was. She could have loved him: she believed he might have loved her. He had returned too late from the war, which Herbert had avoided with considerable address and a disappointment of which he spoke with what she took for the reserve of deep feeling. She had been innocent enough to believe in that. And she loved Piers now, she told herself, without passion which had been poisoned for her, without any desire to rouse it in him, but much as an old woman might love the man to whom she had been married for many years, more concerned for his well-being than for her own. The liveliness of his boyhood which had led her into mild adventures from which her timidity naturally shrank, was now suitably subdued and what had happened to his mind and spirit since those days she could not tell. He seemed the same, kind and tolerant, but with a proper hardness somewhere to be used when it was wanted. He had been the perfect companion of her youth and she could find no fault with him now, but then, she thought, with dry amusement, she was not married to him and if such a chance had been vouchsafed to her she would not have taken it. She would not have risked changing a perfect friend for an indifferent husband or even for a good one in whom the endearing little ways of the friend might become commonplaces or the source of unbearable irritation. She blushed to remember how once, and for a short time, she had listened for certain tones of Mr. Blackett's voice and watched for certain movements of his long hands and found delight in what was only endurable now because she had learnt to enjoy disliking it. And he did not know, he had not the slightest suspicion, that was the best of it, and suddenly, when she and Piers were sitting in the twilight as Rosamund had pictured them and while Rhoda had left them for a few minutes, Mrs. Blackett laughed aloud, a rare occurrence, and it was yet another kind of laughter which Mr. Blackett had never heard.

Lindsay did not like the sound of it and slowly turning his head to look at her, he asked, 'What are you barking at?'

'Barking?' she said, and seemed to listen to the memory of it. 'Yes,' she said, 'it was ugly. I could hear that myself. It sounded ugly and I think I must look ugly too.'

'I haven't noticed it,' he said. 'I've always thought you a very comely wench.'

'And you do still?'

'Certainly I do.'

'But do I look nice?'

'That is implied in the description,' he said.

'Then, Piers, there's no trusting the outside of anybody, not even yours – or Mrs. Fraser's, and she's more than a comely wench, isn't she? What a difficult question for you to answer! You see, I'm not nice, really, and perhaps she isn't, either. Perhaps that happy, amused look she has is a disguise too. Sometimes,' Mrs. Blackett went on slowly, 'I'm quite frightened because I feel so wicked. But not,' she went on, and he was relieved to see a humorous creasing round her eyes, 'not frightened enough to try to be good.'

'Oh, don't try that,' he begged. 'Just go on being what you are. I find it most satisfactory, if that means anything to you, and so I'm sure does Rhoda. She's devoted to you, that child.' ·

'We have so much in common – too much,' Mrs. Blackett said. 'But with Rhoda I can't pretend. No,' she told herself aloud, 'I can't do that. Perhaps I ought to but I won't. Where's the sense in trying to make something that won't be very good and spoiling something else that is?'

'I'm rather in the dark,' Lindsay said quietly, and she parried that suggestion by saying, 'Yes, it's getting late.'

'And you want me to go?'

'I want Rhoda to go to bed. She won't go until you do. But I should like to stay here all night and steal quite a lot of time.'

'Then why don't you? You'd have to wrap up well, though.'

'Ah, I meant with you,' she said simply. 'Talking when we want to or just feeling safe.'

'Safe? You're not nervous, are you, alone with these two girls?'

'I meant safe in my mind. Exorcised. There's something in confession, after all.'

'Not much in yours,' he said.

'But enough — for you. Come again soon. D'you think, with all this growing fuss, Herbert will hurry home?'

'You can answer that better than I can, but I'm pretty sure it won't be necessary.'

'And you sound sorry.'

'I don't like the look of things. I don't like the smell of things. We're told the meek shall inherit the earth. What did that mean exactly, I wonder. Our meekness looks like allowing someone who's very far from meek to inherit someone else's earth. So long as it isn't our own! And it won't stop there. You might as well try to cure a man-eating tiger of his bad habits by throwing him a few unimportant people. They wouldn't be seriously missed and he might be satisfied. Well, I'm going. Good night. Sleep well.'

'Not if I can help it,' Mrs. Blackett said lightly. Where was the sense in having a bed to herself, to be able to turn when she chose, put on the light, sit up and read and, best of all, stretch out her limbs without the danger of encountering another body, if she lost consciousness of these privileges in sleep? There would be plenty of opportunity for sleep when she would be glad enough to have it.

'What's Cousin Piers been saying?' Rhoda asked as her mother remained in the hall after he had gone and seemed to be lost in thought. 'Anything worrying?'

Mrs. Blackett looked up. Quite evidently, nothing was worrying her. From under raised eyebrows she gave Rhoda the mischievous look no one else ever saw and her teeth, catching a corner of her lower lip, seemed to deprecate her own daring.

'What are you thinking about?' Rhoda asked.

'Something rather funny.'

'Tell me, then.'

Perhaps. I'm not sure,' her mother said, and like Rhoda, like

James Fraser, she wished there were a back entrance to the house, for how could she get that double bed removed and two small ones brought in, without the knowledge of the whole neighbourhood? But did she care about that? Again, she was not sure. And it would be a very expensive business. Mr. Blackett, who liked to believe he lived in Spartan simplicity, was inclined to confound the simple with the best when it was a question of his comfort and the cost of that thick box spring and excellent mattress was on a different scale from most of the modest household expenditure, but then, as he had said, that bed was meant to last a lifetime and at the remembrance of those words and all they meant, Mrs. Blackett nearly decided to get rid of it, together with the big sheets and the blankets and the plump, featherweight eiderdown. This was the chance to do it and she would welcome, rather than dread, the ensuing storm, but no, she could not do it. If not in all her thoughts, in all her actions she was a lady. She could not sell what was not hers; she could not take advantage of his absence to offer him what he would think, what indeed, among other things, was intended to be an insult, with the knowledge of his children and the still more humiliating knowledge of the neighbours. He would certainly not like Mrs. Fraser to witness the exchange of one bed for two and he would be right. It could not be done in that way and she doubted whether it could be done in any other; and if it were, generously and kindly – a most unlikely happening – she knew she would be disappointed. The life she had made for herself would need some readjusting for, with such a change in him, she would have to change the tactics she had perfected and, in that deep part of the mind where motives lie snug and hidden, was the fear of being robbed of one of her many grievances. She wanted to keep as many as she could get. That desire was unacknowledged. It simply turned in its place and settled down again, but she was genuinely shocked at having contemplated playing such a trick on him. It would have been, and she could hardly have condemned it more strongly, unforgivably bad manners.

'No, it wasn't funny,' she said to Rhoda, who questioned her next morning because it seemed a pity to miss a joke when so few cropped up in the family. 'I thought it was, just for a minute, but,' she said with truth, 'it wouldn't bear explaining.'

'All right,' said Rhoda, quite sure she would have understood very well and a little hurt at not being trusted, but just as the look she had once seen her mother give her father had shown her that there might be dark and dangerous corners for those who seemed to travel easily on an open road, she realized now, for she had grown much older lately, that there might be unexpectedly lovely and amusing ones for those who made an apparently weary pilgrimage. Loyally, she tried not to make guesses and there were other matters to occupy her mind.

'Don't you think,' she said, 'the Frasers' is a very nice house? They have the balcony for one thing and that room leading into the garden.'

'Yes, those are great advantages,' Mrs. Blackett agreed.

'Then why don't we just go and take it? Why should they have what we like very much?'

Puzzled for a moment, Mrs. Blackett soon took her meaning. Rhoda had been studying the newspapers as well as sitting at Miss Spanner's feet. 'Yes, why indeed?' she said.

'And I'm sure Father would say we are superior people and ought to have what we want. He would, wouldn't he?'

'No, I don't think he would say we ought to have what we want.'

'What he wants, then.'

'No Rhoda, that isn't fair. He doesn't get everything he wants — far from it.'

'Well, let's leave him out. You and I think we'd like that house.'

'But unfortunately,' said Mrs. Blackett, 'we haven't the excuse of pretending they are ill-treating some of our relatives who live there.'

'No, only Cousin Piers, and he doesn't seem to go there now. I should have thought he'd have liked Miss Spanner. But we could easily make up something else. When you're telling lies it doesn't much matter what they are. We could say — well, what could we say?'

'Spying on us from the balcony might do.'

'Yes, and jumping on to our flat roof. Only I don't think we're strong enough to frighten them, not when they're all at home, so we'll just have to let them keep it. I'm rather glad. D'you think they'll ask us to Chloe's wedding? Flora will be furious if she's not back in time for it.'

'She'll be back long before that,' Mrs. Blackett said. Already a fortnight had gone by.

'Unless things begin to happen,' Rhoda said hopefully, 'and they get caught somewhere.'

'They would have to happen very quickly and of course we shan't be asked to the wedding, but I want to give Chloe a present, something, if I can find it, as pretty as she is. Shall we go and look in the shops?'

'I'm not much good at shops,' Rhoda said, 'I wouldn't mind, though, if we could leave Mary at home. I think three people are awful in a street. There's always one in front of the others, or behind, and it's so straggly and uncomfortable.'

'Then let's go into the country,' said Mrs. Blackett. 'Let's fill the next few days with going to places we haven't seen.'

'But nothing instructive,' said Rhoda. 'And what about Cousin Piers? Why shouldn't we go there?'

'Yes, we can do that too.'

'It's a long way, though. I don't think you could walk there and back.'

'I can walk much farther than you think,' said Mrs. Blackett. 'But I shall hire a car. Yes,' she said recklessly, 'I'll hire one every day if we want one and we'll do exactly as we like.'

'And not bother about picnic lunches but go to hotels for meals,' Rhoda said.

'And have the very best of everything,' Mrs. Blackett said

with enthusiasm. 'I'll go over and see Mrs. Fraser. She will be able to tell us the best places. And it won't matter how early we start or how late we get back,' and she was delighted to find that Herbert had left his latchkey in his stud box.

CHAPTER XXXV

CHLOE'had left the shop with the good wishes of Miss Pringle who was to be transformed from an employer into an aunt and was glad to remember she had always been kind to the girl who was marrying her nephew, and she accompanied the good wishes with a generous contribution towards the trousseau, but Chloe, preparing her own home, was often absent, cheered or depressed, Rosamund was not sure which, by her mother-in-law's boundless faith in the nobility of man and the benevolence of Providence. Paul was still away, so Sandra was the only child at home and though she had her little pleasures, for she had many friends, her mother, seeing her sharp little face rather pale under her freckles, wished she could have a holiday in a keener air than that of Upper Radstowe.

'It's such a waste,' she said, 'to have those raw-boned aunts of yours in Scotland and make no use of them.'

'Oh, I don't want to go away now!' Sandra exclaimed.

'Why not?'

'Well, there's Chloe's wedding.'

'You could come back for that.'

'And I don't know those aunts.'

'You haven't missed much. But I'm not going to write a humble letter asking them to have you for a visit, only in the case of dire necessity.'

'And in that case,' Sandra said, 'I'd stay with you. Miss Spanner says she doesn't understand what they're saying when she listens to the wireless, but then, she doesn't need to. She says it's the nastiest noise she's ever heard.'

'She must have forgotten what it was like to hear her dear old father talking intimately to the Almighty.'

'She says they howl,' Sandra said with grave disgust.

'And that's what I wanted to do the only time I heard him.'

'How you hate him!' Sandra said. 'You won't forgive him, will you?'

'Never,' said Rosamund.

'And you won't be serious.

'Not very. Not yet.'

'Like a pack of wolves, Miss Spanner says.'

'Now how does Agnes know that? She's never heard a pack of wolves.'

'And,' Sandra went on, knowing that it was for her benefit that her mother uselessly adopted this light manner, 'I think it's horrible for human beings to go on like that.'

'It's not nice,' Rosamund agreed.

'It's frightening,' Sandra said, 'and I wish we were all together.'

'I don't know that it would be much good, to sit about all in a cluster, like playing clumps. And the boys are having a glorious time. I'm glad they wrote to Agnes and thanked her for it. She's very pleased. And I don't want them to come back yet.' But she knew it was her father of whom Sandra was thinking. She was thinking of him herself. She had heard nothing more from him since he had sent his message. He must, she thought, have found that his congenial surroundings could be enjoyed without her help, or he had tired of them or, as seemed more likely, he was too much absorbed in the developments of the European situation, too much excited, for thought of anything else. His nature needed excitement, it always wanted things a little in excess. There had never been a snowstorm when he had not hoped it would be a heavy one, or a fog when he had not wanted it to thicken and, if she knew him, he now hoped for war. The repulsion of an intelligent being for such waste and misery, the consciousness that it was being deliberately provoked, that there was no real quarrel anywhere except the perpetual one between good and evil, would not overcome his instinct to defy a threat, his pride in his country and his primitive liking for a fight. And in such circumstances, she knew he was at his best, thoughtful for others, forgetful of self, displaying virtues which failed him in the domestic sphere where they were as badly needed. And Heaven alone knew, she said to herself, what he was doing now; prying about, perhaps, in places where he had no business to be and offering his services to people who did not want them.

'Do you know where he is?' she heard Sandra saying in a thin, timid voice.

'I know where he was. I wrote to him a little while ago.'

'Did you?' said Sandra with a flash of pleasure. 'Then write again and tell him to come back.'

'That would be the most successful way of making him stay where he is.'

'Then tell him to stay there, of course,' Sandra said, but Rosamund could not bring herself to write again, not even to please Sandra. She had already fulfilled her promise to Piers and she would do no more. She did not want Fergus back — how could she? — and if he came she would not know what to do with him, nor would the children. Probably he would not know what to do with her or with them, for he must have changed too, and with a certain reluctant tenderness she wondered whether he would still be able to make her laugh, not at his wit, though he had his share of that, but at the nonsense he could not have produced without it. It was a long time since she had really laughed and she wondered too whether Felix, smarting under satire or a snub, had ever heard these sounds of silly merriment and been enraged by them. And yet again she told herself that Sandra was quite right. Somebody else always paid. No doubt she had often made Fergus happy at the cost of Felix and she knew who now had the first claim. Fergus had forfeited his and, in the past, perhaps Felix had persuaded himself that, in her view, he had none. She had sailed along too carelessly, avoiding rocks on one hand and forgetting the sandbanks on the other, yet, if she had gone more timorously, would the results have been any better? No, she decided impatiently, life had to be a dangerous affair. The wrong people might and did get hurt, but it was not her business to protect them or to lick their wounds; they must do that for themselves. She wanted no one to lick her own.

'Here's the postman,' Sandra said. 'Perhaps there will be a letter. No, there's only one for Felix, for Mr. Felix Fraser. I don't think that's the right way to address a full-blown lawyer. And what a grand envelope! And purple ink! That makes it worse. And squiggly writing and Please forward with a squiggly line underneath.'

She handed the letter to her mother who tried not to see the postmark. She could not help seeing, with disdain, the unnecessary precaution of a large blob of mauve sealing-wax on the back of the envelope.

'Redirect it, Sandra,' she said, 'and post it at once.'

'I feel,' Sandra said, as she carefully copied the address on Rosamund's desk, 'as if there can't really be places with awful names like this. There's plenty of time before the post goes and here are Mrs. Blackett and Rhoda coming across the road.'

'But Agnes is coming down the stairs.'

'Oh!' Sandra laughed. 'You think I'd better get rid of it? Yes. All right. I'll let them in and then I'll post it. I expect, you know, it's from a client,' she said.

'Perhaps it is,' Rosamund replied. It was from someone who did not know his address and that both puzzled and pleased her. Purposely, she had not redirected it herself. Felix would be less vexed at seeing Sandra's writing on the envelope, but she felt sure it would be an inappropriate message from a world he had forgotten for a time and the lavender-scented envelope would be painfully irrelevant in a climbers' hut, amid nailed boots and coils of rope and festoons of shabby clothing, while outside the sun brought different odours from the warm earth or a fierce rain pelted them back again.

'Yes, I've had a letter from both the boys,' Miss Spanner was telling Mrs. Blackett, 'and James has done some rather funny sketches. They might amuse you. I'll go and fetch them. Oh no, here they are, in my pocket.'

She knew they were there. She had taken care to have them handy ever since they had arrived. This was her first chance of showing them to anyone outside the family and Rosamund found it pathetic to guess how often Agnes had read them to herself. It was quite sad, her pleasure in them, and they were good letters, not mere hurried acknowledgments of what they owed her and much longer than any they had written to their mother, a fact which ministered to Miss Spanner's enjoyment. 'But if Chloe or I had written them,' Sandra remarked shrewdly, 'she wouldn't have made half such a fuss.'

They described the life in the hut, the cooking and the washing up in which they were well practised already, the fetching of groceries from a distant shop and of butter and milk and eggs from a neighbouring farm and how, on this errand, some cunning was necessary to avoid a bad-tempered bull. 'Felix,' James wrote, 'is better on the rocks than I am, but I'm better with the bull.' Early in the morning they bathed in the stream close by, still with a wary eye for the bull, and on fine evenings they bathed again in the shadow of the mountain on which they spent their days.

'Of course I don't approve of it. I think it's tempting Providence,' said Miss Spanner, showing the sketches to Mrs. Blackett who, having looked with proper interest at these scrawled indications of steep rocks with figures that might have been flies on them, proceeded to make her inquiries about suitable expeditions and Miss Spanner handed the letters to Rhoda, telling her she could read them if she liked.

'I wonder what breed of cows they have up there,' was what Rhoda said when she had done. 'Would they be Highland ones, do you think?'

'I haven't the faintest idea. I'm terrified of the creatures, but I'll ask him when I write. Good letters, aren't they?'

'Yes, and it must be fun there,' Rhoda said.

'And next year, why shouldn't we go too?' said Sandra, who

at home and in the holidays seemed quite a different person from a member of the sixth form at school. 'There must be somewhere where we could stay. Would you like it?'

'Like it!' Rhoda cried. 'But I'd never be allowed to go there,' she added gloomily.

'And what,' said Miss Spanner in her cheerful way, 'is the good of talking about next year? I suppose the mountains will still be there, but I don't know what else will,' and there fell on the little party one of those silences which it is more tactful to maintain than to break, until Rosamund suggested that they might have some coffee to cheer them up.

But Mrs. Blackett rose to go. She had left Mary alone in the house and must go back; moreover, though this was a private thought, she did not deserve the coffee. At present she did not need cheering up. Now, ashamed but not repentant in the presence of this woman with three sons, she could not share the anxiety Mrs. Fraser concealed so well. She had an anxiety of her own, comparatively tiny, completely personal and shockingly petty, but as persistent as the great one overhanging the world. Her honest desire for peace was inextricably entangled with her desire to keep Mr. Blackett far away.

CHAPTER XXXVI

NOT until some days later did Rosamund remember that she had told Fergus nothing about Chloe's marriage. It had not occurred to her to tell him. That was the measure of the distance between them and under her grief that this should be so, her sense of waste, the bitterness of wisdom acquired too late, there was her stubborn anger; there was pity for him too; though, as the days moved on, she had not much time to spare for him. On what should have been happy shopping excursions with Chloe, startling newspaper placards confronted them at the street corners; there was the usual noise as cars, in low gear, climbed the Slope but, in spite of it, there seemed to be a hush over everything, out of doors, in the shops, in people's voices, and Mrs. Blackett, getting less frequent letters with no marked passages in them, wondered that Herbert did not return. Whatever happened, he would be in a strong position, either that of a man courageous to the point of folly, an aspect of himself which would make amends for a mistake in judgment, or of a man whose calculations had been correct. She read his letters rather more attentively. They had met some charming people and this was very nice for Flora. They were mentioned often, but a little vaguely, and Mrs. Blackett knew he was sunning himself in more than a warmer climate. She knew, from her study of him, that he must be turning himself into a carefree holiday maker or a man who should have been an artist and had the attractive melancholy of frustration; into anything, in fact, productive of what he wanted from his companions. Mrs. Blackett smiled, a little surprised and not for the first time, that with this appetite for admiration he had not sought more opportunities for getting it, but she understood that too. It was better to imagine what he could have if he chose than to risk a failure which even he would find hard to explain away. And now he must be very happy. She was sure he would not put up with uncongenial companions for Flora's sake and it was odd to think that the duration of her own happiness probably depended on these people whom she had never seen.

'Don't you think,' Rhoda said, 'we'd better ask Cousin Piers if we can go there soon?'

'Yes, I do,' Mrs. Blackett said.

They had had several little expeditions and twice Sandra had joined the party. Between her and Rhoda, frankly on Sandra's part and cautiously on Rhoda's, there was a growing friendship.

'And didn't I tell you,' said Miss Spanner, 'that you ought to make a friend of her?'

'Yes, and perhaps that's why I didn't do it,' Sandra said sweetly. 'Besides, you can't make friends with people. They just happen.'

'Thank you for the information,' Miss Spanner said tartly. She was a little jealous. It was not likely that Rhoda would seek her out when there was a friendly contemporary in the house. She was wrong there, however. Rhoda was faithful and for her Miss Spanner remained a fount of wisdom and a fascinating character.

The doors of both houses were now left on the latch; Mrs. Blackett might find Sandra in the garden with Rhoda and Mrs. Fraser often found Rhoda in hers and working busily there, for though the garden was tidy it had never been anyone's special care and, delighted to have permission to do what she liked with it, Rhoda was only drawn from it by the chance of learning to ride Sandra's bicycle. Round and round the Square she wobbled, becoming a little steadier each time and trying not to smile too broadly at a pleasure hitherto denied her.

'Wouldn't he be vexed!' she exclaimed gleefully, as she alighted where her mother stood to watch, and at the sight of her happy face Mrs. Blackett had not the heart to reprove her for speaking so unceremoniously of her father. And Mrs. Blackett herself was doing what would have vexed him. She was sometimes discovered in the Frasers' house, listening to the broadcast news. With great diffidence at first she had accepted the invitation to come in when she chose, but it was impossible to remain awkward or shy with the Frasers. They seemed to take her presence for granted. This was another privilege she cherished and it would not last much longer.

'Yes,' she said, 'we can ask Cousin Piers if we can go there when he comes to-day.'

'And go to-morrow?'

'If we can.'

Rhoda, waiting for him, saw him draw up his car in front of the Frasers' door and mount the shallow steps. 'Bother!' she exclaimed. Judging from her own feelings, he would be there for some time, but she had her consolation. The postman who had just brought a letter from her father had also brought a picture postcard for her. Miss Spanner had been as good as her word. The picture was of a mountain with three peaks and though she gave this due attention, she was more interested in the message on the other side. 'Rather lean kine,' it said. 'Poor pasture. Back soon.' It was signed 'James' without the surname and that pleased her. It was nice of Miss Spanner to have remembered, nice of James to write, nice to be friends with Sandra and to ride a bicycle and, best of all, because these nicenesses depended on his absence, to have her father far away. 'I shan't even try to look pleased when he comes back,' she said to herself. She knew it would be no use. She had never been able to twist her features into the expression of anything she did not feel and she was to learn that this particular effort was not necessary.

Rosamund Fraser had seldom found it necessary to look happier than she was and her face, when she opened the door to Piers Lindsay, would have been instructive for Miss Spanner if she had not happened to miss this opportunity. A delicate moment in her stitching, her pathetic desire to make things pretty for Chloe and her pride in her own work had prevented her from leaping up at the sound of the brake and she did not arrive at the top of the staircase before Rosamund, putting out both hands, had said, 'Thank God!'

He took her hands but dropped them quickly, saying calmly, 'What's the matter?'

'Just starvation,' Rosamund said, speaking lightly but feeling a violent love for him because, almost too easily, he was able to keep their compact.

'Not yet,' said Miss Spanner, descending upon them remorselessly. 'Have you brought us some fresh news?'

'Only fresh vegetables,' he said. 'I've really come to look at the basement.'

'It's a flimsy old house,' Rosamund said.

'Yes, you'd be safer with me. I expect I could tuck you all away somewhere.'

'I'm not going to leave my property,' said Rosamund. 'You could go, Agnes. Sandra would chaperone you.'

244

'Me?' Miss Spanner said. 'I shall be on duty. Yes,' she said a little grandly. 'I offered my services to the city in the spring.'

'And I never thought of it!' Rosamund exclaimed and then, inevitably, she said. 'I wonder how they'll dress you up.'

'Even at a time like this!' Miss Spanner sighed and, not with tact, for she did not know it was necessary, but with the dignity befitting a potential heroine, she went into the sitting-room and left the others to go downstairs alone.

'She's a wonderful person,' Rosamund said.

'I think you'd be safest under the stairs,' he said. 'And there's the door in the garden room and the area door as well.'

'You think it's coming then?'

'No, but if it does start and they have any sense, they'll send their bombers over at once. There are three chances. They give way, we give way, or neither of us does. Which do you think's most likely?'

'The worst,' Rosamund said. 'And yet, when I think of the boys, I suppose that's what I ought to pray for.'

'They're not back yet?'

'They'll come if it's necessary,' she said in quick defence.

'Of course,' he said, following her into the garden room and standing with her in its doorway.

'What are you thinking of?' she asked.

'Things I haven't smelt or seen or heard for many a long day,' he said.

'Nasty noises? Nasty smells?'

'No, no, not those. All good. What Felix and James are getting now.' He was thinking of the dusty smell of heather and the smell of wet earth, the gurgling of hidden water, the tinkling of little stones dislodged by sheep, the scratching of nails on rock and plump cushions of damp moss under bare feet. Twenty-four years ago he had been called away from all that. 'And they may be scratching the very same places on the rocks that I scratched,' he said.

Further similarity of circumstances needed no more expression

245

than the look she gave him and though it was steady and there was no appeal in it, he found himself obliged to say, 'My poor love!' with all the tenderness she had been wanting.

She gave him a little nod of thanks. 'Oh, that's something to be going on with,' she said.

'You haven't heard from Fergus?'

'Just to tell me there's no hurry.'

Controlling his anger, he lifted and dropped his shoulders. This was no time for pressing his own claims. 'Any vegetables?' he asked.

'Ask Agnes. I'm going to stay here for a little while. I'm not going to spoil what you've just said with vegetables.'

'I could easily say a good deal more.'

'I know, but it was all there. Agnes will like the chance to talk to you.'

'I'm not particularly anxious to talk to her.'

'You needn't. Just grunt now and then. She'll interpret that according to her taste.'

He went away but he paused in the passage and she heard him knocking here and there, testing the strength of the defences they might need and she wondered whether Fergus had any thought for their safety — he would have none for his own — and again she pictured him as she had first seen him, his arrogance arrested by the sight of her, and she asked herself which of these two men she would have chosen if Piers had been marching there too. She knew it would have been Fergus and she would have been right then as she was sure she was right now. Yet, if Fergus had not left her, she would have done no more than consider Piers with the speculative eye of a woman who instinctively looked at men in their possible relation to herself and in another twenty years' time, she thought with amusement, if Piers ran away in his turn, she might find her true lover in some greybeard ready to fill the gap. But even if he tired of her, Piers would not run away. He would make the best of the situation, he would be kind and patient, but she would take good care that he need not exercise those qualities. Life could not be lived quite naturally with success. It had to be dealt with as an art and that was what she had had to learn.

She was roused from these reflections by the clatter of footsteps on the stairs. 'Have you come to do some gardening?' she asked as Rhoda appeared.

'No. To ask you to Cousin Piers's party.'

'Is he having one?'

'Yes. I really thought of it, but he's quite pleased. The day after to-morrow.'

'The day after to-morrow. That will be the sixteenth.'

'Yes. That will give George time to make the cakes.'

'Are you inviting the guests?'

'Well, Sandra wanted to come and I thought Miss Spanner would like it and he said I could ask everybody. Do come, Mrs. Fraser. You see, Mother's going to have a car. We couldn't let Cousin Piers fetch us and bring us back and if you come there won't be room for all of us.'

'Then I suppose I'd better stay at home.'

'But I don't want to go in the car. I want to fill it up with people and then Sandra and I can go on bicycles and I can hire one. Mother doesn't think I ride well enough, so I want a good excuse.'

'Then of course I must come.'

'And Chloe?'

'No, Chloe will be in Wellsborough.'

'Well, there'll be Mother and you and Mary and Miss Spanner. That's heaps. I wish we were going to-morrow, though.'

'It's nice to look forward to things.'

'When you're sure of them,' Rhoda said grimly and, returning to her mother, she said, 'We'll have to go, whatever happens. We can't give all that trouble for nothing.'

'No,' Mrs. Blackett said, and she read again the letter she had just received. 'We may begin our return journey in a day or two,' Mr. Blackett wrote. 'I want Flora to have a glimpse of Paris, so be prepared — as though you would not be! — for our arrival any day after you get this letter.'

'Of course you must go,' she said, 'but if I know when they are coming, I must be at home to meet them.'

Like Rhoda, she did not know how she was going to do it and, at that moment, in spite of the memories she had stored, memories of broad brown hills overlooking the Channel, the west front of the cathedral in the valley below, the worn stairway there like fallen leaves and the added sense of freedom the hills had given her, she almost wished Herbert had never gone away. She would have to try to get used to him all over again.

CHAPTER XXXVII

PEOPLE to whom travelling is a new adventure are much more conscious of the interest they expect to evoke on their return than of their own pleasure in reunion with those they left at home and Mr. Blackett and Flora, who for three weeks had been living in perfect comfort and safety in a friendly country, had the pleasant conviction that they looked different from the other passengers who alighted at Radstowe station and anticipated a sort of awed excitement when they arrived in the Square. Flora leant forward in the cab as they went through the streets, like a royal personage anxious to let the people see her and hoping some acquaintance would catch a glimpse of her, the hat she had bought in Paris and might as easily have found in Radstowe, and the unaccustomed touch of red on lips that did not need it. A faint aroma of jauntiness still hung about Mr. Blackett. He leant back as though he still lounged in a deck-chair and there were no newspaper placards trying to force themselves on his attention. He was not returning in a hurry. He had, in fact, outstayed the limit he had set himself and he had the satisfaction of knowing that wherever he had been and in whatever company, he had set an example either of a gay courage or of calm common sense. It had been a little hard on Bertha, perhaps, to stay away for so long, but he hoped for the

248

greater welcome and he felt that a slight flavour of resentment in it would not come amiss.

'I think it's a good thing we've come back,' said Flora who was not ignoring the placards.

'Oh yes,' Mr. Blackett said lightly, 'one feels quite glad to be back. There's no place like home,' he added, smilingly putting this remark into inverted commas.

'And nice to have a real English tea with bread and butter.'

They had reached the top of the Slope and turned from the main road into another where the trees, drooping over the pavement, showed here and there a yellow leaf and, almost at once, they were skirting the Green where children were playing on the grass and nursemaids, barricaded by perambulators, occupied the seats under the trees.

'It all looks extremely shabby,' said Mr. Blackett with disapproval as he sat up and straightened his coat.

'Yes, very,' Flora agreed, making sure her hat was at the right angle, for already the car was turning into the Square and, a moment later, it had stopped, but the front door was not opened, all the lower windows were shut and the house had an unmistakable appearance of being empty. The cab was driven away and the suitcases stood on the pavement while Mr. Blackett, after fumbling fruitlessly in his pockets, was forced to the indignity of ringing his own bell and feeling that every eye in the Square, and especially one eye, was delightedly on his back. He heard the buzzing of the bell within the house but no answering footsteps and he turned, stiff with anger, to see Flora mounting the area steps.

'That door's locked too,' she said, and they both glanced across the road where the windows on to the balcony were all wide open and a westerly breeze gently stirred the curtains. It was a difficult moment for Mr. Blackett. He could not give way to the rage urging him to stamp and shout and snap his fingers in a frenzy and after considering the possibility of forcing his study window and climbing in, he gave up that idea for fear of failure, yet outside the house, what seemly attitude could he adopt?

'Oh, isn't it horrid of them!' Flora cried. There were no younger sisters to notice the new hat, her air of experience and the little changes she had made in her appearance: there was no kind mother to ask if she were tired and other interested questions while she hastened to feed the travellers and Flora was deprived of the only pleasures she had foreseen in coming home. 'But perhaps something dreadful's happened,' she said, and as she anxiously made this suggestion she saw more of her father's red lips than he usually showed and much more of his teeth through which he assured her he had no doubt about that. 'Then what can we do?' Flora asked stupidly.

'Remove the suitcases,' Mr. Blackett said, and he picked up two of them and carried them down the area steps. 'And as there is nowhere else to sit, I shall sit here,' he announced.

'I suppose,' said Flora, realizing that the dreadful happening was simply the family's absence, 'I suppose we really ought to have sent a telegram.'

'Nonsense!' Mr. Blackett said sharply.

'Well,' said Flora, after taking a critical look at him, 'how would it be — you wouldn't mind would you — if I went across to the Frasers? They must know something I should think.'

'You can do as you like about that,' said Mr. Blackett, taking a seat on the more solid of the suitcases.

In that sunken retreat he was out of eyeshot and anyone who had seen his discomfiture could enjoy it no longer, but he was acutely conscious of what his appearance must be, seated on the shallow suitcase, his knees almost touching his chin, his head level with a notice written in Bertha's hand and pinned to the door, informing the baker no bread was needed. This notice added to his disgust. Where was Connie? Surely she had had holiday enough. Only a milk jug with a plate on it would have been more vulgar than this correspondence with the baker and he felt passionately that he, of all people, should be spared this kind of thing and he knew his acquaintance of the last week or two would be horrified, perhaps disillusioned, if she could see him now.

He stood up at the sound of footsteps, but they were only those of Flora who came to tell him she could get no answer at the Frasers' house. 'But I'm sure we could get through here,' she said, indicating the window which did its best to lighten Connie's cavern; but Mr. Blackett was determined to suffer. He sat down again. He had reached the point when the longer he was kept outside the house the better he would be pleased.

'Then we might as well go and have tea somewhere,' Flora suggested.

'And leave the luggage?'

'We needn't go together.'

Mr. Blackett's reply was to take a book from the unoccupied suitcase and arrange his expression into one suitable for the perusal of good literature, but he did not turn a page. He was, in fact, almost giddy with the anger he outwardly controlled. He had pictured Bertha in a state of excited anticipation, preventing her from leaving the house lest, absent on the shortest of errands, she might miss the happy moment of his arrival, and she had gone, they had all gone, leaving a message for the baker and none for him though, indeed, that would have been an added insult. It would have acknowledged the likelihood of his return and now it was just possible to believe that his last letter had not been received. But whither and why, Mr. Blackett asked the page he was not reading, had they all disappeared? It was quite impossible for him to imagine any attraction greater than waiting for him in the home he had provided and, to do Bertha justice, that had hitherto seemed to content her well enough. Yet this was the day she had chosen for leaving it and he was obliged to sit, cramped, outside the kitchen door, in order to conceal his humiliation and to shame her when she appeared. And when would that be? Already, though only a few minutes had passed, he foresaw a limit to his endurance and Mr. Blackett told himself with conviction that, at any other time, this desertion could have been forgiven, but now, with the whole world holding its breath — and for his own purposes he momentarily admitted that it might well do so — Bertha was revealing a heartlessness and a frivolity which deeply pained him. A natural anxiety for him and Flora ought to have kept her at home: a fear of impending catastrophe ought to have made pleasure seeking impossible. And the companion of his travels seemed to have deserted him too. Wondering what Flora was doing, Mr. Blackett raised himself hastily and his grey felt hat came into somewhat sharp contact with the underside of the front-door steps. On these Flora had disposed herself with what she felt was a continental out-of-doors ease and she was fortunate in her position for, just as Mr. Blackett knocked his head and almost as soon as he heard a heavy tramp of feet, two young men appeared on the Frasers' side of the Square, marching in step with packs on their backs. Nothing could have been better than to be discovered there, in her new hat, with a new air of unconventionality and just returned from the possible imminence of danger, and yet, for a moment, Flora forgot herself and the impression she hoped to make. She forgot that one of these young men was James with whom she had fancied herself in love and the other was Felix who, like every young man she saw, might fall in love with her. She saw them as symbols of millions of other young men, keeping step and carrying packs, and in spite of all her father's assurances, she saw them as sacrifices to the folly and wickedness of mankind and her face was as grave as theirs when, having no hats to remove, they lifted their hands in greeting and turned to their own door, then, as it did not open, felt vaguely, like Mr. Blackett, in their pockets.

'We're locked out too,' Flora said, approaching laughingly.

'We shan't be locked out for long,' said James and, stepping back, both he and Felix traced the route to the balcony as their father had done long ago, but he had traced it with the eyes of love; these two saw it with eyes which hereafter would never look at a rock or a quarry without planning how to reach the top of it; even a distant window ledge would inspire them to speculation. They were in possession of a new craft and, resigning this chance of practising it, Felix said regretfully, 'The area door's sure to be unlocked.'

It was not locked and they disappeared, but Flora had hardly time to feel aggrieved at being left thus unceremoniously on the pavement before Felix, and she was glad it was Felix, returned to ask whether he could do anything to help her.

'At least you can come and sit in our house,' he said, 'and we're going to have some tea.'

'I'm dying for tea,' Flora said, her head dropped pathetically sideways. 'We've just come home. From France,' she added.

Ignoring this interesting remark, Felix glanced across the road where Mr. Blackett's head and shoulders had an extraordinary effect of being detached from the rest of his body. What could be seen of him might have been a life-size, painted bust, his beard all the blacker for the red spots on his cheeks and, in this colour and lack of animation, Flora suddenly recognized a likeness to one of those plaster saints she had seen in the churches in France. It seemed impossible that it could speak, but Felix optimistically approached it with an offer of hospitality. Flora heard and admired his pleasant, courteous tones and waited, without much anxiety, for her father's reply. He had to choose between being pinned in that area for an indefinite time and accepting a favour from a member of a family he had always disparaged, between an absurd and an inconsistent situation. She was almost sorry for him, though she knew he was able to explain any action to what ought to be other people's satisfaction. She had learnt a good deal about him, in these past weeks and, except that he held the purse strings, she knew he was not really much more formidable than one of the plaster saints. But it immediately appeared that he was a more genial man in France than he was in Upper Radstowe and he found a way out of his difficulty by accepting hospitality for the suitcases and taking Flora out to tea.

'I wish we hadn't come back,' Flora said viciously.

'Not much of a welcome, certainly,' Mr. Blackett agreed.

But Flora could not have asked for a better one. It had been spoilt by her father who had been so pleasant with strangers and could hardly be civil to his neighbours, who had adopted the manner of a person without prejudices, delighted to let his daughter enjoy the company of a charming woman's son while he enjoyed the company of the charming woman, but treating the Frasers as though they had offended him unforgivably. And they were much more attractive than the charming woman's son, who had been at no pains to hide his preference for being alone with his sketch book. He had been duller than James who had at least mitigated the boredom of his farming talk with an occasional attention until, so she had taught herself to explain things, she had decided that these little oases occurred too rarely in the desert to make the journey bearable. She had always admired Felix more, she told herself, and she glanced at her father with annoyance as she walked beside him and thought his very face had changed. It was as tightly shut as his own front door.

'I don't think this climate suits you,' she said. 'You don't look nearly as happy as you did in France.'

'It was of the greatest importance to seem cheerful there,' he said.

'Were you pretending all the time?' she asked with admiring surprise, and without waiting for an answer she stopped to buy a newspaper outside the teashop and it struck her as curious and absurd that in his company, a few weeks ago, she would never have acted with this mild independence, nor would she have heard with indifference his scornful certainty that she was unlikely to read the truth.

'But if we went back at six o'clock,' she said, 'I expect the Frasers would let us listen to the news.'

'I have no desire to hear it and still less to hear it in their house,' Mr. Blackett said.

'Oh well,' said Flora, 'I suppose it doesn't matter so very much to you. Not like last time when you might have had to fight. You were lucky, weren't you?'

'I don't know whether it's lucky to do one's duty,' Mr. Blackett said severely.

'Lucky if the duty happens to be nice though,' she said, speaking in all innocence for, in his place she would have acted

254

in the same way. 'And horrible,' she said, 'to get all messed up like Cousin Piers.'

'You need not waste any pity on him,' said Mr. Blackett, pushing aside his plate and practising scales on the table cloth.

'I don't,' said Flora, smiling sweetly at him. She had made him even crosser than he was before and it served him right.

CHAPTER XXXVIII

'DRIVE slowly,' Mrs. Blackett said.

She was alone for a moment beside the car which had crunched up Piers Lindsay's rough bit of road to take the party home and, as she spoke, her lips trembled and she had to shut her eyes to keep back her tears as she realized the futility of that command. Throughout the afternoon, since their arrival at the cottage, she had been in this emotional state, after nearly twenty years of rigid self-control. Rosamund was not the only person who could read Lindsay's face and though what Mrs. Blackett saw was a new page to her and it was turned immediately, it was quite legible for an instant to a woman who might have received that message, or something like it, long ago and knew that, soon now, she would read in Herbert's face, his bland certainty of his right to her person and his assumption that where his mind went hers would be sure to follow. And when she looked back at that afternoon which was to have been a last snatched happiness under the double threat of war and a returning husband, she could not remember whether, actually, the sun had shone or clouds had lowered: she supposed she had behaved like a reasonable being but she had not felt like one. She had not been roused to jealousy of Mrs. Fraser for evoking that swift look; it was too late to want it for herself; she knew enough to doubt whether it meant happiness for anyone. What it had done for her was to light into emotion the dead fuse of unhappiness which had twisted itself round all her thoughts and many of her actions and, with that coil now hot inside her, the rest of the world seemed dark and the people round her unreal. She was like a person who had received and must not acknowledge a shock which had made her slightly light-headed, and now, standing beside the car which was to carry her into the endless future, she said, 'Drive slowly,' and could have wept at the necessity for such an order and the folly of it.

The driver did not reply to that remark. He said gloomily, 'The King's back in London. Yes. And I've got sons.'

She looked at him then, and instead of a sort of Charon, ferrying her from one world to another, she saw an elderly man with more to lose than she had, whose possible sufferings for and through his children made her own private trouble insignificant, no worse than being forced to eat distasteful food and having to discipline herself to stomach it.

'Yes, three sons,' he said.

'I have no sons,' she confessed humbly, but he was not interested in her lack of them.

'I reckon we're going to reap what we've sowed,' he said, 'and a nasty crop it'll be, war or no war.' Suddenly he seemed to recollect his duties. 'Yes, I'll drive slowly, Mum,' he said.

'No, no,' she said. 'It doesn't matter, but don't get too far ahead of the bicycles.'

Thus it happened that Mr. Blackett, who had recovered the suitcases and resumed his seat, popped up at the sound of an approaching car and saw his second daughter, her skirt well above her knees, pedalling furiously behind it and nearly beating it at the post with a little shout of triumph. Then she saw him, saw Flora sitting on the doorstep and, tumbling from her bicycle, she stared at him in frank dismay and he would have remained accusingly immobile if Mary, first out of the car, had not saved the situation from Mrs. Fraser's mocking glance and Miss Spanner's sharp one, by throwing her arms round his neck, instinctively playing the part of her father's pet.

'Oh Herbert, have you been waiting long? Couldn't you get

in? How unfortunate!' Mrs. Blackett said calmly, and turned from him to pay the driver.

'That will do, that will do,' Mr. Blackett said indulgently loosening Mary's grasp but glad his face had been momentarily hidden by this onslaught. He managed to remove his hat, to smile awkwardly at his wife's unsuitable companions and to reply to Mrs. Fraser's inquiries about the Channel crossing, before she was diverted by the appearance of her sons and hastened towards them.

'I'd give a good deal,' said Miss Spanner a little later, 'to be inside that house for the rest of the evening. But still,' she was thankful for small mercies, 'I call it a very good finish to the afternoon. And a dull time I should have had of it if it hadn't been for George. I had a good talk with him while you were looking at the cows.'

'You mean you asked him a lot of questions.'

'No,' Miss Spanner said with candour. 'I saw at once he was the kind of man who would know how to dodge them, but with more Georges in the country we shouldn't be in this mess now. As if,' she said, giving her nose a specially violent knock, 'this Noah's ark business is going to get us out of it. It's childish. Poor old Noah had to get his information somehow, I suppose, but we know well enough the flood's rising all the time and it's ridiculous, it's shameful, to pretend we're going to do any good by flapping about in the air and politely asking those villains to turn the taps off. And if that man comes back with the dove's message we'll know he has been hoaxed, we'll know it's an artificial olive leaf in his beak. I shall, anyhow. So will George, so will you, so will everybody who hasn't shut their eyes and stuffed up their ears and been full of brotherly love and stupidity for the Lord knows how long. I can't understand it!' Miss Spanner exclaimed. 'All this trust in the false and tenderness for the ruthless. Why? We'll believe any lies those crafty devils tell and laugh at the people who know the truth — or say it's they who are wicked. Upon my word, it's just as though we've been drugged. And why don't you say something?' she asked sharply.

'You're saying it for me,' Rosamund replied. 'You know that, and saying it very well.'

'Very well!' Miss Spanner echoed derisively. 'I haven't the proper language at my command.'

'And you'd better save up what you've got. You'll need it. I'm frightened, Agnes. Of being ashamed,' she added.

'You needn't explain. And I suppose you didn't get a chance of talking to Mr. Lindsay?' Miss Spanner asked artfully, for there was no knowing what had happened while she was occupied with the satisfactory George.

'That wasn't necessary either,' Rosamund replied.

'Oh, you know what he thinks, do you?'

'Yes, I know what he thinks,' Rosamund said, and in her voice there was a quietly possessive note she did not trouble to control, the one she had been repressing all that afternoon which for her, as for Mrs. Blackett, had been a strange one and not quite real, overhung by a great anxiety and yet fretted by little jealousies, little desires, of which she had not thought herself capable, to assert her claims. After that first look Lindsay did not know he gave her — a momentary flash of contentment — she received, quite rightly, no more attention than any other of his guests. She would have been disappointed if he had behaved less than perfectly and it was the very perfection of his behaviour which had made her childishly eager to acknowledge him as her own.

'And I suppose,' said Miss Spanner, 'you flatter yourself you know what the boys think too.'

'Pretty well.'

'And Fergus?'

'Oh yes, I know all about him.'

'Remarkable insight into the masculine mind,' Miss Spanner said tartly, 'but I'm afraid we'll have to wait till nine o'clock to get any more news of Noah.'

'Yes, I can't help you there,' Rosamund said, 'except to be sure there are plenty of good intentions, concrete blocks of them.'

Before nine o'clock, Paul, sunburnt and excited, had arrived unexpectedly. The young schoolmaster had considered it his duty to be nearer home and Paul, loudly applauding his brothers' return, wanted to know what they meant to do.

'Shut you up,' Felix said, and left the house with a bang of the front door. A few yards away from it, he met Chloe without her lover. Each said 'Hullo,' to the other, hesitated for half a minute, silently, with lifted eyebrows and raised shoulders, expressed all that was necessary and passed on and Flora, at her bedroom window, pausing in her unpacking and envying Chloe an opportunity that meant nothing to her, thought it unnatural that this brother and sister should not linger for a few words after a separation. Chloe and Felix, however, like all the other members of their family, could afford this apparent indifference. It came a little hard on Sandra but she had adapted herself to the independence and reserve and unspoken loyalty of her elders and though she was surprised to see Chloe arrive alone, she knew better than to ask a question.

'All the boys have come home,' she said.

'Yes, I saw Felix just now,' Chloe replied calmly and went upstairs.

Wondering at herself, she stopped outside Miss Spanner's door. Queer sounds came from within but her knock was heard and she entered to find Miss Spanner on the floor beside her wireless set.

'I never took the Tower of Babel seriously before,' she said, 'but it's here, right enough. They're jabbering in every language in Europe. Why couldn't they have decided to speak English and have done with it?'

Chloe's light, pretty laughter induced Miss Spanner to shut off these alien, uglier sounds. 'What have you done with your young man?' she inquired.

'I'm not sure,' Chloe said. 'Miss Spanner, if you were a girl —'

'Now it's no good starting like that,' Miss Spanner warned her. 'I never was a girl — not what you'd call one. I was born a plain spinster, somewhere about thirty years of age.'

'And never in love?' Chloe ventured to say.

'I was on the brink once, but cowardice saved me. Not mine.

His. And I've lived to thank God for it. I was unhappy at the time but I've seen his children and as his wife's a much better looking woman than I am, goodness knows what he and I would have produced. The queer thing about life, one of the queer things, is the way good and bad change places.'

'Is it?' Chloe asked. 'Then what can we do about it?'

'Nothing,' said Miss Spanner. 'Take your chance. Run your risks. And whether you've been wise or foolish you'll find out later.'

'Too late,' Chloe said.

'That can't be helped. And another queer thing,' said Miss Spanner who shared Chloe's surprise and pleasure in this sudden intimacy, 'is that though life's a tricky business, it's a mistake to be too pernickety with it. Use a broad brush and slap on the colours now and then.'

'Yes,' said Chloe, 'I think you are quite right. So why don't you?'

'Me?' said Miss Spanner. 'I'm only a spectator.'

'But other people see you,' Chloe said, looking thoughtfully at this figure on the floor in a crumpled, dingy, brown dress who, but for her face which was unusually animated, was rather like a collapsed and neglected scarecrow. In good, unusual clothes, her hair arranged with calculated severity and her lips brightly coloured, she would have had a distinction of her own and Chloe longed to set to work on her.

'And perhaps big earrings,' she said aloud.

'So that's why you're staring at me! That's what you're thinking about!' Miss Spanner exclaimed. 'You're just like your mother. Here's the world going to rack and ruin and you're bothering about clothes!'

'Second nature,' Chloe said. 'I can't help it.'

'And I thought you were taking an intelligent interest in my remarks.'

'I was,' Chloe said. 'I came on purpose to get them.'

'Did you indeed?' said Miss Spanner, trying not to sound mollified and flattered. 'What's the matter?'

'We've had a quarrel. At least I have. My young man doesn't quarrel. He just listens patiently. So stupid! If he had any sense he'd get angry too. I'm not sure that I'm going to enjoy living with a man like that.'

'Oh, if it's enjoyment you're after!' Miss Spanner said.

'What else? And there are lots of different kinds. Being unhappy together might be a sort of pleasure.'

'So you're prepared for that?'

'Of course.'

'Then what's the trouble?'

'He thinks we'd better be unhappy without each other, because of the situation, if you please!' Chloe said in delicately mocking tones. 'Because we don't know what's going to happen. Who ever does? Who cares? He's so damned cautious and conscientious and he shouldn't be.'

'And he won't be,' Miss Spanner prophesied. Beauty like Chloe's would have inspired that thin-necked deacon to a gay defiance of old Mr. Spanner.

'But he has been, already. He ought to have said, "Let's be married to-morrow," and now I don't think I'm going to marry him at all.'

'Then,' said Miss Spanner slowly and praying for guidance, 'you're not willing to take risks, either. There are all sorts you know!'

'Perhaps,' Chloe said. 'I hadn't thought of it like that.'

'And if it's perfection you're after, you may as well realize that you'll never get it, but I think you're getting pretty near.'

'Do you? So do I, really, but I was vexed. Yes, perhaps I ought to take my kind of risk, too. It's not so exciting, though!'

'It's much more important. It will keep you busy for a lifetime.'

'Rather fun,' Chloe admitted. 'What a good thing I came to you! I had a feeling you'd put me right. Thank you, Miss Spanner, dear. But mind, it's a secret.' She bent down to kiss her and left her with a warm and fragrant sense of triumph.

CHAPTER XXXIX

THE children's mother had to appear as faultless in the children's eyes as he could help to make her. That had been the principle on which Mr. Blackett had always acted, any other would have been a reflection on his own judgment, and difficult as it was not to show his displeasure on this occasion, he made an effort and he was annoyed to find that this was the less necessary because Bertha was behaving with quite an unusual urbanity and ease. She had offered no apology and expressed no regret for her absence and, but for Mary, who had her uses, he would not have known, for he could not ask, where his family had been and why Bertha had gone to the expense of a hired car. He reserved his questions and criticisms and the matter of Rhoda's bicycle to be dealt with, for a more private hour. He listened with what apparent interest he could summon to Mary's account of their various outings and Cousin Piers's farm and Mrs. Blackett listened with real interest to all Flora had to tell. Rhoda was the skeleton at the feast. She was miserable and she could not pretend to be anything else. Here they all were, having one of their prim meals again instead of their picnics in the kitchen or the garden and she knew that the cause of her father's lack of instructive comments on his holiday was the seething annoyance he tried to hide. She made only one remark throughout the meal. Roused to unbearable irritation by Flora's little affectations and superior air, she said scornfully, 'Anybody'd think you'd been at least as far as the North Pole.'

'There's no need for jealousy, Rhoda,' her father told her. He knew how to vex her. 'It will be your turn next.'

'I'm afraid that may be a long time away,' Mrs. Blackett said. 'Next year, if all goes well.'

'But that's so unlikely,' she replied, quietly taking the liberty of having an opinion.

Mr. Blackett merely dropped his smooth eyelids and kept them dropped. His wife's statement, taken in any sense, was not one of which he could approve, nor would he discuss it at the moment, but he said, offering his words with modesty, 'I have a strong belief in the efficacy of good thoughts,' and he raised his eyelids, to think how very ordinary his wife looked, though comely in a humdrum way, and how unappreciative she was, mutely inviting Mary to a second helping of pudding while he spoke, and he remembered the thin, elegant creature, so remote from any connection with puddings, to whom he could certainly not have uttered his last words — they would not have been suitable — but who understood a side of him unknown to Bertha, the important side which had been repressed by circumstances and duty and he was amazed at his own steady business and domestic achievements and resentful against those who had made them necessary and took them for granted. The other woman had expressed her surprised admiration. Physically indolent or delicate or perhaps both, her mind had been very alert and it had been exhilarating and, at first, a little shocking, to look at her, relaxed in her chair, not beautiful but exquisite, consciously decorative from head to foot, and hear her lazy voice discussing morals and religion as well as books and pictures with much greater licence than he had ever allowed himself in his thoughts. But he would not be behindhand with her. He hurried after her and caught her up and roamed with her freely, even where there was a suggestion of trespass. She had hinted at an unfortunate marriage; he was significantly reserved about his own, for a woman can say things which a man must not. He knew he would never see her again. Far back in his mind there lurked a dreadful suspicion that he might have seen less of her if he had not been the only available man who was possible as a companion, but she had given him a standard by which Bertha was definitely dull and Mrs. Fraser, vital and provocative as she was, seemed almost coarse. Minute by minute, however, he knew he was returning and must return to the Upper Radstowe edition of Herbert Blackett who had a strong moral sense and strict views of propriety for his family and, as an example to it, for himself. He could no longer be the essential artist, susceptible to all forms of beauty and restricted by no conventions. He was a middle-aged man in the paper trade with a wife and three daughters to guide and provide for and an unacknowledged anxiety about the future in the just possible folly of taking up another country's quarrel. In such lamentable circumstances, he was anxious, too, about his own position as a false prophet. It might have been wiser to be less positive but things had become more critical than he had ever expected and his mind had always been attuned to those of the country's leaders, he had approved so heartily of all they had done and left undone during the past years that he had felt sure he was safe with them, and in his household he could not bring himself to speak without authority. It obviously did not do to speak in other tones. This had just been proved by Bertha's lack of attention to his last words, uttered with what he thought would be impressive quietness. He did not speak again and when he retired to his study, with an eye for any disorder and dust in it, nobody and no coffee followed him.

There was a little dust, as he found by running a finger across a shelf, but there was no disorder. Everything was exactly as he had left it and the room and his books were a solace to him; the emptiness of the Square and no more than the usual sounds of distant traffic were like a promise of peace. It was difficult to believe that, elsewhere, there was agitation, that messages were being buzzed across the world, that countless people anxiously awaited news. There seemed to be no reason why he should not have his coffee and he left his study to discover the cause of this delay. He heard the clatter of china and cutlery from the basement where Rhoda and Mary were washing up and, overhead, footsteps were going to and fro, drawers were opened and shut, furniture pushed here and there.

'What are you doing, Bertha?' he inquired when he met her on the landing.

'Taking away the things I had left in Flora's room,' she said, 'and making up your bed.'

'My bed?'

'The big one,' she said.

'You haven't been sleeping in it?'

'Oh no,' Mrs. Blackett said.

'Why not?'

'I couldn't. I didn't want to,' she replied and, without looking at him, she hurried past him.

He was touched, ashamed of his late disloyalty. As a wife, Bertha had the qualities he most desired in one and this shyness which made her perennially a girl had a value he knew he would not find elsewhere, it was a tribute no one else could pay him, not Mrs. Fraser whose beauty and gaiety teased him, nor his late sophisticated companion who had put him on his mettle and enlarged his vision of himself. So, smiling a little slyly, her neglect and unpreparedness forgiven, he followed her into the bedroom, but there his eagerness was checked. The bed was not in its usual position. It now faced the windows instead of standing against the wall, an arrangement which did not suit him, and Mrs. Blackett was plumping up the pillows instead of waiting modestly for the embrace he had intended for her. Nevertheless, he did not wish to lose his moment and he said amicably enough, 'Why thus?'

'For a change,' she said.

'The very last thing I wanted!' he said, and took a step towards her but, with a practised hand, she flung the sheet across the bed and the little breeze it made, her concentration and the unagitated deftness of her movements cooled his ardour. She might have been a landlady preparing for an unexpected and not too welcome lodger.

'Surely all this,' he said, 'might have been done before.'

'It will be done in time,' she said, and she wanted to add, 'It will be done all too soon!' She wanted to cry out her detestation of sharing that bed with him, of any sort of contact with him. She saw, in a serious quarrel, what would be, at least, a temporary escape; she felt she was losing her grip on herself and that power of getting an amused satisfaction from deceiving him which had supported her for so long. These last weeks had put her badly out of practice and while, meticulously, she spread the blankets, she knew she must recover her skill. What else could she do? Her plight was that of many other women ill-mated. She had three children and she had no money, but she remembered that elderly, patient man saying quietly, 'And I've got sons,' and as she looked up Mr. Blackett saw an indefinable change in her face. It had been placid as it always was but stiffer, and it had softened now that her immediate little task was done. He was touched that she should make so serious a matter of it and his tenderness returned.

'Bertha,' he said, his arms round her at last, 'you're pleased to see me?'

'You didn't seem very pleased yourself,' she said.

'No. I was disappointed. I was, I must confess, a little hurt. And then, I was astonished to see you arriving with the Frasers, and in a car. I was astonished and not pleased to see Rhoda on a bicycle. I hope,' he added in sudden alarm, 'you haven't bought it for her.'

'I haven't, though it wouldn't have cost nearly as much as Flora's holiday.'

'But you see,' Mr. Blackett said gently, 'I happen to disapprove of bicycle riding for girls. However, we need not discuss all that to-night. We mustn't quarrel to-night. But we have never quarrelled yet, have we?'

Mrs. Blackett did not answer. She went on with her own thoughts. There were those boys, too, across the road and, thinking of them, tall and tanned and as lithe as tigers, she was able to ignore the unpleasant boredom of being fondled by Mr. Blackett. It was petty to care what happened to her own body when lovely young ones like theirs were threatened, yet it was better that the ugliest of physical disasters should overtake them than that their minds should be indifferent or poisoned or imprisoned. The choice had to be made between temporary material ease and permanent spiritual evil. So Mrs. Blackett thought while her husband became aware of something new in her reception of his caresses. She did not try to escape them, she did not accept them with her charming shyness; she was simply allowing them to happen.

'What is the matter with you?' he asked irritably. It was the first time he had ever come so near acknowledging defeat from her.

Rocking slightly as he let go, then standing still where he had left her, she said, 'I was thinking.'

'There is a time for everything.'

'Yes, that's why I was doing it,' she said.

'And a time, if I may remind you, for my coffee,' he said.

And it was time for something else, as Rhoda's voice warned her from the stairs. 'Are you coming? It's nearly nine o'clock,' she called.

'No, I'm not coming to-night,' Mrs. Blackett replied. She went on to the landing and said with a half-mischievous look which Rhoda could interpret as she liked, 'I've forgotten to make your father's coffee.'

Rhoda immediately responded with a grimace. 'But it's very important to-night,' she said.

'I know, but there's nothing I can do about it, is there? And I do know how to make coffee!'

'Well, I can go, can't I?'

'Of course.'

'But mind you don't tell Flora.'

'Go quickly,' Mrs. Blackett said, and she stood, like a sentry, at the head of the stairs until Rhoda was safely away.

Mr. Blackett, darting to the window as the front door was shut, was in time to see his daughter entering the Frasers' house without ceremony. It was too late to call her back and Mrs. Blackett did not give him an opportunity for reproach. With her purpose achieved, she went down to the kitchen. She had come to the conclusion that with Rhoda it was absurd, because it was useless, to present a united parental front, nor was it salutary for Mr. Blackett to believe in its existence and when he followed her into the cavern he rarely entered she said at once, 'Rhoda will bring back the news. I expect you saw her go across the road.'

'Why should you expect that?'

'Because so little escapes you,' she said sweetly, and she told herself that she had only to fool this man to the top of his bent and she could do what she liked with him except make him into the kind of man she wanted. For less than that, the price would be too heavy. She would never be able to change the contents of his mind of which self was the chief ingredient and already her own mind was warped enough by her passive deception of him. She would have been a better woman, she thought, if her behaviour had seemed worse and perhaps — this was an altogether new idea and a disturbing one — he would have been a better man, and, all at once, she felt deeply sorry for him in his unconscious isolation. There was no one in the world, except himself, who really cared for him, there were very few who cared for her. They had each lived in a mean little world, his of self-satisfaction, hers of pandering to it for her own amusement and hers, she feared, was the meaner. Twenty years ago they might have helped each other but he did not know he needed help and she was too young, too wretched to give it, too sure he would not understand her if she asked for it, and here they were, looking at each other across the kitchen table, complete strangers bound to each other for life. She was nothing to him, really, but a competent housekeeper and a licensed release for a highly sensual nature and if, at this moment, he had crumbled into a little heap of dust, easily disposed of, she would have issued from the confinement of a cell into endlessly open country. And this honestly cruel thought softened her heart a little until he hardened it again by running his tongue swiftly across his upper lip and telling her that he did not like this running to and fro between the houses, that Mrs. Fraser was not a suitable acquaintance for her or for his daughters.

'No,' Mrs. Blackett agreed, 'I often wonder why she bothers to be so kind and friendly — your coffee's ready — because really she must think we are all very dull.'

'Dull!' Mr. Blackett repeated.

'Stodgy,' said Mrs. Blackett unexpectedly. 'You see,' she added innocently, 'she doesn't know you very well.'

'No indeed,' he said. 'I have taken, I have had to take, some care to prevent it. That is the kind of woman she is.'

'The kind you find so attractive,' Mrs. Blackett said quietly.

CHAPTER XL

THE room seemed to be full of people when Rhoda entered it and all the fuller because two of the seated figures, those of James and Paul, rose at once and embarrassed her a little by an attention she had seldom had the chance to receive. She liked it, however, and other signs of welcome, especially Miss Spanner's sharp nod and the friendly grin of James, but almost at once Big Ben began to strike and everyone fell silent. James, motioning Rhoda to the chair he had left, stood against the mantelpiece, his head bent attentively, his profile towards her. All the Frasers were there except Felix, and Rhoda thought, not for the first time, that here, too, a house without a father in it was a very pleasant place and for a little while she hardly heard what the impersonal voice was saying. She was more interested in seeing how the people in this room were listening to it. Miss Spanner had dropped her darning. She looked rather fierce, as though she had a grudge against the distant speaker; Mrs. Fraser and Chloe sewed steadily; Sandra watched their faces and Paul watched James, in his view the most important person present, the one who might be actively and, to Paul, enviably concerned in what was going to happen. And Rhoda, when she looked at James, was surprised to find herself unhappy. As she saw him standing there he seemed to her to have grown much older, to have changed into a man who would not want the friendship of a schoolgirl or bother to tell her all the things she longed to know about the farm. She felt unhappier still when, at the end of the news he, like the others, said nothing and then went out of the room. He would not have done that if she had been a grown-up visitor. He would have waited for her to go, perhaps he would have seen her safely across the road instead of leaving Sandra to watch her from the doorstep. She was hurt but she did not blame him. He could not be expected to think about her at a time like this and she had never wanted him to think about her in what she would have called a silly way, nor had there been anything of that kind in her thoughts of him, yet now, the distance she saw widening between them, the graveness of his manner as he listened, his easy, firm pose against the mantelpiece, gave him, hardly consciously to herself, the charm, the perfection of the unattainable.

She crossed the road with the slowness of her disappointment yet she was too quick to hear Sandra calling her to come back.

'Where's Rhoda?' James had said. 'I wanted to show her some photographs.'

Then Sandra had called but Rhoda had already, rather sadly, shut the area door.

'She can see them to-morrow,' James said. 'Can you get her across here? I don't want to meet the old man or Flora.'

'Yes. We're rather friends. She's nice but,' Sandra said regretfully, 'not pretty.'

'If she were pretty she wouldn't be so nice.'

'Why? Chloe's lovely!'

But niceness for James at this stage did not involve any particular virtues except interest in what interested him. 'Oh, Chloe's not bad,' he agreed, and went back to the sitting-room to hear Miss Spanner saying, 'As far as I remember, there's no mention of gulls in the story of Noah's Ark.'

'It couldn't mention all the animals,' said Paul. 'Far too many, but there were two of every kind so there must have been two gulls.'

'H'm,' said Miss Spanner, 'I wonder how many there are in this ark of ours.'

'Ark?'

'Island,' said Miss Spanner.

'Must be millions,' said Paul.

'I believe you,' said Miss Spanner.

'I didn't know you were interested in birds,' James said.

'Only in certain kinds.'

'Buzzards any good to you? We saw them in the mountains.'

'No, I don't specialize in those,' she said.

'Agnes is talking in riddles,' Rosamund said. 'She hardly knows a sparrow when she sees one.'

'But I do know a gull.'

'Heaps of them on the river,' Paul said. He was puzzled and a little uneasy. Longing to talk about the news, instead of, so inappropriately, about birds, to ask questions and offer opinions, hopeful that something really exciting was going to happen and that it would last long enough for him to have a share in it, he had a feeling that his remarks would not be welcomed and might be considered in bad taste and with the arrival of Felix at that moment he decided on discretion and said good night.

'And have a bath,' Felix said. 'You must be filthy.'

'Not as filthy as you'll be soon,' Paul said, making for the stairs.

'And Paul's baths are my business,' Rosamund said. 'You never speak to the boy without snubbing him and I won't have it.'

'I must, I suppose, have caught the prevalent germ at some time,' Felix said suavely.

Chloe looked at him angrily. He was breaking the family convention of keeping a decent silence about their father and Sandra, of course, had recognized the allusion. It was painful to see how quickly her thin little face could sharpen, but part of Chloe's anger came of her disappointment that it was Felix who had opened the front door and not the man for whom she had been listening.

'Oh, come and have a drink,' James said.

'Thanks. I've had several already.'

'Has he, do you think?' Rosamund asked when he had gone into his bedroom across the passage.

'Probably. Not too many, though. He's all right.'

'All right! I call it all wrong,' Miss Spanner said.

'And now,' said James, 'you're going to tell us about your

271

great-uncle who shot the tiger and wouldn't have had a hand steady enough if he'd ever indulged in alcohol. You were going to tell us that, weren't you, Miss Spanner?'

'I did think of mentioning it,' she admitted.

'But I'll bet you anything he had a celebration that night.'

'What's the good of betting about something we'll never know?' Miss Spanner said and covered up this lapse in loyalty by saying hastily, 'Besides, I don't bet. There was never any betting in my family and never any drinking, not so much as a wine glass in the house,' and she looked at Rosamund and waited in vain for one of her usual retorts, but she was not listening. She was kneeling in front of the fireplace and lighting the wood laid ready in the hearth and Miss Spanner ostentatiously looked at the clock. Chloe looked at it too, but for a different reason.

'Just as we're all going to bed,' Miss Spanner remarked.

'And in your house you never had a fire from the end of April till the beginning of October, did you, Miss Spanner?' Sandra said.

'Never,' she replied. 'It was the eleventh or twelfth or thirteenth commandment, I forget which, we had so many extra ones.'

'I'm cold,' Rosamund said.

'You don't wear enough underclothing,' said Miss Spanner.

'Down my back,' Rosamund said, and turned to let the growing warmth play on it.

'I'll make some tea,' Sandra said, 'and we'll all sit round the fire. That would be nice, wouldn't it?'

'Yes,' Chloe said, 'and I'll come and help you.' She felt, all at once, that it would be comforting to be alone with Sandra. 'I'm rather cold too,' she said.

'Are you? Then go back. You shouldn't be in this basement,' Sandra said anxiously.

That was the worst of Sandra. It was impossible to hint at any kind of trouble without distressing her unduly, yet there was about her an almost visible aura of sympathy and in the glow of it Chloe felt she would be warmed.

'Just give me a hard hug, will you?' she asked casually.

Sandra obliged her willingly and said, 'I don't believe I've ever done that before.'

'No, and don't you dare to do it again without an invitation,' Chloe said, 'I felt so cold,' she said again.

'And I'm sure,' said Sandra, warming the teapot, 'it would be better if we talked instead of pretending, about what we're all thinking of, I mean.'

'If we were all women we could. It's not so easy with young men there because you've either got to sound heartless or frightened.'

'Then the boys should start it.'

'They think it wouldn't be kind to Mother.'

'That's silly,' said Sandra.

'Men are,' Chloe said. 'They're so old-fashioned. The nice ones,' she added.

Sandra accepted this enlightenment without comment and carried the tray upstairs.

'Tell Felix,' Rosamund said. He had an awkward temper but he did not sulk and Paul, coming downstairs in his dressing-gown, his head wet and glistening, his face flushed and his eyes sleepy from his hot bath, met the elder of his brothers in the passage and no one ever knew or would ever have suspected that the memory of Paul like this, with the contours of his face softened babyishly, often flashed into Felix's mind at strange moments as the years wore on and Paul grew dangerously older, and put a special venom into what Felix had to do.

'I'm only fetching a book,' Paul said quickly.

'They've been making tea,' Felix told him. 'You'd better come in and get your hair dry.'

'Can I? Oh good!' Paul said gratefully. James was easier to get on with but a kindness from Felix was doubled in worth.

It became quite a gay party round the fire, with Felix and James describing their holiday in detail and laughing, somewhat excessively, the others thought, at episodes which fell rather flatly on the ears of those who had not had all their physical senses sharpened by happiness and some sense of danger and their sense of humour more easily satisfied than usual but, in spite of the tea and the fire and the laughter, Rosamund still felt cold. She could not forget the darkness outside this bright room, not the kind, normal darkness of night but a darkness impregnated with an evil so positive that she believed she would be able to smell it if she went into the Square, and with evils less definite too, the follies and weaknesses and half betrayals of the past, now having their sneaking triumph, and out in that darkness some- where was Fergus who ought to have been here. Her common sense and experience of him told her that he need not be pitied: these were the exciting conditions in which he flourished, yet she could not help seeing him as a waif and she longed to be able to call him in.

'We'll have to tell Lindsay all about it,' she heard James say.

Yes, there was Piers too, she thought, but she need not worry about him. He was self-supporting; that was, perhaps, the quality she liked best in him. He could be buffeted by chance and keep his footing. He was the kind of man most admirable to women, the kind who will accept being sacrificed, even un- reasonably in their own eyes, without those signs of grievance so painful to the sacrificer.

'He'll be here to-morrow,' she said.

'Let's have him to supper, shall we?' James said.

'I expect he'll come if you ask him. Do you know it's eleven o'clock? We must go to bed.'

At that hour, Mr. Blackett decided that he must go to bed too and as he stood at his bedroom window, undressing in the dark for fear of waking Bertha, he saw the light in the sitting-room go out and the one in Mrs. Fraser's bedroom come on. How long would that burn? he wondered. He would not be able to watch it from the bed in its new position but he had gained more than he had lost, a precious, new and unexpected piece of infor- mation at which he chuckled silently. A great deal of what had puzzled him unwillingly in Bertha's conduct, not everything but quite enough to satisfy him, was now explained. How dull, and it was only fair to himself to say how modest, he had been! He had not suspected her of jealousy, she had seemed too placid for that emotion, but to-night she had been tripped into revealing it. For Mr. Blackett this was a delightful discovery. It gave their relations the piquancy they had lacked and it showed an acuteness he had suspected just as little, though on this discovery he did not dwell. Jealousy of Mrs. Fraser accounted for the new position of the bed and her professed liking for the woman was merely a covering for a very different feeling. And, more than likely, her carelessness about the time of his arrival and the coldness of her greeting had been caused by the comments in his letters on his new acquaintance and her feminine capacity for reading between the lines. Poor little woman, he thought with happy anticipation of amusement. It would do her no harm to believe she had offended him with that last sharp remark and, very carefully, he lifted the bedclothes and insinuated himself beneath them while she, breathing with the regularity of sound sleep, did not know whether or not to regret the retort he had wrung from her, but his fatuous conceit had been intolerable and she had difficulty in sustaining her even breathing when she thought of it.

CHAPTER XLI

MR. BLACKETT's first thoughts on waking were a continuation of those to which he had gone to sleep. At an age when most men and women, with resigned dismay, see themselves jogging into the future on a monotonous road promising no surprise or excitement, a road on which all the signposts pointed to duty and duty was only a repetition of yesterday, he had received just what he wanted in the way of stimulus. His signposts still pointed towards duty but the road had suddenly become much more interesting and he sprang out of bed, full of energy and good humour. And the news seemed to him to be satisfactory. The signs were favourable, he told his family, when he had opened his news-paper.

'Who for?' Rhoda asked.

He did not reply in words. The look he gave her was intended to convey his astonishment that such a question should follow his remark, that there could be any doubt that what he considered favourable could be anything but right for all concerned. 'A ruthless opponent,' he said after a suitable pause, 'and I have never considered him one, would neither have consented to con-tinue negotiations nor would he have shown this charming con-sideration for the fatigues of an older man. That in itself is a very promising gesture. An essentially kindly people, I've always said so,' he added, wishing Rhoda would not look at him with so much earnestness. In anyone else it might have been explained as due attention to the family oracle, but he had never been able to deceive himself satisfactorily where Rhoda was concerned. He was distrustful, though he did not go so far as to suspect her of putting that question simply as a test. For information, as for everything else, she preferred Miss Spanner and, too young to realize a fraction of what war would mean, she half hoped for it just to prove her father humiliatingly mistaken and, perhaps, to open doors for herself which, otherwise, he might succeed in keeping shut.

'Mr. Blackett,' Miss Spanner reported a little later, 'looked very genial and perky when he went by just now.'

'It's remarkable how you see everything,' Rosamund said, 'and you look rather perky yourself.'

'Yes, it's one of the better dispensations of Providence, the interest we all take in our own affairs and the scrapings of happi-ness we can get under the very jaws of death, as you might say.'

'I'm glad you have some scrapings,' Rosamund said.

'Oh, yes, I get some,' said Miss Spanner.

What had cheered her when she woke was her little, secret triumph over Rosamund. It was the old maid, not the mother, to whom Chloe had given her confidence and her heart was warm for the girl who had always seemed remote, courteously tolerant of Miss Spanner's presence, until last night when she had developed such charming qualities that Miss Spanner was now willing to deny her none. But Chloe had waked to the pain of wondering whether she had lost her lover: Rosamund to the worry about Felix which had been vaguely pursuing her through the night. Yes, these small personal joys and troubles took first place though this, which might or might not be trouble, was connected with the greater one: it was at times like this that a young man might make sure of a moment's joy or commit some folly he recognized for what it was but believed he would not have much time for regretting. This morning, though he had a few days of holiday left, he had gone to the office.

'I wish,' Rosamund said to James, 'you had stayed away a little longer.'

'So do I, but you know what Felix is.'

'No. I wish I did.'

They were in the garden again and again James was greasing his boots. 'Mad as a hatter at times,' he said. 'I'll do his boots, too, while I'm about it and then I'll put them away,' he looked at her with something like a wink, 'for another time. Oh well, it was good, it was good, it was good!'

'Do you think Felix feels like that?'

'Of course. Either you feel like that or you have no use for it and he had plenty. Great natural aptitude, too. Smithers was quite impressed. A bit foolhardy, though, when he got the chance and that's wrong, that's not in the code. And it was good discipline for him to have to do what he was told and keep his mouth shut. Then he took it into his head that we ought to come back at once and back we came.'

'Well,' said Rosamund, 'one never knows. One of you might have been killed if you'd stayed.'

'And what a lost chance of glory that would have been,' James said with his sardonic yet good-natured grin. 'No In Memoriam notices with those nice little bits of poetry attached.'

'Don't James,' Rosamund said sharply. 'I wouldn't indulge in any of those messages myself, but I can understand them and,

277

after all, they are almost the only reminders we ever get that there was once a war. It has been blotted out as though we ought to be ashamed of it. Ashamed of it!' she cried. 'Of a lot of other things but not of that. Yet your generation, how I don't know, has been very subtly inoculated with the idea that we were in the wrong and those villains over there have posed and been accepted as the injured party ever since. And not only your generation. Strangely enough, mine too. Agnes was quite right about the gulls.'

'Oh, that's what she was getting at, was it?' James said slowly.

'We've gulled ourselves,' Rosamund went on, not heeding him, 'and been gulled for the last twenty years. Too lazy, too tired, to bother or foresee. And nearly all the best men gone, the ones who knew what they were fighting for and would have lived for it. It was easier to think all would be well. And we're being gulled now. You needn't look so sceptical and amused. You'll find I'm right.'

'I'm not sceptical,' James said. 'I'm not amused. I'm interested.'

'Yes, exactly! Just interested in a detached sort of way.'

'Interested in you,' James said. 'You don't often get excited and I didn't know you felt like that.'

'No. My fault. In that way I've been as bad as anybody else. Let's pretend, we seemed to say, we didn't fight a war for decency and justice. It's not quite decorous to speak of it. And we've pretended so hard — and it's the only thing we've really given our minds to — that we've made ourselves believe it. Most of us. I haven't. Agnes hasn't, Piers Lindsay hasn't or,' she hesitated, 'your father. We're all the more to blame for keeping quiet and blurring over the violation of a treaty as though it was just an unfortunate little breach of manners or a forgivable misunderstanding. Have you ever heard anybody mention it? No. You all seem to think we were fighting for something we had no right to. It's true that, at the end, we were fighting for our existence — we had to — and surely we had a right to that, but at the beginning it was for an ideal of decency and good faith. And it wasn't fair to you or to the future, to let you grow up in ignorance of that. All I did, sometimes, was to ask you to make allowances for your father, and that seemed to amuse you too, as though he'd been doing something rather funny when he got his wounds. But perhaps,' she said, seeing how gravely he was listening, 'I'm not being fair to you.'

'Go on,' he said encouragingly, and she laughed, though she had been near tears in her indignation and remorse and this unwonted speaking from her heart.

'You'd all starve if I did,' she said. 'I must do some shopping.'

'I'll come with you,' James said. 'I expect you think carrying a basket is just the job for a degenerate young man.'

'No, James, I knew you were all right under the skin. And Felix too. I knew you would want to get back but I think you were in too much of a hurry.'

'As I've told you, that was Felix and now he's mewed up in an office before he need be. What a life, anyhow, and the last thing I should have thought he'd choose.'

'Ah, there are two different sides to him, the hot and the cold. That's his trouble, or may be,' Rosamund said, and she wondered whether the fixed candour with which James looked at her was not a little overdone and he did not pursue the subject.

'I'll tell you what I'll do,' he said. 'I'll ask Lindsay if I can go and help him until term, or anything else, begins. I meant to have a go at the garden but someone has done that already.'

'Oh, that's Rhoda. She loves a garden.'

'But she wants to be a farmer.'

'Does she? Who told you?'

'She did, of course. I've got some photographs of the farm to show her. Cows, chiefly. She likes cows.'

'You'd better go across now instead of coming with me.'

James shook his head. 'The less I see of Flora, the better I'm pleased.'

'I'm not surprised and no doubt she feels like that about you.'

'I hope so. In her own way, you know, she's really very pretty, but utterly and completely unattractive. She tries too hard.'

'You ought to have discovered that a little sooner.'

'I know. But I never really liked her much and what's a kiss or two anyway?'

'A great deal sometimes, when they're the first ones,' Rosamund said. She could not help a passing thought of Rhoda and fancied he suspected her of it, but she was not mentioned. Rosamund would not have cared to suggest and James would have disgustedly denied the possibility of any such tampering with her young integrity.

'The tradesmen,' Rosamund said as they set out, 'will be so full of optimism that I'm afraid I shan't manage to be pleasant and then I shan't get as well served as usual.'

'You can say we must hope for the best.'

'Yes, without knowing what it is. But we never know that. We never can. Not here. I do wonder what's on the other side of the grave, don't you?'

'Certainly not,' James said. 'I'm too much interested in this side of it.'

'Oh, I'm interested in it too. I feel sometimes that I'd like to live for ever, but naturally one wants to know the result of an examination.'

'But if it lasts a lifetime it's not reasonable to expect the result to be very good. The strain's too great.'

'No doubt the examiners make allowances for that, but it's not my own marks I really care about. What I want to know are the right answers. I'm sure a great many of them will be surprising.'

'Well, that's something to look forward to,' James said dryly.

She was not sure that this remark was made in reference to himself but that she should be forced to hear it in that sense filled her with helpless rage. It seemed as though a comparatively small quantity of evil, if it were determined enough, could overwhelm a far greater quantity of good which, by its nature, was more passive and, with a maternal passion she seldom allowed to run riot, she looked at her son as he adjusted his long stride to hers, the empty basket swinging from his hand, and thought how thoroughly decent he was, kind and humorous and tolerant. Why should his life be at the mercy of this evil? And these characteristics of his were those of his countrymen as a whole, of the policeman on point duty who gave her his special, smiling salute, of the butcher and the fishmonger and the errand boys who whistled gaily as they kept their customers anxiously waiting for their goods and she unknowingly quoted Mr. Blackett who had used the words in another connection, when she said, under her breath, 'A kindly people.'

'What?' James asked, bending towards her.

'Nice people,' she said with a little inclusive gesture.

'But far too many of them,' James said, his mind still among the hills where the voices were the melancholy, protesting ones of sheep and the many different voices of water, the gay, the desperately hurried, the chuckling, the serene and, most poignant in his memory, the slow drip of it, high up on the cliffs where its reservoir was some giant sponge of moss, brilliantly green. Every few seconds there was a drop and then a tiny splash on the rocks below. That dripping and the crying of the sheep were mournful sounds and he knew that to anyone alone and lost up there in a mountain mist the water's voice would be slyly sinister and the sheep's calls would have fear in them, but for him they had all the romance of an unhappiness he did not feel, like the charm of sorrow put into lovely verse.

'And what are they, what are we all doing?' he asked.

'I don't know. I often wonder,' Rosamund said.

Stationary or moving cars and carts almost filled the broad street; people entered shops and left them, stared at the goods displayed in the windows, met acquaintances and formed chattering obstacles on the pavements and a great part of this activity was caused by the necessity to live or die. And the activity did not end in the streets; it was prolonged in innumerable kitchens and began again to-morrow. It seemed a strange use of existence, she thought again but, as Miss Spanner would have said, it was probably one of the more merciful of Providence's dispensations. Many people found their happiness in it, comparatively few could have spent their time to any other

281

purpose, she was glad herself, as she had been glad before, to be thus occupied and she knew that out of this mass of mediocrity, and so redeeming it, there sprang, occasionally, those rare human beings who, fed materially by others, were able, in their turn, to feed hungry eyes and ears and minds.

'The fact is,' she said, 'and I'm afraid I'm repeating myself, we never really know what we're doing, but if we didn't behave as though we did, why, there'd be no standards. We shouldn't have the satisfaction of judging other people and I'm not going to give up that privilege in a hurry. And there are standards, there must be,' she continued to herself, realizing that James was not listening. 'The other side of them may be different from what we think, but we must abide by the side we see,' and she went unwillingly but dutifully into the red and yellow horror of the butcher's shop.

CHAPTER XLII

MRS. BLACKETT could be envious of all sorts of people and all sorts of qualities, for her spirit was humble and she seldom had the pleasure of making comparisons in favour of herself. She was envious of Mrs. Fraser's looks, of the way in which she wore her clothes, of the freedom in her household, of that look Piers Lindsay had given her and, most of all, her lack of a resident husband, but jealousy of all this was another matter. Jealousy finds it hard to contain its own pain and must scatter its poison where it will do most hurt, while envy need not have any bitterness in it. There was none in hers and jealousy was a feeling so alien to her nature that, in spite of her long study of her husband, the idea that he might suspect her of it had not once entered her mind and she was slightly puzzled when he bade her good-bye that morning and gave her a smiling, quizzical look instead of the customary kiss. She did notice that he looked more human, less unattractive than usual, but this might only have been because he kept his distance instead of approaching her with the tacit reminder that he was setting out, in all tenderness, on her service. Then, as, roused to curiosity, she stood at the dining-room window to see him go, light broke upon her, making her cry out, as though a fierce flash of lightning had startled her, but this sound had ugly laughter in it. She had been as stupid as he was. She had thought him angered by her retort; she had merely raised his self-esteem, if that, too, were possible, and, strangely, she was at first almost more vexed on Mrs. Fraser's account than on her own; as though, she thought indignantly, the woman whom Piers loved could find any attraction in Herbert Blackett! And while she was ashamed of having married a man Mrs. Fraser must despise, she discovered that the sillier he was, the more completely she could feel detached from him. This was a better state to be in than one half loving, half ashamed, emphatic about his virtues to the inevitable accentuation of his faults. There were faults Mrs. Blackett could have borne with patiently, opposed frankly and even liked but, search as she might, she could not find either faults or virtues in Mr. Blackett which were human or lovable.

'He isn't real,' she muttered, sitting down in the nearest chair, anger and grief churning together in her breast. He had been manufactured and set going by some kind of clockwork which his own particular energy sustained but, though he could tick with precision and regularity, it was with definite limitations of feeling and action. But she must be wrong. No one could be as hopelessly mechanical as that and she blamed herself again, awed by the responsibility of human beings towards each other, yet aware of the danger of exercising it.

She looked up as Rhoda came into the room and though her mouth was set in its naturally sweet curves, her widely opened eyes seemed half blind and Rhoda, ready to defend, cried anxiously, 'What's the matter?'

Mrs. Blackett lifted and dropped her clasped hands. 'I felt as though I couldn't go on,' she said. 'I suppose I'm tired. But I shall telegraph to Connie this morning,' she said more briskly, 'and when she comes there won't be so much to do.'

'Has he been nasty to you?' was Rhoda's disconcerting reply. 'You weren't tired when we were alone and you could walk for miles and miles.'

'He is never nasty to me, Rhoda,' Mrs. Blackett said with truth, 'or to anyone.'

'He is to me, but I don't care. I'm rather glad, and if he wasn't to you, you're miserable because he's just — well, just nasty. I can't see a single nice thing in him.'

'Oh Rhoda,' it was what she had been thinking herself, 'your father has always done his very best for you.'

'Then I don't think much of it. And Flora's the image of him. She'll be perfectly horrid when she's older, she's bad enough already, unless she gets turned inside out. How happy we were, weren't we? It's so easy to be happy, really. And I hate being done good to. What's nice is to like people. It doesn't matter so much about being liked, though,' she added, 'that must be nice too.'

'Then we ought to do our very best to like everybody.'

'Do you do that?'

Mrs. Blackett hesitated for a moment and then said, 'No,' but in the straight look she gave her daughter there was something that asked for mercy from more questioning, an appeal which was not really necessary: they understood each other but when Rhoda said, 'I don't know how you manage to be so good,' Mrs. Blackett was abashed by praise altogether undeserved and it was impossible, it would have been wickeder than the thing itself, to tell her how this appearance of goodness had been maintained. She did say, however, 'Manners are important, Rhoda. They're like — they're rather like a garden roller. You use it and it's hard work but you find, as you push it, that you are treading on much smoother ground.'

'Do you?' Rhoda said. It was a metaphor she could understand; it was also a reminder. 'I meant to roll the Frasers' grass to-day but now I don't think I shall.'

'Why not?'

'It's different, now they are all at home.'

'You can slip in through the basement. No one will take any notice of you.'

'Except Flora,' Rhoda said. 'I wish she had her bedroom at the back and I wish you could have the study for your drawing-room.'

'I'm afraid you would meet with serious opposition to both those plans,' Mrs. Blackett said demurely.

'And I know it's silly of me to care, but Flora spoils things.'

'I don't think she'll follow you this morning. I'll send her on an errand of some kind.'

'All right. I'll go when we've done the dusting,' Rhoda said, but it was not Flora's company she feared: it was her thoughts, now very distantly nearer to the truth than they had been before and Rhoda hated the apparent likeness in her own situation to what Flora's had been a little while ago. She wanted to see James and he did not want to see her, but she did not want this in Flora's way and she was sure James's indifference was no more than the natural one of a man towards a betwixt-and-between nobody like herself. How could it be anything else? She was not important enough to be avoided, and she wished everything could be as it was before he went away and while he was away, before he had been forced to listen so gravely to the news, with so grown-up an air that she was half afraid of him. Everything was horrid, her father at home again, her mother unhappy, Miss Spanner prophesying disgrace and the happy freedom of the Frasers' house and garden gone.

It was not decreed, however, that this youthful pessimism should have time enough to harden on her like a crust and it gave way, because it was youthful, under a fairer prospect for herself. She went in by the area door and met Paul in the passage.

'I've come to roll the grass,' she said, and he was at once eager to do a job he would have grumbled at being asked to undertake.

'But I rather wanted to,' Rhoda said.

'No, let him,' Sandra said, from the kitchen stairs. 'He doesn't know what to do with himself.'

'But,' Rhoda said, 'that's why I came. I mean — well, all right. I suppose I'd better go back.'

'But I was just coming to fetch you. You went away so quickly last night and James wanted you.'

'Did he?'

'Yes, and I shouted but you didn't hear.'

'No, I didn't hear,' Rhoda said.

'So now you must wait till he comes back. Let's go into the garden.'

'Yes, I don't suppose Paul will do the rolling properly.'

He had not even fetched the roller from its corner. He was flicking pellets of earth at a cat which sat on the wall and, despising his marksmanship, yawned at him impudently, and then settled itself more comfortably for sleep. So Rhoda fetched and propelled the roller after all, careless of her red, hot face and the strands of damp hair sticking to it. She was full of energy in the knowledge that she had not lost a friend.

'The ground's too hard, really, but I like doing it,' she said.

'You'll get over-heated,' said Miss Spanner from her bedroom window. Paul managed to hit the cat on the exact spot he had chosen as his target and went away; Sandra said, 'Do stop and I'll get you something cool to drink'; then James appeared and sat beside her on the roller.

Afterwards she wondered anxiously whether she had been unpleasantly hot and decided that, as he did not move away, it must have been all right. At the time, she was too much interested to think about herself at all, hardly to think of him except as a particularly nice source of information. They sat with their backs to the house and the sounds from within reached her vaguely. Someone was calling to Chloe, telling her there was a telegram for her and the boy was waiting and later Miss Spanner's voice was heard again. 'What else do you want?' she asked sharply, and Chloe answered, 'I like people to stick to their guns.'

'You're never satisfied,' said Miss Spanner, but when at last Rhoda realized that it was time to go home and she met Chloe in the hall, she remembered Miss Spanner's words and thought Chloe looked more than satisfied and she was glad because she was happy again herself.

In the hall of her own home she encountered Flora who laughed in an unpleasant way. 'Do look at yourself in the glass,' she said.

'Why should I? I don't want to.'

'I'm not surprised. Your hair's in streaks and your blouse is outside your belt.'

'Only a bit of it,' Rhoda said cheerfully and tucked it in. 'I've been rolling the grass.'

'And you ought to have been helping Mother with the cooking.'

'Oh, mind your own business,' Rhoda said.

'And it's rather funny that the grass needed rolling to-day.'

'It didn't really,' Rhoda admitted.

'Any excuse will do, I suppose,' Flora said. 'And anybody will do for James Fraser to talk to about his silly old farming. I hope you realize that. You needn't look so angry. I'm telling you for your good.'

'No, you're not. You're telling me for your own,' Rhoda retorted, but she checked the rest of the words which were ready to tumble from her lips. The preservation of everything that was simple and friendly in her relationship with James in her own mind seemed to her much more important than saying nasty things to Flora and with a great effort and disgust for the necessity of this deception, she said good-humouredly, 'Well, I don't mind listening to him. I expect his family gets tired of the subject. And Sandra made some lemonade and we had it in the garden.'

'So long as you understand,' Flora said kindly, 'but I think Father's quite right, you know.'

'What about?'

'He's never liked them, the Frasers, has he? And since I've seen a little more of the world and met such very different kinds of people, they do seem to be very ordinary, almost common, always talking to their friends on their doorstep and things like that. And very funny friends, some of them. And Mrs. Fraser hardly ever wears a hat. Of course,' she added hastily, 'that's all right abroad where everybody's unconventional, but not when you're middle-aged and living in Upper Radstowe. It's rather showing off, I think. And then there's that awful Miss Spanner.'

Here Rhoda had to keep her arms close to her sides to prevent herself from smacking Flora's face, but her feelings for Miss Spanner, too, must be concealed. She knew a declared affection was a vulnerable spot and Flora would be very glad to know of it.

'Still,' Flora ended magnanimously, 'it doesn't really matter to me, one way or the other. Why should it?'

'No, I don't see why it should,' Rhoda said, surprising herself with just the right accent of agreeable indifference.

'But of course,' Flora said, 'we must be neighbourly and as we are not allowed to have a wireless of our own, it's very convenient to be able to hear theirs.'

CHAPTER XLIII

'I WONDER,' said Mr. Blackett that evening at the meal which Rhoda always dreaded and at which, though she had a hearty appetite, she never properly enjoyed her food, 'I wonder, Mary, how much you can remember about the interesting places Flora and I saw when we were in France.'

Mary looked puzzled. 'But I wasn't there,' she said.

'Silly child!' Mr. Blackett said. 'You know I wrote special descriptions of them for Mother to read to you.'

'Well, she didn't. Did you, Mother?' she asked, turning to the other end of the table.

'No, I didn't,' Mrs. Blackett said pleasantly, 'because I very much dislike being read to myself.'

'I don't mind if it's exciting,' Mary said.

'Ah, there I'm afraid I shouldn't have obliged you. The fault of my pen, of course, for the places themselves were exciting enough.'

'What happened in them?'

'Many interesting things, no doubt, but what I tried to express was what happened to me when I looked at them.'

'What did?'

'Nothing, I'm sure,' Mr. Blackett said acidly, 'which is likely to happen to you.'

'Hope not, if it was horrid,' Mary said.

Mr. Blackett made a little sound of vexation but he managed to produce a feeble smile in response to Flora's look of sympathetic exasperation. 'Well, well,' he said, and did not return to the subject until he was alone with Bertha. 'I was a little hurt,' he said then, 'about my letters. I took some trouble with my little narratives and I flattered myself they were rather well done.'

'And I expect you enjoyed doing them.'

'I did. It was a pleasure to me and I hoped to give pleasure to other people.'

'And instruction,' said Mrs. Blackett.

'Yes. And though I have been disappointed there I may get some more pleasure for myself by reading them again.'

'Then what a pity I didn't keep them,' she said.

'You didn't keep them?'

'I never keep letters.'

'You get very few to keep,' he retorted.

'Very few,' Mrs. Blackett said.

'And these, if I remember aright, are the only ones you have ever had from me since we were married.'

'I know,' Mrs. Blackett said with a heartfelt mournfulness for which he was momentarily at a loss to account. However, he did his best with this remark.

'And surely,' he said, 'it was better to have been together than to have exchanged letters though, for me, there was a charming novelty in writing them.'

'But not in getting them?'

He laughed. 'Well Bertha, you haven't the pen of a ready writer, have you? I was always delighted when I saw your envelopes — there were not many of them by the way — and a little disappointed at what I found within. But it did not matter. I am not entirely lacking in imagination.'

'No indeed,' Mrs. Blackett said.

'And yet I have not quite enough, not quite enough, to understand why you should have destroyed the letters. You see,' he said gently, 'I have not been able to do the work which would have been my choice. I should have much preferred to write something different from the dreary stuff I have to put on paper and, rather ironically, about paper, though I have done it with a certain amount of success. Possibly I should have been less successful if I had followed my inclinations,' and as Mrs. Blackett did not dispute this statement though he gave her time, he added, 'I could not have afforded to have a wife and family,' and with gratification he saw her draw the deep breath of some-one who has escaped disaster by a hair's breadth. 'I might,' he went on with amusement but watching for more signs of dis-tress, 'have been living in the traditional garret,' and he was surprised to hear her say in decided tones, 'You wouldn't have liked that.'

'Perhaps not,' he said sharply. 'And you wouldn't have liked it, either, would you?'

'But I shouldn't have been there.'

'Really, Bertha, I might be talking to Mary! If I must be more explicit, what I meant was that you would have missed all the comfort and happiness we have had together.'

'Yes.' Mrs. Blackett sighed again. 'I should have missed all that.'

'And it's probably all for the best as it is but when I was away in new and beautiful surroundings and with leisure and the sort of freedom an artist needs, I did feel that I could get some of my impressions into words, inadequately, of course, but not so very badly. I had hoped you would appreciate them or at least appreciate the effort, so I felt hurt, Bertha, and yes, even a little angry. I had looked forward to reading them in a moment when what, for want of a more suitable word, I must call the inspiration had left me.'

'The inspiration,' said Mrs. Blackett, 'seems to have died away during the last part of your holiday.' She knew what she was doing. While he talked, she saw herself confronted by three choices and two were false and one was honest. She could be responsive and a little awed; she could display those signs of jealousy he fancied he had detected in another direction, or she could let out all the cruelty she had accumulated in twenty years, but the time for that had not come, that must be kept for a more fitting occasion or for one when she could no longer contain it, and she chose the middle course because she thought, hating but determined to indulge herself, it would make her laugh now and add to her weapons for the future. 'Your letters lately,' she said, 'were very short and hurried.'

He did not answer immediately. Then, looking down and smiling self-consciously, he said, 'I was certainly very pleasantly occupied.'

'So I imagined,' said Mrs. Blackett, thinking how silly he looked, and she, too, dropped her eyelids but she did not smile and Mr. Blackett, understanding everything, could not altogether regret the loss of his efforts at fine prose. He would have liked to know whether she had destroyed his letters in a spurt of anger, handling them roughly, or with her usual gentle deftness and before he could say anything either provocative or reassuring, he heard her sigh again, a sound he found very satisfactory.

'What is the matter, Bertha?' he asked hopefully.

'I was just thinking what a lot of people there are in the world altogether, and how important they all are to themselves.'

This was not so satisfactory and he said testily, 'Really, women's minds seem incapable of concentrating on the same subject for more than a minute at a time. And where are the girls going?' he asked, as their figures passed the window.

'To hear the news, I suppose.'

'What news?' Mr. Blackett said scornfully.

'That's what they want to find out.'

'Don't be silly, Bertha. You know quite well — at least I hope you do — that I consider all this fuss quite unnecessary. We are in good hands. This is a mere excuse for gadding across the road.'

'You shouldn't expect young people to stay at home all the time.'

'It depends on the home,' said Mr. Blackett. 'However, I hope that unfortunate episode with one of those loutish youths, I can never distinguish one from the other, was merely an episode.'

'Oh yes,' Mrs. Blackett said, 'and it was never of any importance. He soon got tired of Flora.'

'Tired of Flora!'

'Yes, people who are always thinking about themselves become very wearisome.'

'I'm surprised,' Mr. Blackett said with reproach, 'to hear you speak like that about your daughter.'

'She is your daughter too.'

'I know that very well,' he said with a look so slyly reminiscent that she very much regretted a remark which had, in fact, been meant as an accusation. 'And,' he went on, 'she made quite a different impression among the friends we met abroad, I can assure you.'

'Perhaps other people stole her chances,' said Mrs. Blackett.

'I don't understand you.'

'Never mind.' She stood up and went to the window. She had half a mind to follow Flora and Rhoda. Piers was there, she knew, though he had left his car elsewhere. That was a pity. It would have annoyed Herbert to see it there.

'What are you looking at?' Mr. Blackett asked.

'At nothing I can see,' she said without turning round.

'You are rather mysterious to-night,' he half complained.

'Never mind,' she said again as though she spoke to a child. Just on the other side of the wall on her left hand, so near that it was a wonder she could not hear them, were the two people she liked best in all the world, Rhoda and Piers. There was, she decided, a difference between love and liking. She supposed she had some natural love for Flora and rather more for Mary; she was anxious for their well-being and happiness; but, as Rhoda had said, it was liking that really mattered, the trust and security that went with it, and she wished with all her heart she could like the man who sat behind her. 'Was she fair to him? she asked herself. Had she ever tried to get below those varnished coats of conceit and self-esteem with which he was plastered? And what would she have found if she had succeeded? How good it would be, she thought, if she could drop on her knees in front of his and put her arms round his waist and laughingly try to shake him while she told him what an old goose he was but how much she liked him, all the same. But he would not care to be called a goose and she did not like him. She could not have really liked him in any circumstances and, bound to him as she was, her body at his disposal, what might have been a mild antipathy was an increasingly strong one. She wished he had not gone away. She felt as though the poison in her system, not altogether deleterious while it was under control, had now, with her temporary freedom, flooded her whole body and she was in danger of complete corruption, and she understood how people could go to a priest to be shriven. But that way was not for her. Sooner or later, she would have to find another.

'You are looking at nothing for a long time,' Mr. Blackett remarked.

'But I'm seeing something now,' she said with a note of pleasure in her voice, for Connie, carrying a heavy suitcase, had just come into sight. 'It's Connie. What a good creature she is! She needn't have come till to-morrow.'

'I think she ought to have been here long ago,' said Mr. Blackett. 'And the precious news must be over by now. It's time the girls were back.'

'Oh,' said Mrs. Blackett, starting for the door to welcome Connie, 'do try to be more liberal.'

'Liberal?' he said.

'More generous.'

'What an extraordinary thing to say to me!' Mr. Blackett exclaimed in genuine astonishment, but she had gone.

It was pleasant to be with Connie in the kitchen, to hear about her holiday and her relatives and her opinion on the state of affairs, even though she had forebodings about her brother who was a reservist and fears for her nephews who were growing up, and while Mrs. Blackett was there, listening with sympathy and some affection for a faithful friend, Mr. Blackett had the vexation of seeing Piers Lindsay escorting his daughters to their door.

'Really,' he said later to Mrs. Blackett, 'I've come to the conclusion that someone ought to tell him about Mrs. Fraser.'

'What about her.'

'She has a husband.'

'Perhaps he knows.'

Mr. Blackett laughed. 'I'm quite sure she has kept that fact pretty dark.'

'I don't see why she should.'

'Of course you don't, thank Heaven! But I do. She doesn't want to frighten him away. The victims who get entangled in her web are what she feeds on.'

'Then,' said Mrs. Blackett, 'you think she ought to have no men friends?'

'No nice woman can have men friends,' he replied.

'Miss Spanner lives there too.'

'I should hardly call Miss Spanner a woman,' Mr. Blackett said with a smiling sneer. 'But of course you were referring to her as a chaperon, and in that capacity she may justify her existence,' and Mrs. Blackett, going upstairs to wish Rhoda good night, told herself it would be impossible for anyone to tease or persuade him out of his prejudices.

She found the room in darkness. She felt her way to the head of the bed and stood there for a moment, thinking Rhoda might be asleep but, as an ominous little sound reached her, she bent down and found her face was wet.

'Isn't it awful?' Rhoda gasped.

'What, child, what?' Mrs. Blackett asked anxiously.

'Not being able to cry properly because of Mary. There's only one place in the house I can sometimes get to myself and it's not comfortable enough to cry in.'

Mrs. Blackett crossed to the other bed. 'Mary's fast asleep,' she said. 'But why are you crying? You never cry.'

'Everybody,' Rhoda persisted jerkily, 'ought to have a private place.'

'Yes, indeed they should. But why are you crying?' Mrs. Blackett asked again, sitting on the edge of the bed and stroking Rhoda's hand until the sobs subsided.

'You're sure she's asleep? I'm so ashamed,' Rhoda whispered.

'Ashamed?'

'Of Flora,' Rhoda said, and Mrs. Blackett was immediately conscious of relief. 'And I can't explain, exactly, but it was all wrong and horrid. Showing off. And they were all there, Chloe and Mr. Stephens and Cousin Piers and all the others and Miss Spanner, of course, and suddenly she began sort of teasing Felix, and she's hardly ever spoken to him before, and hinting she'd seen him somewhere, with somebody to-day, as if he'd been doing it on the sly, laughing, you know, in a silly way, but spiteful underneath. It was awful. It doesn't sound anything when I tell you,' Mrs. Blackett, however, thought it sounded far too much, 'and it didn't last long, but it made me feel as if my inside had all shrivelled up and I was ashamed to look at anyone and Felix stared at her as if he'd like to kill her, quite slowly and politely, I mean the killing, and Cousin Piers changed the subject and everybody began to talk. And now we can never go there again!'

'You can,' Mrs. Blackett said.

'Are you sure?'

'Of course. You'll find it will be all right.'

'Then I'll try to go to sleep and forget it, as though it had nothing to do with me, but it has, you know, in a way.'

'Yes, in a way,' Mrs. Blackett admitted.

'And have I worried you? I wouldn't have told you if you hadn't come in just then. Have I worried you?' she repeated.

'I'm sorry about it,' her mother said, 'but I shan't cry.'

'No, you can't,' Rhoda said crossly. 'You've nowhere to do it in, have you? You're worse off than me.'

CHAPTER XLIV

FLORA knew she had made a mistake. She had made one with James, though this she did not regret, and now she had made one with Felix. She had her father's capacity for mental juggling, but she was not easy as she undressed, with frequent pauses to contemplate herself in the mirror and favourably compare her vivid colouring with the pale yet, she had to own, somehow attractive young woman she had seen with Felix that morning. She had a lively instinct in such matters and she knew, from the way they walked in silence, that they were not casual acquaintances, and she felt a bitter enmity for that girl who, she was sure, was not a lady, nor was she as pretty as she was herself.

She turned from the mirror as she heard her mother go to Rhoda's room and, after a while, pause on the landing, but she only called out a good night and passed on and Flora let out the breath she had been holding. There was a part of her that could not but respect her mother's standards of behaviour, old-fashioned though they were — or, more truly, it was her mother herself who evoked respect. A reproach from her would have been unpleasant, but apparently Rhoda had told no tales. She was probably too stupid to realize there was one to tell and Flora would not have realized it herself but for Felix's cold stare and the very reserved good night of Cousin Piers. She was not sensitive to the surrounding atmosphere. She saw her mistake now, not as one of essence but of situation. Where she had been wrong was in teasing Felix in the bosom of his family. He would have been quite different if no one else had been there;

he would have liked it, she was sure, but she had not been able to control her desire to show herself lively and knowing, to attract his attention and relieve her jealousy of someone who seemed to be getting what was her own due.

Downstairs, though with no sense of error and not actually looking in a mirror, Mr. Blackett was experiencing some of the feelings he would have been disgusted to discover in his daughter. Across the road, the family dispersed without reference to Flora. Miss Spanner had plenty to say but she was biding her time until Rosamund was in bed. Below, in the garden, Chloe and her lover were saying a long good night and Miss Spanner made as much noise as possible while she undressed to warn them that she was not far away. Then the murmur of voices ceased, she heard Chloe coming up the stairs and hoped for another knock on her door, another confidential little talk, but happiness was self-sufficient, Chloe did not knock and Miss Spanner, though disappointed, consoled herself by reflecting that she was only being treated as most people treated God. He was a very present help in time of trouble, forgotten when times were good.

She braided her hair, donned the drab dressing-gown and then, as she cautiously reconnoitred the landing, she saw Felix making for his mother's door; another disappointment but one highly provocative of speculation, and with speculation Miss Spanner knew she would have to be content. She decided to get into bed but it was some time before she opened her book. Deliberately she put out of her mind all the little events of the day, James and Rhoda sitting on the roller in unsentimental oblivion of what went on around them, Flora's coy impudence, and those murmuring voices in the garden which, now that they were silent, had changed from those of the man and girl she knew to an echo of all such murmurings in the past, a prediction of all to come, with every pair of lovers believing they were saying new things in new tones. In such murmurings Miss Spanner had had no share: she had been denied much happiness, spared much sorrow, and it seemed to her that she was like the neuter gender personified. She had put forth nothing and mentally she was the more able, though less able than she thought, to view greater events impersonally. On this occasion she did not try to view any of them. The little ones in the garden, in the long sitting-room, dropped quietly out of sight as though they had left the stage by some mechanical device; the crowded contents of her bedroom lost shape and meaning and she gazed at the opposite wall without seeing the smudged oil paintings or the ghastly clarity of the framed photographs and, in her way and very humbly, Miss Spanner tried to pray, putting up no definite petitions, aware that, unlike her father, she did not know what gifts the Lord ought to vouchsafe, but hoping that justice and mercy would be among them. That was all she could do. The pictures returned to the walls, the furniture appeared again, she felt her recurrent pleasure at being in this house, surrounded by her own possessions, but unpossessed herself by tyrannous affection. Opening her book, she forgot everything but the printed page and her sharp ears missed the sound of Felix shutting his mother's door.

He had entered her room without waiting for an answer to his knock. Three of his long strides took him to the head of her bed, yet he gave the impression of having come a long distance at great speed and he began to speak at once.

'That damn little — ' but Rosamund put up a hand.

'I agree, but don't say it.'

'Why not?'

'Horrid word.'

'Horrid girl.'

'Poor thing,' Rosamund said. 'Don't bother about her.'

'But it's doing me good to be in a tearing rage. I've wanted to talk to you and I couldn't, but temper's like drink. It loosens the tongue.'

'I prefer a temper.'

His own seemed to subside. 'And it's only fair to tell you,' he said.

Rosamund nearly shut her eyes to shut out the disclosure he

298

was going to make, but that would not help him and she looked at him without, she hoped, betraying her anxiety. 'I don't particularly want to be treated fairly,' she said. 'In fact, I don't know how there can be fairness or unfairness between you and me.'

'But you ought to know first. I may be getting married.'

'May be? What a — what a contingent sort of remark,' she said.

'Yes, so you needn't tell anyone.'

'No.' The drawn look she had sometimes seen on his face had given way to the expression he might have worn in contemplating a dangerous surgical operation, resigned to the prospect, almost bored by the thought of it, and she said, 'Oh Felix, must you?'

'Not the kind of must you're thinking of.'

'I couldn't help thinking of it, could I?'

'I suppose not. Things are not very well arranged. We ought not to become physically adult while we're still mentally callow and then get punished for it. Oh, I know I'm mentally callow still but a little less so than I was.'

'And I won't have you punished!' Rosamund exclaimed.

'Ah, I didn't say I was going to be,' he replied quickly. He looked at her gravely but, though perhaps he did not know it, there was a sardonic twist at the corners of his mouth and this statement, she guessed, was the foundation stone on which he must try to build his loyalty.

'Can't you tell me any more?' she asked. 'Who is this girl?'

'I feel pretty sure Miss Spanner has given you a certain amount of information,' he replied, 'and I don't know whether to hate her for it or to love her for giving me that holiday and, in a way, I could hate her for the holiday too.'

'You mean,' Rosamund said, 'that it made a difference.'

To her distress, he dropped his face into his hands. 'Of course, of course,' he muttered against them. 'And what a name to have given me!' he exclaimed childishly. 'I've always hated it.'

'It was rather stupid,' she admitted, 'but it was meant as a

299

kind of thanksgiving. And I'm still thankful,' she said emphatically.

He lifted his head. 'She would have hated those hills,' he
said, 'and I knew, as soon as I saw them, that I never wanted to
see her again.'

'Then don't,' Rosamund said.

'So easy, isn't it? But you can't treat people like that.'

'Yes you can.'

'But it wouldn't be — well, honourable, would it?' he asked,
and he seemed to her to be pitifully young.

'How can I answer that? You haven't told me enough, but I
think it's possible to be honourably dishonourable.'

'I'm not so sure,' Felix said. 'And I didn't bother much about
it while I was there. When you're climbing you can't think of
anything but what you're doing. And bathing in those streams
washes everything else off. And yet before I went away, as
soon as I knew I'd passed my final and needn't come on to you
for anything, I'd been badgering her like a madman to marry me.
Like a madman,' he repeated. 'And even when I got her letter
I could forget it nearly all the time. There's a sort of healing
magic there.'

'I remember the letter.'

'But Sandra redirected it.'

'I thought you'd rather.'

'So I did. I hoped you wouldn't see it.'

'And in the letter?' Rosamund ventured.

'I got the promise I'd been asking for.'

'And where does the contingency come in?'

'War,' Felix said, and there was a pause before Rosamund
murmured, 'But I wonder why.'

'A sort of Victoria Cross, for valour!' Felix said. 'And then,'
he said in a rush, 'you wonder that I shut Paul up when he's
pleased at the prospect. Yes, a cross! That's rather good! Oh,
I'm a cad to be talking like this! You'll forget it, won't you?'

'If I have to.'

'It's all my own doing,' he said but, as though she were to

300

blame, he asked angrily, 'And what sort of state of mind d'you think I'm in? I'm very nearly praying that we'll knuckle under.'

'I expect we shall,' Rosamund said, and she was very nearly praying for it too. She wondered why that girl had changed her mind. Influenced by what Agnes had told her and by what Felix was feeling now, it was impossible not to be suspicious of base motives. To be romantically the bride of a soldier, to be the pensioned widow of one, might be a brighter prospect than marrying a man with a very small income and his way to make. Or had absence, that untrustworthy guide, misled her? Yet why should absence succeed where the presence of this attractive creature had failed? He was just like Fergus, she thought, with a little heartache, impulsive but capable of a deadly cold and where he did not love completely she could imagine what that mortal chill would be.

'You must get out of this,' she said, and saw at once that the imperative mood was not the one to use with him for he answered sharply, 'That's impossible. We have to reap what we sow.'

'Not necessarily. You can plough up the ground before the crop arrives.'

'And what would the ground feel about it?'

Her clenched hands, lying on the sheet, tightened a little. This was to keep back a smile or a word that would betray her sad amusement. Even in his misery and his desire to escape he could not forgo the belief that he was deeply loved and though she had it in her mind to tell him he would leave the ground prepared for someone else who might already be negotiating for the use of it, she was silent for a time and then decided that she must speak, that leaving something unsaid was as likely to be wrong as saying it. 'Felix,' she said, 'go and tell her the truth. I'm sure that's the right thing to do.'

It was now he who felt amusement and he did not try to hide it. 'You mean that's the way to get me out of a mess and so you can persuade yourself it's right. And a pretty fool I should make of myself,' he muttered, and she knew he was remembering with shrinking all the protestations he had made and did not know how to withdraw, and she thought with him that things were not very well arranged. The eager generosity of youth could become a usurer demanding more and more interest on what had been freely given; critical faculties began to take command over physical desire and she had no doubt that Felix had already heard the genteel accents to which the satisfaction of his eyes had deadened him and if he could subdue his pride and see his obligations beyond the present moment, he would be lucky in having been so speedily disillusioned.

'Believe me,' she said, 'it's better to be a fool for half an hour than an unhappy man for the rest of your life.'

'And that,' he said, 'may not be for very long. I wonder you haven't suggested interceding for me.'

'You don't wonder anything of the kind,' she retorted. 'You knew there was no danger of that.'

'No,' he said more gently, 'but I oughtn't to have come crying to you like this,' and as he stood over her, before he bent down to kiss her, she saw from his set face that an attempt at a smile might crumble into actual weeping, so it was she who had to do the smiling and, after he had gone, a little weeping.

CHAPTER XLV

WHAT she wanted was somebody to talk to, but not Fergus. He would have said the boy was a fool and must pay for his folly. The somebody she wanted was Piers Lindsay. He would listen and simply by listening he would comfort her but, half superstitiously, she had put a ban on private interviews and she thought grimly a lot of good that self-denial had done for Felix! Moreover, she had given him her word to tell no one. There was nothing she could do, either for him or herself. She had to wait, trying not to find a way of believing that the sacrifice of one country and the honour of her own was a reasonable price for her son's liberty. And he could get it with a few words, she thought angrily, and spare her this hateful complication to her suspense, a lifetime, long or short, of misery for himself and she had no patience with his false idea of chivalry, largely mixed as it was with unconscious conceit. She feared there was a wakeful night before her, but the consciousness of her helplessness brought sleep quite suddenly and deeply and when she woke she was not aware of having dreamed. Often she dreamed of her father and waked in dreadful trouble because she had quarrelled with him or he had scolded her, a cruel way of meeting him of whom she always thought with tenderness and who had always dealt tenderly with her. She never dreamed of Piers, seldom of her children or of Fergus but to-night she thought she must have been with him in her sleep. She had so strong a sensation of his nearness that she left her bed and went to the window, then stepped out and leaned over the balcony. There was no one below or anywhere in the Square. The night was very still; the lamplight shone with its peculiar effect, in deserted streets, of secret anticipation; no steamer hooted and no lion roared; she could hear no footsteps, but the feeling of his nearness stayed with her when she returned to her room and put on the light and saw that it was nearly three o'clock, and she smoothed her hair before she opened her door and listened from the landing to the silence within the house. All she could hear was the ticking of the clock in the hall. Hardly noticeable in the daytime, it now sounded very loud, inexorably marking the passage of time, the approach of the unknown. A little more quickly than usual her heart was doing the same thing, all the hearts in the house were doing it; though she could not hear them, they were all beating towards the future. For five of these hearts she was responsible and she went quickly back to her room and shut the door as though she could keep out all she feared for them and for herself. And there was much of that. Though she had smoothed her hair instinctively when she thought Fergus might be near, she had been afraid to find him

303

in the house. He would be the stranger who had parted from her in anger, the man who had asked for his release and so, as it were, sanctioned her love for another and then, outrageously, ignored her. No, she did not want him back, she did not want to see him, yet she would never be quite rid of him and little as she was given to belief in telepathic messages reaching anyone like herself, she was almost persuaded that this waking to a sense of his nearness must have been such a message and it was a long-time before she could sleep again. Her own problem dwindled when she contemplated that of Felix; she tried to see his as insignificant compared with the mass of misery that might fall on the world, and if he were awake now, turning from side to side as she was doing, she had no doubt that he, too, was trying to think more of his country than of himself, to prefer its honour to his own escape, though that was already easy enough. He had only to give a little push to a door not quite fast. It had been shut on him with reluctance and on conditions and it was these against which his pride ought to revolt, but she could do nothing, nothing. She was helpless in this, as in the greater matter, though, perhaps, far back, she had her share of blame for both.

She found rest at last by sending her mind across the river, over the tops of the trees on the other side, over fields dun-coloured with stubble, to the little house sheltering Piers and George, and she pictured Piers showing the sad side of his face, the other pressed against the pillow, while George lay on his back, the ends of his moustache as sharp as the bayonet he had once used and would be ready to use again and, though she received no message from that quarter, she knew the substance of it would be exactly what she wanted. That was nearly as good as getting it and with the thought that emotionally and mentally she was as sure of Piers as of her own eventual death, she went to sleep at last and woke to the ringing of church bells for early Sunday service, a pleasant sound to her because she could lie in bed, pitying all the people who pattered through the streets in obedience to that summons and leaving her family to forage for their breakfasts when they chose. Her own breakfast, she knew, would soon be brought to her by Sandra who would then prepare another tray for Chloe.

'Only this Sunday and next and then I shan't do it for Chloe any more,' Sandra said.

'One job less. You ought to be thankful,' said Rosamund.

Sandra did not find it necessary to reply. Instead, she said, 'And Miss Spanner's going on as usual because the boys are wandering about in dressing-gowns. She might do it herself if she had a nicer one, but she says it's slovenly.'

'So it is, but it's nice, once a week.'

'And now she's started about wastefulness.'

'Tell her to mind her own business.'

'And how cross you'd be if I did! It's all these separate teapots that worry her. She says if we all had breakfast together we'd save about a quarter of a pound of tea and the day will come when we'll need it. D'you think that's true?'

'I think it's very likely. In the meantime I'm going to use all I want and in the meantime, too, Sandra, don't look like that. We must make things as happy as we can for Chloe.'

'I don't think we need bother much about that,' Sandra said. 'I think her happiness is inside herself.'

'And that's where it should be. Still, we may as well do what we can.'

'James is all right,' Sandra said. 'He has his own kind of happiness inside himself too, but Felix isn't like that.'

'No, it's you red heads who are the worriers,' Rosamund said, but she did not point the difference between these two. Felix's worries, naturally, at the moment, were for his own affairs; Sandra's would always be for those of other people. 'If only you would realize,' she said aloud, 'that you can't do much for other people in their troubles, but quite a lot in their happiness. You won't believe that, though, until you're as old as I am and you'll wear yourself to a thread and you won't be pretty.'

Sandra laughed. 'That won't matter much.'

'It will matter a great deal, to you and everybody else. Besides you'll create the very atmosphere you don't want.'

'I know,' Sandra said. 'I'll try not to, but I did think Felix looked rather extra glum this morning.'

'Perhaps he had a bad night,' Rosamund said a little dryly.

'Why?' Sandra asked anxiously. 'He's much too young for that, isn't he?'

'Much,' Rosamund agreed, and when Sandra had gone she would not allow herself to sigh. She must abide by the doctrine she had been preaching. She could not help Felix in his difficulty but she could increase Chloe's happiness by finishing the preparations for the wedding gaily and, in doing this, she found herself, at times, more generally hopeful. She would have been sorry to agree about anything with Mr. Blackett, but the pause in discussions did seem as though there were hesitation on the other side, and while she had no faith in her country's leaders who had never yet fairly faced a situation, centuries of tradition were behind them and might stiffen their weak backs, force them to outface a bully whose word was known to be worthless and who was so foul with evil it seemed as though he must perish of his own rottenness. And to expect anything good of that corruption was, after all, to expect sweetness from carrion. To approach it was to risk infection and as, during the next few days, she read the newspapers and heard people talking in the streets and shops, she began to fear that the traditions of her country were out of fashion, that some other infection already pervaded it, not a positively evil, certainly not a cruel one, but an aggravated form of the inertia which was responsible for so much. She knew there must be many people who felt as she did, but there were not nearly enough of them. In her own house she found them. She learnt that though she had not properly combated the prevalent idea that an enemy must be right and had been too silent about the past, too much afraid of sentimentality to voice her great pride in her country and her love for it, her children's inborn ideas of decency and justice went beyond their own private affairs. They were nervously on the alert and, though they said little about it, she knew these young men of hers were thinking less of their own

306

skins, even Felix was thinking less of his future than of those standards by which they had lived, which they accepted as their inheritance and now feared might be repudiated. She did not know how to be thankful enough for that. There was comfort, too, in buying a lettuce from Piers Lindsay, another occupant of a world she understood, and having a few words with him across the vegetables, and there was always Agnes who, reserved during the daytime for Chloe's sake, had her say at night and listened, grimly amused, to Rosamund having hers with the eloquence of an easy-going person really roused, an accumulated indignation and a physical as well as mental loathing for the gang with whom we parleyed.

'And the dove sets off again to-morrow,' said Miss Spanner.

'On another flight of imagination.'

'That's about it.' She gave one of her startling bursts of laughter.

'It's not funny,' Rosamund said.

'Funny! I wasn't trying to express mirth. That was meant as derision at the thought of the poor dove among those beasts of prey, sniggering behind their grinning fangs.'

'I wonder,' Rosamund said. 'I wonder if those grins are not a little nervous.'

'Of the British lion? They know he's gone to sleep and if they're not sniggering now they'll do it yet.'

'That's what I'm afraid of,' Rosamund said. 'And isn't it horrible to think that not one of those brutes can have enjoyed honest laughter for years. Perhaps never. There can't be honest laughter where there's cruelty and anyhow they haven't any humour in our sense, the whole lot of them.'

'It's a very peculiar sense,' Miss Spanner reminded her.

'Yes, we're a peculiar people,' Rosamund said with satisfaction, 'but what are we going to do, Agnes? How are we going to live, if we lose our pride in ourselves?'

'Get it back somehow,' Miss Spanner said, giving her nose a specially hard knock.

CHAPTER XLVI

SANDRA had been at pains to show Rhoda she was not involved in Flora's error. 'Let's do something,' she said towards the end of that week. 'I'm glad school begins to-morrow. Everything's ready for the wedding and these are such horrid days to get through. I suppose it's rather cowardly, but I want to get away and pretend this is just a nice ordinary day with no special need to listen to the news. Let's go to Mr. Lindsay's on our bicycles. He'd give us something to do.'

'But I've had to take my bicycle back to the shop,' Rhoda said.

'You could hire it again, couldn't you?'

Rhoda made a rapid calculation of how much pocket money would be left when she had paid for the wedding present she was giving Chloe. 'I'd like that better than anything,' she said fervently, 'but I'd have to get back rather early, quite by five o'clock.' That, she thought, would give her a wide margin of safety, before her father's return.

'Well, that's easy,' Sandra said. 'We shall have had enough by then because I expect it will be weeding. Of course James stays as long as there's anything to do.'

'James?' Rhoda said.

'He's working there.'

'Is he?' Rhoda's tone was now mournful. 'Aren't men lucky! They can do whatever they like.'

'So can we, sometimes, and this is one of the times. We'll take our lunch and then no one need bother about us. Your mother wouldn't mind, would she?'

'No, she wouldn't mind.'

'Then let's go.'

Rhoda shook her head. 'Not there,' she said.

'But you said you'd like it.'

'Yes, I know, but you see —' Rhoda stopped there. She did not want Sandra or anyone else to see what she saw herself, the possibility of another smirching word from Flora. She would be sure to discover that James was working with Cousin Piers, perhaps she knew it already, and though Sandra could guess nothing of this, she saw in Rhoda's eyes an appeal for the acceptance of her decision and the asking of no questions and she said quickly, 'All right. We'll go for a long walk instead.'

'Where there are fields,' Rhoda said.

'The fields are getting farther and farther away, but I know some woods and when we get out of them we see the sea.'

'On this side of the river,' Rhoda decreed.

'All right,' Sandra said again, loyally trying not to solve a puzzle to which she began to find a clue.

It was a good day they had together, talking very little but unembarrassed by their silences, and these young things who should have been looking forward hopefully to the future, agreed with unconscious pathos, when they parted in the Square, that it would be a nice day to remember.

Flora, who had had a very dull one, looked with what was supposed to be amusement at Rhoda's red face and untidy hair as, rather footsore, she limped into the dining-room where the others were just finishing tea, with her father, most unexpectedly early, at the table. It was a good thing she had not hired the bicycle, a good thing she had not crossed the river, for while Mr. Blackett merely raised his eyebrows at her appearance, Flora said at once, 'You look as if you've been farming. Have you? Because if I were you I wouldn't.'

'I know you wouldn't, but I'm lucky not to have any looks to bother about.'

'There's something in that,' Flora said. 'Have you been just with Sandra Fraser all the time? You must have been bored. You have a queer taste in companions, but perhaps you think it's worth your while. Where have you been, really? Over to Cousin Piers again, I suppose.'

'You can suppose anything you like.'

'And you can answer a civil question when it's put to you,' Mr. Blackett said sharply.

'Flora's questions aren't meant to be civil,' Rhoda said calmly.

309

'This tea's cold. I'm going to make some more and have it with Connie in the kitchen.'

'Yes, a very queer taste in companions!' Flora laughed after her.

'And you,' said Mrs. Blackett, 'will never have any at all unless you can cultivate a more generous spirit,' and at this unwontedly severe remark, Flora showed the genuine astonishment of her father when he was accused of the same fault.

She was exactly like him, Mrs. Blackett thought, in character and in looks. They were both gazing at her with eyes a little defensively veiled, there were the same high spots of colour on their cheeks and there was the same over-redness of their lips.

'Oh!' Flora burst out at last, 'of course no one must say a word against Rhoda!'

'It would be pleasant to hear you say anything else,' was Mrs. Blackett's reply, 'but she is used to it and I think she minds much more when you attack her friend.'

'Friend!' Flora exclaimed and she looked at her father. She felt this was his cue.

'Friend?' Mr. Blackett repeated in a grave tone.

'Yes,' Mrs. Blackett said, 'and I am very glad she has such a nice one.'

'I don't believe Rhoda cares two pins about her,' Flora said.

'Don't judge everybody by yourself,' Mrs. Blackett begged, and before either Flora or her father could frame a retort there was an exclamation from Mary who had been an interested but puzzled witness of this scene.

'Here's Chloe Fraser coming now,' she said, and Mr. Blackett, taking a glance through the window, had a momentary vision of youth and happiness speeding towards his door. 'What can she be coming for?' Mary wondered.

Mrs. Blackett knew. A few weeks ago she would have regretted Chloe's arrival at this moment; now she was rather pleased. She was pleased, too, when having met her at the door and taken her into the drawing-room, they were followed there by Flora and Mr. Blackett in time to hear Chloe say, 'Such a lovely present, Mrs. Blackett! I had to come over at once. I don't know why you should be so kind,' and to see Mrs. Blackett kiss her as she said, 'I wanted to be sure you would see something very pretty every time you looked at it.' Then her warm, gracious tone changed to a colder one. 'I don't know whether you have ever met my husband,' she said.

'We know each other very well by sight, I think,' Chloe said smiling at his slightly exaggerated bow, smiling, but with difficulty, at Flora. 'And you'll come to the wedding, Mrs. Blackett?'

'I shall come to the church to see you married. On Wednesday, isn't it?'

'Yes, on Wednesday. Whatever happens.'

'Whatever happens,' Mrs. Blackett said with approval.

'And thank you very very much,' Chloe said, clasping her hands tightly in the hope that Mrs. Blackett would believe in the sincerity of her thanks. 'But I shall see you before then, shan't I? You'll come and see the other presents?'

'Yes, I should like to do that,' Mrs. Blackett said, accompanying her to the door and there, without spectators, kissed her again and wished her happiness. 'And I think you will have it,' she said.

'Yes,' said Chloe, 'I know I shall, if it's only for a few days,' and she returned as swiftly as she had come.

Mrs. Blackett went back to the drawing-room prepared, even anxious, for questions, and at once, as though she suspected she had been robbed of something, Flora demanded, 'What did you give her?'

'An old gilt mirror,' Mrs. Blackett replied.

'And you meant she'd see herself when she looked at it?'

'Yes, that's what I meant. I wanted to give her something as pretty as she is and nothing but her own reflection seemed to do.'

'I can see no reason why you should have given her a present of any kind,' Mr. Blackett said.

'And, anyhow, she isn't as pretty as all that!' Flora cried.

'No?' Mrs. Blackett inquired gently. 'But you see, Flora, she has charm, too, and that is more important. And,' she went on, looking beyond these two unfriendly faces, 'that comes from within and has a beauty of its own and lasts for ever. So,' she said more briskly, 'I have paid my little tribute to it,' and she ended this interview by going, not too quickly, to the garden door and standing there for a minute before she descended to the garden. She had given them every chance to speak, but neither of them had taken it. Mr. Blackett merely gave a slight cough and turned it into a hum. It was not what she had said, but her manner, which was remarkable. There was, Mr. Blackett realized, a new kind of authority in it or, rather, a new sureness of herself, and he took a sly look at Flora to see whether she had received the same impression, but Flora was asking herself, with aggrievement, in what particular quality of Chloe's she was lacking, and if she really lacked it, how she was to get it.

She lifted her bowed head. 'I don't think she's as wonderful as all that, do you?' she asked resentfully.

'A pretty piece,' Mr. Blackett said tolerantly. 'Somewhat lacking in colour, I think.' He liked Mrs. Fraser's blue eyes better than Chloe's grey-blue ones, her vivacity better than Chloe's quietness.

'Yes, I think so, too,' Flora said eagerly.

'Both,' Mr. Blackett went on, 'in her appearance, which is of very little importance and, if I am not mistaken, colourless in character. And you and I know that character and intellect are the first necessities.' He patted her shoulder. 'I much prefer my own daughter's qualities,' he said and would not embarrass her by looking for signs of her modest gratification.

She made a mocking face at his retreating back. How stupid he was, she thought. Anyone could deceive him. She was sure that woman in France, pretending he was a kindred spirit, had simply been using him to pass the time and he had no idea that she herself cared nothing about character except that it seemed to have some connection with this indefinable thing called charm, but she knew that it might be valuable for the future to keep him in this state of ignorance. And what was this charm? she wondered again, going upstairs to find it if she could, and so successfully finding it in her looking-glass when she saw the brilliant enamels of skin and lips, the greenish eyes under the black hair, that she thought her father must be purblind and her mother bewitched by those people across the road. And they must be purblind too, she decided with a heavy heart. What was she to do with the prettiness no one else seemed to appreciate? There must be someone somewhere who would take her view of it and, while she shared her father's political opinions, and thought it would be wicked to become involved in someone else's quarrel — though it was noble to try to avert it — she did see, in the possibility of war, the possibility of escape from home, a chance of getting those experiences which were her due.

Mr. Blackett, in his study, could see no advantages in that disaster. He looked at his bookshelves and could not find anything to suit the uneasy moment. He had come home earlier than usual, to his own quiet kingdom, where his eyes would not be affronted by sensational newspaper placards or his ears vexed by speculative chatter. His midday meal had been ruined by the reminiscences of his contemporaries who usually shared his table, by their interested and quite superfluous inquiries about his activities in the last war and by the polite reserve with which they accepted his explanations. He had thought all that was over years ago and he had not been able to produce for these men the remark with which Bertha had always been well satisfied, about the hard necessity for some people to resign all hope of glory.

He had come home to be soothed and he had been disappointed. Rhoda had returned from an expedition and a companionship of which he disapproved, looking like a tramp and in a quarrelsome mood and Bertha's reproaches had been directed towards the wrong person; she had attacked Flora. And if he had not come home early he would never, he supposed, have heard about the wedding present and this savoured of deceit. He wondered how much it had cost and whether he was expected to pay for it. He did not intend to do so. And then, with a quiet dignity, Bertha had taken the stage and made her little speech and her

313

leisurely exit, a new Bertha, he thought, and yet, rummaging in his mind for incidents and words he had put aside as useless and now found he needed, taking them out and looking at them, they became more significant than he had believed. Once she had told him Flora was like him and he had been pleased, but lately she was finding faults in the girl. Did that mean she was finding them in him too? She had accused them both of lack of generosity and when had she ever acknowledged a virtue in him or given him a word of praise? And in the romantic sanctity of their bedroom, had she not laughed at him? Mr. Blackett, who had been pacing the room, stood still and saw, not the carpet at which he looked, but a dark well of unknown depth. Half fascinated and quite horrified, he stared down, knowing that the longer he looked the darker and deeper it would become, until, with self-preservation more urgent than curiosity, he stepped back into safety. He remembered her gratifying signs of jealousy and the carpet closed over the pit.

CHAPTER XLVII

ON the next Sunday, the last of September, Rosamund heard a more imperative note in the early call of the church bells and she fancied that there must be more hurry than usual in the answering pattering feet, as though prayers to be efficacious, and they needed to be that, must be particularly punctual, as though a special effort of pleading, could persuade God to renounce his laws and make life meaningless by wiping out all responsibility for past acts and thoughts.

'But perhaps I'm wronging them,' she said as Miss Spanner entered, wearing her Sunday frock and looking reproachfully at Rosamund in her nightgown.

'Wronging them!' Miss Spanner exclaimed. 'You couldn't if you tried. In the first place, you're incapable of imagining enough vileness.'

'Thank you, Agnes, but I wasn't thinking of that gang. I was thinking of the people who go to church to pray; sneering at them a little, I'm afraid, but they may not be asking for miracles. They may just be asking for the right spirit, but I wish they would do it from their comfortable beds and let other people sleep in peace.'

'Peace!' Miss Spanner cried.

'Is it? Will it be?'

'Who for?' Miss Spanner asked. 'Would you call it peace if some kind friend decided that you must give up half your house and nearly all your freedom with the expectation of losing all of it to the accompaniment of a little torture, just to save him from getting mixed up in a dispute for which there's no justification except filthy greed? Well, that's the role we're playing. No justification! No justification!' Miss Spanner cried in a fury. 'And half the world, more than half, is behaving as though it's perfectly reasonable to grab anything you fancy. And the greed won't stop there. You'll see. Why should it? But the victim hasn't consented yet to being carved up. Queer, isn't it? Selfish. You'd think he'd be grateful for being allowed to keep a little bit of his own body. And I hope he'll prefer to keep it all.'

'And that will mean war.'

'Yes.'

'And we're not prepared for it.'

'No.'

'I think I'd better get up,' Rosamund said.

'And why need we be prepared,' Miss Spanner continued, 'when we can appease the wolves by throwing other people at them? But the appetite can grow by what it feeds on — we'd better remember that. When I was a child I used to believe that a steady human eye could control the most ferocious brute. Did you believe that, too? The cowed animal, acknowledging its superior, simply slinks away. We're trying that trick as well and the animal must find it very amusing. He knows these particular human eyes haven't outstared any aggressive creature yet. The old Noah was lucky. He had all the beasts of prey safely under

315

lock and key. But I don't believe you're listening. And oh,' Miss Spanner said contritely, 'I suppose it's easy for me to talk like this. It's different for you.'

'Isn't it the way I've always talked myself?' Rosamund said wearily. 'It's the way I still feel, but there are complications, Agnes, complications, and I do hope Piers will take it into his head to come over this afternoon.'

'Piers?' Miss Spanner said sharply.

'That's Mr. Lindsay's name.'

'I didn't know you used it.'

'Of course I do when I get the chance and that's not often.'

'And how,' Miss Spanner inquired, 'do you imagine he's going to help?'

'Oh, just by existing, just by being himself and making you feel there's still hope for mankind.'

Miss Spanner's jaw dropped slowly. 'So that's what you call him, that's what he does for you,' she said, and at the sight of her mournful face Rosamund said quickly, 'For everybody, I should think.'

'Not for me,' said Miss Spanner firmly. 'A bit of a nonentity, I call him. He hasn't much to say for himself.'

Rosamund laughed. 'You're quite right, Agnes. That's just it. There could hardly be a more selfless person.'

'And how do you know that?'

'Because I'm a clever woman.'

'Bah!' said Miss Spanner and went to the window. 'You're not in love with him, are you?' she asked in a tremulous voice.

'What would be the good?'

'Good? It would be wicked! — You're a married woman.'

'I do hate that expression,' Rosamund said. 'I always think it sounds slightly indecent.'

'But are you?' Miss Spanner asked.

'Yes, yes, nothing's happened.'

'I mean in love,' Miss Spanner said unwillingly.

'No,' Rosamund said with a sort of scorn. There was a difference between loving and being in love. She would not have smoothed her hair for Piers when she rose in the night. Then, she asked herself, was she in love with Fergus still? 'No,' she said aloud, but she liked to remember the strangely enduring pleasure he found in looking at her. She hoped, she knew that Piers found pleasure in it too, but she had been scrupulous in trying not to provoke it and with him it was not the first consideration. He would be sorry, but he would not love her less, if she lost what beauty she had kept.

She had shut her eyes and now she opened them to see, with astonishment, that Miss Spanner's eyes were full of tears. These overflowed and Rosamund, through her alarm and pity, could not help deploring the grotesqueness of her friend's appearance, the unchecked tears falling towards the childishly drooping mouth.

'I was afraid, I've always been afraid since he started coming here,' Miss Spanner whimpered. 'I even told lies to warn him off.'

'Lies?' Rosamund said, and Miss Spanner nodded her head several times. 'What lies?'

'Oh, never mind,' Miss Spanner said miserably.

'And do you think they were successful?' Rosamund asked, hardening herself against this exhibition of emotion.

'How do I know? And it doesn't matter so long as you don't care yourself. Because,' Miss Spanner cried, 'what was going to happen to me if you went and married someone else? I had a right, hadn't I, to try to keep what I'd got at last?'

'Heaven knows you haven't had much,' Rosamund said, touched as she always was by the thought of Agnes's youth and forgiving the lies which had done no harm.

'And I'm not making a fool of myself now, because I'm un-happy,' Miss Spanner explained, 'but because I'm so thankful to feel safe.'

'You're lucky,' Rosamund said. Life could never be really safe, though it was true that there were fewer points of danger for Agnes than for her, and perhaps that was not so lucky, after all. 'Don't cry any more, my poor dear,' she said. 'Whither I go thou shalt go —'

'And where's that?' Miss Spanner asked in a new fright.

'Into the future,' Rosamund said. 'And my people shall be thy people and all the rest of it.' She realized the rashness of this promise but she was not sorry she had made it. She had not rescued Agnes from that dark house on the Green to thrust her into a greater loneliness and she found herself remembering that Fergus had always liked her curious friend. It was one of the nice things about him, that capacity for recognizing her quality under an exterior which troubled his eye for beauty and a manner which suspiciously resisted his friendliness.

'My people are yours already, aren't they?' she said. 'They like you very much.'

'They put up with me,' Miss Spanner said. 'It's all I can expect.'

'Don't be an affected idiot. I never so nearly dislike you as when you adopt a humble attitude. Go and put on your dress for the wedding and let me see what's wrong with it.'

She had added to her complications. She had accepted responsibility for Agnes, but was she fit for it? In the past she had not properly accepted her responsibility for Fergus and she might fail Agnes too. She had drifted past all the mistakes she knew Fergus was making: she had allowed herself to drift into love for Piers and allowed him to love her in a highly involved situation through which she could not see her way. She had never looked far enough ahead and her only right to criticize those who had made the same mistake in larger matters was her readiness to admit her faults and, until she was roused by the return of Miss Spanner in a garment needing immediate action, she felt too much of a failure to dare to face another day. But she was sure of herself in the matter of clothes and, on her knees, in spite of Miss Spanner's protests, her reminder that there were more important problems to be faced than the length of a skirt and that this preoccupation with it was an unworthy frivolity at such a time, she tackled it with zest.

'I can't make a war or stop one,' she said, 'but I can make you look less of a fright. There! Now undo the hem and turn it up again. Did you happen to try on this dress before you bought it?'

'No,' said Miss Spanner. 'Couldn't be bothered. The girl in the shop said it was my size and I knew she'd sneer at my underclothes. And, talking of girls in shops —'

'Why should we?'

'Oh, all right. I was only going to say that Felix is oftener at home in the evenings than he used to be.'

'Yes, bad for him, with a pack of women.'

'Better a pack than one,' said Miss Spanner. 'And just when the shops are shut, too, so perhaps we needn't worry.'

'Have you been worrying?' Rosamund asked as though surprised. 'And those sleeves must come out too. The shoulders are all wrong, and in future, Agnes, take me with you when you go shopping.'

'I'll take you to-morrow if you like and you can have a look at her.'

'A nice pair of old cats we should be. Looking for the wrong mouse, too, very likely.'

'Then you admit there's a mouse,' Miss Spanner said quickly.

'Sure to be,' Rosamund said. 'You're a queer mixture, Agnes. You reverse the usual order of things. You'll be furious if the Government plays any dirty tricks but you'll play them yourself out of mere curiosity.'

'Curiosity!' Miss Spanner exclaimed. 'I should call it the kind of maternal care you've never given your children.'

'The kind your mother gave you, peeping and prying! There's something a bit Spannerish about you, after all.'

'You're the only person I ever talk to and I'll never tell you another thing,' Miss Spanner declared. 'All the same —'

'What? Turn round slowly. Yes, that will do, but don't lose all the pins when you take the dress off.'

'All the same,' said Miss Spanner, 'I shouldn't be surprised — but no, I won't tell you.' She would not speak, she tried not to think of the admirable plan she had made for Rhoda. Rhoda was still loyal. It was no longer an adventure to reach Miss

Spanner's room, but she still found pleasure in it, still stared and listened in spite of the other attractions in the house and no tricks, clean or dirty, even privately, must be played with her simple candour. 'But if it happens,' Miss Spanner said, 'perhaps you'll remember that I foresaw it.'

'I will. That gives you unlimited scope as a prophet. And I suppose it's time I got dressed.'

'High time,' said Miss Spanner ungratefully. She stepped on to the balcony and returned. 'Blacketts, just starting for church,' she reported.

'And I know what he'll be praying for,' Rosamund said.

Mr. Blackett, as a matter of fact, did not feel inclined to pray at all. This was nothing new. He did not find it a necessary exercise. Church going was discipline for his family, a sign of his belief in law and order, a personal protest against the careless tendencies of the times and he had his reward in listening to beautiful, familiar words. This morning all he heard was his wife's voice as she joined in the hymns and the responses and he heard it with irritation. He liked this acquiescence in the woman he had married, yet he had an admittedly unreasonable feeling, on this occasion, that she was declaring her independence of his silence. He was very uneasy; he was as much aggrieved as Flora when she could not get what she wanted, and though his expression was that of a man who accepts injury with dignity, he raged inwardly to think that his comfort, his business, his security and his own prophecies were imperilled by the obstinacy of a country no one would be the worse without. And at breakfast there had been an argument he had not been able to quell, a new experience. Flora, who seldom failed him, had expressed views which were his own, but Rhoda — he glared along the pew and saw her as glum and silent as he was himself — had dared to have very different ones and had still more daringly suggested that he hated anyone to disagree with him, and declared that she had a right to her own opinion. He would have forbidden her to come to church but for his conviction that she would have been delighted to stay away. She would have slipped across the road where, he had no doubt, she had been injected with these false notions.

'Rhoda,' he said to Mrs. Blackett as he watched his daughters walking homewards, 'is quite insufferable.' On the way to church, the children walked behind their parents, on the way back they went ahead. 'Look at her now. In the road instead of on the pavement. Still too bad tempered to walk beside Flora, I suppose. I don't like the way she is developing. She is going to be an arrogant, unattractive young woman, I'm afraid, the very type I most dislike. I don't know how I came to have such a daughter.'

'I worked very hard on her,' said Mrs. Blackett, with unusual candour, 'before she was born, though I don't believe that sort of thing is really effectual.'

'Evidently not,' said Mr. Blackett. 'You had better start working all over again. And in the first place, this constant communication with our neighbours must be stopped. You know I distrust them. Tell her so.'

'I think you must do that.'

'After her behaviour this morning I refuse to speak to her.'

'Very well,' said Mrs. Blackett, smiling a little. People who never fought were never beaten. They had reached the entrance to the Square. 'Dinner will be a quarter of an hour later than usual,' she said. 'I'm going into the Frasers' house to hear the news.'

CHAPTER XLVIII

'THE funeral baked meats,' said Felix, looking at the simple preparations for the wedding, 'did coldly furnish forth the marriage table, only it's the other way round. Wedding first, funeral after. A pity,' he said to his mother with a wry grin, 'we couldn't have had a double wedding while we were about it.'

'It's the bride's mother who gives the entertainment,' Rosamund said.

'Clever!' he said, grinning again but, his grin said, he was not to be caught like that.

She thought he seemed a little drunk but she was sure this manner, unusual with him, though she had often seen it in his father, was a mixture of desperation and exhilaration. The conditions that doomed might also save him. Twenty-four years ago a gay recklessness, this kind of flippancy, had been the resource of young men who knew their lives were not worth many days' purchase, and here it was, all over again, yet the prospect had not dimmed Chloe's radiance and Rosamund saw Felix looking at her with an envious curiosity as she came calmly downstairs in her soft blue dress and little hat, half smiling and, as it were, illumined by an inner glow.

'I don't want to give you away,' he said. 'I'd like to keep you.'

Flora, disdaining to go to the church with her mother as a mere spectator, watched the proceedings from the dining-room window. She saw Miss Spanner, Sandra and Paul set off on foot, they had not far to go; then a car came for Mrs. Fraser and James, another for Felix and Chloe, and she thought it was a very shabby affair. It was like a servant's wedding, she decided, when she saw the boys in ordinary suits and the charwoman, left in charge of the house, standing on the doorstep to see them go, and if she had been familiar with an author she could not appreciate, she would have said, changing the words a little, 'No white satin, no lace veils, a most pitiful business.' But when the cars had gone and the heads had disappeared from many of the windows in the Square, it was her own situation that became pitiful. She felt as though she were alone in an empty world and it seemed a long time before Chloe and her husband returned, then Mrs. Fraser with a little lady in flowing garments and a large lace hat and a tall, vague gentleman who fumbled in his pockets for the car fare and suddenly remembered that he was a guest. These, she supposed, were the bridegroom's parents and then, in little groups, the other guests arrived, many of them young, and why was she not there? Why was she not talking merrily to Felix or even to James? Then she saw her mother walking with Miss

322

Spanner and Cousin Piers and with them entering the house and she ran upstairs and hastily changed her frock. Somebody would wonder why she was not there too, perhaps Felix, she thought excitedly, would come and fetch her, but the minutes passed and nothing happened except the arrival of Rhoda and Mary who, back from school, flung their books into the area and joined the party. She was certainly not going to follow them and as she was the only member of the family who had not been invited, she would not go now if she were asked. She heard the hum of voices through the window of the long room, she saw changing figures on the drawing-room balcony and at last the doorway, the shallow steps and the pavement were full of people watching the bride and bridegroom drive away under a shower of flower petals. And still the young ones lingered, finding plenty to say to each other, plenty to laugh about, Felix and James, but not Rhoda, among them, and Flora cautiously, enviously, peered at them until she saw her mother and Mary leave the house and she retreated to the drawing-room, whence there was no view of the Square, and she was found there, deep in a book.

'It was a pity you didn't come,' Mrs. Blackett said. 'It was a very happy party. Mrs. Fraser saw me in the church and asked me to the reception.'

'Reception! How grand!' Flora said.

'She didn't call it that.'

'Well,' said Flora, 'I suppose she had to ask you. You'd bought the invitation, hadn't you?'

'Bought it?'

'With that present,' and when her mother did not answer, she said, 'Where's Rhoda?'

'I think she is still there. I expect she will come back with your Cousin Piers.'

'Did they ask their other tradesmen too?'

'I didn't notice any of them,' Mrs. Blackett replied patiently, and then, very gently, she asked, 'Why are you so unhappy?'

'Why shouldn't I be?' Flora replied sullenly before she let herself go and cried, 'I haven't any friends here. I don't fit in with these humdrum people. It's the wrong kind of life for me. And nobody wants me at home. Rhoda hates me and Mary doesn't count and you just try to be kind and Father likes me because he thinks I'm like him.'

'And so you are,' Mrs. Blackett said.

'Then,' said Flora accusingly and with enjoyment, 'I suppose you just try to be kind to him, too.'

'No, I don't try,' Mrs. Blackett said, and left Flora to make what she would of that.

'And,' Flora went on, 'I hope there'll be a war, not because I think it would be right; I don't. Though Father's stupid about some things, he's quite right about that, but I might be able to get away from home and meet some really interesting people, the kind I like.'

'It would be the best thing for you,' Mrs. Blackett said.

'Wouldn't you mind?' asked Flora, ready for another grievance.

'I should be very anxious about you.'

'You'd be more anxious if it was Rhoda.'

'No. I shouldn't be at all anxious about Rhoda.'

'Well, no,' Flora said after a little thought, and with a smile, 'you wouldn't need to be, would you?'

Mrs. Blackett gave a sad little shake of her head. She knew it would be misinterpreted: she knew anything she could say to Flora would either be taken as an affront or slide off the polished surface of her self-esteem.

'And it's a pity Rhoda doesn't realize that herself,' Flora said, and added with apparent irrelevance, 'I very soon got bored with James Fraser and had to let him know it.'

Mrs. Blackett heard this remark with concealed amusement not unmixed with pity, but she was startled when Flora said, 'And now it will be James who will soon get bored with Rhoda. Haven't you noticed? All this friendship with Sandra? It's so obvious. But it began ages ago with pretending to like Miss Spanner. As if anybody could!'

'I can and do,' Mrs. Blackett said with an unmaternal desire to slap Flora's face.

'Oh, that's quite different,' Flora said. 'I meant anybody young.' Mr. Blackett had wondered how he came to have a daughter like Rhoda: Mrs. Blackett knew all too well how she came to have one like Flora. She was not worried about Rhoda. The time for that would be when the child began to take an active interest in her appearance. There was no sign of it at present and between then and now many things were going to happen. There might be no James for whom she would wish to brush her hair and make sure her blouse had some firm connection with her skirt; there might even, she realized, as Piers Lindsay prowled about the basement, be no Rhoda herself.

'Not so bad under the stairs,' he said, 'but I think Blackett ought to have an expert up to look. Your own idea, of course.'

'Yes,' Mrs. Blackett said. 'Have you looked at Mrs. Fraser's basement too?'

'Some time ago,' he said with a little lack of tact.

'So you think it's coming?'

'It looks like it. It looks as though we've done our worst without success, yet who knows?' he said with mock hopefulness, 'we may still find something worse to do.'

'I don't see how.'

'Of course you don't! You wouldn't be you if you did,' he said, and kissed her but, while she was proud of these words and touched by this reward, she knew that in other circumstances, married to a man with whom it was her pleasure to agree, she might have been able to arrange matters in her mind to suit his views. It would not have been easy, for though she was not a politically minded woman she would have had to subdue her instinctive convictions in favour of what looked like expediency. It happened to be her pleasure to agree with her cousin and he had taken the agreement for granted because he believed in her, a tribute quite unlike any she had ever had from her husband who, in praising her, always seemed indirectly to applaud himself, and she would have felt quite gay if gaiety had been possible in such an hour.

'Is Mrs. Fraser very anxious, do you think?' she asked.

'She didn't look it, did she?'

'No. It was a nice little wedding.'

'I don't know much about weddings. I believe this is the first I've been to since I was at yours.'

In the darkness of the basement Mrs. Blackett shut her eyes but she was no more blind than she had been on her wedding day; indeed she saw too much, too clearly, with them shut and she opened them quickly and said, 'I haven't been to many myself, but do you know what I do? I'm rather ashamed of it and always hope no one will recognize me when I join the crowd at a church door and wait to see the bride come out. I suppose it's the same sort of fascination as there would be in watching someone gambling for high stakes.'

'But the dice box is still over the dice,' he said.

'Yes, but the gambler's face is interesting. Chloe looked quite confident of her luck.'

'So did you,' Lindsay said, starting up the stairs.

And so she had been, but the difference between her and Chloe, she was sure, was that between ignorance and knowledge.

'And it was some time before I forgave you,' he said.

'Really, Piers?' He could see her face clearly now and she did not conceal her pleasure.

'I suppose I was in a sentimental mood, just back from war, and found my pretty cousin stolen.'

'Only a mood? And some time doesn't sound very long,' she said.

'It wasn't very long. You're sorry about that, aren't you? What brutes women are in matters of love! You'd like me to be suffering still, wouldn't you?'

'It would be very nice for me,' she owned with conscious demureness.

'So I thought but, to be rude and honest, I wasn't long in recovering and I still love you, like a brother.'

'Yes,' she smiled and sighed together, 'very much like a brother and a reserved one, but perhaps brothers always are. Perhaps those boys across the road don't tell their sisters much.'

'The difficulty about telling is that it so often involves telling about someone else.'

'Otherwise you might?'

'I'd trust you with anything. Good-bye.'

He kissed her again and she said solemnly, 'This is one of the best days I've ever had,' and its goodness was increased when she saw a slight contraction of his face and knew it expressed sorrow or anger for her: she knew too that though sorrow might be, anger was not justified. If her husband searched his conscience he would find no reproaches in it except for those errant thoughts he had not and never would turn into actions, and if she had been asked what complaints she had against him, she could only have replied that it was the man himself, irritating her to a frenzy she had turned into a vicious pleasure. He had not wronged her beyond giving her a character to meet his needs, yet it was a big wrong, condemning him and, to some extent, excusing her.

She watched Piers Lindsay go and without bitterness saw him glance down at the kitchen and then up at the balcony. He had loved her mildly for a little while; given the opportunity, he might have loved her for much longer, but she thought it possible that she was happier in imagining what might have been than in the chance of putting it to the proof.

CHAPTER XLIX

WHEN Mr. Blackett turned into the Square that evening, walking with the quick, hard step of his indignation with events, he slackened his pace suddenly at the sight of Mrs. Fraser and Rhoda talking together on the pavement, Mrs. Fraser leaning on the long handle of a broom she clasped. Both turned their heads at the sound of his approach and Rhoda ran across the road and disappeared down the area steps, but Mrs. Fraser, as he expected, lingered – and this was to his surprise – took a few paces towards him, an attention which made some amends for his daughter's conduct. Rhoda, he thought, might have had the decency to wait for him; it looked very bad to run away like that but her manners, her carelessness of appearances, were always deplorable. He was, in truth, glad to be free of her cool scrutiny. He had not, however, to meet Mrs. Fraser's usual amused and inviting eyes. She hardly smiled as she greeted him; the little lines round her eyes seemed to be more deeply graved, to be the effect of time and not of laughter.

'Wait just a minute, Mr. Blackett,' she said. 'Stay there. I want to sweep the pavement,' and turning from him and pushing the broom in front of her, she cleared away the coloured shreds of flowers he had not noticed, most of them already flattened into a mosaic. 'There,' she said. 'Now you can pass,' and he said in a puzzled tone, 'This is very kind, but surely it wasn't necessary.'

'I thought it was. A sort of Sir Walter Raleigh act, but he laid down a cloak and I removed the obstruction.'

'A very pretty obstruction,' he said.

'Yes, we've had a wedding.'

'Indeed?' said Mr. Blackett. 'Not a very happy occasion for a wedding I'm afraid.'

'Not a happy occasion for anything,' said Mrs. Fraser, knocking the head of her broom against the kerb and going into the house. 'Were you watching?' she asked Miss Spanner. 'I hoped you would be. When I saw him coming I simply couldn't bear to let him tread on what's left of Chloe's flowers.'

'He must have thought you were crazy.'

'He doesn't know what to think but it won't be that.'

'I wonder how he'll like the surprise he'll find at home,' Miss Spanner said.

The distance to his own door was all too short for Mr. Blackett. He wanted time for consideration. That was an extraordinary thing to do, to stop him and clear a way for him, as though he would have noticed those faded petals unless, indeed, he had chanced to slip on them. That was a possible explanation of Mrs. Fraser's action, but why had she referred to the historic incident? he asked himself, taking a long time to find his latchkey. It was almost, to put it mildly, a declaration of special respect; he fancied there must be something symbolic in it; and she had not laughed. She had looked older but more charming in this serious mood and possibly this was the true one, revealed to him at last, but these thoughts, on which he meant to dwell in the solitude of his study, were swept from his mind as soon as he opened the door. The neat, narrow hall did not look like itself. A pair of soiled gloves lay on the little table, there was a basket on the floor beside it, a coat had been flung over the banisters and a shabby suitcase seemed to be awaiting transport upstairs and he was staring at these objects and conscious of a low, continuous sound, when Mrs. Blackett appeared from the passage between the sitting-rooms. She was laughing, silently, as he had seen her do before and, remembering that night, he asked severely, 'What is causing you this amusement? What,' he pointed to the disorder in the hall, 'does all this mean?'

'Hush! Come into the study. One of the horrors of war,' she said, and frowning at this untimely joke, he followed her. 'It's your sister Maude,' she said.

'Maude!' he exclaimed, and forgave her flippant description of their guest's arrival. 'Maude! And you can laugh! Well, she talked her husband to death and now, I suppose, she is going to kill me.'

'She was afraid of being killed herself, by bombs.'

Mr. Blackett's lifted eyebrows expressed surprise that his sister should think this mattered. 'Most inconsiderate,' he said. 'And where,' he inquired, 'is she going to sleep?'

'I've arranged about her bed. She must have Flora's room.'

'And Flora?'

'Flora will sleep with Mary. Mrs. Fraser is kindly letting Rhoda have Chloe's empty bed.'

Mr. Blackett did not speak for a moment and it seemed to her that he had to remember to look annoyed before he muttered, 'I suppose it can't be helped. But for how long?' he asked desperately, 'for how long?'

'We could hire a room for her somewhere in the Square.'

'No, no,' Mr. Blackett said hastily.

'Then we must just live from day to day.'

'A most unsatisfactory way of living,' he said.

'Is it? It's what I've been doing for nearly twenty years.'

'Yes.' He smiled. 'I can believe that. You have always had someone to do the planning and thinking for you. Well, I suppose I must go and see her. But what a thing to do! And without warning!'

'It would have been worse, longer, with a warning,' Mrs. Blackett said.

'Yet you could laugh!'

'Yes, she hasn't the faintest idea that we're not delighted to see her. I thought that was funny. Is it a family peculiarity, that sort of obtuseness? Flora has it too.'

'I don't know what you mean, Bertha. You are very unfair to Flora, lately. You will be saying next that I have it myself,' and when Mrs. Blackett laughed again he thought that, this time, she was quite right.

Flora, escaping from the drawing-room and the ceaseless flow of her aunt's voice, went upstairs to help her mother in preparing the visitor's room. 'Why should Rhoda go to the Frasers?' she asked. 'Why shouldn't I?'

'You wouldn't like to share a room with Sandra, would you?'

'It wouldn't be any worse than sharing one with Mary.'

'But you hardly know Sandra and don't seem to want to. And what about Sandra herself?'

'Well, what about her?'

'She might not like it.'

'I don't see why she shouldn't,' Flora said, and Mrs. Blackett had no doubt about an inherited family failing.

'I never get a proper chance,' Flora complained.

'A chance? What for?' Mrs. Blackett asked, and Flora did not reply.

To Rhoda, her mother said privately, 'Don't look too pleased.'

'I wasn't going to. I'd thought of that already. He might easily make me sleep on the drawing-room sofa.'

'He?' Mrs. Blackett said reproachfully. 'It was Flora I was thinking of.'

'I don't care about her a bit. I don't care about him, I mean Father, either. I only mind about being stopped and I half wish I could be because I've never stayed in anybody's house before and perhaps I shall do wrong things. And I do hope, for your sake, that Aunt Maude likes going to bed early.'

'She'll find I like going very early,' Mrs. Blackett said. 'In fact I intend to be something of an invalid.'

'And she'll turn you into one if she stays for long,' Rhoda said gloomily.

Aunt Maude, however, created an extraordinary unanimity of feeling round the supper table that evening and Mrs. Blackett actually met and responded to her husband's occasional glances of despair, but she tempered these unwilling signs of sympathy by finding a strong physical likeness between the brother and sister and enjoying the enforced silence at the head of the table. In a pause, for somehow Aunt Maude ate a hearty meal, Mr. Blackett did get in a sentence.

'Rhoda,' he said, 'don't go across the road without me.'

'But,' Rhoda said, raising her voice above the renewed accompaniment, 'it's only a few yards.'

'That's not the point.' He, too, raised his voice. 'In the circumstances I think it would be the proper thing to hand you over formally, as it were.'

'Every night?' said Rhoda, and Mr. Blackett blenched at the horrid portent in these words.

'I can eat no more,' he said, pushing his plate aside and glaring at his sister, and as he went towards his study, Rhoda said, 'I want to be there in time for the news.'

'One mechanical noise is no worse than another,' he snapped back and slammed the door.

'Nearly human,' Rhoda murmured to her mother, but she did not know how long this approximation would last; she hoped he would leave her on the doorstep and knew, when she saw him gallantly pick up her little bag, that her hope was vain. He would not have carried the bag unless he had meant to be seen with it and as he meant to be seen, she was glad he was carrying it. She wanted to feel proud of him and while she distrusted his motive in accompanying her and doubted whether he would make a favourable impression, though she knew he would try, there came into her mind one of those fancies which disappear with youth but are sturdy enough while they last to defy unlikelihood. In those few seconds while they crossed the road and stood at the Frasers' door, she thought this might be the beginning of a new relationship with him. He might, all the time, have wanted to be friends with her and with her friends, and had decided to show his good intentions and she gave him a wide, encouraging smile as she rang the bell, but Mr. Blackett hardly noticed it, pre-occupied as he was, like an actor standing in the wings and nervous about his entrance.

'Generally I just walk in,' Rhoda said. 'They're that kind of family.'

'So I have always imagined,' Mr. Blackett said, and his tone convinced her that he had only come to emphasize his good manners and to have an excuse for escaping from Aunt Maude. He did not know himself why he had come. Another second's delay before Sandra opened the door might have sent him back but, changing her look of surprise into one of welcome, she took him into the sitting-room where he said to Mrs. Fraser with grave playfulness, 'I have come to deliver my daughter into your hands,' and suddenly he remembered how once he had told her he disapproved of another daughter's friendship with her son and it seemed to him that there was a flash of remembrance, without amusement, in Mrs. Fraser's eyes. Sandra and Rhoda had gone upstairs and he was alone with her, as he had been then, but now four walls enclosed them and she looked strangely defenceless: more strangely still, she seemed willing to be in that state now

332

and, with a lift of the heart, he saw that he was right and that all the other moods she had shown him were the protection she could keep up no longer. Here was the real woman, controlled but betraying herself in the sad eyes which had grown much darker, and while this was a triumph it was one that frightened him and his unacknowledged relief was great when this swift, silent communion was broken by the sound of footsteps in the hall and the opening of the door.

Mrs. Fraser's two tall sons, and at the moment they looked to him rather like policemen, entered the room and she failed in the adroitness it was hardly fair to expect. She gave no light explanation of his presence but said, 'It must be nearly nine o'clock,' and one of the young·men turned on the news.

Sandra and Paul and Rhoda came in quietly and everybody sat down, Mrs. Fraser picked up her knitting and Mr. Blackett, an unwilling neophyte at this ceremony, prepared himself to hear the worst, to behave, on hearing it, as a strong man should, but, as the news proceeded, he found there was no need for strength, only for relief and hope and, glancing about him joyfully, he was astonished to·see no sign of relief or joy on any of the other faces. Then, with a peculiarly sharp click the news was turned off and Mr. Blackett, wanting to spring to his feet and shout as, so they had just heard, hundreds of other men had done at this tidings, found himself compelled, by some force he did not understand, to remain where he was and to be silent. He saw Mrs. Fraser's lips compressed at the corners and her eyebrows raised and one of the young men — Mr. Blackett always pretended he did not know which was which — said quietly, 'I should think that's going to settle it.'

'I think so too,' Mr. Blackett said gladly, but this remark passed unnoticed and no one turned to him for mature masculine comment. The other young man was giving his mother a queer look. He was frowning, yet he seemed to be holding back his breath. Then the door was opened and Miss Spanner, unbecomingly hatted, popped her head round it.

'What's the news?' she said.

'Another interview has been graciously granted,' said Mrs. Fraser.

Miss Spanner gave one of her alarming hoots of laughter, then smiled laboriously. 'Now I call that very kind,' she said. 'And I suppose I've been wasting my time. Oh, good evening, Mr. Blackett. But it was interesting. Civil defence,' she informed him, 'but how monstrous, how obscene, that human beings should have come to a pass when they've got to fit enormous snouts on to their faces and look like a pig's nightmare! It's degrading!'

'I think,' said Mr. Blackett, making himself heard at last, 'we are mercifully to be spared that degradation.'

'And what other kind are we going to exchange for it? And how far does the mercy extend, I wonder?' she said, and her remarks which she had no right to make and her appearance which was an offence, roused Mr. Blackett to a state of irritation which Rhoda recognized and no one else seemed to notice, and he carried it away with him after he had given and received somewhat distracted good nights.

CHAPTER L

HE did not go home at once. He had to sort out the impressions and emotions crowded into the last half hour before he faced the placidity of his wife, who had never looked at him with such defencelessness, and the battery of his sister's monologues. He strode down Chatterton Road, past the foot of the Avenue, where he had had the misfortune to see Flora with that young man, and when, after mounting the short, sharp ascent to the Downs, he reached their flat expanse, he thought it looked like a vast encampment on which the hawthorn bushes were dark tents, but there were no watch-fires and no sentries; they were not necessary. The encampment slept in peace as he felt well assured all the world he cared about would do ere long. He thought thankfully of the lives saved but he did not think of those which would be lost, starved, perhaps, in the flesh, and still more certainly in the spirit, and his thankfulness was not great enough to swamp his memory of Miss Spanner's scepticism and the arrogance of it in that plain spinster. She had no right to any opinion and still less to offer one to him. And then he had to adjust Mrs. Fraser's regrettable irony to the charmingly appealing aspect she had shown him, but this was not difficult. The appeal was to him as a man, the irony was for a situation she did not understand, and as he stood still under a cloudy sky, with no one else in sight and a moving circle of light from the cars on the surrounding roads enclosing him, he was momentarily astonished at his own perspicacity. He had seen through Mrs. Fraser's mocking manner, he had always said there would be no war: there was no doubt he was right in one case and soon, he believed, he would be proved right in the other. But this astonishment was disloyalty to himself; it suggested an uncertainty he quickly disowned, and he felt enriched, enlarged, attractive and wise. His wisdom would have to be acknowledged by his family, his attractiveness would have to be controlled. Perhaps just a few words might be uttered in corroboration of the looks which had passed between them; then their lips must be sealed against each other and their looks diverted and, thus making pictures in his mind, Mr. Blackett directed his steps towards the road for, in the darkness, the uneven ground was apt to jerk him into the practical necessities of the moment. Yet, as he went homewards, out of the darkness into the lamplit street, a change came over the spirit of his dream. He remembered the cold and unresponsive atmosphere in Mrs. Fraser's sitting-room; the grim silence of the young men who should have been overjoyed; his own daughter, silly child, following their lead; the insignificance – he had to admit it – of his presence in that company. Mrs. Fraser, at least, ought to have looked at him for sympathy and guidance. Had she been cautious or was she mentally under the domination of her sons and that impossible old maid who added to her pleasantries an appalling squint? For all the attention paid him he might as well not have been there, yet how different Mrs. Fraser had been when they were alone. How fortunate that the door had opened when it did! In the next few seconds what would he have said or done? He preferred not to answer this question though he could have done so quite satisfactorily. Either as a man moved irresistibly to an avowal or as one strong enough to refuse what she seemed to ask, he would have been pleased to see himself but, as he knew truth was waiting for him just round the corner, ready with its disconcerting mirror, he gave it the slip with a quick change of thought and entered his house without a glance across the road.

'I'm afraid I stayed rather a long time,' he said to Mrs. Blackett with a conscious air, for though he had run away from some of his own thoughts there was no reason why she should not be led into pursuit of them.

She was sitting up in bed and she laid aside the book she had been holding. 'All alone in the dark?' she said. 'That was a funny thing to do. I saw the sitting-room lights go out some time ago.'

'So you were watching for me?'

'No, I happened to be opening the window at that moment. I expect they are very tired and glad to go to bed. So am I.'

'And what has made you so tired?' he asked.

'You will find out to-morrow when you entertain your sister for a whole evening. To-morrow I shall take Rhoda on her long and dangerous journey across the road.'

'You choose to be sarcastic, Bertha,' he said, smiling indulgently and with reassurance, 'but I hadn't intended to go again. There is no need for you to worry about that.'

'Don't make me laugh,' Mrs. Blackett said. 'I shouldn't be able to stop.'

'Bertha!' he exclaimed. 'What on earth has come over you?'

'A very strong sense of the ridiculous,' she replied. 'It's a healthy sense to have and I ought to have cultivated it more. It doesn't help youth very much, but what a comfort in middle age!'

'I don't understand you,' he said curtly.

'Don't try,' she answered amicably.

'But I have always understood you, until lately. Lately you

have been a little different. I haven't,' he asked almost timidly, 'I haven't hurt you in any way, have I?'

'You couldn't,' she said with impressive earnestness.

'No, not willingly,' he said, touched to see her looking at him with a sweet seriousness, and he was grateful for the calm permanence of her affection, though he remembered that she had cause for gratitude too. 'Nevertheless,' he said, 'you are a little different. You used not to have these queer fits of laughter.'

'You ought to be glad to see me so — so happy,' she said.

'But you don't let me share in your amusement.'

'I would if I could but then, if that were possible, there would be no need to laugh.'

'I don't understand you,' he said again, wishing he had a dressing-room in which he could remove his clothes in privacy.

'No,' she agreed kindly. 'Was there any news?'

There was indeed. It looked as though they need not be burdened with Maude much longer. It was great and promising news, he told her, as he sat on his side of the bed and changed his trousers for the legs of his pyjamas, and then, safe from ridicule, he stood up, asking her whether he had not always said war could be avoided. Patience and perseverance would, it seemed, reap their reward, after all.

'And what will that be?' Mrs. Blackett asked. 'And who gets it?'

'Bertha! Really! I'm afraid Maude has tired you out. You are not really as stupid as all that. Yet the plain fact is that women never seem to see things in true perspective. I should have expected Mrs. Fraser to be overjoyed at this prospect. Not a sign of it. But then—' He paused, thinking of her in that gentler aspect.

'Yes?' Mrs. Blackett said.

'I distrust the influence of that dreadful person who lives with her.'

'Just a pair of ignorant women,' Mrs. Blackett murmured.

'Exactly. Although—' Again he paused. It did not suit him to call Mrs. Fraser ignorant. 'No, what they are suffering from in that house is lack of a mature man's point of view.'

'You must try to supply it,' Mrs. Blackett surprised him by saying.

'I wish I could,' he said, drawing back the curtains and seeing a light still burning in Mrs. Fraser's bedroom.

Mrs. Fraser in bed, Miss Spanner in her usual chair, were temporarily silent. Felix and James, much to Miss Spanner's embarrassment — caught in her dressing-gown and with her hair in plaits — had unexpectedly joined the party and there had been a lively interchange of speculation and a unanimity of distrust about this third flight of fancy.

'It's the first time they've ever come in when I've been with you,' she complained.

'It's the first time this particular situation has arisen. And you're just as modestly dressed as usual and look quite as nice.'

'That's not saying much.'

'No, I didn't mean to say much. And you don't seem to realize that, to them, women of our age are not women at all, just nice old things. But I'm glad they came. It made a little cosiness in a very strange world. And I'd give a good deal to know what Fergus is doing now.'

'No good, I'll warrant.'

'And now you're being spiteful and I won't have it.'

'That's all very well, but if you're going to start thinking about him again —'

'I've never stopped for long.'

'Then I'm not safe after all!' Miss Spanner cried.

'Yes you are, yes you are. And for goodness sake, don't begin boo-hooing again.'

'I think,' Miss Spanner said with dignity, 'that's rather a mean remark.'

'Then you shouldn't be nasty about Fergus. You don't understand him.'

'Well enough,' said Miss Spanner.

'It's never well enough with any of us and, actually, for a minute or two to-night, I almost liked that silly ass.'

'What! Noah?'

'Good gracious, no! Dear Mr. Blackett. When he came in he really looked quite sorry for me. I didn't want him to and I wish I hadn't given him the chance. I hate being pitied, but it was a sign of grace, and I was tired after the wedding and it's so devilish to have to choose between your country and your sons, and I hadn't time to arrange my face before he saw it and, for a minute, he looked as though he understood and would like to say so.'

'Then why didn't he?'

'No time. The boys came in. We've always considered him detestable, but we may be wrong.'

'It would take more than a sympathetic look to make me change my opinion,' Miss Spanner said, 'and that's the kind of look I never get. But oh yes, we may be wrong. We may be wrong about Noah. All the virtues may be vices and all the villains saints, and weakness is wisdom and cowardice is a superior kind of courage, and filthy cruelty doesn't matter so long as it happens a long way off and not to us. There's no such thing as right or wrong. They are only words to juggle with, two jokers in one pack and very handy, and the sooner we're all blown up the better. But to tell the truth, what's worrying me at the moment is my belief that we're being diddled and the elected representatives of the country will live to blush for their happy cheers to-night.'

'No they won't,' Rosamund said. 'Blushing's out of fashion. They haven't blushed for any of their retreats yet. Nowadays an excuse is a justification and the sinner's always right and the sinned against is always wrong. Anyhow, we chose them. We're not quite innocent. Go to bed, Agnes. Perhaps in our dreams we'll get back to the world we used to know. But I haven't quite given up all hope.'

'What of? You don't imagine, do you, that this means relenting on the part of the relentless? It's just an attempt to avoid war until they want it and as we've been very obliging so far, they don't see why we shouldn't oblige them a little more. Diddled!' Miss Spanner said again. 'So what are you hoping for?'

'Just a little decent shame,' Rosamund said. 'What an ambition! And I'm afraid that's aiming rather high!' and she felt bitterly towards Felix whose stupid pride prevented her from keeping her indignation unalloyed.

CHAPTER LI

Rhoda, lying awake after Sandra had gone to sleep, was afraid the next night might see her on the drawing-room sofa. Though she did not know why her father had chosen to accompany her, she knew the mood in which he went away. Nobody had taken much notice of him and this, which had made her thankful, had made him cross. Inexperienced but acute and, like her mother, well read in her study of him, she knew he could not value anyone who did not value him and even the importance of the moment would not excuse this neglect: indeed it increased the offence, for he had expected to be asked for comment and to be listened to with respect. And that was not all. The room had been cold with scepticism, Miss Spanner had vexed him and he was quite likely to say he did not approve of the influence of the house but, as he would not make that decision if it involved him in difficulty or inconvenience, she saw a chance of being here each night until Aunt Maude went home or, as might be necessary, some other safe place was found for her. It was a nice house to be in, Rhoda thought and — again like her mother who had grudged wasting any of her happiness in sleep — she lay awake, enjoying being with Sandra and knowing that, below, there was Miss Spanner and, still farther below, there was James. She felt a great contentment in being near these three friends, and there was a sort of happiness in the house itself although, as Miss Spanner had instructed her, there could be no happy outcome to the situation. There was still the possibility that the boys might have to go and fight and while, as Miss Spanner's faithful disciple, she was ready to believe that necessity would be rooted in righteousness, the horror of it had suddenly lost its vagueness. This was when she and Sandra and James and Felix were talking on the landing, as seemed to be the family habit, before they went to their separate rooms and, for the first time, she looked at these young men with eyes appreciative of their comely youth, their little tricks of gesture and expression and, while she was still too immature to be moved by these physical aspects, she was approaching that state in her realization that they were both good to look at, their voices were pleasant to hear and they were a little mysterious in their different sex, and she knew she would not be happy, even working on the land, if these two were in danger of death or mutilation. But as she lay awake she was not thinking of this new pleasure in observing them; she was thinking that the secret of the house was the lack of enmity in it and the easy way they all had with each other. There was no Flora, Rhoda thought enviously, and no father presenting himself as wisdom and constantly revealing his weakness. Yet it might have been worse that evening, she thought, growing drowsy. He had not had a chance to be his didactic self. He had been dominated, she half regretted, by the combined forces of people who were quite indifferent to his opinion, and over whom, luckily for them, he had no control.

However, she found he had nothing but amiability for her next morning, at breakfast, when he was not eagerly reading the newspaper. He was anxious but optimistic and that, he found, was the general state of feeling in the business world. So Rosamund found it when she did her shopping. There was a peculiar hopefulness in the butcher's handling of the meat and she fancied the errand boys were shriller than usual in their whistling and more dilatory in their methods and she hurried home where, throughout the rest of the day, she busied herself with packing up Chloe's wedding presents and possessions, thinking there might be a letter from her to-morrow, remembering her own first nights and days with Fergus and doubting whether the conscientious accountant could be his equal as a lover, yet knowing there was no end to the surprises in human beings. And she thought of Felix going coldly to his marriage, if need be, taking his pleasure with a revengeful mental cruelty and hating himself for the cruelty and the pleasure and she was enraged because she was as helpless in this matter as in the other which might be settled this very night. Yet, though she called him foolish and wrongly proud, she recognized that he alone could decide where his honour was engaged and that it was as dear to him as her country's was to her, that he might see her attitude towards his affair as she saw the attitude of such as Mr. Blackett in the national entanglement. She thought, too, about Piers Lindsay who would be sure to come to-morrow for, whichever way things went, she would have need of him. It would always be her need he thought of, not his own, and dwelling on this certainty with gratitude, she realized how easy it would be to sacrifice him, for he was not only selfless: he would find an indignity in struggling for what he wanted unless he could be convinced no one else would suffer. And who else would? she asked impatiently. It would not be Fergus who had replied to her obliging letter — had it been too obliging? — with that curt telegram. What right had he to think she would wait indefinitely on his will? In her anger, she was near breaking one of Chloe's fragile treasures, but this rare state of anger did her good. She felt freer, less involved in circumstances, and when Mrs. Blackett arrived just before nine o'clock, she found Mrs. Fraser surprisingly, almost disappointingly, gay.

Only she and Miss Spanner and Paul and Sandra were in the room, for James had said to Rhoda, 'I can't bear any more of this listening. We shall hear everything soon enough. Let's go into the garden and pretend it's a nice world,' and Mrs. Blackett, escaped from her sister-in-law, feeling herself stunned, as though she had spent the day in near neighbourhood to a powerful waterfall, was thankful to sink into a chair and be wrapped, for a few minutes, in the quietness of the shabby, pretty room before the announcer began his tale.

'But what kind of world would you like it to be?' Rhoda asked.

342

'One with peace in it but not too much plenty,' James said.

Again they were sitting on the roller for there was no other seat and again they had their backs to the house which, on this side, was quiet and in darkness but, from some other house, they could hear a broadcast voice without distinguishing the words and the incoherent, steady sound was like insanity protesting it was sane.

'I don't want to fight men,' James said. 'I want to fight the earth. No, not to fight it. I want to make it give me the value of the sweat I've put into it. That's all and that's fair, isn't it?'

'Yes, that's fair,' Rhoda said.

In front of them were the small trees of the garden, the bigger trees in the gardens that backed the houses beyond and hid them, but, here and there, a light from a distant window came through the branches.

'When it's dark it's like being in the country,' Rhoda said. 'I've never really lived in the country. Once we had our holidays on a farm and I expect that's where I got the taste for it.'

'Neither have I, till lately, but that's where I've always wanted to be.'

'Oh, of course,' Rhoda said, and, after a pause and the rekindling of James's pipe, the bright, pale flare of the match and then the red glow of the tiny fire in the bowl, she said, 'I can't think of anything nicer than working hard all day and being very tired and then sitting outside for a little while before you go to bed and thinking of all the things you've got to do to-morrow.'

'Then you're lucky, because you can do that now.'

'But there's nothing I want to do to-morrow except come back here in the evening, perhaps. We've got an awful aunt staying with us, you know.'

'Yes, I know. But you wouldn't want to do everything that has to be done on a farm. How about carting muck?'

'I like the smell,' she said. 'And nice to know you're going to feed the ground.'

'Yes, yes,' he said. She had the root of the matter in her. 'You'll have to be a farmer.'

343

'How can I?' she asked gloomily. 'But you can,' she said, enviously.

'I'm not so sure. If I'd listened to the news I might be nearer knowing. That's partly why I didn't.'

'Oh,' Rhoda said, and she hoped the other part was a wish to talk to her. 'But farmers —' she began.

'But I'm not a farmer. I'm no more use at present than anybody else. Besides —'

'No,' Rhoda said. 'Yes. I see. You couldn't. But perhaps — And anyhow, afterwards. But there's not much hope for me. I might be allowed to be a gardener and that's the nearest I'll get to it.' She was leaning forward, her hands on her knees, and he could see her abrupt, short nose outlined against a sky that was not quite dark. She was like a person bound but ready to start off as soon as the bonds were loosed. 'The nearest I'll get,' she repeated.

'Then,' he said, 'you'll have to — oh, wait and see. You don't know what may happen.' He had been going to say that if she could not be a farmer she would have to marry one and he had stopped because, with the words on his lips, he had thought, unemotionally, that he would rather like to marry her himself, some day, when they were both old enough. She had the qualities he liked in man or woman and though she was not pretty, she had a compensating eagerness, like a colt's, and he wished he could give her the equivalent of a lump of sugar or a carrot and a friendly pat, but he liked her too much to do that and he said, more to himself than to her, 'And you're still at school.'

'And rather a dunce,' she said. 'I ought to be much higher up. Sandra's only a year older than me, but I'm more than a year behind her. Still, I'm beginning to get a bit more interested. I expect you were good at school.'

'Just average,' James said.

The distant protestations of sanity stopped abruptly and, as if in derision, a lion roared.

'Funny, rather nice,' James said, 'to think my grandfather used

344

to sit out here and listen to that noise. Different lions, though, I suppose. Has my mother ever told you about the wire door he made for her bedroom, to keep out the snakes and things? Hasn't she? She tells it to everybody. He must have been a good father to have.'

'Was yours nice, too?' Rhoda asked, and after a pause, James said, 'Mixed,' and knocked out his pipe. She took that as a sign that the interview was over but, as she went towards the house, James said, 'And if I have to go away, don't forget me.'

'Forget you!' she said. 'When I once like a person I never stop.'

CHAPTER LII

THE policeman on duty at the cross-roads near the church thought Mrs. Fraser must be looking for something she had lost. Her head was down and she walked with quick, short steps instead of moving with the easy swing which was quick too, but looked slow because it was obviously effortless. He had no chance to give her his usual special salute and it was lucky there was no traffic at the moment for she went across the road without looking to right or left. Perhaps, he thought, she had lost one of the earrings she always wore. An observant man, he had never seen her without them of one kind or another. Yes, she was searching the ground, for normally she carried her head high and looked about her with interest and pleasure; he was sorry to see her in any kind of distress, and, wishing he could help her, he watched her as she went across the Green until he had to turn his attention to his business.

The policeman was right in thinking she had lost something but wrong in thinking she was in search of it. She knew it was not to be found and her head was low because the loss shamed her and she did not want to see shame on other faces or, worse still, not to see it. She had been wandering about the house, upstairs and down, into the garden and back again, pacing the long sitting-room, touching things, trying not to cry and now she had hurried out in search of comfort on the hill. She had gone there often in times of trouble, though there had never been a trouble like this one, and she had gone when she was happy, increasing her happiness with the sight of the gorge and the river winding its sluggish way to the channel, the bridge flung so lightly across the chasm and the pale, distant hills. 'I will lift up mine eyes unto the hills,' she said to herself, but when she came to the place from which she hoped to see them, they were not there. They had retreated, as she wished she could do, behind a thickness of cloud, and that was fitting. There was nothing she could raise her head for, nothing, she thought, dropping her hands heavily on to the railings and seeing in the massed trees on the other side of the river not the golds and yellows of autumn showing here and there, but a dishonourable tarnish creeping over them. And in her mind she saw the whole of the country she loved so well, its wide moors, its hills dotted with sheep and threaded by streams of cold, clear water, its placid little rivers broadly bordered by meadows richly coloured with cattle and dazzling in early summer with yellow and white and green; she saw the villages tucked cosily into valleys and the spires or towers of their grey churches rising above the clustering trees; manor houses, benign with age and experience in their open parks; great cathedrals like couchant guardian monsters, dominating the cities they overlooked or unmoved in the midst of them; everything that was beautiful, explaining and being explained by its people, seemed to her to have that tarnish on it, or to be blurred, deadened, to have lost its loveliness and its meaning and she thought the breaking of the waves all round these shores had the sound of hissing in it.

Tears started into her eyes and rolled down her cheeks; she could not keep her mouth steady, but she pressed the tears away with the backs of her hands, for people were passing behind her and, having cleared her eyes, she wondered whether she need have bothered, whether she would not see tears on other faces and, for once, strangers would be friends in a common trouble.

She could hear children laughing and shouting round the squat tower, not knowing they had lost the chief part of their inheritance; she looked at the middle-aged man and woman who leaned over the railings near her and they seemed well content as they exchanged their homely comments, and she turned from them to face the footpath and watch the passers-by — an old man, puffing at his pipe, a young one, walking slowly, his nose in a book, a few youths indulging in a little horseplay and emitting loud, mirthless laughter, a tired mother who could not be expected to look much further than the necessity to get her lagging children home to bed, two well-dressed women of uncertain age, talking with cheerful animation in crisp, cultured tones, confident of themselves and their place in a satisfactory world, and she thought, for a moment, that it must be she who was wrong, that nothing untoward had happened and that this day was the same as any other, or a better one than most. She did not meet a glance which, like her own, looked for someone with whom to share a sense of loss and indignity and personal guilt and it seemed to her strange that, behind her now, the cars and carts were still rumbling slowly over the bridge. There should, she thought, have been a hush over the land, not a two minutes' silence of homage and thanksgiving, but an astonished silence of grief and shame. But am I wrong? she asked herself again as a man went by, relief in his quick footsteps and happiness in the set of his mouth and the brightness of his eyes. This man, the two cultured ladies, a plump, smiling matron chatting to another, were these the reasonable people and was she turning a wise compromise into a tragedy? But could what was wise be wrong? And she was convinced that wrong had been done. Possibly, right might eventually be its strange offspring but, however good the child, the sin of the parent must remain, an indelible, black mark in history. And then, as she looked up from her sad contemplation of the footpath, she saw coming towards her and walking lightly, a young man and a girl, their faces bright with the promise of a happy future. She had known them both since they were children and their parents before them, they had been at Chloe's wedding, and before she could cut across their path or get ahead of them they had seen her. She had to wait for them, to hear the news of their engagement because everything, they said, was all right now, to feel indignation and pity at that phrase and to conceal, in their enchanted hour, her own unhappiness, but when they had passed on, she told herself she must go back to the shelter of her own house where no one would tell her that everything was all right. Felix was free from the bond he hated, he and James were physically safe for a time, at least, but she must, she thought, smiling at her own conceit, be like that Corsican who said he was a patriot before he was a father. She might have had to suffer horribly for Felix, to have known great fear for both her sons, but she would not have been ashamed. She was thankful her shame included neither of them. And Felix had not only been right, according to his standards but, a rare occurrence, he had been rewarded: the country had chosen expediency and, unlike its sturdy self, had lost its head in the belief that its reward was not only here and now but stretched into the future and she feared that, sturdy no longer, it was dwindling to its decline.

She managed to give the policeman a smile, but would not risk hearing a disillusioning word and she reached home to see Felix lifting his bicycle up the area steps. He was going to meet James, he told her, at Lindsay's place and unless they were asked to stay there for the night, they would bicycle on until they found somewhere to sleep and to-morrow they would be on the hills.

'Poor things as hills,' he said, 'but still, hills, and there will be no one there. I want to get out of this. Everybody's drunk, or will be, with alcohol or idiocy.'

She nodded. It was the best thing he and James could do.

'And,' he said, with an awkward smile, 'I feel a bit drunk myself, on neither. We'll be away to-night, perhaps to-morrow night too. I've arranged it with the office. There were a few more days holiday owing to me and they're so damned cock-a-hoop I wonder they didn't offer me a partnership to celebrate the occasion. And don't worry. There are no rocks, worse luck.'

'No, I shan't worry, but Felix,' she said a little timidly, 'have you seen that girl?'

'Why should I?'

'Well, isn't it odd not to?'

'The conditions don't exist so the contract is broken. I'll never see her again if I can help it,' and she knew it was not only the mountains that had cured him but the humiliation of being accepted on her terms.

'You are just like your father,' she told him.

'Me?' he exclaimed.

She laughed. 'Yes. Unforgiving. Didn't you know? And remember there may be a war yet.'

'Yes, that would clean us up, wouldn't it? But, you see, it won't be this one,' he said with his malicious grin, swung himself on to his bicycle and looked round to wave before he disappeared.

She went into the quiet house and wondered why she had rushed out of it, for nothing was changed here. She knew her father would have felt to-day as she did, as her sons did and as she knew their father must, and the grandfather clock, which had been her grandfather's, ticked with an effect of steady continuity. It was the only sound she could hear, as it had been that night when she waked to the certainty of Fergus's nearness and, through the association of ideas, it was the clock that now seemed to warn her of his presence. Very quietly, she opened the sitting-room door, almost expecting to find him there, but the room was empty, there was no one in the drawing-room, no sign of Sandra or Paul, the house seemed to be deserted until she found Miss Spanner in her bedroom, sunk in a chair, with the paws of the smaller feline which decorated the back of it, hanging limply, with a hint of sympathy, against her shoulders.

'We saw it was coming but we couldn't really believe it,' she said. 'It's the worst thing that's ever happened. It's much worse,' she said slowly, 'than if you'd turned me out.' That had been her standard of unhappiness and she had gone beyond it and Rosamund thought there was a kind of nobility in her friend's plain face, and then, spoiling her fine expression with a squint, Miss Spanner said, 'Here's a fine new chapter in our fair island's story!'

Characteristically, Rosamund had seen her trouble physically as visual beauty smirched. For Miss Spanner the greatness of her country was expressed, recorded and crystallized in its literature. She loved the essential geniality of it, the controlled splendour, the courage, the good sound core to it – and had that gone for ever? Was it to be a monument to the past, without possibility of issue?

'Our fair island's story,' she said again and, this time, mournfully. She sat up. 'Felix left a message for you.'

'Yes, I've seen him.'

'And,' said Miss Spanner, 'if I had a bicycle I'd be off too.'

'You certainly would,' Rosamund said.

'Don't try to be funny. This is no time for being funny.'

'I agree. It's penance we ought to be doing, not celebrating a triumph. It wouldn't be so bad,' she said, moving with difficulty about Miss Spanner's crowded room, 'it wouldn't be so bad if they'd say it's damnable and disgraceful, but in our lamentable circumstances it couldn't be helped.'

'But it could have been helped.'

'I know that! I know that! I'm only asking for a sign of shame at having any dealings with those gangsters. How they must be laughing! Actually helping them, helping them, Agnes, to save our own skins! And we'd had warning enough. Our skins ought not to have been in any danger. And what about the skins of the other people? Do you remember how I asked you what we were going to do if we lost our pride in ourselves? Well, we've lost it and you said we'd have to get it back. But how? That's what I want to know. How, how, how?'

'Take care of my ornaments,' said Miss Spanner. 'I don't want to lose them as well. Nobody but an idiot can suppose the

350

trouble's stopped. This is only the beginning and we'll get another chance.'

'And refuse to take it.'

'I'm not so sure,' Miss Spanner said slowly. 'I can't believe we've gone rotten altogether. And if we take it we'll save the whole world or go down in glory,' and somewhat abashed by the expression of these beliefs, she rose and straightened the skin on the back of her chair.

CHAPTER LIII

MR. BLACKETT was in high spirits. There had been no difficulty about the removal of his sister. She was as anxious to return to the stuffy little flat she had feared she would see no more as he was to precipitate her departure and he celebrated a double cause for rejoicing by giving her a first class railway ticket. He had played lightly with the idea of accompanying her, in a different compartment, for though he disliked crowds and had a proper scorn for mass emotion, this was a unique occasion and he would have liked to mingle with people who were not indulging their primitive instincts in the usual way of crowds, but marking their approval of political skill and wisdom by honouring the man who represented both. Such impulsive actions were foreign to his character, however, and he went home-as usual to find no special jubilation there. On the whole, Flora was disappointed, Mrs. Blackett said nothing and Rhoda was feeling a little guilty because she could not help being glad that James need not go to war and Mr. Blackett, remembering that he had always foreseen a peaceful outcome, could not, with dignity, express too much joy, and limited himself to a calm benignity.

'You see, I was right,' he said to Mrs. Blackett when they were alone.

'Of course,' she said with quiet emphasis.

He was gratified and looked at her with approval. On the whole she was everything a wife should be, yet — was it because she was his wife? — she did not stir him unless he provoked himself by overcoming her reluctances. She had all the domestic virtues but she lacked that conscious femininity, that tribute to the masculine, which he found in such abundance in Mrs. Fraser.

'I shall go across the road and ask if I may listen to the news again,' he said, 'and I think perhaps,' he looked at her slyly, 'you might like to come with me.'

'I shouldn't like it at all,' she said.

'No? Very well.' He felt dangerously bold. He had warned her and she must take the risk.

It was Mrs. Fraser herself who opened the door and, pleasantly granting his request, took him into the sitting-room.

'Paul's here,' she said. 'He will turn on the news for you. Paul, this is Mr. Blackett,' and she left him with the boy who had good manners but to whom he had nothing to say and who, quite rightly, had nothing to say to him.

Paul was quite definitely disappointed at the news. He thought war would be a fine thing with both his brothers in it and a chance, with any luck, of being in it himself, but he knew his disappointment had a different quality from theirs and from his mother's and he did not speak of it. He sat at one end of the room, Mr. Blackett at the other, the disembodied voice between them, and Mr. Blackett's happiness was streaked with wonder at Mrs. Fraser's conduct. With this child's presence to protect her, surely so much caution was hardly necessary and it was not courteous. He had an odd feeling that he was in disgrace and being punished and he kept silence and did not linger but, as Paul was taking him to the door, Mrs. Fraser — had she timed this descent? — was coming down the stairs, pointing her toes, one hand on the banister rail, moving, he thought, with calculated grace.

'May I congratulate you?' he said solemnly. 'For the mother of sons, this is a happy day.'

She had reached the hall and, slowly lifting her head and lowering her eyelids, she said quietly, 'I knew my sons could not last for ever, but I hoped England would,' and she stood there while he wished her a disconcerted good night and, in his hurry, stumbled over the steps.

He was vexed about that; he was vexed because he had not stood his ground and assured her that England was safe for many years to come; there was a written guarantee for that. Instead, he had accepted what seemed like a scornful dismissal and unable, for once, to put a flattering interpretation on her manner, he went to find what comfort he could from his wife.

She looked up from her sewing. 'Well,' she said, 'I suppose you found it satisfactory.'

'Satisfactory? Oh yes, yes, a great achievement. A wonderful personal triumph. Enormous enthusiasm!' He fidgeted about the room but, gradually, he found something soothing and sympathetic in the movements of her plump, dexterous hands. 'But I was treated myself with very little courtesy,' he said.

'I am surprised,' said Mrs. Blackett.

'Nothing surprises me in that woman. I was shut up alone with her schoolboy son, if you please!'

'She did not invite you. You were making use of her. You have never shown her much courtesy yourself.'

'I have already given you a reason for that,' he said, pursing his lips.

'Yes, and isn't it possible,' she said, with a little catch in her voice as she bent over her sewing, 'isn't it possible that she too is doing her best to behave as she should?' She did not look up because she knew the mixture of primness and gratification of his expression, his lips a little moist, would be more than she could bear, and then, without conscious intention, moved by all the warring emotions of the last weeks, a cruel desire to hurt him and yet, it might be, to save him and at the same time to cleanse herself of the poison in her mind, she did look up. She knew the moment had come and she was going to speak at last and she gave him that full glance of which she was so sparing, in which he saw, for the first time, a resemblance to Rhoda's steady stare, and his silly smile stiffened into an uncertain one.

'And the strange thing is,' he said, 'you don't seem to mind.'

'Mind!' she echoed. 'Mind what?'

'Surely you can't ask me to be more explicit. I should have thought you had been explicit enough yourself.'

She let her sewing drop from her hands. 'I don't know whether to laugh or cry,' she said. 'You see, you don't really live in the same world as I do.'

'Not entirely,' he agreed. 'I live in two worlds. In one I get my living — and yours, and there you and I and the children meet, but into the other, the one in which I ought to have lived all the time, I can fortunately retreat when I choose. But why laugh? Why cry? Particularly, why laugh?'

'Because you are such a fool, Herbert,' she said gently. 'Such a fool.'

'Yes, I know.' This was a disadvantage he had to bear. 'I know I am an unworldly fool.'

'That sounds very nice,' she said, 'but it isn't what I meant and it isn't true. Your world is made and entirely occupied by Herbert Blackett and anyone else who sees him as he sees himself. But nobody does, nobody. How could they? The reason you don't like Rhoda is because she sees someone quite different and you know it.'

He stared at her in amazed alarm. 'Bertha,' he said, and when he spoke he let out more breath than voice, 'Bertha, have you gone mad? Do you know what you are saying?'

'Yes, indeed, I do,' she said pitifully. Now that she had begun she must go on but she found it was more difficult than she had expected. She had believed that when she could contain herself no longer all her pent-up feelings would burst out in a happily angry flood. Now, faced with his anxious astonishment, she found it necessary to harden herself, to remember his bland self-satisfaction, the caresses she hated, his skill in giving everything a significance which ministered to his self-esteem, his complacent misapprehension of her character.

354

'I have been studying you very carefully for years,' she said.

'I am aware of that. I have not been ungrateful. Materially, I have had every possible consideration, but wasn't that your fair share of the labour and your duty? And one does not live by bread alone,' he said, and he saw her smiling, for this stupidity strengthened her. 'However, you have not been yourself lately, I think you ought to see a doctor, and I shall ignore the cruel things you have been saying. You will be sorry for them when you are calmer and I shall try to forget them.'

'You won't succeed in doing that,' she said, 'but you'll do what you always do.'

'Forgive?' he suggested, trying to smile kindly.

'What you are doing already.'

'I am trying to do that.'

'You will avoid the truth,' she said. 'But how can you help it? You don't know what it is. Do I? Does anyone?' she asked a little wildly.

'Now Bertha, quietly, quietly,' he said. 'I can explain it all. You have worried yourself, quite unnecessarily, about this fear of war, and my unfortunate sister has worn you out. Now you must go to bed,' and Mrs. Blackett in a despairing whisper, said, 'I'm afraid it's hopeless.' She had not properly realized that the faults of which she meant to tell him were the very ones which would make the telling useless. 'And yet,' she said, 'I don't feel I can live in all this falseness any longer.'

'Oh Bertha, how absurd you are,' he said gently. 'There is no falseness. I have never said a word to Mrs. Fraser I should not have liked you to hear and I have given her no opportunity to say one. I know you have been a little jealous but I didn't think that would do you any harm!'

'Oh, don't be so ridiculous!' she cried. She was angry now and not more for herself than for the other woman. 'As though I should care! As though she would look at you except to laugh at you! I know she thinks you are a conceited prig and that ought to have been very humiliating for me but, as it happens, it isn't. I just don't care! And you think she was resisting temptation when she left you to-night! Yes.' She spoke quickly, giving him no chance to interrupt her. 'The temptation to tell you what she thinks of people who are rejoicing, as you are, to-day. She couldn't very well do that in her own house and so she left you. That was the only temptation she had, I can assure you.'

'If that explanation comforts you, let us leave it at that,' he said. 'You are not fit, just now, for argument,' and speaking very slowly and clearly, as though he wanted to force some sense past the delirium of a feverish patient, he said, 'There is nothing at all for you to worry about. Do you hear that, Bertha? Nothing at all. Let me take you up to bed. A good night's rest and then the doctor in the morning. Come,' he said, going towards her with outstretched hands.

'No, no,' she said, and he was not resentful. He knew that people even a little overwrought shrank from those nearest to them, and he saw that he would have to be very gentle with her for a time, though when had he been anything else?

'I might have known this would happen,' she said, 'that you wouldn't listen. It won't do you any good but it will do me a great deal. It has amused me, all these years, deceiving you, but I can't bear it any longer. It makes me feel so wicked.'

'Deceiving me?' he cried. And into his mind there rushed the extraordinary possibility that such ideas as those with which he had played had taken form and substance in his wife's actions, and strangely enough, the very outrageousness of the thought gave it a horrid probability. 'You're not telling me,' he said in a hollow voice, 'that you have been unfaithful to me?' He put his hands over his face and from behind them his muffled voice asked, 'Who is it? Is it Lindsay?' and he heard her say sharply, 'Don't!'

He took a peep at her through his fingers which shook a little. She seemed quite calm, her lips were set in their usual half-smiling curves. She had never changed the way in which she wore her hair. Parted in the middle, it was drawn back softly from her smooth forehead as it had been when he first saw her and he could believe that what had attracted him then might well attract someone else. When he could forget himself he was not stupid and the difference he perceived in her as she leaned forward, looking beyond him, was a positive quality instead of the negative one to which he was accustomed and there crept upon him a conviction of her perfect self-control, worse than his suspicion of mild insanity.

'What are you thinking of?' he asked, dropping his hands.

'Of you,' she said.

'There's no one else?',

'No, no. There are more ways than one of being unfaithful. And all that side of me was killed in Florence.'

'In Florence?'

'I loathed it. I've gone on loathing it. No, of course you didn't know. You have never known the first thing about me. You have never troubled to find out. You were happy, so I must be happy. You were charmed with yourself, I must be charmed with you. And I've let you think so. I liked to see how stupid, how self-satisfied you could be.'

'I don't believe it! You don't know what you're saying. You said you loved me. Why did you marry me?'

'I was so ignorant,' she said quietly. 'And then I had so poor an opinion of myself that I think anyone reasonably presentable would have done. But perhaps I ought to have gone on pretending, so that you could go on being happy. I wonder. You are not a bad man,' she said, hating her own patronizing tone. 'You work hard and I'm sure you are honourable in your business and you do all you can for the children, in your own way, definitely in your own way.' She sighed. 'That's just it. For you, there's only one way. You are not self-indulgent in the usual sense, but how you indulge yourself in every other! You can't see a pretty woman without thinking you must attract her and protect yourself! I think that annoys me more than anything else because it's so fatuous and so untrue. And you've never thought of me as a separate person. That,' she said, 'is why you can't retort with nasty things about me now. There are plenty,

but you don't know what they are. For you, I haven't a character. I'm an appendage, but I've been thinking about you
intensively for nearly twenty years.'

He stood up and began to move about the room with short,
agitated steps painful to see and when she said sternly, 'Sit down,
Herbert. You must listen. This is the first and last time,' it was
painful that he obeyed her, going with uncertainty to his chair,
and she felt sorry for him when she saw his cheeks drawn under
his eyes and his over-red lips sagging.

'And do you know,' she said, and now her manner was
friendly and confidential, 'how it all started, this frightful conceit
of yours! I think I do.'

She paused but he did not speak. Mad or sane, what did it
matter? He had dropped into that dark little pit from which,
a short time ago, he had turned his gaze.

'I expect you were predisposed that way,' she said, 'but I
think you had to make yourself a protective covering when you
got out of going to the war.'

That roused him 'War!' he cried. 'It is a wicked, hateful thing
and I was right.'

'But you told me at the time it was your painful duty to stay
at home. It wasn't. But I was so simple, I believed you.'

'It's the duty of every man,' he stammered, 'to oppose it.'

'But you didn't do that,' she said quietly. 'I could have
understood that. And now the very word enrages you. And
you hate Piers Lindsay because he went and bears the marks of it.
Your principles are not really finer than other people's. And
you're thankful for what's happened now because, somehow,
it seems to justify you. And the hide you began to make for
yourself then has grown thicker and thicker every day. And I
don't suppose I've penetrated it,' but he had gone and whether
she had merely irritated his surface or made a hole in his defensive
armour she did not know. She heard the slamming of the front
door, but she was not alarmed. He would not do anything
desperate. He would probably return with everything arranged
in his mind to his own satisfaction and she was not satisfied with

herself. She felt rather ashamed, but she knew she felt more kindly towards him than she had done since their wedding day and could see him simply now as another faulty human creature like herself.

CHAPTER LIV

MISS SPANNER had said there would be trouble across the road one day and it had come for Mr. Blackett, though not in the way she had planned and, if she had heard of it or of a much more exciting domestic drama, it would not have diverted her, that night, from her alternating anger and despair as she thought of her fellow country men cheering as a victory what was an inglorious defeat. The colour returning to Rosamund's cheeks when Piers Lindsay arrived in the evening, her restlessness calmed, the sense she did not try to hide of something almost like content, had not stirred Miss Spanner to anxiety, because these changes were unobserved. She was not looking for signs and portents in her own small affairs. Passages from the Old Testament she knew so well were sounding in her ears, words of lamentation and denunciation.

'What luck!' she had exclaimed suddenly.

'Luck?' Rosamund said in sceptical surprise.

'Getting the Bible translated when we did,' Miss Spanner said.

The words, even without the aptness she found in them were a solace denied to Rosamund. She had her own in Felix's freedom and Lindsay's love, but whatever alleviations they could find, neither of these women, who laid no claim to wisdom, who were without any special training, these ordinary products of the ideas on which they had been nurtured, Rosamund, unobtrusively by her father, Miss Spanner through her books and both in the traditions of their country, would ever be shaken in their conviction that those traditions had been forsworn. But, exhausted by the emotions of the day, they were both asleep before Mr. Blackett had returned from wandering through the streets.

Exactly where he went he never rightly knew. He heard the front door bang behind him with an awful sound of finality and it seemed to him that it was Bertha who had thrust him out, her rough hand which had slammed the door on him, that hand hitherto so soft and deft, and for a time he proceeded in a queer shambling trot, very different from the normal, assured gait of Mr. Herbert Blackett. And those cruel words had come from her whose speech had seldom been less gentle than her words! It was no wonder he moved with such uncertainty for he felt that the ground was shaking under his feet. Yet he could not believe all this had really happened. It must be a nightmare. He could not live without the steady foundations on which he had built his life, without his supports and props and, since he was quite certainly alive, he must surely be under some delusion. This questionably happy idea soon deserted him. Here, when he lifted his dropped head, he saw houses and streets he knew, taking on none of the fantastic shapes incident to dreams and, realizing that he was indeed awake, he straightened his back though he did not slacken his pace. He pushed past merry groups of people who were celebrating their release from fear; he heard distant sounds of revelry from the city and the shouting and the laughter added to the confusion in his mind and this very gradually cleared to the necessity of accepting a horrible reality. He could not change it, for all his adroitness, into anything but what it was. He did not try to defend himself against anything his wife had said. Whether it was true or false was not his present concern. What had brought a great lump of misery into his chest, what drove him round about the roads of Upper Radstowe, was the thought of the woman whose fancied love and admiration had been the unacknowledged background to his life. She had been hating and despising him for years, his wife, who had made a home which had seemed as near perfection as it could be and to which he must eventually return. For, he asked himself, standing still and breathing hard, as though he had temporarily evaded his pursuers and could afford a moment's rest, what else could he do? And as he stood there, instinctively seeking the shadow of a drooping tree, it seemed to him, who was rarely imaginative except about himself, that the world must be thronged with people who, for a while, might wander in the protective darkness of the night but, sooner or later, must go back to houses they hated, to houses where they were not wanted, because there was no other shelter for them, and he was one of them, like some sad old dog who had been beaten for a fault he did not know he had committed, but must trundle home meekly to his kennel.

Stealthily he put his key in the lock and found he need not turn it. The door was opened for him.

'Why, Bertha, Bertha!' he stammered in meek surprise, remembering that, in all their days together, she had never been at a door to welcome him.

'I was listening for you,' she said, and when she saw the queer, homeless look he had, she was aghast at her presumption in tampering with another person's soul and she knew that if he was humiliated, so was she, but sensibly she said, 'Shall we go into the kitchen and have something hot to drink?' and hearing the new friendliness in her own voice, she gave him an amused, questioning glance, as though to ask whether he heard it too, and with, as it were, an uncertain wag of his tail, he followed her down the basement stairs for, again, what else could he do?

An hour or two later, Miss Spanner was roused by the opening of her door. She turned on the light beside her bed and, starting up, exclaimed in alarm, 'Why, Felix, what's the matter?'

'Good God!' was the reply, and immediately, with great presence of mind, Miss Spanner reduced the room to darkness and for a long time after the door had been shut again, she sat up in bed, leaning forward, her thin arms stretched out in front of her. Somewhere beyond her door was an all too evident sign and portent in her own small affairs, and they were very small, she kept reminding herself. They were of no importance, nor was she, and she insisted on subduing her anxiety when she remembered that many, very many, other people as obscure as herself, were doomed to suffering compared with which anything that might happen to her was much less than a pinprick and, indirectly, she was partly responsible for that suffering, she deserved the pinprick, and in that sincere belief she fell asleep at last and waked to see Rosamund entering with the early morning tea.

'An attention I didn't expect to-day,' Miss Spanner said, drawing in the corners of her mouth.

'Why not? I should think you are more than usually in need of it. Did you get a dreadful shock, my poor dear?'

'Not as bad as he did, I'm glad to say,' Miss Spanner replied.

'Of course, he went straight to our old room. It's queer that I never thought that might happen. I'd always imagined he'd come up by the balcony but, you see, he'd kept his latchkey.'

'You ought to have bolted the front door.'

'That wouldn't have kept him out for long.' She smiled, with her lips, in what Miss Spanner considered an annoyingly complacent manner, but there was no amusement in her tired eyes. 'A few nights ago,' she said in a dull voice, 'I suddenly felt sure he was in the house. When he really came, I knew nothing about it until he was standing beside my bed.'

'Ah, he didn't get as far as that with me,' said Miss Spanner. 'But what a thing to do! Just like him! I thought, for a minute, it was Felix and what he thought I don't know, except that you must have changed a lot since he saw you.'

'And he couldn't laugh!' Rosamund said. 'That was the awful part of it.' For a moment she hid her face in her hands. 'He couldn't laugh! But then,' she said, 'that was why he came.'

She went to the window and looked out on a grey morning. It was very quiet here, at the back of the house, but she fancied she could still hear Fergus's retreating footsteps. Often, in the past, she had listened eagerly for their approach and she had strained her ears for the last of them when he was going back to war, but never with so much sorrow as she felt now. Then, because he carried all her love with him, there was a sort of triumph in letting him go. It had been harder to send him away with no more than her pity and, yes, some kind of love, but not the kind he wanted or — anger stirred in her again — the kind he had expected. Yet she had been touched to the point of complete forgiveness when, looking down at her miserably, he had said, 'I had to come to you. I got the last train down. I knew you would be all right about all this.'

'I wish,' she said, still looking at the garden but speaking to Miss Spanner, 'I wish one could be sure where one's responsibility ends or whether it ever ends at all.'

'I'm sure you've none for him,' Miss Spanner said. 'I imagine that's someone else's business now,' and as Rosamund half turned her head, Miss Spanner saw that she smiled again. 'Isn't it?' she cried.

'No,' Rosamund said.

'And you're pleased!'

'Not altogether. I wish I could feel anything altogether. How much easier it would be!'

'But you're pleased,' Miss Spanner repeated. 'Of course you would be. You're that kind of woman and I can very well guess what he's been saying.'

'No you can't, Agnes,' Rosamund said quietly.

'I've read every love scene in English literature and that's much more than you've done.'

'I know, but then — ' and there Rosamund stopped. She could not tell poor Agnes that she had never heard a lover's voice and Fergus's voice, alas, had been a lover's still. 'I can't get warm,' she said, gathering her dressing-gown round her.

'And no wonder, if you've spent the night in that garment. Come and have your tea. Well, I suppose this means I've got to pack. And I'll go quietly. And I don't mind as much as I thought I should because, since yesterday, I don't care much about anything. I just want to get into a hole and hide. We didn't know what a lot we thought of ourselves, did we, till this happened? I went to sleep and forgot it all and then that man had to come and wake me up. And what do you think the boys will say when they come home? Lucky they weren't here. They'd have taken him for a burglar and there'd have been a fight. There'd have been a fight anyway, I expect, and quite right too.'

'Yes, that was lucky. And I don't think Sandra or Paul can have heard anything. It was cold there. I lit a fire.'

She and Fergus had knelt in front of it and watched the wood catch and then the coal, his arm round her waist, her head against his shoulder, his left hand and her right one held out towards the flames as though, in this posture, they renewed their vows before some sacrificial altar.

'I've cleared away the ashes already,' Rosamund said, 'because Sandra would be sure to see them. But I think I shall tell her. I think she would be happier if she knew her father had been here.'

Miss Spanner snatched at the past tense. 'Been?' she cried.

'Yes, he's gone,' Rosamund said, and she sank into a chair decorated with one of the great-uncle's cats. 'But,' she said, with an attempt at laughter, 'I made him have a good breakfast first.'

'H'm,' said Miss Spanner with a return of pessimism, 'and when do you expect him back again?'

'I don't know, Agnes,' Rosamund said patiently.

Those few minutes in front of the fire had been very sweet. While they lasted, she and Fergus seemed to be young again and when she looked at him and saw all the characteristics she had loved, the set of his mouth, the lines round his eyes, the hair which had lost most of its bright colour but was still thick and strong, and he looked at her and found a like pleasure in her face, she could have yielded physically to his old charm, but he had laughed then, the old, delighted laughter of possession, and the temptation passed. He had no right to laugh like that. He had forfeited his possession, yet he still took it for granted. He had humbled himself by coming to her in his need and he either expected generosity from her or saw no cause for it.

Does it depend,' Miss Spanner asked reluctantly, dreading the answer, 'I mean has his coming back anything to do with me?'

'No. You weren't mentioned.'

Miss Spanner grunted again. 'And I suppose the rest of it isn't my business.'

'No,' Rosamund said.

'And I'm not curious.'

'Oh no, never,' Rosamund agreed heartily.

Miss Spanner leant back against her pillows. 'I only want to feel safe,' she said.

'Safe!' Rosamund exclaimed. 'Why bother about your little bit of safety here when we're all in mortal danger? A lot of us think there isn't any, but there is, and that was Fergus's only consolation.'

'So he's on the right side, is he?'

'Don't be silly,' Rosamund said.

That was what had made it so hard not to drift again and take the temporarily easy course, but she had seen the consequences of drift. He would not have gone away but for the results of that tendency in her nature; he would not have come back if the country had not drifted into its perilous, false safety; she had allowed herself to drift into love for Piers but, except for his sake, she did not blame herself for that. That was the fault of everything she liked in him. But what was she to do about him now? she asked herself, while Fergus strode up and down the room, raging at one moment against the Government and, at the next, telling her he had never really ceased to love her, shrugging away her reminder of his request, showing himself bitterly hurt when she remained unresponsive and apparently unforgiving. Was it not still drifting to leave her attitude unexplained and drifting in a direction which would take her treacherously far from Piers? Yet she offered no explanation. She could not be fair to Piers without being cruel to Fergus and, not sure whether justice or kindness were the greater virtue, she tipped the scales a little in favour of kindness because, in this way, she gained nothing for herself and sacrificed, as women like to do, the person she loved best, and she remembered how Sandra had complained that gain for one always involved loss for another. Fergus's gain was not very great but, as she watched him who had been ready to fight, had come home to fight and might have to do it yet and was almost in tears because he could not do it now, she knew it was impossible to cast him out altogether, to tell him she wanted to be free, now, when he was in trouble, when the future was so uncertain, when there was misery enough in the world and would be more. And once again, as she had done so often years ago, she pictured him lying dead or wounded, with no one, this time, to call his own.

But how childish he was to suppose that all would be well here, in future, because the past was submerged in the present trouble! The tide would inevitably ebb and his grievances would be revealed, like a bit of wreckage on the shore. And there would be other grievances. What part did he imagine he could play in the home he had left two years ago? Felix and James were men; they would never accept his authority and he would never resign it. He had forfeited their allegiance too and while they lived in the house he would have to remain outside it.

She had made that clear and, surprisingly, he had acquiesced. Perhaps he had been unable to fit himself with dignity into the picture; perhaps he was acting with the generosity which lay at the roots of his character. She did not know, but with Piers she would have known.

'I suppose,' she said to Miss Spanner, 'life is quite clear to some fortunate — or are they stupid? — people. I simply grope. I have to find my way by feeling and probably the way is wrong.'

'So long as you are doing your best,' Miss Spanner said with unwonted gentleness. She was in the dark and Rosamund's sad face — and how seldom she had seen it sad — warned her that she must remain there.

'Yes, my best!' Rosamund said scornfully. 'That's what people always say they're doing when they've made a mess of things and want to clear it up, and though part of me feels that nothing much matters now, I know it does and more than ever. But I know, too, that my best is a very poor thing at that.'

Ought she to have fought for Piers? she asked herself. Had she been taking the easiest way again? All she was sure of was that it was the way her groping took her and Piers, with that strength which is not afraid to look like weakness, would tell her that what was right for her must be right for him. He would not say a word in his own cause or try to argue with instincts which were not susceptible to reason, and she said, 'I'm going for a walk this morning, Agnes, into the country,' and the cast in Miss Spanner's eye wavered and became fixed.

She might meet him in the lane and they would lean over the gate again as they had done when he first told her he loved her. There would be no oats now to listen and whisper; they must have been gathered long ago. The field would be bare, but she had never yet looked at a bare field without wondering what the next crop would be and feeling sure it would be a good one.

AFTERWORD

Nothing very much happens in her books, and yet, when you come to the bottom of a page, you eagerly turn it to learn what will happen next. Nothing very much does and again you eagerly turn the page. The novelist who has the power to achieve this has the most precious gift a novelist can possess.

Somerset Maugham was writing, of course, of the work of that consummate miniaturist and ironist, Jane Austen. Yet his words could equally well describe the art of E.H. Young — another novelist who worked on a small scale (Jane Austen described her own method most vividly as, 'The little bit [two inches wide] of Ivory on which I work with so fine a brush') but within whose novels we find that largeness of human experience, albeit viewed crisply down the wrong end of a telescope. Beneath the small strokes of delicate brush-work, and underpinning E.H. Young's stories of West Country provincial life, are the perennial darker issues which flow also through Jane Austen's drawing rooms: the threat of war, deceit, the inevitability of loss, human disappointment, blindness and misery.

Chatterton Square was Emily Young's last novel, published in 1947, two years before her death from lung cancer. It is a work of maturity, with less sparkle than *Miss Mole*, and less instant charm than *The Misses Mallett*, yet a depth of insight, a *gravitas*, which (arguably) makes it a greater work than those earlier books. For its title the novelist broke her custom (her first two novels excepting) of naming her books after their significant characters: *The Misses Mallett* (1922), *William* (1925), *The Vicar's Daughter* (1928), *Miss Mole* (1930), *Jenny Wren* (1932), *The Curate's Wife* (1934) and *Celia* (1937). The switch is perhaps significant. For although *Chatterton Square* does have a heroine, Rosamund Fraser, we are asked to look far, far beyond her; in any case, she is not the novel's most memorable character. It is typically subtle, even oblique, of E.H. Young to distinguish in her title the nondescript fictional square in Radstowe where her characters live, but which hardly features as a symbolic entity in the book the way that Egdon Heath (for example) does in Hardy. In a sense she is, by this simple device, making a statement about ordinariness: Chatterton Square has 'seen better days', it has been deserted by 'fashion and prosperity', and is not really a proper square at all, but an unfinished oblong. So the physical setting for the novel mirrors its emotional theme: a coming-to-terms with the everyday messy complexity of human life, all illusion gone. Just as the inhabitants of Chatterton Square have to accept the shabbiness of their surroundings, so they must needs accept the limitations of their lives.

Emily Hilda Young was no stranger to the kind of passionate compromise that can lurk beneath an ostensibly conventional facade. She was born in Northumberland in 1880 — the year George Eliot died, the year Thomas Hardy published *The Trumpet Major*. The third child in a family of six girls and one boy, Emily received a conventional middle-class education, at Gateshead Grammar School and then at Penrhos College in Wales. Her father was a partner in the shipbrokers', Simpson, Spence and Young, and (one can safely presume)

370

approved Emily's marriage at the age of twenty-two to someone in a respectable profession — J.A.H. Daniell, a solicitor.

Daniell's home was in Bristol, or rather, in Clifton — the high, leafy and 'classy' area of that city surrounding the Downs, and as remote from the teeming poorer areas as Hampstead is from Hackney in London. We know nothing about their marriage; there is no evidence to suppose it was not happy, although the fact that E.H. Young's work has as a recurring theme the profoundly unsatisfactory and difficult nature of the state of marriage might lead one to suspect that life in the solicitor's house was, at the very least, not bland. Emily Young published three novels during her marriage and pursued interests like rock-climbing and riding — until the outbreak of the First World War changed things irrevocably. Whilst Emily worked in stables and a munitions factory, her husband went to France, to be killed at Ypres in 1917. Then, after sixteen years in the city, Emily left Bristol forever. Yet clearly the place, and her experiences there, had taken an unshakable hold on her imagination, for of the seven novels she was to publish after the war, six are set in Bristol — which she calls Radstowe, echoing the original name Bristowe.

Emily Young did not remarry after her husband's death, unless one is to count a deep and permanent relationship with a married man as a spiritual union as significant as any conventional marriage. George Eliot would have said so. Just as she took the decision, in 1854, to leave for Germany with George Henry Lewes who was unable to divorce his wife Agnes, so Emily Young took a decision that was almost as extraordinary, given the mores of the period: to live in a *ménage* with a married man and his wife. George Eliot's liaison was open, and ruined her reputation in polite society for many years, until literary fame meant that great ladies could at last put aside their scruples about entering her drawing room. But in a sense it was easier for the Leweses; they inhabited a literary world where unconventional behaviour was tolerated, if not accepted. Emily Young spent the rest of her life loving a man, Ralph Henderson, who was headmaster of a public school, Alleyn's, and whose career would have been ruined by any breath of scandal.

Ralph Henderson had been at Bristol Grammar School with J.A.H. Daniell; he was an enthusiastic and highly skilled rock-climber like Emily, and it seems likely (although biographical details are sparse) that her husband introduced her to the man to whom she was additionally drawn because of a shared interest. There is no doubt that their relationship began before the war, whilst Emily's husband was still alive, for in 1914 the two went openly on holiday together, joined by Emily's nephew Philip. When Emily was 'free' she went to live, ostensibly in a separate flat, in the Hendersons' house at Sydenham Hill, South London, where Mrs Daniell (as she was always known) was an accepted part of the household. For twenty years, until Ralph Henderson retired from Alleyn's, the association continued in this tolerant, outwardly conventional way — Emily and Ralph able to take holidays together with close friends, the Gotchs, who were both teachers at Alleyn's and who seem to have acted the role of conspiratorial chaperones.

Whilst Mrs Daniell lived thus, E.H. Young produced her novels steadily, hiding behind the anonymity of her maiden name. So it went on, until Ralph Henderson left Alleyn's and went into semi-retirement from 1940 onwards; then he and Emily (both in their sixties) went to live alone in Bradford-on-Avon in Wiltshire. They were still near their friend Mr Gotch, who was now headmaster of the Bentley School, Calne; they lived — we must presume happily — in peaceful seclusion until Emily's death in 1949. With other writers this story might have been the stuff of high drama: the Scott-and-Zelda form of turbulence that makes powerful literary biography. It is characteristic of this most English writer, E.H. Young, that a private life which must have contained great passion as well as some pain should have been so successfully hedged round with a concealing thicket of reticence and accommodation.

Yet in the work there is always the question of marriage . . . what it is and what it does to people. There is no doubt that, in *Chatterton Square*, the writer who had herself been married when she first met Henderson, and who had to live *with* his marriage, portrays marriage itself as a prison. Two couples are contrasted, almost set in opposition to each other, just as their houses jut in different directions at right angles to each other in one corner of Chatterton Square. In one house lives Rosamund Fraser, a fading beauty in her early forties, whose husband Fergus has left her and their five children because, with unexplained selfishness, he has decided to pursue his creative interests abroad, away from the demands of family life. In the other house live Herbert and Bertha Blackett (E.H. Young has a talent for bestowing singularly ugly names on her doomed characters, even to the point of caricature) with their three daughters, Flora (pretty, but self-centred and so

373

doomed, like her father), Mary (a curiously undeveloped character) and quiet Rhoda, full of integrity, who rejects her father's teaching.

Herbert Blackett, with his fixed ideas, overweening vanity, covert and therefore dishonest sensuality and strong streak of cruelty, is a brilliant creation. E.H. Young's remorseless dissection of the Blacketts' arid marriage ranks with anything in twentieth-century fiction, particularly for the skill with which she indicates physical repulsion — all the more powerful for its delicacy. At the beginning of Chapter V the mousy Mrs Blackett takes the centre of the stage for the first time, and we glimpse, in one paragraph, the misery of her life. Mr Blackett has been 'in sentimental mood', which is E.H. Young's way of stating that he has demanded and received his conjugal rights. When he is asleep his wife moves to the edge of the bed, trying to calculate the number of nights she has spent there with him, and she envies Rosamund Fraser who can sleep alone. Later it emerges that Mrs Blackett's memory of her honeymoon in Florence (which *he* thinks she recalls romantically) is one of 'surprise and disgust and despair' — that of a woman who is revolted by 'the process . . . of begetting' and knows there is no escape in the future. It is a terrible prison sentence, summed up in the phrase, 'her body at his disposal'.

Yet E.H. Young would be a lesser novelist were she to leave it at that. It is one thing to create a man who is a monster, and a downtrodden, unhappy wife; quite another to perceive the subtle collusion that is often at the core of such a desolate marriage. For although Mrs Blackett is right to detest her conceited ass of a husband, she also *needs* to detest him — her loathing being all that

374

she has (apart from her daughter Rhoda) to give her essentially cowardly and dishonest life a meaning. Should Mr Blackett once be 'generous and kindly . . . she knew she would be disappointed'. In a few devastating sentences, the novelist reveals the complex truth about Mrs Blackett:

> The life she had made for herself would need some re-adjusting, for, with such a change in him, she would have to change the tactics she had perfected and in that deep part of the mind where motives lie hidden, was the fear of being robbed of one of her many grievances. She wanted to keep as many as she could get.

When finally, at the end of the novel, Mrs Blackett summons the courage to tell her husband exactly what he is like, knowing that he can understand but a part, Mrs Blackett is relieved: 'she knew she felt more kindly toward him than she had done since their wedding day and could see him simply now as another faulty human creature, like herself'. The moment when the rejected Mr Blackett, shocked and humiliated at last, returns to the house where he thinks he is hated, to be met at the door by his wife for the first time in their marriage, is one of the most moving in E.H. Young's work.

With the deftness which has characterized her handling of both sets of inhabitants of Chatterton Square, E.H. Young switches immediately from this scene to the moment in the Fraser household when the absent Fergus returns, blundering by mistake into the room he used to share with Rosamund but which is now used by Miss Spanner, Rosamund's unmarried friend. This cross-cutting throughout the novel has something of the technique of film, and serves to emphasize always the paradoxical interconnectedness yet separation of the characters. Cleverly, Emily Young contrives to deny us 'sight' of this Fergus, for by morning Miss Spanner discovers that he has been and gone. He first wanted a legal separation, then refused Rosamund the divorce that would have freed her to marry Piers Lindsay; now he has returned because of the threat of war in Europe, yet Rosamund says that the children would not accept him living with them again. She still loves Fergus, yet she loves Piers more (we sense); the return of Fergus seems to banish forever the possibility of happiness with Piers.

Or does it? *Chatterton Square* does not end bleakly; on the contrary, although we know that war is inevitable and that people are doomed as inevitably to their private misery, E.H. Young chooses to end her last novel on a note of hope that is all the more beautiful and fragile for the blackness which surrounds it. Here again, events in the macrocosm add poignancy, urgency, irony, to what happens in the microcosm: 'it was at a time like this that a young man might make sure of a moment's joy or commit some folly he recognized for what it was but believed he would not have much time for regretting'. The shabby act of appeasement at Munich (referred to with Young's habitual obliqueness), approved by Mr Blackett yet a source of shame to the Fraser household, will not — we know — avert the course of war. By the end of the novel we cannot know if Rosamund's sons will be killed, whether James might return perhaps to marry Rhoda, whether Piers or Fergus may repeat the heroism they both showed during the First World War, when Herbert Blackett avoided conscription. Important as all these questions are, treating as they do matters of destiny and duty, we are left wondering two small things. First, whether the poor Blacketts may eventually find some peace, if not happiness, together. Second, whether Rosamund Fraser may find that her vague hope is justified – a hope, not for ecstasy, but for that groping towards contentment which is the most that some of us can hope for. Rosamund sighs, 'I have to find my way by feeling and probably the way is wrong', conscious that her path is one of constant compromise: still E.H. Young leaves us in no doubt that she approves this particular personal morality. Rosamund Fraser says that she knows that doing one's best is perhaps not enough, if one's best is a 'poor thing'; on the other hand, this character has been presented to us as the novel's heroine: gentle, honest, loving, beautiful inside as well as out. In her, weak though she may seem, are those qualities which guarantee survival – even in the face of international evil and private failure. It may seem a fault in the novel that the character of Piers Lindsay is so sketchily drawn, but the very fact that Rosamund's two men, Piers and Fergus, are mere ciphers serves to heighten our perception of Rosamund herself, just as in *Middlemarch* the strong character of Dorothea contrasts with that of the weak man she loves, Will Ladislaw. Thus George Eliot makes a statement about the propensity of many women to burn out their souls in loving men who are, essentially, their inferiors – a view with which E.H. Young would almost certainly concur.

That love is always limited is one of the messages of *Chatterton Square*. The love between woman and woman (Rosamund and Miss Spanner), between mother and children, between man and woman: all disappoint, all throw into sharp relief the individual's yearning loneliness. Yet by accepting that, by casting off all romantic hopes and viewing a landscape devoid of any softening greenery or whispering crops, we open ourselves to the chance of joy — just as Rosamund Fraser does at the end. It is typical of this fine and subtle novel, which does not turn aside from the darker undercurrents of life, that the penultimate word of the text should be that bold little monosyllable: 'good'.

Bel Mooney, Bath, 1986

ALSO OF INTEREST

OTHER NOVELS BY E.H. YOUNG

MISS MOLE
New Introduction by Sally Beauman

"Who would suspect her of a sense of fun and irony, of a passionate love for beauty and the power to drag it from its hidden places? Who could imagine that Miss Mole had pictured herself, at different times, as an explorer in strange lands, as a lady wrapped in luxury and delicate garments . . . ?"

Miss Hannah Mole, a farmer's daughter, has for twenty years earned her living as nursery governess or companion to a succession of difficult old women. Now aged forty, a thin, shabby figure, she returns to the lovely city of Radstowe with its hills, trees and arching suspension bridge. Here she is, if not exactly embraced, at least sheltered and employed by the pompous nonconformist minister, Reverend Corder, whose motherless daughters are sorely in need of care and good food. But even the dreariest situation can be transformed into an adventure by the indomitable Miss Mole. Blessed with wit, intelligence and the splendid capacity to call a spade a spade, she wins the affection of Ethel and of her nervous sister Ruth, transforms life at the Vicarage, and triumphs in her own entrancing way . . .

THE MISSES MALLETT
New Introduction by Sally Beauman

There are four Misses Mallett. First come Caroline and
Sophia – large and jolly spinsters with recollections of a past
glamour which sustain them as the years slip by.

Then there is Rose. Beautiful Rose with her knot of dark hair,
pale complexion and lovely grey eyes. So much younger than
her stepsisters, she calmly awaits the event – or the man –
that will take her away from their life of small social successes
in the city of Radstowe. But she is independent and fastidious:
no man, not even the eligible Francis Sales, can entirely
capture her heart.

The fourth Miss Mallett is Henrietta who arrives to share the
conventional home of her three aunts. With her Aunt Rose's
beauty and her own wilful spirit, she determines against
spinsterhood. Encountering Francis (no longer so eligible),
she falls under his spell. As Rose and Henrietta circle round
Francis they are forced to decide between sense and sensibility
– and each of them makes the perfect choice.

JENNY WREN
New Introduction by Sally Beauman

"Jenny, too, wanted pleasure, pretty clothes, laughter, admiration and love, but she would not stoop to get them. She would wait, holding herself erect, until these gifts came to her unsought."

On their father's death, Jenny and Dahlia Rendall, with their mother Louisa, move across the river to the heights of Upper Radstowe. Here they try to make a living by taking in lodgers. But their neighbours eye this all-female household with alarm and distrust — especially when a local farmer takes to calling on Louisa, now an attractive, if not entirely respectable widow. Dahlia takes it all with a pinch of salt; fastidious, conventional Jenny cannot. Embarrassed by her mother's country ways, smarting at every slight, both real and imaginary, she longs for a different life. Then Jenny falls in love with a handsome, young squire — but certain of his prejudice and a prisoner of her pride, she dares not reveal her name . . .

THE CURATE'S WIFE
New Introduction by Sally Beauman

"Life would be a much simpler matter with her will, her thoughts and her footsteps following Cecil's, but how very dull this docility would be, how bad for both of them!"

Dahlia Rendall has moved not many yards from her family home, Beulah Mount in Upper Radstowe. While her sister Jenny sojourns in the English countryside, the lovely unconventional Dahlia launches forth on what appears to be the most conventional of marriages — to a curate, the Rev. Cecil Sproat. As Cecil struggles with his sermons, Dahlia battles with domesticity, her naturally irreverent wit, and her weakness for handsome young men. And Dahlia's vision of marital perfection is at odds with Cecil's. But she has intelligence, determination and a sense of humour — all useful weapons in that age-old battle of the sexes called marriage.